POT-BC

Jo Edwards

Published by Weasel Green Press

POT-BOUND

Cover Art by Regina Wamba of Mae I Design
Edited by Mike Rose-Steel
Interior Text Design by Richard Edwards

ISBN: 978-1-908212-20-7

First Edition:
10 9 8 7 6 5 4 3 2 1

For Rich, the human sunbeam.

"The roots of a pot-bound plant wind themselves round and round the inside of the pot making an impenetrable wall. They are unlikely to spread out into new soil; they can only circle endlessly, travelling to nowhere."
The Royal Horticultural Society

CHAPTER ONE

This was not how my life was supposed to be. I'd always thought that by the time I'd succumbed to the wide-fitting section in Clarks, I'd be living in the swanky part of town, welcoming shiny-haired friends into a gleaming kitchen of chrome and posing provocatively in a Cath Kidston pinny as they admired my magnificent muffins. I'd imagined savings building up smugly in the bank, a loving and devoted husband at my side, the eager participant in our thrice-weekly sex sessions involving several seamless changes in position each time.

Instead, here I was. In the wanky part of town. Owner of a damp, dark end-of-terrace hovel with a disconcerting smell. Savings account turned on its head to become a fearsome credit card debt. All alone; the loving and devoted husband exposed as a lying, deceitful rat. The closest I'd been to sexual stirrings was when I'd watched James Martin drizzling hot sauce over two quivering crème caramels on last week's Saturday Kitchen.

At least I still had my career! How many hours *had* I worked this week? About fifty so far over the four days; I'd taken today off so I could move house. Although, it didn't exactly feel like a day off; I'd received a steady stream of calls throughout the morning:

10.00 am "Kate, Martin's not turned up for work. I've been calling and calling him, but there's no answer. Did you give him the day off?"

"No, I didn't."

"Oh, hang on, it's alright, we've found him! He was in the toilets, constipated again. His mobile was in his pocket but he couldn't hear it over the straining."

10.30 am "Kate, head office need the monthly sales figures urgently. I can't find them anywhere."

"Have you looked in the monthly sales figures folder?"

"Er, no, I'll try there, then, shall I?"

11.00 am "Kate, is it alright if I send Alan home? He thinks he's got nits."

"But Alan's bald, isn't he?"

11.30 pm "Kate, a customer wants to know if his health policy covers him for this outbreak of cholera that's reached the UK. Who should I phone for advice?"

"*Cholera?* Are you sure?"

"Oh yes, it's quite deadly, apparently. You start to get spots, then lesions, and then the crown of your head dies from fungus. Everyone here's extremely worried."

"You don't mean chalara dieback, do you?"

"Yes, that's it!"

"I think it's just ash trees that need to be concerned." *And Trunky Tracy, perhaps.*

I turned my phone off in the end. I'd begun to suspect that my team actually enjoyed torturing me.

It was a relief when the removal men finally left. One of them had reminded me of a Grand National winner, with his buck teeth and flared nostrils and his younger side-kick had done a very good impression of a sprinkler, leaving dribbles of yellow urine over the seat of the toilet I'd just scrubbed. I'd had enough of their chirpy, cheeky-chappy banter: "These are nice mugs Missus, they'd look even better with something

in them!" and "Where do you want us to put this telly love,
back in the seventies where it belongs?" Ha bloody ha! My
cheeks ached from hours of phoney grinning; I'd been
anxious to make them believe I was perfectly comfortable in
the company of blue-collar workers and not at all repulsed by
songs about explosive diarrhoea "comes out your bum like a
bullet from a gun" or by the heady aroma of Brut and stale
sweat. My other cheeks were also rather painful after I'd
caught my foot in a hole in the threadbare stair carpet and
descended the last five steps on my arse.

I sat down gingerly on a box which had a list of items
sellotaped onto it. I had started the list with meticulous
attention to detail; the first item read 'Dark blue medium-
sized glass vase with white swirls', but I had clearly lost
patience with the whole process, the list ending abruptly with
'Misc crap s/board'. My wedding dress was draped over a
box in its plastic sheath. I could see it had a large brown stain
on the front, at about crotch-level. Perhaps it was rust;
neither had been used in such a long time. Red Rum had
asked if he could use it to clean his van - the dress, I'd
assumed, not my crotch. I looked round at my life; all my
worldly possessions crammed into cardboard boxes which in
turn were crammed into the largest property that I could
afford on a single salary - and it was about the size of a doll's
house. Where was I going to put all my stuff? I had a sudden
flashback to the very first house I'd bought, a shoebox of a
starter-home that was so small you could answer the front
door whilst sitting upstairs on the loo. And now, over twenty
years later, I was living in something almost as tiny. I simply
hadn't evolved. I may as well stop shaving my arms.

I started to poke about in the boxes without much

enthusiasm. The Ex had swiped most of the best stuff in the St Valentine's Day massacre. He'd chosen the 14th of February as the day we should meet up and separate the spoils of our thirteen years together. His plan had been, I think, to use this date to tug at my heartstrings and engineer a reconciliation. He had turned up with a bottle of wine and wearing his I-think-I'm-George-Clooney winsome smile. I noticed that he'd produced the wine from a Happy Shopper carrier bag, having been to the local Londis. He never did make any real effort. On our twelfth wedding anniversary (linen and silk) I'd wrapped myself, naked, in the lovely new 100% Egyptian cotton bed linen I'd purchased from M&S and sat seductively on the bed waiting for him to arrive home. I waited and waited, thinking that perhaps he'd stopped to buy something silky and sexy for me to slip into. When he finally appeared, he'd presented me with two Union Jack tea towels that he'd picked up at the service station when stopping for petrol. He said: "You're not ill, are you? What's for tea?"

When he'd arrived on the evening of the 14th, I'd made neat stacks of all our possessions in the lounge, ready to be divided up. He'd shown no sign of wanting to make a start and instead had opened the wine, sat down at the kitchen table and started to talk about 'our good old times'. His memories consisted mainly of sun-drenched, care-free holidays - "Do you remember that wonderful hotel we went to, what was it called..." and "Do you remember that fabulous restaurant we ate at, what was it you ordered...". I let him reminisce for a bit before asking: "Do you remember that super weekend we had in Cornwall? You know, the one with Debbie and Paul? You shagged Debbie senseless on the sofa while I was asleep upstairs. What a lovely memory."

His mood had changed abruptly. "How typical of you to throw that in my face!" he'd hissed. "I'm doing my absolute best to make things right between us and all you can do is rake up the past!" He was filled with self-righteous indignation. "Well, I feel sorry for you, I really do. Whilst the rest of us move on with our lives, you're going to end up a very lonely, bitter old woman."

Old woman? I was only forty-three, for Christ's sake! Admittedly, I had been searching high and low for a salad spinner and had recently enjoyed a documentary about whiskered bats (I felt an affinity with them) but even so, I still shopped at New Look occasionally. Well, I looked in their window on my way to Monsoon. It had turned rather ugly at that point. There was a prolonged spate of mud-slinging which culminated in me telling him I didn't care what he took, just as long as I didn't have to look at his stupid, pudding face ever again. It felt good at the time but I was seriously regretting it now. He'd raged through the house in a furious temper while I sat in the kitchen drinking his toxic wine. I hadn't paid much attention to what he was taking. Now, I was one of the few remaining people in the UK (and probably the universe) who didn't own a flat screen TV. My ugly, squat Ferguson set had a video recorder built into it. When had I last watched a video? Our wedding one, probably, before he'd recorded the Spanish Grand Prix over it. Gone too, the lovely retro Roberts radio, the funky cubed iPod speakers, the framed photo of us beaming next to Michael Palin, (we'd managed to position ourselves alongside him at the luggage carousel at Heathrow whilst our friend stood opposite and snapped us, he never even knew)... oh, but they were only things, just material things that I could live without. I had my freedom and my independence; no more picking up fetid socks from the floor or being made to feel guilty for serving up pasta with a dollop of Philly again. Nor did I have to suffer the indignity of having someone prod my stomach and say "Alright, Jabba?" My new life started today. I had to look forwards; I had to stay positive.

There was a knock at the door. I opened it to find my friends Karen and James brandishing a bottle of Sainsbury's champagne at me.

"Hi Kate, it's us!" cried Karen. "We've come to christen your new home! And by that, I don't mean we're going to have sex in it!"

"Unless you're up for it, of course," said James, hopefully, earning himself a thump on his arm from his wife. "Christ, it was difficult to find you; we've never been out this way before - it's really quite rural, isn't it? Nice big field opposite you."

"And there's no danger of it being built on," added Karen, "not with that bloody great pylon in it. Get this open, Kate; we'll have some bubbly then you and I can try out the local pub while James puts your bed together."

"I can't go out, Kazza," I protested, standing back to let them into the narrow hallway. "Look at the state of me, I've been cleaning all day and I absolutely reek of Toilet Duck."

"Nonsense," she replied, her ample form all but filling the tiny space in the hall. James, tall and lanky, ducked too late and whacked his head on the staircase. "You've got to meet the locals; see if the natives are friendly. Come on, pop your cork! If you can remember how to, that is!"

I cautiously slid back the wobbly French windows in the

lounge and eased the cork out of the champagne. It shot up
the tangled garden and disappeared into the gloom. We all
cheered. As I didn't have a clue where the glasses were, James
washed up the mugs that the removal men had been using
and we poured the bubbles into those. I showed them round
the house, which took the best part of ten seconds. I could
tell from their ashen faces what they thought of the place.
Karen was holding her hand over her nose.

"I'm sorry about the smell, I don't know what it is.
Maybe the previous owner is buried under the floorboards."

"It'll be a dead mouse," said James, as he peered at a
large crack in the ceiling, inches from his head. "I expect
you'll come across it sooner or later. It could be up in the
loft, of course. Er, you did get a full structural done, didn't
you?"

"Oh, it's all cosmetic!" Karen exclaimed, feigning
brightness. "It won't take much to cheer this place up, Kate!
How about a trip to Ikea tomorrow?"

"I hate Ikea," I said sulkily. "I can never find my way out
of the bloody place. And I'm skint, anyhow." I may as well
not have spoken; Karen was already getting carried away,
twirling round, her hoopy hippy earrings jiggling madly as
champagne slopped from her mug.

"A few colourful rugs and throws dotted about the place
and a big mirror to open up the hallway. Some lovely scented
candles or perhaps, just to start with, something more
industrial strength. Strip off all this shitty brown swirly
wallpaper, make a feature of the wall over the fireplace, that's
all the rage you know, paint it plum perhaps, that would
cover those stains..." I let her chatter on, leaning, exhausted,
against a couple of boxes annotated for 'Bedroom 3'. I only

had two in this house and one of those was more like a closet. When she finally ran out of steam and champagne, we left James to make a start on the bed and headed off to the pub.

Stepping onto the drive, a figure suddenly popped up at the rickety fence to our right making us both jump. We found ourselves looking at a small, ferrety man, with dark oily hair, a centre parting and very thick glasses. "Hello there!" he called. "I'm Mervyn. I live here, in the middle house - I'm known as Mervyn in the middle!" He gave a great honking laugh, like a goose in a gang bang.

"Hi, I'm Kate," I said, "and this is my friend Karen."

"Aha! All girls together is it?" *Honk honk.* "So I'm going to be living next door to a mad party house, am I? Lots of girly nights and sleepovers I expect!" *Honk.* "Well, as long as you don't play your Durham Durham records too loudly!" *Honk honk honk.*

"No, I won't be living here, Mervyn," said Karen with a twinkle in her eye. "Kate's moving in on her own. She's a single lady you know, well, at least she is at the moment!" She winked at him. *Oh God.* "What about you, Mervyn? Great tank top, by the way! Are you footloose and fancy free too?"

Mervyn gave a rather nervous honk of laughter and wiggled his hands in his trouser pockets. "Well, I wish I was of course, but I live with my dear sister and er, she takes some looking after you know. You girls! Always keeping us men busy, aren't you! Stopping us getting into trouble!" *Honk honk.*

"What's your sister's name, Mervyn?" I asked.

"Sissy."

"Oh, sorry - what's your sissy's name?"

He blinked at me from behind his glasses. "Sissy."

Karen snorted. I decided it was time to go. We said goodnight to Mervyn and started up the lane to the pub. The clocks were due to go forwards at the weekend but even though it was almost officially summertime, the air was cold and dank. The Dog and Gun was an old-fashioned type of pub, with a public and a saloon bar. We chose the saloon. The portly landlord acknowledged us with the briefest of nods and served us vodka and tonics. I peered over the bar but couldn't see any wine bottles. "Where do you hide your wine then?" I asked, jovially. He tapped one of the pumps. *Jesus, wine out of a tap?* I gave an involuntarily shudder.

"At least it won't ever be corked!" Karen laughed, seeing the bright side as usual. The landlord gave a bored shrug. We sat down at a ring-stained wooden table and looked round at the few other drinkers in the bar. We brought the average age down by fifty years.

"Well, it's early yet," said Karen, taking a large gulp of neat vodka before adding some tonic. "Just you wait - there's bound to be some landed gentry types who come in here for a drink after a hard day beating up commoners. They'll take one look at you and whisk you away to a life of luxury and endless games of Spin the Pauper. Give them one whiff of that Toilet Duck and you'll be driving them crazy, you'll see."

"I don't want to drive anyone crazy, Karen, I just want to adjust to life on my own. At my own pace. It's really quite a scary thing, finding myself single after, well, after centuries of always being part of a couple. There's no safety net now; there's just me to pay the bills, cover the mortgage, fix the car. What if I get the sack? What happens then?"

"Then you'll find another job," said Karen firmly. "Or

walk the streets. Plenty of blind men want prostitutes. Stop panicking, you'll cope, you know you will. At least you've managed to buy somewhere and you're not having to rent some scummy flat." I knew she was referring to The Ex, who, despite flogging mortgages to other people for almost twenty years of his life, had been unable to raise a mortgage himself. *Oh, how I laughed.* He was renting a flat in an area he'd referred to on Facebook as 'Water's Edge'. Out of curiosity, I'd driven past it one evening. The bland seventies-built block of flats had clearly been modelled on the Maze Prison. It backed onto a small muddy stream, which had become the final resting place for scores of Asda shopping trolleys.

Karen swirled her drink around and gave me a rather strange, sideways look.

"What?"

"I wasn't sure whether to tell you this or not," she said slowly. "I wondered if you already knew, but as you haven't mentioned it, I assume you don't."

"Know what?" I felt a sudden tension in my stomach. What was she about to say?

"Your ex," she said, looking at me closely. "He's with her. He's with Debbie, The Fucking Trollop. Apparently, her husband found out about their fling and threw her out. Or she chose to leave, I'm not sure which. She's staying at the flat at Crappy Creek, with your ex. They're back together."

It was like being punched in the guts. For a moment, all those dreadful feelings came rushing back; the suspicion, the doubt, the humiliation - the crippling nausea. I took a large gulp of vodka, trying to quash it all back down.

"What about the Devil Child?" I asked, hoping I sounded nonchalant and not like an overwrought sheep.

"The kid's at the flat too. I guess they'll be arguing over who doesn't get custody!" She gave a short burst of laughter, then pulled up short and studied my face. "Are you ok?"

"Yes, I'm fine," I lied. I was shaken. I knew The Ex would eventually find somebody new, but I hadn't figured on him getting back with The FT; I thought they were all over and done with. I took another big swig and pulled myself up straight. "Well, I reckon they deserve one another. I doubt it will last very long, not with that ghastly toddler in tow; you know how rubbish he is with kids." I thought of The Ex in his pokey flat, having to share his 'man-space' with garish plastic toys, constantly tripping over Barbie's Dream House, driven mad by sticky finger prints on his iPad ... not to mention all the tears, tantrums and bed-wetting. I suddenly felt enormously cheered and raised my glass to Karen.

"Well, bums up! Here's to a new start; freedom for me and a life of depressing, domestic misery for him!"

"Bums up!" cried Karen. The regulars looked over at us disapprovingly. Karen beamed at me. "The best thing you can do now is move on, m'dear. Get yourself out and about, don't hide away listening to your old Durham Durham records; go out and meet lots of lovely new people. Why don't you join a dating website? They're terribly popular."

"*No way!* That's so sad, so desperate."

"It's not! Apparently, forty percent of couples meet on the Internet these days. It's the way forwards."

"Well, I don't want to."

"Why not?"

"Because I don't want to be groomed by a paedophile!" I might have hissed that a bit too loudly, as several pairs of bloodshot eyes swivelled in our direction again.

"Don't be silly. Anyway, James and I are throwing a dinner party next Saturday. Nothing fancy, just a few friends from work. You must come."

I noticed she wasn't looking me in the eye. "Who's going?" I asked suspiciously.

"Oh, like I said, just some friends from work and er, someone James plays cricket with."

"What's that loud ringing sound? Ooh I know - alarm bells! Don't tell me you're trying to fix me up with someone, it would be so hideously embarrassing-"

"Rubbish, of course I'm not!" Karen cried, unconvincingly. "It's just that Nigel..." *Nigel?* "is such a lovely guy and he's been single for a while now..." *I'm not surprised with a name like Nigel!* "and both James and I thought you two would really hit it off."

"Bloody hell, Karen," I groaned. "I can't believe you're trying to set me up with someone already. I've been out of the dating game for years and years, I can't remember what it's like, I wouldn't know what to say, how to act-"

"Oh, come off it Kate, nothing's changed! Short skirt, high heels, laugh at his jokes. Simples! Great stuff, we'll count you in for next Saturday, then."

I attempted to protest but all resistance was futile. Oh God, a blind date. Called Nigel. Not exactly the exhilarating new start I'd hoped for. We walked back to the house to find James stressed and sweaty, surrounded by bits of bed frame and slats of wood. I didn't know why I needed a double bed; it took up the whole room and even after The Ex had moved out I'd continued to sleep right on the edge of the mattress rather than spreading myself out. I didn't tell James that though, it would seem a bit ungrateful now. I held steadfastly onto the frames while he rammed the slats into place.

After James and Karen had left, I crept, exhausted, into bed. I was expecting some much-needed peace and quiet, but the radiator in the bedroom clanged so loudly I thought someone was in the room banging saucepan lids on the floorboards. When the creaks, groans and gurgles from the cistern finally died down and I fell asleep, I dreamt my hips got stuck between the walls on the landing and I couldn't move; I struggled and struggled but I was trapped. The fire brigade had to blast me out with a water cannon. I woke up in a cold sweat and the dead mouse smell in my nostrils.

CHAPTER TWO

Every single part of me ached as I arrived at the offices of Perypils Insurance on Monday morning. I'd spent the weekend scrubbing and scouring and was now as high as a kite from bleach fumes. I'd been extremely liberal with it, attempting to smother the pungent smell, but it hadn't worked and I knew I was going to have to venture up into the loft this evening. After a lukewarm shower, I'd hosed myself down with Sure deodorant, Impulse body spray and the last of my Chanel No 5, but I was still worried I smelt a bit rodenty.

I called "Morning Stanley!" to the guy sat behind the reception desk, who fixed me with a sour stare.

"I want a word with you. I caught two of your people tailgating again this morning. Both tried to get through the pass door when they thought I wasn't looking, but I caught them red-handed. They gave me a load of lip as well, the cheeky buggers. I want something done about them."

Good morning to you too! "Well, that's very disappointing to hear, Stan. Did you take their names?" I approached the reception desk and realised Stalin Stan was standing, not sitting.

"Of course I took their names. It was the same two that always cause trouble; that German one with the bolt through his ear and his sidekick with all the tattoos. I don't know how he gets away with it, some of those tattoos are quite obscene, they must breach the dress code. If I had my way, they'd be forcibly removed. Always forgetting their passes those two, it's not good enough, it's about time something was done about them."

Great - Ben and Danny, two of my finest. No surprises there. I took the stairs up to the fourth floor where my teams were spread over two wings, totalling almost two hundred staff. Last year, I had one hundred. Had my salary doubled too? *Had it buggery*. Extra holiday, perhaps? A bigger bonus? Nope. Just twice the workload and the constant urge to self-harm.

I tried to devote an equal amount of time to both my departments, so I spent alternate weeks seated in each wing. This week, *thank God,* I was amongst the Property teams. I felt a bit safer here. The other wing housed Customer Complaints, who were not to be approached without a crucifix and garlic. I looked around for Ben and Danny's team manager, The Lazy Shit George, who should have started at 8.00 am. It was twenty past and there was no sign of him. I sighed. If you want something doing...

I logged into my system and called Ben and Danny to my desk, seeing out of the corner of my eye, the unread email count rocketing skywards. The two lads shuffled over, tugging at their floppy fringes and fidgeting with their studded belts.

"Right. Who forgot their pass this morning?"

"Er, that was me," mumbled Ben.

"And you tried to follow Danny through the door using his pass?"

"Well, I didn't want to trouble the guy on reception, he looked very busy and-"

"So you tailgated. What's your understanding of

tailgating?"

They both looked at their feet. "It's not allowed."

"And Danny, did you put on a German accent when you spoke to Stanley?"

"Um, er, I might have done, perhaps. Sometimes I do slip back into my native tongue."

"You were born and bred in Gloucester, weren't you?"

"Well, yes, but after I was hypnotised at the Munich beer festival, I find that, on occasions, I do suddenly break into a German accent-"

"Oh for God's sake, Danny, that's enough." I lost patience. "You know not to tailgate and you've been very rude to Stanley. It's completely unacceptable. You can both go and apologise and pray that he accepts it. Otherwise, I'll have no choice but to start disciplinary action." Although Christ knows when I'd have the time, the number of unread emails was already up to one hundred and sixty three.

"But he'll never accept an apology!" cried Ben. "He's such a Nazi. He'll just go on and on at us like he always does, we can't even get a temporary pass off him without thumbscrews! He's always picking on us."

"I'm afraid that's tough luck, guys. Hopefully it will teach you to remember your passes in future. Now, off you go. And make it convincing. And in English. Hang on a minute; what's that on your arm, Ben? Is that a new tattoo?"

"What, the Bart Simpson one? Nah, had it ages."

"No, the one next to Bart. Is that a-"

"That? Oh, er, that's an ancient symbol. Represents the Greek god of, um, tools."

"It's a penis, isn't it?"

"What? No, no, it's not. Do you think it looks like a

penis? Some women think everything looks like a phallus, don't they? I think it's a condition, phallusitis, or strapadicktome, or something."

I kept a straight face. "You'll have to keep it covered up while you're at work."

"But no one will notice, it's really small."

"Life-size then, is it? Just cover it up please, Ben."

They sloped off to face the wrath of Stan, who had probably lined up a firing squad in eager anticipation. Phallusitis! Cheeky beggars. Still, I was impressed that I'd recognised a penis after all this time. Talking of which, there was still no sign of The Lazy Shit George. Another of my team managers, The Drain, entered the office and removed his greasy anorak. He took his Pot Noodle out of his Asda bag-for-life and placed it on his desk next to Friday's flaccid banana and his tea-stained mug. His wife used to make sandwiches every day for him as part of his packed lunch, but she had left him just before Christmas, running off with her dance instructor. The Drain said he'd known something was amiss when she stopped bothering to peel the foil from his Dairylea triangles. I watched him hobble awkwardly towards the drinks machine. "What's up Martin?" I called out. "Has your back gone again?"

He changed direction and limped to my desk, a pained expression on his pasty face.

"No, it's my leg," he replied, clutching at it with a dramatic grimace.

"Oh dear, has your sciatica come back?"

"No."

"It's not thrombosis again, is it?"

"No." He scratched his bald patch, looking embarrassed.

"Actually, I've been having salsa lessons."

Don't smirk. "Oh, well that's, er, very energetic of you!" I said brightly. "How did you hurt your leg?"

"I'd really rather not say."

"Did you twist it or something?" I pressed him.

"If you must know, it was one of the lady dancers," he said, sounding indignant. "I was partnered with this, er, this rather large woman, which I thought was most unsuitable as I was half her size. She had these great, big hairy hands... I tried to protest, but the instructor said there wasn't anyone else for me to dance with, even though there were several young ladies sitting around without partners. I was told they were being rested."

"And what happened?"

"Well, it was my partner, you see, she was most aggressive; wouldn't let me lead and almost wrenched my arm out of its socket during the Ricky Martin medley." He gave an indignant sniff. "It turns out *she* used to be a *he*."

"Oh, er, right. But how did you hurt your leg?"

"I trod on his foot. He kicked me."

I managed to keep a straight face until he had limped out of sight but my email inbox quickly wiped the smile off my face - two hundred and twelve unread! *Jesus.* I'd only taken one day off! It was ridiculous, how the hell was I going to get through that lot? I clicked on the only one that actually mattered; the month end sales result. Great stuff! March's performance had been good and my teams had, somehow, finished on target. I thought I'd share this news with Brett, my boss, so I emailed him:

Good morning Brett
    Great news from Cheltenham - we achieved 101% of target in
    March! Now looking forward to an excellent April!
Cheers
Kate

It was a pathetic attempt to obtain some praise, but what the hell. If he sent a congratulatory email back I could circulate it around the teams to demonstrate how much the management team appreciated their efforts. As I started to assemble my inbox into some sort of order, I saw his reply drop in. I opened it eagerly.

Kate
    The target is now 110%. The Chief Exec issued a directive to
    all sites on Friday. So you've underachieved. Can you let me
    have your plans to address this performance gap by 9.30.

Brett
Sent from my iPhone

I stared at the screen in dismay. I felt like an over-eager puppy that had just presented its master with a stick and was waiting all waggly-tailed for a pat on the head. Instead, my master had chucked the stick over the edge of a cliff. A ten percent increase in target! Just like that? How could it be done? I took a deep, calming breath, picked up the phone and dialled his mobile number. It rang several times before being answered with a breathless "Hello?" It was rather noisy in the background, I thought I could hear an announcer - was he at a station?

"Brett, it's Kate. Hello? Brett? Are you there?"

"Hello, yes? Who is it?"

"It's Kate."

"Ah, yes, hi Kate! Really enjoyed last night babe; you were fantastic. Shall I come to yours tonight? I'll bring the oil."

Woah! "Er, wrong Kate, I think, Brett." *I bloody well hope it's the wrong Kate!* "Kate King. From work. You remember me? I've been working for you for the last two years."

"Oh, oh yes, of course, hi Kate. Can you just hang on a minute?"

I could hear him speaking with someone. Their voices were muffled, but I thought I caught "both ways on Barnstorming Bob."

"Right, Kate. What's up?"

"I'm calling about the sales target, Brett and the sudden increase. I'm really concerned about how I'm going to achieve it, especially when there's a freeze on recruitment. My staff numbers are down."

"Yes, yes," Brett now sounded as if he was standing next to a busy road. "I understand your concerns but it's a bit of a no-brainer I'm afraid, Kate. The Chief Exec has issued a directive for all sites to achieve a hundred and ten percent, no exceptions. Failure to do so is career-threatening."

"But I don't know how I can do it, Brett," I tried hard not to sound too whiney. "Ten percent is such a massive increase. What can I do to create that sort of improvement?"

"What about the complaints teams?"

"What about them?"

"Well, they haven't got a sales target, have they? Give them one. That should do the trick."

"You want the *complaints* team to sell?" I was incredulous. "But, but, they're not trained or anything and I don't think it's really appropriate-"

"Got to go, Kate, I'm running late. We can discuss this later. Can you send me your prediction for April's results?"

"What? But April only started a few minutes ago! How can I predict-"

"Bearing in mind you've got to be at a hundred and ten percent."

"Um-"

"Good, good, I'll put you down for a hundred and ten. I'll be in Cheltenham next week, so we can talk it all through then. Everything else ok?"

"Er, well-"

"Great stuff. Cheers then!"

He was gone. *Bloody hell.* I wondered how my team managers would react to the target increase. They'd already taken on bigger teams and were beginning to creak at the seams. Last year I had five team managers in the Property department. Now I had just three. I looked round at them. The Drain was finishing a cup of tea. As he tipped up his mug, I could see it had 'I'M A TWAT' printed in red on the base. I suspected it had been a Secret Santa gift from his team.

The Lazy Shit George had arrived and was seated at his desk, next to his youngest, prettiest, blondest team member. I saw I had an email from him. I opened it.

Kate
Soz I was l8. 4got to change clox! G.

He was already on a formal HR plan for underperformance; he really wasn't helping himself. Thank God he had such excellent communication skills with which to redeem himself! Why get up and walk twenty feet to apologise when you can email? My third team manager, Hissing Cyn, had annual leave this week. She'd said she didn't have anything planned, but was intending to spend some time in the public galleries at the Crown Court. She enjoyed the bankruptcy cases most of all.

I knew I couldn't put it off any longer; I was going to have to see how the Customer Complaints teams were doing. I stopped at the drinks machine to brace myself with a strong coffee. Big Andy, a fellow whipping boy, was collecting a cup of hot chocolate that looked as if it had been scooped up from a muddy puddle.

"Katie, old girl!" he boomed. "How did the move go? You look bloody knackered!"

"I am. It went okay, thanks for asking. Still surrounded by boxes and a horrid smell, but hey, I'm in."

I relayed my conversation with our boss. He laughed. "Typical Brett, wave a magic wand and the sales fairy will uplift performance by ten percent! Did you say he's coming down again next week?"

"Yes! I can't understand it; he's been down twice already this year. That's double what he managed for the whole of last year."

"You know why, don't you, old girl? He can't work at the Manchester site any more, not since that nasty business with what's-her-name's husband and he's not welcome in Bridgend after he told that Stevie Wonder joke and Boss-Eyed Brenda reported him to HR. And as for Birmingham, well, every time he parks his car there, it gets vandalised. He seems to think it's the kids from the school over the road but I don't think they would have written 'Brett is a prick' down the side of his car in whiteboard pen, do you?"

"He might think twice about coming here, too, after my teams have shoved his magic wand up his bottom. Anyway, I've got to shoot, I'm just on my way round to Sleepy Hollow."

"Jesus, without a stake and a hammer? I'll say a prayer for you."

It was wonderful to drive home in the light; it seemed as if summer was just around the corner. I felt quite elated until I opened the front door and the smell hit me. Surely it was even worse today? There was nothing for it; I was going to have to go into the loft. I took my torch from the car and dragged a chair upstairs, standing on it to remove the loft hatch. I poked my head cautiously up into the dark space, recalling a horror film I'd seen where a woman had done exactly the same thing, only to find a faceless ghoul creaking backwards and forwards in a rocking chair. I couldn't see a thing. There didn't appear to be a light and it was clear my £3.99 garage-bought stubby torch wasn't up to the job. I rather thankfully abandoned the project and went to change out of my work suit.

I pulled a pair of jeans from the narrow airing cupboard and stepped into them. As I zipped them up, I caught sight of a large black mark on the left leg at shin level. Damn, what was that? I peered closer - oh my God, a spider! I screamed out in horror and thwacked manically at the great hairy beast with flailing hands. I shot down stairs, shrieking and slapping myself all over in case it was still clinging to me. I *hate* spiders. Horrid things; they look so evil, always hunched up, hideous great legs that suddenly scuttle across the carpet towards you. *Ugh.* I stood trembling at the bottom of the stairs. Whatever was I going to do? The Husband had always dealt with spider emergencies. Smaller ones I could hoover up, but this was a monster; I knew I wouldn't be able to put a glass over it, I'd never force myself close enough.

With my arms wrapped protectively around me, I crept gingerly up the stairs. Oh God, there it was, on the landing. It was massive. I cried out in revulsion and ran back downstairs and out of the front door. I had to get help - *please let Mervyn be in, please.* Barefoot, I ran down my drive and up Mervyn's. He didn't have a doorbell, so I hammered on the glass panel in the front door. A stone squirrel squinted reproachfully up at me from the doorstep. There was no answer. He must be in, his red Fiat Panda was on the drive and I could hear music - was that Liza Minnelli singing?

I knocked again, more prolonged this time. Nothing. I stood back and looked up at the windows. A curtain twitched - someone was there! I poked the letterbox open and shouted "Mervyn! Sissy! It's Kate from next door. I need some help please!" I tried to peer through the flap and thought I could make out a pair of feet on the stairs encased in sensible Hush Puppies. I couldn't tell if they were men's or women's.

"Sissy, is that you? It's Kate from next door. Are you there?"

"Er, just a minute Kate." It was Mervyn. *Thank goodness.* I stood back from the door with a huge sigh of relief. I sensed movement inside the house but it seemed like an age before Mervyn finally opened the door, his head appearing in the narrow gap. He peered out nervously.

"Oh Mervyn, I'm so sorry to disturb you," I babbled, "but I really need some help. There's a big spider in the house and I can't bear them, my husband always used to do things like that, I just can't go near it, could you please, please come and get it for me, I'd be ever so grateful."

Mervyn blinked rapidly behind his thick glasses. "A spider you say? A big spider?" He swallowed. "Um, er, how big, would you say, exactly?"

"It's like a wig with eight legs! Could you come and get it for me?"

"Um, right, er, yes, ok. I'll, um, just go and tell Sissy where I'm going."

He closed the front door and I went to wait by mine; I wasn't going inside on my own. I hopped from foot to foot until Mervyn eventually appeared, wearing a pair of extremely heavy-duty gloves, which ended almost at his elbows. He looked as if he was ready to do some falconry, not trap a spider under a glass.

"Thanks for this Mervyn," I said, "it's really good of you. It was at the top of the landing when I last saw it."

"Right," he stood at the open front door, but didn't go in. He slapped a gloved fist into his palm in the manner of Robin when he'd just received an order from Batman. I pushed the front door wide open and stood back, nodding at him to go ahead. He hesitated, then stepped carefully inside, looking all around him.

"I think it's upstairs, Mervyn," I told him again, following him inside. I noticed he'd put his beige tank top on inside out. He nodded and started up the stairs, a bead of sweat breaking out on his upper lip. Strange, it wasn't exactly a warm evening. At the top of the stairs, he stopped and crouched down.

"Can you see it?" I asked from the bottom of the stairs.

"Y-yes," he stammered.

"Shall I fetch a glass to put over it?" I called.

"Er, yes, yes," he sounded breathless. He must be ever so unfit if a small flight of stairs made him pant. I went to the kitchen to fetch the largest glass I could find and picked up my credit card statement from the table; he could slip that underneath, it was thick enough. I took them up to Mervyn who was still crouched at the top of the stairs.

"Here you are, Mervyn." I said, holding them out. "Is the glass big enough, do you think?"

He turned a white face towards me, taking the glass and statement in his gloved hands, which were shaking. It all looked rather cumbersome.

"Shall I hold your gloves for you?" I asked.

"No!" he snapped so sharply that I jumped in alarm. He recovered himself and pushed his glasses back up his sweaty nose. "I'll keep them on," he said, adding by way of explanation, "Eczema."

"Oh, I see. Can you get the glass over it, then?" I could see he was still too far away from the spider to be able to cover it with the glass. Perhaps he had poor eyesight. "I'll just be downstairs, Mervyn," I said, unable to bear the sight of the spider any longer and not wanting to be too close if he aggravated it.

"Yes, right, ok then, here goes." He edged a bit closer to the hairy monster and braced himself. I went downstairs and stood in the hall. I heard the glass go down on the floor with a bang and then a piercing girly scream rang out. *Jesus!* Had he seen the outstanding balance on my credit card statement?

"Are you all right?" I called up in concern.

"Yes," he squeaked. I heard him bang the glass down again. Then again. It must be giving him the right run around. I heard several exclamations, incensed grunting and then a vehement cry, followed by sustained, frenzied thumping. I looked up at the ceiling in alarm - I thought he was going to come right through it. He finally appeared, red-faced and perspiring heavily, holding the glass with the contents hidden by his glove.

"Got it," he announced breathlessly. "I'll just let it go outside."

Let it go? He'd just stamped the living daylights out of it, for Christ's sake! Stick some thread up its bum and you could probably make a kite out of it. I watched him make a great show of pretending to release it in the bushes.

"Off it runs!" he said cheerfully. *Floats more like, like a dry leaf in the wind.*

"It won't get back in the house, will it?" I asked innocently, unable to help myself.

"No, no, it's scuttled off in completely the opposite direction! Off to find a nice warm shed, no doubt."

I thanked him profusely, called him an "absolute star" and he looked very pleased with himself, even managing to unleash a few feeble honks of laughter before he hurried back next door to "give Sissy her afters". I really hoped he meant apple crumble and custard.

As I rubbed Vanish carpet stain remover into the spidery remnants on the landing, I began to wonder how I was ever going to cope without a man. I couldn't go squealing next door every time I came across an insect. I had to be strong and self-sufficient now, like a super hero. Or heroine. Which one would I be? I'd be Robust Woman! That was it; I had to be more *robust*. I took the cloth and the Vanish back downstairs to put away under the kitchen sink, dropping them and screaming in terror when I saw another spider on the kitchen floor. It turned out to be the top off a tomato.

CHAPTER THREE

Saturday evening

I was sitting on my bed as if it was a life raft. There were boxes and suitcases full of clothes piled up all around the bedroom. It hadn't been the easiest of weeks; the increase in sales target had gone down like a ton of hot horse shit and when I'd tentatively approached the complaint team managers about making sales they'd reacted like I'd suggested group sex with The Wurzels. As Brett was due in Cheltenham next week, I'd organised a colleague coffee session so the teams could air their concerns directly to him. That's if we could get past the usual inane questions about why they weren't allowed to wear leggings or why the porridge-eaters couldn't use a different dishcloth.

The pressure was getting to everyone. When I'd arrived at work yesterday morning, I'd passed The Drain who was limping awkwardly towards the door, clutching his anorak.

"I'm going home," he said, without stopping.

"Oh dear, is it your leg again?" I called after him.

"Followed through." He disappeared down the stairs.

And as if work hadn't been challenging enough, home was not fairing any better. My parents had been over today so I could show them round my new residence; I don't think it was admiration that had made their mouths hang open. My father's first words were "Bloody disaster that flat roof over the porch. Deteriorate like buggery, they do, surprised it hasn't caved in already." That was before he'd even seen

29

inside the place. I think he soon realised that having a flat roof over the porch was going to be the least of my worries.

My mother had bought me a lovely pink camellia in a pot. I placed it on an even patch of rubble on the patio where it sat looking nervously around at the thuggish weeds straining up towards it from between the gaps in the crazy paving. Behind it, the menacing jungle waited, ready to advance and engulf it in darkness. Mum stood in the lounge, gazing around in bewilderment. "When are you going home, dear?"

"I am home, Mum. This is where I live now."

"Don't be so silly, dear! This isn't your wallpaper. When are you going home?"

I knew another change would be too much for her to take in; she'd only just stopped asking after The Ex. Each time I told her we'd split up, she'd get upset all over again. It had, at least, provided my father with recurrent opportunities to refer to The Ex as that "useless idle pillock", which I never tired of hearing.

 Dad ventured into the loft and rigged up some makeshift lighting so at least we could see what was up there. The answer was nothing. There were no dead bodies, or faceless ghouls or any "bleeding insulation" as my Dad called down in disgust. No wonder the house felt so cold. At least the smell had begun to abate or perhaps I had just become accustomed to it. I had a cup of tea and a piece of Battenberg with my mother as we watched my father walking disapprovingly around the garden. "Bloody slugs," he announced on his return. "You've got to watch out for those bastards, Kate. They've mutated into monsters this year, they'll eat bloody everything I tell you, everything. Come across from Europe, they have, probably encouraged by the French; they're always sending us their shite. Look at that Renault we had, a complete heap of rubbish. And there's Arsène Wenger, of course."

"And Kermit the Frog," added my mother.

Dad decided it was time to take her home. I waved them off, saying I'd see them at my brother's 40th birthday party and promising faithfully to keep my guttering clean. Now, it was Saturday night and to round off a perfect week, I faced the ultimate horror of a blind date. *Why was I doing this?* Had I ever been on a blind date before? I thought back, trying to conjure up the faces of those long-forgotten boys I'd been out with - the greasy-haired car mechanic who'd presented me with a song he said he'd written for me which I'd thought was incredibly romantic and slept with him, but as I was getting dressed I heard the exact same lyrics on one of his Motorhead records; the good-looking farmer who I'd fancied for ages but who'd asked me, when we'd eventually got it together, if I owned anything "fleecy" I could slip into; the one night stand who I thought looked like Paul Young, but in the sober light of day was more like Paul Daniels - but yes, actually, I had sort of been on a blind date before. A friend had tried to fix me up once, at a party. It had been with her boyfriend's mate, who was called Gareth and when I'd walked into the party in my green rah-rah skirt and black lace fingerless mittens, my friend had pointed out two blokes who were stood together in a corner of the room. I went over to them and asked which one was Gareth. They took one look at me, pointed at each other and exclaimed "He is!" I could still hear the howls of laughter reverberating around the room, as Suggs sang "You're An Embarrassment".

What was I going to wear? I stood in front of my bulging wardrobe; there were many more garments hanging from rails in the second bedroom. I was going to have to undertake a mass cull, as the house simply wasn't large enough for all my clothes. Karen had called tonight a dinner party, so jeans were definitely out. I didn't want to look too over-dressed, *too desperate*, but neither did I want to look like a buttoned-up willy-frightener. I pulled out a dark green, knee-length woollen dress. It was shapeless, but I could chuck a belt on and perhaps liven it up a bit with a funky necklace. I'd seen Gok do it enough times on the telly and his victims usually turned out alright.

I re-applied another layer of make-up, then quickly removed some eye-liner when Beetlejuice glared back at me menacingly from the bathroom mirror. I attacked the ever-present dark circles under my eyes with great splodges of concealer, a product that should be prosecuted under the Trade Descriptions Act for concealing precisely sod all. I was in a foul mood, I didn't want to go. Why hadn't I said no? I was too weak. *I must change.* I didn't want anyone pulling my strings anymore; I'd had enough of that during my marriage. I Googled: 'assertiveness'. A huge amount of information flashed up; there were books, courses, exercises – ugh, something dodgy-looking - there was obviously a massive demand for this sort of stuff. So it wasn't just me, then. I clicked on a questionnaire entitled 'How Assertive Are You?' Question number one was: You have stayed at home all day waiting for the electrician. He doesn't turn up. What do you do?

a. Feel mad but decide to wait and see what happens. *Oh yes, and perhaps he'd like to fondle my breasts when he finally shows up?*

b. Phone and ask where he is. *"Yes, hello there .. oh, you're in the pub, are you? No problem. So sorry to have troubled you."*

c. Phone and arrange another appointment, telling him you've taken time off work. *Why the hell would you want to arrange another appointment with this waster?*

d. Phone. Shout about unreliability and slam the phone down. *Surely that's what everyone would do? It must be the right answer.*

I just about had enough time so I completed all ten questions. As I answered mainly D's, I was given a score of eight, which indicated that my behaviour was mainly aggressive. What a load of old bollocks! I was never ever aggressive; the stupid scoring must be wrong. Such a waste of time. I rammed my feet into a pair of black high heels and booted an empty lap-top bag right across the room. I was sick of tripping over the bloody thing.

I decided I'd drive to Karen and James'. I really would have loved to have a drink, but I knew that after the first two glasses of wine my tongue would no longer fit my mouth and the slurring would start. There was no way back from that. I wanted to be able to hold a proper conversation, not just do the glazed-over, unfocussed nodding that I performed when I was drunk, repeating "Oh ... right" which means "Even though I'm trying to look sober, I haven't taken in a single word you've said". As I reluctantly left the house, I saw a curtain twitch in one of the upstairs rooms next door. Mervyn's sister, perhaps? I hadn't met her yet, although I knew she must be a fairly large lady, judging by the Himalayan-sized bra I'd seen hanging from their whirligig. I unlocked the car and set off to the dinner party with a Gareth-sized sense of doom.

Karen opened the door to me, her face flushed red from the heat of the kitchen and I guessed, grape juice, as she seemed rather merry. "Kate, you made it! Everyone's here already. Nigel was here first, actually," she gave me a conspiratorial nudge as she pulled me inside. "He's obviously pretty keen!" *Oh God.* Karen was always so loud; surely he would have heard her say that? She took my coat and practically shoved me into the lounge where the others were gathered.

"This is Kate everyone! James, get her a drink would you babe, I've got to go and stir the risotto, otherwise it will stick to the pan like shit to a blanket!"

A grinning James got up from the sofa to peck me on the cheek. He introduced me to two smiley couples whose names I instantly forgot and then to a very pretty blonde woman called Faye, who was dressed in a white shirt over blue skinny jeans and funky cowboy boots. She had her nose pierced. I immediately felt middle-aged.

"And this is Nigel." As James finished his introductions, a tall slim man struggled up out of a leather beanbag to shake my hand. He was in his forties, with dark hair that was beginning to grey a little at the temples. He was wearing a pale blue shirt, rimless glasses and a cheery smile. He offered me his beanbag, which I declined. I wasn't about to sit down on an unpredictable moving object that would, no doubt, emit a loud farting sound the minute my bottom sank into it.

I perched on the arm of the sofa and turned my attention to one of the couples, asking them how they knew Karen and James. This was safe territory. I realised I no longer had any idea how to behave in a potential date situation; I'd thought it would all come flooding back to me.

Damn it; why hadn't I Googled 'How to resuscitate your libido after it's recently committed suicide' or something useful like that? Too late now.

A rather shrill-sounding Karen called us into the dining room. The table was beautifully arranged but my heart sank when I saw nameplates. Of course, how predictable, she had seated me next to Nigel. I felt so awkward, but he was entirely at ease and chatted away about his work (Forestry Commission), his son (twenty three, no longer lives at home – hooray!) and his passion for cricket (bats at number three but can also bowl if required).

He asked me about myself - Insurance (very dull), soon-to-be-divorced (very embittered), just moved house (very skint). In comparison, the lovely Faye was absolutely intriguing. She taught art at the same school as Karen, having spent several years travelling around Asia "for spiritual inspiration". She was named after the actress Faye Dunaway as her mother was a huge fan of Bonnie and Clyde. It could have been worse she figured, as her mother was also a fan of Butch Cassidy. All the guys were fascinated by her piercings, of which she had several. Most she couldn't show us, but she did pull up her shirt to reveal her belly button ring. I noticed her tummy was very brown and flat. I could feel my own expanding. The chunky, elasticated belt I'd put on kept rising up over my spare tyre and I tried to tug it down surreptitiously when no one was looking. I realised that Karen had invited Faye so that Nigel and I didn't have the pressure of being the only single ones there. It was a smart move, but I wished she'd chosen someone less engaging. Someone older. And fatter. Preferably with a smattering of zits. And halitosis.

Nigel, I noticed, found it very easy to chat to everyone. I admired the way he could keep a conversation flowing and be interested as well as being interesting. He really did seem very nice; I tried hard not to picture him in just his batting pads. I couldn't tell if he fancied me or not, but he did briefly hold eye contact for a little longer than you would normally expect. I felt a sudden rush of excitement. Gosh, it was quite an unfamiliar sensation; I thought everything had dried up for good.

When the meal was over, we found ourselves stood together, backs against the primrose Aga as we laughed at James' attempts to operate his fancy new coffee machine. He'd managed to find the instructions for it, peering at them drunkenly before exclaiming, "Bollocks to this, they're in Swa-fucking-hili!" and shoving them down the waste disposal. He was now attempting to pour water into the part that I thought the coffee should go in, whilst swaying precariously from side to side. The others had retired to the lounge, apart from Karen, who came into the kitchen to tell James to hurry up with the coffee. She looked pointedly from me to Nigel and then gave me a very knowing smirk. I ignored her, praying Nigel hadn't noticed.

We stayed in the kitchen together, enjoying our chat and in no rush to re-join the others. He really was rather lovely; I wasn't used to having a man actually listen to me and respond to what I was saying. The Ex-Husband just used to grunt or go "mmmm" without lifting his head from his iPhone/iPad/laptop/newspaper/Haynes manual; I'd come to believe that I was just a very boring woman. No wonder I'd been so worried about going on a date, but what do you know? The very first one and I'd met someone I really liked. I had even managed to be engaging whilst being stone cold sober! He appeared to like me too; at least, he hadn't run away screaming. Neither had he seemed to want to follow Faye into the lounge with his tongue hanging out like the other guys had done. Perhaps the piercings alarmed him. Was he going to ask to see me again? The evening was beginning to wind down, so time was running out. Should I ask him out? *Be bold* - the new, independent me. He'd told me he lived in Borden, on the outskirts of the forest; that wasn't too far from me, we could easily meet up in a lovely country pub, there were lots out that way. I cleared my throat, feeling my heart pump a little faster.

"So, Nigel," I said, smiling in what I hoped was a suggestive, seductive manner. "What do you do for entertainment in Borden, in the evenings?"

"Well," he replied, taking a sip from his glass of wine and pushing his glasses further back up his nose. "There's a really good dogging scene."

You what? Had he said "dogging"? I stared at him, searching his face for signs that he was joking. I couldn't see any.

"Yes," he continued, "it's really quite developed now you know, especially around the forest, of course. Some really excellent places. I could show you, if you're, er, interested, that is." He looked at me closely, trying to gauge my response. I was utterly speechless. *Dogging?* Had he really just asked me to go dogging with him? I knew I'd been out of the dating game for a while, but even so ... didn't people normally go for a drink, or for a meal? Perhaps had a cheeky snog if things went well. But dogging - was that normal these days? Did he expect us just to watch, or to participate? Oh God, what should I say-

"Karen!" I cried, making Nigel jump out of his skin. Karen had entered the kitchen and I could have kissed her. She looked at me, startled.

"We were just talking about Nigel's role at the Forestry Commission," I babbled, grabbing her arm. "And it's a lot more interesting than just tree-hugging, I can tell you!" *Hell yes!* "Anyway, I've got to go now, so thank you so much for such a lovely evening and it was great to meet you Nigel." *You bloody weirdo.* I backed away and dipped into the lounge to say goodbye to the others. Karen came to see me out, looking very concerned.

"What on earth's wrong, Kate? You haven't got the shits, have you? I bloody well told James that cream was off, but he said it would be fine, it was only a week or so past its sell-by, there was only the tiniest bit of fur-"

"No, I'm fine, just, er, a bit tired all of a sudden." I tugged at the door latch. *Let me out of here.* "I'll call you tomorrow. Thanks again. Night!"

Oh my Christ. I drove home, my head in a whirl. What a disastrous foray into dating territory; I couldn't tell Cliff Richard from Gary Glitter! How was I ever going to survive unscathed? Perhaps I shouldn't bother and just stay single. It was far safer, required a lot less effort and I could wear my comfy old grey pants without shame. But who was going to look after me in my old age? What if I became ill and couldn't cope on my own? I couldn't imagine my brother caring for me, and as for his mad wife... it would be like a re-enactment of 'Misery'. I sighed as I turned into the lane. It was only a first attempt and I shouldn't give up hope so easily. I must be more resilient. *More robust.*

As I pulled up in front of my house, I saw a shadowy

figure at next door's window, peeking out from a gap in the curtains. I could make out long hair and the curves of a sizable bust so assumed it must be Mervyn's well-endowed sister. I gave her a cheery wave to let her know she'd been spotted but the figure instantly ducked backwards. Great, there were weirdoes all around me. I thought of Nigel, in the forest, creeping up to someone's car, breathing heavily, windows steaming up ... stop, stop. My stomach gave a lurch and I had to let myself into the house very quickly. I think Karen might have been right about the cream; I was in grave danger of doing it on my own doorstep.

CHAPTER FOUR

Monday

I was due to meet Brett at 9.30 in the canteen to discuss the sales targets. I'd arranged a colleague coffee session for 11.00 so he could speak to some of the staff about the targeting and explain the rationale for the increase. Greed, of course, was the rationale, but it would be interesting to see how he described it.

I waited for ten minutes and then called him on his mobile.

"Yes, hi Kate, I'm not far off."

"Where are you?"

"Er, just a minute..." big pause "smells like Wolverhampton."

"But that's an hour away at least!" I cried.

"S'pose so."

"Well, I'd better put the coffee session back a bit, because we need to discuss the issue first, before you face the staff. I'd arranged it for eleven-"

"You stupid bloody bitch!"

"*You what?* Now look, there's really no need for that sort of-"

"Why don't you learn to drive, you stupid bloody woman! Yes, you, dipshit! Get your heap of crap out of my way..."

I pressed the off button. I realised I couldn't put the coffee session back as it would run into the lunch hours and then there would be carnage on the phones. Oh well, Brett would just have to go into battle unarmed. I returned to the complaints teams, who were already buzzing from a high volume of calls. I'd inherited the department from my nemesis, Cruella, at the beginning of the year after we'd gone head to head for the same job. I'd won; the fact that she was pregnant almost certainly had nothing to do with the company's decision. Although I'd only managed the teams for a few months, I was beginning to understand what might have turned her quite so demonic.

"Kate! Pat's phoned in sick again. Her boil's got worse. Her husband tried to burst it with a knitting needle whilst a neighbour held back the folds of flesh but Pat thinks it's infected now. She's having to lie face-down on the bed until the doctor comes. So I suppose you'll be expecting me to run her team as well as my own?"

I studied the pencil-thin figure of The MC (Mini-Cruella, or The Miserable Cow, both titles fitted perfectly). She always dressed in a dark skirt suit that swamped her tiny frame, and an ever-present Victorian cameo brooch aged her well beyond her thirty years.

"Thank you for letting me know, Joy. Perhaps you and Jan can share Pat's duties for today. Where is Jan?"

The MC gave a sniff. "She's in the loos trying to sort out an argument between Becky and Gemma. Apparently, Becky made an unkind remark about Gemma's new veneers on Facebook - called her Jaws or something - so Gemma posted a picture of Becky exposing her breasts in Nando's. You can't really see it's Becky because the T-shirt's pulled up over her face and she's saying it's not her breasts as her implants aren't as lopsided as the ones in the picture."

Poor Jan. She was my rock, my saviour. I felt terribly guilty; she had been planning to take early retirement and should have left in March, but I'd pleaded with her to stay on and help me manage the complaints department until she had eventually relented. I knew she regretted it; comments such as "What, leave all this to sit in the garden with a good book and a large gin and tonic?" sort of gave it away.

Brett the Boss arrived just before eleven, mobile glued to his ear. I pointed him toward a desk and plugged in his laptop for him. Even if he hadn't been on his phone, there was no time for us to talk, as the coffee session attendees were already making their way to the meeting room. I hovered over him until he ended his call and escorted him to the room before he could take another.

"We'll stop at the drinks machine Brett, so you can grab a coffee."

"But we're going to a coffee session, aren't we? Won't there be coffee there?"

"Er, there was that directive, do you remember? It came from you. No more coffee at coffee sessions, to keep costs down."

"Oh, right."

The atmosphere in the meeting room was mutinous. Twelve disapproving faces, arms folded defensively across chests, met our entrance. The MC was there, sucking on a lemon, but she was the only team manager. Where was The Rock? We needed someone else on our side!

"No Jan?" I asked The MC.

"No, she's stuck on a complaint call - Mr Bullock. He's very unhappy because we keep spelling his name wrong."

"Right, well, let's make a start then, shall we guys?" I said as brightly as I could. "For those of you who haven't met him before, this is my manager, Brett." *Please, please stop reading your text messages and acknowledge the staff, you arsehole.* "Brett! The guys do have a few questions for you, particularly the increase in their sales target and the introduction of sales into the Customer Complaints teams-"

"Concerns."

"Yes, they are concerned-"

"No, it's called the Customer *Concerns* team now. We don't use the word complaints anymore at Perypils. Too negative."

"Er, right, well ... over to you then, guys! This is your session, so who wants to ask the first question?"

"I do." The MC was straight in. "I'd like to know how we are supposed to sell products to customers who are complaining? They're already upset when they call us - how are they going to feel about getting a sales pitch on top of everything else? Surely it's just going to give them more cause for complaint."

"Mmm, mmm," Brett nodded, rubbing his chin, pretending to look thoughtful. "But you see, there's your challenge! Handle their complaint - sorry, concern - really well and the customer will be eating out of your hands! It's a great opportunity to promote our products; turn that frown upside down!"

Had he really just said that? I cringed, head down, suddenly fascinated by my fingernails.

"I had a customer on the phone this morning who was complaining about the length of time it took us to settle a claim for his dog's operation. His dog, Scottie, needed a second operation and he couldn't afford to pay for it, because we hadn't paid out for the first one." This was Andrea speaking. Dramatic pause. "Scottie died." There was a collective, sorrowful "Aww" around the room. "The poor old guy was sobbing his heart out down the phone to me. Tell me, should I have tried to sell him something? What should I have sold him?" Everyone looked questioningly at Brett.

"Well ... oh gosh, look sorry, I'm going to have to take this call, it's really urgent." *His phone hadn't made a sound!* "Back in a mo."

You bastard. Everyone looked expectantly at me as Brett hurried from the room. I took a deep breath. "Not every scenario will be appropriate," I managed. "You're going to have to be the judge of when it is and when it isn't; you're the ones at the sharp end and we trust you to make that decision." *Good, good, butter them up with some insincere flattery.*

"But-" started The MC.

"Our customers are entitled to the best possible service we can offer," I continued, cutting her off. "And yes, that does involve telling them about products that suit their needs, even if their initial call was to complain about something."

They didn't look convinced. "With respect, Kate," began The MC pompously, "you don't have much experience of handling complaints. Clare ran our department for eight years and she would never have agreed to us having a sales target. *She* would have understood that it's impossible."

She also used to fly around the building on her broomstick, only stopping to pull the legs off an agency member of staff. Bloody Cruella. Would she always continue to haunt me?

"Look, I know it's a big change for you and it feels scary, but we can do this, we really can. You'll get lots of training and support and of course, all your sales are incentivised. You'll be able to earn a bit extra for your summer holidays, or put some aside for Christmas, perhaps." I could see that had made them think a bit.

"Will the canteen be doing a Christmas lunch again this year?"

I blinked at the sudden change in topic. "Er, who asked that, was that you, Foggy? I don't know, I'm afraid, you'll have to ask the canteen manager. But he might not know yet, AS IT'S ONLY APRIL."

Morten Fogarty was undeterred. "And will it be dress down again, for the two weeks over Christmas?"

Why the hell are you asking me this now? "Do you need eight months notice then, Foggy? Are you thinking about designing a reindeer costume, or something? Need to grow some antlers?" Everyone laughed, diffusing some of the tension in the room. Brett re-appeared, obviously encouraged by the titters.

"How's it going?"

"I was just saying to the guys that they'd get full support and training."

"Oh. We'd better take that offline." *Uh-oh.* That sounded ominous. I quickly covered it with a bright: "Next question!"

I managed to keep Brett behind in the meeting room after the session had finished by hiding his phone under a piece of paper. He thought it must have fallen on the floor, so as he was hunting around under the table, I took the opportunity to fire some questions at him. He confirmed that there was no budget for additional sales training and that it would have to be supported "in-house". He said, very casually, that the Property team could train the Concerns team.

I rubbed my temples. "Just to clarify then Brett, I need to get the Property team, whose own target has just increased by ten percent, to take time out to train the Concerns team - all one hundred and three of them?"

"Yes, that's right. You should aim to complete the training by the end of May; got to hit the ground running big time." Brett was still scrabbling about under the table on all fours - he really was talking out of his arse.

Back at my desk, I took a blank piece of A4 with the intention of drawing up some sort of training schedule, but an hour later it was still blank, apart from a doodle of a stick woman dangling from a noose. I'd been interrupted by The Snake who'd slithered across from the other wing to tell me that George ("I'm not gossiping, you understand but...") had been making references to drug usage on his Facebook page. Very thoughtfully, she'd printed some of the pages for me.

"I can't see any mention of drugs, Cyn," I said, after I'd read them. "What made you think there were?"

"They're here, look. I've highlighted them," she hissed. I read them again. It appeared to be an exchange between George and someone called Big C, but the grammar was so appalling, I couldn't make head nor tail of it. The Snake had highlighted "Suz is air head but i is amp head!" and "wanna rock 2nite?" It meant nothing to me, but then to be fair, I'd have only recognised "chasing the dragon" which I remembered from Grange Hill. I sent a disappointed Snake away. I didn't have the time for any more Facebook bollocks; it was the bane of my life and anyway, I'd have been far more shocked if she'd told me George wasn't on drugs.

I gave up on the training plan, deciding to salvage something from the day by helping The Rock and The MC with some of Pat's Welcome Back duties. Interviews have to be conducted with staff who have been off sick, and are performed in the hope of frightening them back into good health. I picked up Pat's list and took the top one, Ian Price. He'd been absent on Friday, calling in to say his back "had gone". Hallelujah! Not a disgusting bowel problem for a change. Nor anything messy and menstrual. Which one was Ian? That was him, standing at his mate's desk, animatedly chatting away whilst, above their heads, a flashing digital board told him eleven customers were queuing. He swung round in alarm as his friend warned him I was approaching. "Oh, er, Kate, I was just stretching my back! Doctors orders, you know; mustn't sit still for too long or it'll seize up. Got to move around."

"Yes, well, perhaps you could do it without interrupting your colleagues. Shall we do your Welcome Back interview?"

We set off down the department toward the meeting room, a journey that took a frustrating amount of time, as Ian seemed scarcely able to walk. He clutched at his back and hobbled along bow-leggedly, like a toddler with a very full nappy. Once in the room, he sunk into the chair with a good deal of "oohs" and "ers" and looked at me, his face creased in pain.

I smiled at him. "So, how's your back? All better now?"

He missed the joke. "It's awful Kate, just terrible. I simply couldn't make it in on Friday and I've been in absolute agony all weekend. I managed to struggle in today because I know how busy we are on Mondays and I didn't want to let the team down."

How heroic. I started to work my way down the Welcome Back questions. "What caused your bad back?"

"It just goes every now and then."

"Goes where?"

"You know, it just sort of gives way without warning. I could be doing the simplest of things, such as bending down to do up my trainers or pick up my skateboard and it just suddenly goes. I can hardly move when it happens. It's incredibly painful, you know." *Hmmm, not to mention incredibly convenient. Didn't the test match start on Friday?*

Next question. "So what treatment are you receiving?"

"Um, well, the doctor said to rest."

"I thought you said he told you to move around?"

"Er, yes, I mean, he said to rest it at first but then to make sure I moved around."

I looked at him with something bordering on despair. How many of these bloody interviews had I done over the years? It was just possible this could be the one thousandth. I had a vision of balloons suddenly falling down from the ceiling and streamers flying into the room. Congratulations! You've listened to one thousand pieces of complete bullshit! You've won this lovely padded straight jacket and a euthanasia voucher.

"Hasn't the doctor recommended *anything*, Ian?" I asked, unable to prevent a sigh escaping. "Has he actually examined your back or sent you for a scan?"

"Oh yes! He said if it happens one more time then he'll definitely do all that." He held my gaze, wincing a little as he rubbed his poor aching back. A thought struck me. "Gosh Ian, look at your muscles!" I exclaimed, a sudden change of tack. "They're massive!"

"Oh what, these guns?" he said, brightening up and flexing his biceps. "I'm glad you noticed, I've been working on them for ages."

"Well, they're extremely impressive, I must say. Do you work out a lot? Silly question! Of course you do!"

He leant forward. "Bench presses," he said, with a knowing nod. "If you do them regularly enough, you soon build yourself up. I'm lifting one hundred and twenty kilograms now."

"One hundred and twenty kilograms!" I whistled, even though metric weights meant nothing to me. "I doubt I could even manage one of those!"

"Well, I did four hundred yesterday!" he scoffed. "No problem!" *You dopey git.* His face fell as he realised what he'd said.

"You did four hundred bench presses?" I feigned astonishment. "But you said you were in agony all weekend, you said you could hardly move!"

"I mean, no, it couldn't have been yesterday, it must have been last week-"

I shook my head. "Give it up, Ian for goodness sake. Why were you really absent?"

I could see him racking his tiny brain for something plausible. "I didn't feel well," he eventually mumbled. "You know, a bit low. Depressed, maybe. And anxious." He nodded, warming to the theme. "I said I had a bad back because I was too embarrassed to admit the truth."

Oh, here we go, he'd played the depressed-and-anxious card. That meant there would be another set of pointless questions to work through now. I felt my shoulders slump. I wanted to scream "Now I'm bloody well depressed and anxious! There's absolutely nothing wrong with you is there, you vacuous, bench-humping, skiving little shit!" But alas, I couldn't say that out loud. For some reason, HR didn't like things like that, the fastidious bastards. I gazed gloomily at the long list of 'Mental Health Issues' questions.

"Very well, let's start again, shall we? And Ian - you can stop rubbing your back now."

My buttocks had only just brushed the seat of my chair when The MC came rushing over. "Kate, can you take this complaint call for me? I've tried to placate the customer but he's insisting on speaking to someone higher up. He's extremely angry."

"What have we done to him?"

"Well, he originally called to complain about the length of time his claim was taking to come through. The poor man has been registered as blind, so he made a claim on his health policy about six weeks ago."

"Yes?"

"Sean took the call. He apologised and everything, but-"

"But what?"

"He asked the customer if we could quote him for his car insurance."

Oh God.

CHAPTER FIVE

How terrifying did this feel? Going to a 'do' on my own. Unaccompanied. How on earth do single people do it? Didn't they live in perpetual fear of being left standing on their own, pulling the I'm-actually-fine-with-having-no-one-to-talk-to face, or fiddling with their mobiles - you're never alone with a phone! Is it something you ever get used to? I knew some of my brother's friends and I'd seen them fairly recently at his wedding, but I couldn't say I knew them well. My Dad had phoned to say that he and Mum wouldn't be there. He thought it would be too much for her, especially as earlier today she'd become very upset when she thought Danny Baker was trapped inside their privet hedge. It was next door's radio.

I didn't want to go, I was too scared. But I felt I had to. It was my brother's 40th and I had to make the effort; I mustn't become a strange recluse like J D Salinger or the blonde one from Abba. I could be single for years, maybe forever. I had to socialise, get to know new people. But what if nobody spoke to me? Did I have the confidence to go up to a stranger and start a conversation? What would I talk about?

I Googled: 'How to start a conversation when you are as dull as shit'. I found a five step process:

Step one: Introduce yourself. Look approachable and smile broadly.

Then promptly get returned into the care of the community.

Step Two: Remark on the location or occasion. *What a great party! Lidls must have completely sold out.*

Step Three: Ask an open-ended question. These should begin with: when, what, why, where. *What am I doing here? When can I leave?*

Step Four: Synchronise. Listen to what the other person is saying. Use their name and give encouraging statements. *Is that so, Dave? That's amazingly dull, Dave. Excuse me while I stab myself to death with this toothpick, Dave.*

Step Five: Beware of your internal monologue telling yourself negative things. *You're boring the pants off them. They can't wait to get away from you.*

I read the five steps several times and committed them to memory, hoping I would be able to recall them for use at the party. The next dilemma: what to wear? I stood in front of the wardrobe waiting for inspiration to strike. The location wasn't particularly glamorous (the function room of a pub) but it was a party, so perhaps I should go for a dress. Which one? I mustn't look too tarty as I didn't want to appear sex-starved and husband-hungry, so that ruled my trusty little black dress out. Anyway, it no longer covered as much thigh as it used to. Perhaps repeated dry cleaning had shrunk it.

I eventually selected a cheerful shift dress that had zigzags of bright colours on it. I had worn it to the office several times but no one from work would be at the party so that didn't matter. It had a very useful flappy bit of material across the stomach that helped disguise bloating disasters - what a brilliant design! I'd spent most of the previous year attempting to shift a stone in weight (I failed, despite the obvious calorie-burning effects of the daily self-loathing flagellation) and trying to reverse the ageing process. I'd spent hundreds of pounds on new beauty products that promised to make me 'look younger by the weekend' and on child-frightening teeth whitening treatments. Well, no more. My new mantra was:

"Life should NOT be a journey to the grave with the intention of arriving safely in an attractive and well preserved body, but rather to skid in sideways, chocolate in one hand, wine in the other, totally worn out and screaming 'What a ride! I wanna go round again!' "

I'd found this anonymous quotation on the back of a birthday card and liked it so much I'd stuck it up on my fridge door. I wasn't too sure about the skidding in sideways bit, I've never been spontaneous, but I wasn't going to waste any more of my time and energy on some sadistic ideal of what a woman should look like. Besides, I couldn't really afford the maintenance now.

I dug out a pair of nude high heels, which were very much in vogue this time last year and found a handbag that almost matched. I was ready. God, I felt nervous. This was ridiculous; *get a grip you silly cow*. I picked up the B&Q gift card that I'd got for my brother after he'd said he needed to do some DIY. He'd inadvertently left his cordless power drill lying around whilst The Bunny Boiler was pre-menstrual. I reluctantly left the house, carefully locking the front door behind me.

Mervyn popped up at the fence. *How did he know?* Had he been crouched there all day, waiting for me to emerge?

"Aha!" he cried, eyes glinting through his huge spectacles. "Caught you! Off out to some rave, are you?" *Honk honk.* "Going to be dancing the night away with some handsome young man I expect!" *Honk honk honk.* "Trying to make me jealous! Well, lucky him I say!" The honking ended in several snorts. I didn't like the way he fiddled in his trouser pockets every time he spoke to me.

"I'm just off to my brother's birthday party, Mervyn," I said, anxious not to get caught. "It's his fortieth."

"Gosh well, he must be a much older brother then!" *Honk*. I warmed to him.

"Yes well, I must dash," I said, not correcting him. "I don't want to be late."

"Yes, off you go then! Mustn't keep your Prince Charming waiting, must you!" *Honk snort honk.*

I waved goodbye and set off, wondering what Mervyn and his sister did in the evenings. I still hadn't met her; what was she like? Did they get on well together or did they bicker and snipe with one another and argue over whose turn it was to make the cocoa? At least they had each other for company; at least they weren't alone. A spasm of self-pity ran through me and I nearly turned the car around and went home. No - I could do this. *I must do this.* Everything would be fine, it couldn't possibly be that bad. I ran through the five 'conversation' steps again in my mind. I had to give it a go.

I arrived at the pub and parked in the large car park at the rear. Heart thumping, I walked toward the function room from which I could hear the Black Eyed Peas pumping out "tonight's gonna be a good good night". That had to be a positive omen. *Here goes.* Chins up, stomach in, don't trip over. I pulled open the door and stepped inside, displaying what I hoped was a confident, approachable smile. The small room was jam-packed; all the tables were occupied and there was a large scrum at the bar. A handful of women were bopping away on the dance floor. My brother's wife, The

Bunny Boiler, was amongst them. She was wearing an extremely short, skin-tight, black and white dress. Her large breasts were squeezed up to bursting point and protruded out almost as far as her stomach. Was she pregnant? She couldn't be, not by the way she was swigging from that bottle of Bacardi.

I looked around and although many heads swivelled in my direction to see who had just come in, I didn't recognise anyone. Still smiling, I picked my way through the tables toward the crowded bar and stood amongst the throng who were pressing forwards, with some desperation, to be served. People looked at me then looked away, probably wondering who the grinning lunatic was. This was worse than I had imagined. Even in the middle of a crowd, I stood out. It felt as if there was a flashing neon sign above my head: "On her own! No friends! On the prowl! Misfit! Saddo!"

As I edged closer to the bar, I heard a voice to my left. "Hello Kate!" I turned around and found myself looking into the lovely blue twinkly eyes of Kevin, my brother's closest friend and best man at his wedding last year. *Oh, the relief.* Someone I knew.

"Oh, hi Kevin," I said brightly. "How nice to see you again. How are you?"

"Er, yes, I'm good thanks," he replied, looking momentarily confused - had he mistaken me for someone else? "Can I get you a drink?" he asked. "I know one of the barmaids here, she'll let us jump the queue."

"Great, thanks Kevin," I replied, remembering to use his name as per step three of the conversation tips. Or was it step four? "I'll just have an orange juice, Kevin, as I'm driving." *I must ask an open-ended question.* "When, I mean how, no sorry, I mean have you been here long, Kevin?" *God, what a cretinous question.*

"No, not had time to get nearly drunk enough yet!" he laughed, catching the eye of the barmaid, who leant forwards, all smiles, to take his order, ignoring the protests of others in the scrum.

"How are things with you? Your brother told me you'd moved into a new house." He'd put that very tactfully.

"Yes, that's right, Kevin," I nodded, trying to think of something interesting to say about the house. "It's quite small but it's home!" *What was wrong with me? Why was I talking like a complete moron?*

"Does it need much work doing to it?" He looked at me hopefully and I remembered he worked as a general maintenance man.

"Plenty!" I laughed, taking my orange juice from him. "But I'm afraid I'm totally skint at the moment, Kevin, so I can't put any work your way, Kevin!"

"Oh no, no, I wasn't touting for business," he looked embarrassed and quickly took a large swig from his pint, burying his face.

"That's four pound thirty please, Kieron," called the barmaid. I stared at him as he passed over a ten pound note. His name was Kieron! *Oh God.* How many times had I just called him Kevin? Why hadn't he corrected me? I was about to apologise but was interrupted by my brother, who had appeared at my side.

"Sis!" he exclaimed, glancing nervously over his shoulder. "I didn't think you were coming tonight. You didn't RSVP, did you?"

"Oh no, sorry Stu, I forgot," I replied cheerfully. He

looked at me with concern, not seeming at all pleased to see me. I felt most put out. "It's not a problem, is it?" I asked. "I promise not to eat much if that's what you're worried about!" Kieron laughed, trying to cover the awkwardness, but my brother still looked extremely worried. What on earth was wrong with him?

"It's just that, well, when we thought you weren't coming, we invited, er well, Kirsty thought it would be ok if we asked..."

He didn't need to finish his sentence. I'd seen them. There they were, stood in the corner of the room, breezily chatting away to another couple. The Ex, in his naff beige blazer, rescued from the bargain bin of a Moss Bros outlet shop and her - Debbie, The Fucking Trollop, in a sleeveless cream dress, exposing a good chunk of arm flesh. A wide brown belt strained to clinch in her waistline, and she'd matched the belt with chocolate coloured tights and brown high-heeled shoes.

I felt sick to my stomach to see them both. Kieron melted away. Stu was looking at me anxiously.

"Stu," I half choked on my words. "How *could* you?"

"But we didn't know you were coming!" he protested. "And Kirsty's good Facebook buddies with him, she-"

"I couldn't give a shit, Stu!" I wailed, close to tears. "I'm your sister, where's your loyalty? You know he cheated on me with her, you know what an arse he's been. And as for *her*, this is the woman who asked us to go on holiday just so she could shag my husband! How could you invite them here?"

Stu looked wretched. "I didn't want to Sis, it was Kirsty. She wanted to stay in contact with him. I didn't."

No, and you haven't got the balls to stand up to your deranged wife. I looked over at The Bunny Boiler on the dance floor; she'd spotted me and was smiling triumphantly in my direction. Why had she taken sides against me? What had I ever done to her? Apart from referring to her as a bunny boiler of course, but I didn't think I'd ever said it out loud. Only thought it.

"You're not going to make a scene are you, Sis?" my brother asked anxiously. I didn't know what I was going to do and was trying hard not to cry. Kieron reappeared and handed me a glass. "Brandy," he said. "It's good for shock." I accepted it gratefully and took a huge gulp. Then another. I felt the fiery liquid burn its way down my body until it reached my lurching stomach. The desire to weep subsided.

"Don't worry Stu," I said. "I'm not going to cause any trouble. But I will just go and say hello. For old time's sake." My brother started to protest but I was already pushing my way through to The Ex and The FT. They had seen me and stiffened up at my approach, their fake, phoney smiles rapidly vanishing.

"Kate," said The Ex, moving protectively closer to The FT and holding his chin defiantly in the air. "We were told you wouldn't be here tonight."

"And yet here I am," I said sarcastically. "And quite frankly, I'm rather surprised to see you both here, at my brother's party. You know, a family occasion. *My* family's occasion."

The FT looked at me warily. At least she had the decency to appear uncomfortable.

"For your information, we were invited here," said The Ex snootily, "by a member of *your* family. But if you don't think you will be able to behave in an adult manner, then perhaps we should leave."

"Perhaps we should go, darling." The FT touched his arm anxiously.

Darling? God, how pretentious. I looked her up and down. "What a nice dress, Debbie," I said, smiling at her. "And who'd have thought to team it with brown tights?" I looked pointedly down at her legs. "You usually only expect to see chocolate logs at Christmas."

"Right, that's it!" The Ex hissed. "If you're going to be childish and insulting we'll go." They put their drinks down on a table. People close by were staring at us. "We've moved on Kate," he said, *the pompous twat.* "You need to do the same."

"Moved on?" I repeated, looking incredulous. "Don't you mean reversed backwards up a dead end? Didn't you tell me that Debbie meant nothing to you? Nothing at all, you said. Didn't you say that it was just a stupid fling? How did you refer to it? Oh yes, you said it was the worst mistake of your life. And the worst sex!"

The FT flinched. The Ex quickly started to shepherd her out, his face like thunder.

"You're not going?" I called after them. "Oh, shame. Well, bye then and don't forget to put that blazer back in the clothes bin behind Asda..."

They'd gone. I noticed that The Bunny Boiler rushed out after them, the treacherous bitch. I leant up against the wall and swirled the remains of my brandy around in the glass. I was shaking. I still couldn't believe they'd been invited, let alone had the brass neck to show up. *How utterly humiliating.* And all I could do was make remarks about trunky legs and second hand clothes; a pathetic effort. I'd rehearsed that meeting so many times in my head, but in my dreams, I was always hanging off the arm of some attentive young hunk, a shimmering satin dress clinging to my slender frame, the very image of Keira Knightley when she stamped James McAvoy's library book for him in Atonement. *Fat chance of any of that.* Perhaps I should have hired a gigolo for tonight, but given the sorry state of my finances, I'd only be able to afford one that looked like Eric Pickles. As I was considering whether I should leave too, a deep voice boomed into my ear. "Oh, hello there, it's Katie isn't it?" I turned to face a portly, red-faced man, around fifty-ish and with thinning sandy hair.

"It's Kate, actually," I replied. I didn't know who he was and it felt rude to blurt out 'who are you?'

"I'm Finn, we met at Stu and Kirsty's wedding last year, do you remember?" *Nope.* "Your brother often does some work for me. Not that I should say that too loudly of course, as it's all done on the QT!" He laughed a great belly-booming laugh. Now I recalled him. He'd spent the wedding propping up the bar, red wine on intravenous, bellowing at anyone who'd inadvertently strayed within earshot. Which was a radius of approximately sixty-three miles.

"Do you come here often?" he roared. I thought maybe someone in New York would answer him. I tried to recall the five conversation steps. The introductions were done, so step two was to remark on the venue.

"It's a great venue isn't it, for a party?" *You idiot.* The room was far too small, there weren't nearly enough bar staff and there was a strong smell of rising damp. The wall looked like it was starting to sweat and I peeled my shoulder away from it with a shudder.

"Well, it's not exactly the yacht club!" he exclaimed,

taking a noisy slurp of red wine. Aha! He's into sailing. Step three - ask an open-ended question.

"The yacht club, you say? When, er, I mean what sort of sailing do you do?" *Another idiotic question.* I should have used his name, but I hadn't quite caught it. I thought he'd said "I'm thin", which clearly he hadn't, as that's not how people usually introduce themselves and it was obviously untrue, given that his tie only reached half way down his enormous stomach. It may have been a crap question, but it had the desired effect to start a conversation. Although it wasn't a conversation I was required to contribute to, so I wasn't sure if it could actually be classed as a conversation. He boomed at me for some considerable time about his "forty footer" named Lolita (cringe), the size of the galley, his hugely impressive equipment (for navigation, I learnt, not without some relief), stories of raging storms and near death experiences. I blinked each time he got too close and puffed fumes of red wine into my face. His yellow yacht club tie was splattered with dark red dashes. I remembered step four, which was to synchronise and give encouraging statements - "An *eighty* foot wave, wow" and "Gosh, all those pirates, single-handedly, you say?"

Step Five, however, wasn't so easy. My internal monologue was working overtime. As well as it telling me "Christ, this guy's a crashing bore", I could see The Bunny Boiler out of the corner of my eye. She looked upset and drunk and was engaged in an argument with my brother. At one point, they both looked in my direction and she seemed to be about to come over to me, but my brother pulled her back. Oh dear God, was she intending to have a go at me? A cold fist of fear clenched in my stomach - what if she attacked me? She was extremely volatile, especially after a few drinks. What if she punched me, hit me in the face? I might lose some teeth; I'd just given up my Denplan subscription, I couldn't afford it anymore. Would I have to have NHS false teeth fitted? Would they crumble each time I bit into a bar of Dairy Milk? I really would stay single forever if I looked like the guy from the Pogues. I could see Stu trying to reason with her and eventually, to my enormous relief, I saw her flounce off towards the toilets.

"Ah well," The Bore was saying, "you really must, you know."

"Yes, yes," I muttered distractedly.

"Great!" he bellowed. "That's settled then! You'll love it! And you'll get your sea legs in no time, just you wait and see!" I looked at him in alarm. I would love what? Had I just agreed to something?

"Here's my card," he produced a business card from his trouser pocket and gave it to me. It felt warm and moist. "I'll make a great sailor out of you; I think you'll find I'm an extremely rigorous teacher." He gave me a lecherous wink. "Did I mention that Lolita has three *double* berths?"

Woah! I was horrified. Had I agreed to go sailing with him? Or something even worse?

"I'll just take your number," he was saying, taking out his iPhone. "Don't want you slipping through my fingers now, do I! Not when I've just hooked you!" He boomed his thunderclap laugh and looked at me expectantly, waiting for me to recite my number. I would rather have given it to Hannibal Lecter. I stuttered it out, thinking quickly enough to swap around the last two numbers. He punched it into his phone - I prayed he didn't test it by calling me while I was standing there. Bugger these conversation steps, they were a bloody minefield. How could I get away from him? Why was there not a sixth step: 'How to extract yourself before you start to self-harm'?

"My ex-wife was a damn good sailor," he was saying, "but nothing ever pleased her, nothing at all. Not even when I named my first yacht after her, The Crap Shag! Ha ha ha!" I looked around in desperation. The dance floor was full of drunken women, stumbling around to 'I Will Survive', some barefoot, others risking their lives in vertiginous heels. I spotted my brother at the bar, gulping down a pint of lager as if his life depended on it. I interrupted The Bore mid-flow, saying it had been great to meet him, but I really needed to talk to my brother.

"Orf you run then," he said cheerfully. "I'll call you tomorrow to arrange our rendezvous." Another leering wink. I knew he was looking at my bum as I walked away. I clenched my buttocks and pushed a path over to Stu. "Hi Sis," he said wearily. "Are you ok?"

"Yes, I suppose so," I sighed. "Is Kirsty alright?"

He shrugged. "She's pissed. And she's a bit hacked off with you for upsetting our guests, but she'll get over it."

Upsetting their guests! You mean upsetting my love rat ex-husband and his conniving trollop? What about me? What about my feelings?

I was about to protest but my brother was looking past me, his eyes widening in horror. "Oh, Christ no, that's all I bloody well need!"

I turned round. Georgia, the Bunny Boiler's teenage daughter had entered the function room. She appeared to be virtually naked; just a scrap of material covered her chest and her bum cheeks were doing their best to escape from a pair of miniscule denim shorts. She could hardly walk in her huge platform shoes. What was she, fifteen? She looked like a hooker.

"Blimey Stu," I said, "that outfit's way too adult for her, what's her mother going to say when she sees her dressed like that?"

He looked surprised. "There's nothing wrong with her outfit," he said. "It's her boyfriend; Kirsty can't stand him. She's going to go mental when she sees him here."

I hadn't noticed her boyfriend. I followed Stu's worried stare and saw, fighting his way towards the bar, The Lazy Shit George. "It's George!" I exclaimed.

"You know him?"

"Yes, he works with me, well for me." Although I used the term 'work' in its loosest possible sense.

"Kirsty can't stand him," Stu repeated, looking round anxiously for his wife. "Says he's too old for Georgia, as well as being a druggie and according to Facebook, he's with a different girl every night." I could sense the panic rising in him.

"Look," I said, in what I hoped was a calming voice. "You go and find Kirsty and try and get her to have a quiet word with Georgia outside." *Not much hope but worth a try.* "I'll go and talk to George; let him know he might not be too welcome here." I nearly added "as I know exactly how that feels" but I stopped myself. Stu had enough to worry about.

He headed in the direction of the toilets and I shimmied through the crowded bar to reach TLS George. I could see that Georgia was on the dance floor, rooted by her great clumpy shoes to the spot, flinging her arms around like a demented half-dressed scarecrow in a force eight. She was going to catch her death of cold dressed like that.

"Hello George," I said as I reached him. "Fancy seeing you here!"

"Oh, hi Kate," he replied, slouching against the bar in his usual laid back manner. He looked at my dress. "Have you just come from work?"

Damn it, I knew I should have worn something else. "Er, no, no I haven't. Are you here with Georgia?"

"Yeah."

"I didn't know you two were together?"

"We're not really."

"But, you're seeing her?"

"Yeah, but we're not, like, exclusif or nuffin." *What the hell did that mean? Were they in a relationship or not?*

"The thing is George, I know your personal life is none of my business, but I think that Georgia's mother is a bit concerned about the age gap between you. She's only fifteen, isn't she?"

"She's sixteen," said TLS George defensively. "And I'm only twenty four you know, it's not that big a gap." He looked past me, bored by our conversation.

I tried again. "I think that Kirsty, her mother, is going to be a bit unhappy to see you here," *you haven't got a pet rabbit have you?* "So perhaps it might be a good idea if you-"

I didn't get any further; a blood-curdling screech cut me dead.

"What's that dirty little bastard doing here?" The Bunny Boiler stormed through the crowded room, people falling over themselves to get out of her way. She was bearing down on TLS George before he knew what was happening.

"And look who he's with," she leered with contempt, right into my face. The Bacardi fumes were so overpowering that my head jerked back. "I thought you liked them younger than that, George?"

"No, we're not here together, Kirsty," I started to say but I knew immediately it was futile. She wasn't in the mood for listening; her eyes were all glazed and goggly, and one was staring in a different direction to the other.

"We're not here together Kirsty," she mimicked in a mock posh voice. "God, you make me sick, both of you. It doesn't take an idiot to see what's going on here," *you said it.* "You'd shag anything in a skirt wouldn't you George? You're not fussy - innocent teenagers, middle-aged stuck-up tight arses..." *Did she mean me?* She was swaying around alarmingly. I noticed she'd had another tattoo done, over her left breast. It was a fairy with very large wings. Or it might be a daddy-long-legs. She stabbed a finger in TLS George's face.

"You're disgusting. And I bet you're riddled, you've been seen going into the clap clinic. Don't deny it, you were tagged on Facebook." *Was that why he was off sick last week?* "You're a jumped-up little dopehead. And if you give my daughter a dose, it will be the last thing you ever bloody well do!"

TLS George, trying to maintain his composure and look cool, shrugged at her. *Oh no-*

"Don't you shrug your shoulders at me, you little tosser! You couldn't give a shit, could you? Well, I'm going to make you give a shit, *you shit*, see if you give a shit about this!" She tried to fling the remains of her drink over TLS George but he grabbed her arm to stop her. The glass fell to the floor and smashed. She shrieked and took a swing at him with her free arm. He dodged out of the way, barging against me. I fell back heavily on the man behind me who cannoned into a group of guys stood next to him. They started shouting and cursing and then all hell broke loose. Punches were thrown and glasses smashed. Women were screaming. I tried to get away from the bar area but it was too packed. I cried out in pain as someone trod down hard on my foot. Fists were flailing and the music stopped. Suddenly, I felt a strong grip on my arm as I was pulled through the fray and forced through the gap in the bar. I found myself staring at the optics.

"This way, out the back." It was Kieron, my saviour for the second time that evening. He propelled me through the bar and out into the dank, dark yard at the back, closing the door on the riot inside.

"Thank you so much," I stuttered, wincing at the pain in my foot.

"Are you ok?" he asked anxiously.

"Yes, I think so." I couldn't see my foot properly in the dark but at least I could walk on it. "Can I get out this way?"

"Yes, that door leads out to the car park." He pointed to the back of the yard. "Do you think you can drive? I could call a cab for you."

"I think I'll be fine." I didn't care how much it hurt; I just wanted to get away from there. I managed to smile at him. "Thank you for rescuing me, you've been very kind."

"Kieron!" the bar maid appeared in the doorway. "We need you in here; Stu can't restrain Kirsty on his own."

"Er, righto," he replied. "I'll just see Kate to her car."

"No, no, I'm fine, you'd better go and help Stu." I hobbled towards the exit calling over my shoulder, "Please thank him for a lovely evening!"

With huge relief, I reached the sanctity of my car and turned on the interior light so I could examine my foot. A layer of skin had been scraped off and a large purplish bruise was already forming. Ouch, it throbbed like buggery. As I started the car, the door to the function room burst open and the fight spilled out into the car park. I pressed my wounded foot down on the accelerator and quickly drove out past the mass of heaving bodies. My lights briefly picked out The Bunny Boiler, wild-eyed and rabid, as someone behind her grabbed hold of her hair and wrenched her backwards. The grabber looked semi-naked – my God, it was her daughter!

I drove home rather shakily, replaying the evening in my head. My first proper 'do' as a single woman. How bad had it been? Let's see: I'd turned up to find that the host didn't want me there, repeatedly called his best friend by the wrong name, caused two guests to leave, upset the host's wife, got myself involved in a punch-up and agreed to meet a dribbling pervert who was hoping I'd blow his hornpipe before I was lost at sea. What on earth had I been so worried about?

Chapter Six

I faced another week with the Customer Complaints-Concerns teams. I marked them off on my calendar like a prisoner chalking up his time in captivity on the wall of his cell. Pat, The Blubber, had made a brief appearance before having to go home when her labyrinthitis flared up, causing a sudden dizzy spell. She'd toppled sideways off her chair, falling on Gay Ray who was sitting next to her and had ended up with her face in his lap. He was still frozen in shock.

A commotion in one of the teams made me look up. The MC came rushing over. "Kate! Something awful's happened. Linda's just opened an envelope and a pile of white powder fell out! Whatever shall we do?"

Give it to George to stick up his nose? I stood up reluctantly; my foot still hurt to walk on and I'd been trying to keep my weight off it. "Let's have a look, shall we?" The team, who were quite capable of making a paper cut feel like a major medical trauma, were all out of their seats and clucking away like a load of old hens. Some were comforting Linda, who'd opened the envelope while others were backing away. The rest of the teams in the department were all looking over, wondering what was going on. Linda, young and fragile-looking, stood by her desk, hands clasped to her chest as if in prayer. She looked round at me with huge frightened eyes. On her desk I could see a torn envelope with white powder scattered around. It looked a bit like Persil.

"Oh Kate, whatever do you think it is?" Linda asked

anxiously. "I've sniffed it, but it doesn't really smell of anything."

"It could be dangerous," said someone in the team.

"It could be an attack on the company," another called out. "You know, like germ warfare."

"Yes, it could be anthrax," said someone else.

"That's really deadly," added another.

"We ought to evacuate," said someone else.

Linda started to sob. I tried to take control of the situation. "Now look," I said firmly, "It's probably just a prank, or a disgruntled customer trying to make trouble. Let's all keep calm. And turn that bloody fan off Carol, you're going to blow it all round the department. I don't care if you are having a hot flush. Linda, go and wash your hands. Has anyone else touched the powder?" I looked around. Andrea, a large woman with a frizzy perm and wearing a two-sizes-too-small Mrs Doubtfire dress, nervously raised her hand. She looked incredibly pasty-faced. "You go and wash your hands too, Andrea," I ordered. She hesitated. "What's the matter?" I asked.

"Er, I, I tasted it," she stuttered. *You did what? Please God, tell me I didn't just hear that.*

"What do you mean, you tasted it?"

"I, well, I thought it looked like sugar, so I, er, thought I'd see if that's what it was. So I stuck my finger in it. And licked it."

"For f-" I caught myself.

"Just a dab, like," she added, as if that somehow justified her insanity.

"Is Andrea going to die?" someone called out, hopefully.

"Only if I beat her hard enough," I muttered. I sent

Andrea to wash her hands and, as we didn't keep an antidote for anthrax in the first aid box, suggested she drink a glass of water to flush it through. I moved the people who sat closest to Linda and cordoned off her desk.

"Shouldn't we evacuate?" asked The MC anxiously.

"No, I'm going to get advice from Facilities," I told her. "In the meantime, please try and get your team back to work. And keep a close eye on Andrea."

"In case she falls ill?"

"In case she puts it in her coffee."

I phoned Facilities. A recorded message told me that I had to use the online service to report faults and cut me off. I accessed the online site and after much impatient clicking around, I eventually managed to locate a number for 'emergencies'. I rang it and waited in a queue for fifteen minutes, before finally giving the details to the uninterested man at the other end. He said in his monotone android voice: "I'll submit the report. Someone from Facilities will be over."

"But when will that be? What action should…" He'd gone.

Bloody useless. I went to tell the team that someone would be along shortly. They were mutinous. Cries of: "It's not safe here!", "we should evacuate", "I've got really bad asthma", "my husband said we should definitely leave the building and he should know, he used to deliver the toilet rolls to Porton Down". I told them we needed to wait for expert advice before we evacuated, as we might make things worse by spreading any contamination. That shut them up a bit; or at least the horrified cries were reduced to sulky mutterings.

I found a voicemail from my brother on my mobile. "Hi Sis. Sorry about the party. There were only three arrests in the end, so not too bad really. Er, Finn's been having trouble contacting you on the number you gave him so could you give him a call? He said he gave you his card. I didn't know you were into sailing; you used to get sea sick in the bath! Cheers Sis, bye."

Oh God. I'd hoped The Bore had been too pissed to remember. I'd have to think up some excuse for not going sailing; what about an inner ear infection? But they cleared up. Perhaps I could tell him I was emigrating. Or dying. I went to get myself a strong coffee. As I stood at the drinks machine, watching the dirty brown liquid squirting into the plastic cup (wondering, as I always did: how often do they clean these pipes out? Could you get Legionnaires disease from them? How long would I be off sick for? Just a few days or long enough to re-decorate the lounge?), I saw two guys from Facilities rush past me in a blur of luminous yellow. Two burly policemen, belts bristling with truncheons, handcuffs and other evil-looking implements of torture, closely followed them. *Bloody hell - were they here because of the powder?* I abandoned my coffee and hurried after them. Their arrival caused uproar in the department. Everyone stopped what they were doing and anxious faces swivelled to see what was going on.

"Who's in charge here?" snapped Stanley, the officious little twerp from Reception.

"I am, Stan," I said from behind him. "You know this is my department."

He swung round and looked at me distastefully. "Oh yes, this is Kate King," he announced to the others, in much the same way he would warn them to avoid a dog turd. "Where's this suspicious package?"

"It's an envelope which was addressed to the complaints team. White powder fell out when one of my team opened it." I led them to Linda's desk. They all peered closely at the powder.

"Has anyone touched it?" barked Stan.

"Yes, two people have been in direct contact with it," I said carefully.

"They've actually handled it?"

"Yes." *Oh God, I was going to have to be honest.* "And sniffed it, I'm afraid. And, er, one of them tasted it." They all stared at me in horror.

"*Sorry?*"

You heard me. "One of them tasted it."

Even Stalin Stan was momentarily speechless. I heard one of the policemen mutter "Fuck me". The other recovered himself and took charge.

"Right," he said, "until we find out exactly what the substance is, we're going to have to follow our standard procedures. We'll cordon off this department and anyone who has been near the powder will have to go into quarantine immediately. Have you got a room we can use for this? A meeting room or something?"

"Well, yes," I replied. "But what do you mean by 'been near' the powder? I don't want to have to put the whole team into quarantine, so can you be more specific?"

"Well, anyone who has eaten it, of course," he replied, *the sarky bastard.* "And I'd say anyone who has been up really close to it."

"So all of you then?" I asked. They all looked at each other.

"Er, well yes, I suppose so," he said hesitantly, not

looking particularly happy at the prospect.

"Look, isn't this just a little over the top?" I asked. "I mean if it is something nasty, like anthrax, wouldn't everyone be dead already?" *Although I'm not saying that's a bad thing...*

"We can't take any chances," the policeman said, authoritatively. "We don't know what it is and until we do, we're going to follow our standard procedures and limit the risk of further contamination. Let's get to the quarantine room; bring any colleague who's been up close to the powder. Move the rest of the team right away from that desk."

I knew I was going to have to put myself into quarantine, so I left the poor MC to organise her team and explain what was happening to the rest of the department. I took Linda and Andrea with me to the meeting room. It wasn't a particularly large room and with the three of us, two super-sized policemen and the two guys from Facilities, it felt very claustrophobic. They all started to make calls on their mobiles and radios. If the anthrax didn't get us, the radioactive waves would be sure to finish us off.

Linda had started to cry again and between sobs, said she felt sick and dizzy. Andrea held her hand and asked her, somewhat unhelpfully, who her next of kin was. The sobs turned into wails. One of the policemen radioed for an ambulance "just in case". That made us all feel distinctly uneasy. Stan was giving me a headache. He was constantly on his mobile, loudly barking orders to his colleagues in Facilities. I suspected he was relishing his moment of importance. The policemen, clearly bored, decided they were needed outside to help direct operations.

"But haven't you got to stay in quarantine?" I asked.

"We'll be careful not to come into contact with anyone," they said, as they edged out of the room. One of them reappeared a few minutes later to deposit two paramedics who were dressed in green jumpsuits. They examined a distressed Linda and got her to breathe into a brown paper bag. I asked them what the symptoms of anthrax were. They cheerfully told me that "respiratory collapse" was one of them. I asked them if they considered a brown paper bag to be the most effective treatment for respiratory collapse. They said Linda was just having a panic attack. Stan pompously informed them that as they'd come into contact with us, they'd have to remain here in quarantine. For some reason, they seemed quite happy at the prospect. Perhaps it was preferable to attending road traffic accidents and the other hideous atrocities that they faced every day of their working lives. Andrea's perm was a shocking enough sight, but at least they'd been trained to witness horrors like that.

I called The MC to see how her team was. "Oh Kate, everyone's so worried," she said, sounding extremely harassed. "The whole site's been cordoned off; no one's being allowed in or out." *What?* "And it's lunchtime of course, so those who want to go out can't and those who want to come back in aren't allowed. It's absolute chaos, everyone's up in arms. Poor Jenny has missed her appointment with her therapist; she sees him for her nervous twitch and now she's climbing the walls. Steve got her a cup of tea but that was a big mistake, he's got third degree burns now. And the press have turned up at the front gates. They're trying to interview staff but we've been told not to speak to them."

Christ, what a mess. I relayed all this back to the room.

Stan sniffed and said that Facilities would have everything under control, but it certainly didn't sound that way. At least in our little group Linda was calmer now and had stopped the histrionics. Her boyfriend called her, saying he had heard something about Perypils on the local radio. We heard her say to him: "Everyone keeps talking about this Ann Thrax, but I don't know who she is."

Brian, Stan's sidekick, organised some coffee and sandwiches to be sent up from the canteen. The unsuspecting woman who wheeled them into the room on a trolley was told that she'd have to stay with us in quarantine. She was not impressed. "I can't stay 'ere all bleedin' day, I've got to pick the kids up in 'alf an hour."

She had a ferocious row with Stan, as the rest of us nibbled self-consciously on our sandwiches and tried not to look at the pair of them. She refused to stay and left the room, slamming the door hard. Stan was straight on his mobile to make sure they didn't let her out of the gates, but unless they'd put up an electric fence and were patrolling it with Doberman Pinschers, I couldn't imagine anything could stop her.

Linda said that several of her team had hugged her when she'd been upset this morning, so shouldn't they be in quarantine too? Brian said "Yes, probably" but no one did anything about it. The room was crowded enough as it was and it was getting very stuffy. Andrea kept slurping her coffee, which grated on my nerves so much it was all I could do to stop myself from launching across the room and beating her about the head. That would be pointless though; not even a baseball bat would make any impact on that hair.

My mobile rang. It was Brett the Boss. Damn - I really

should have called him.

"What the bloody hell's going on there, Kate?" he snapped as soon as I answered. "Perypils is all over the sodding news! Apparently there's been a radioactive leak at the site?"

"No Brett, it's not a leak. I'm sorry, I should have called you. It's just an envelope with white powder in it. It will be a hoax, or a prank. Someone with a grudge. It's a total over-reaction." I looked pointedly at Stan who wouldn't meet my eye.

"You must keep me posted, Kate. The Chief Exec's been on to me, he's extremely concerned."

"Well, you can tell him we're all fine, we're here with two ambulance men so we're in very good-"

"He's extremely concerned about the disruption to the business; what the hell are your sales figures going to look like today?"

I did my best goldfish impression. "Well, er, it's a bit difficult to say at the moment Brett, I'm stuck in quarantine you see, and-"

"Never mind all that bollocks," he cut across me. "Get off your bloody backside and go and crack the whip. My balls are on the line here Kate, yours too, come to that. I need to know that your sales won't be affected by all this shite. Call me back with your predicted figures, soon as you can." He was gone.

"Was Brett worried about us?" asked Linda.

"Of course he was," I lied.

"When's he coming down, then?" asked Andrea, her mouth full of sandwich. How many had she eaten? Ten? Twenty? The buttons on her dress already looked set to ping off at any moment; they'd take a pane of glass out.

"He was here last week, Andrea. He held that coffee, er, colleague session, remember? You were there."

"But he's only got four sites to manage, so shouldn't he spend a week in each?" bleated Andrea. "I mean, we hardly ever see him, do we? He just rushes in and out, so where does he spend his time, I mean, you'd think he'd stay put in one place..."

I shut my ears; I'd heard the same thing so many times before. I couldn't understand why the staff were so obsessed with seeing Brett; when he did put in an appearance he was either glued to his mobile or his forehead was stuck to his laptop. He rarely spoke to anyone, except to borrow a charger or ask directions to the canteen.

The room was really very warm now and smelled of egg sandwiches, which was rather disconcerting; the sandwiches had been cheese and ham. The MC called me and said a team of men wearing "Sellafield" suits and breathing apparatus had been into the department and removed the powder and the envelope. A specialist team of cleaners was there now. *For God's sake, this was bloody farcical.* Brett called me again. I declined the call then sent him a text saying that the sales figures were unaffected by the incident and we would finish the day on target. I had no idea if this was true or not, but it's what he wanted to hear and it would keep him off my back for a bit.

Time ticked tediously on. One of the ambulance men had fallen asleep even though Andrea was sucking noisily on a piece of orange right by his ear. In the heat of the tomb, someone's personal hygiene was beginning to fail. I tried to open the windows but they were locked. I asked Stan to get someone up to unlock them but he said he was not prepared to be held accountable if someone fell out and killed themselves. He had a point; I felt on the verge of jumping. Was the fourth floor high enough to kill me outright? If not, whose decision would it be to turn off the life support machine? My parents, I suppose. I could just imagine my father: "Can you feel that?" (Whacks my knee with a sledgehammer). "No, nothing, waste of bloody electricity. Switch her off." Linda was prattling on endlessly about her cat, her eyelash extensions, Big Brother ... Andrea was trying to dig out a strand of orange stuck in her back teeth ... Brian was picking at some dead skin on the palm of his hand ... the ambulance man was snoring ... Stan was grinding his teeth ... I couldn't stand this much longer, I was going out of my mind.

I phoned The MC. "How are things?" I trilled, aware my voice sounded unnaturally high-pitched.

"Oh yes, it's all fine now," she said airily. "Everything went back to normal as soon as we got the all clear. Where are you?"

Where am I? "I'm still in bloody quarantine, where do you think?" I shrieked. "What do you mean 'got the all clear'? What's happening?" Everyone was staring at me, all wide awake now.

"Yes, the police said the powder was completely harmless. Some sort of sugar solution, apparently. Why are you still in quarantine?"

"Because nobody thought to bloody well tell us!" I yelled. I terminated the call and turned on Stan, whose face had gone very red. "Bloody hell Stan, Facilities need a good kick up the arse! Or do you think they purposefully "forgot" to tell you that the all clear had been given?" I actually made the speech marks with my hands, that's how low I'd sunk. "I bet they were desperate to keep you shut away for as long as possible because they wanted ten minutes of their day without being forced to goose-step around by a jack-booted jackass with a Gestapo complex! I wouldn't be surprised if it was one of them who sent the white powder! I bet they'll trace it back to the canteen; probably find Greasy Graham's dandruff in the sugar solution. Thank God he didn't send the tapioca! Everyone knows what he uses for that-" I think I must have appeared in danger of losing it, as Stan was backing away from me, his eyes wide with alarm. One of the ambulance men grabbed my arm and said "easy now" as if he was reining in a wild horse.

Stan scurried out of the room and we all followed. I felt myself relaxing as soon as I got through the door; it was so wonderful to be out of there. As my blood pressure began to subside, I said goodbye and thank you to the paramedics and told Andrea and Linda to go home, thinking they'd be grateful. *Wrong.* Linda whined, "Oh, but my boyfriend picks me up and he won't have finished work yet. Can I go early tomorrow instead?"

Andrea sniffed, "I was due to finish soon anyway." Just no pleasing some people.

I limped back into the department expecting some concern and sympathy, but no one even looked up. The excitement was over and their lives were back to normal. I sat down heavily at my desk, crumpled and greasy. My head was banging. I had eighty-six unread emails; it was going to take me all evening to get through that lot.

As I made a half-hearted start, Big Andy bounded over. "There you are Kato, you old slacker!" he boomed. "I heard you'd managed to get the entire building shut down while you sat around on your arse all day! Nice work old girl!"

Ha bloody ha. "Yes, very funny Andy," I said, rubbing my temples. "But actually it was all a bit scary for a while. One of my guys opened an envelope and all this white powder spilled out."

"Is that all it was?" Big Andy asked incredulously. "You're joking, aren't you? We get that all the time in my teams. We don't go through all that bloody hullabaloo!"

I stared at him. "You've had powder in envelopes too? So, what do you do, then? What do you do with the powder?"

"Just blow it off the bloody desk and get on with things, of course! What else?"

CHAPTER SEVEN

Saturday

I was forced to go shopping for a new pair of jeans, an activity I despised. My comfy, sky-blue 'boyfriend fit' pair were totally frayed at the hems and my skinny jeans made my thighs look like two sausages about to burst out of their skins. Why were all my clothes shrinking?

I went to Next first, where I was met by a bewildering array of bootcuts, high-waisted, ultra skinnies, low-rise ... but, joy of joys, I found a style that promised to lift my bum and flatten my stomach - bloody brilliant, magic jeans! I picked up a pair in dark navy and a pair in black, both size 12 and brimming with hope, went to try them on. I pulled on the black pair and just about managed to get them done up. I looked in the mirror expecting to see Jessica Ennis' midriff looking back at me. Instead, a roll of white stomach flobbered over the waistband, just above a squashed, strangulated crotch. I turned round to examine my Kylie-style pert buttocks but my bum was still gazing dejectedly down at my heels. The bottoms of the jeans were very flared; I looked like one of Charlie's Angels - the one that had eaten too many Iced Fingers.

"How did you get on?" asked the girl who was looking after the changing rooms.

"Yes, good," I lied, handing her the jeans. "I just can't decide which colour so I'm going to have a think about it."

Disappointed, I went next door to Top Shop and picked

up a pair of grey skinnies that looked great on their mannequin, teamed with beige ankle boots and a cream biker jacket. In the changing room, I undressed again and attempted to pull the jeans on. They got stuck just above my knees. Bemused, I checked that the zip was undone and then that they really were a size 12. Jesus, I couldn't get them anywhere near my arse; they weren't even within shouting distance.

The super-slim girl outside the changing rooms said, very brightly, "How were those for you?"

"A little on the tight side."

"Oh, shall I get you a larger size?"

"*No!* I mean, no thank you. I've been a size twelve for twenty years; I think the sizing must be wrong on this pair."

Dejectedly, I sloped into Marks and Spencer. An assistant asked me if I wanted any help.

"Have you got any normal jeans?"

"Um, I'm not really sure ... what do you mean by normal?"

"Ones that cover your bum; your whole bum that is, not just halfway up the cheeks and that zip up beyond your first pube."

She showed me to the stretch section. It was full of Granny-jeans, all comfort fit and Chelsea-pensioner blue. An old lady wearing a green paisley headscarf shuffled over to me, wheezing heavily. "Can you tell me where the chicken fillets are, dear?" she asked, peering at me.

"The food section's just over there," I pointed to the back of the store.

"No, the things that go in your bra dear, you know, to boost your cleavage."

I gaped at her. She must be pushing ninety!

"My husband's worn my old ones out, you see dear. I give them to him to squeeze at night; he can't tell the difference, not since his glaucoma."

Oh dear God.

I abandoned my Jeans-for-Sumos search and trudged gloomily to Starbucks, joining the long queue for the counter. I had to face it; I was no longer a size 12. I couldn't afford to buy a whole new wardrobe, so I'd have to bloody well lose some weight. *Bugger it.* I'd thought, with the stress of the house move and the constant getting up and down to change channels because the remote didn't work, I'd be a lot slimmer, but this eating for one malarkey was proving disastrous for my waistline. I no longer ate proper meals, I just picked at things in the evenings. A bit of toast and pâté, a jam sandwich, a couple of Wagon Wheels; all lots of little bits, but they were adding up to a significant calorie-count overall. I had to get into a proper healthy-eating regime before I turned into the Pillsbury Doughgirl.

I ordered a skinny cappuccino and ignored the lovely pastries that were crying out to me from the glass shelves. *A good start - well done me.* There weren't any empty tables so I perched on a stool at the bar by the window and watched an endless stream of shoppers pass by, many of them clad in perfectly fitting jeans. I noticed how many couples went past. Wasn't forty percent of the British population supposed to be single? Perhaps Cheltenham had a lower percentage, for some reason. You needed two incomes to afford to park here.

I couldn't help being struck by how miserable people looked. A little girl, with her bottom lip stuck out as if it had a coat hanger wedged in it, whined and moaned and tugged at her father's hand, trying to pull him backwards. Poor sod, what a brat. I looked more closely at the little girl; her fair, wavy, WI hair looked familiar. Was that the Devil Child? It was! It was Chloë. I looked at the man she was with - *it was him, The Ex.* I tried to hide my face behind my Starbucks mug, praying he wouldn't look my way. He looked awful; unshaven, dishevelled and wearing his grey trench coat that I hadn't seen in years. He'd stopped wearing it after someone had joked he looked like he should be on a register.

Chloë wriggled out of his grasp and ran to the Postman Pat ride outside Boots. I watched The Ex follow her and saw him rub a hand over his weary-looking face. I felt a sudden pang of sympathy. This would be his idea of a day from hell; there was only one thing he hated more than shopping and that was children. Combine the two and it was hardly surprising he looked so miserable. He used to spend every Saturday on the golf course. At least, that's where he'd told me he was. He'd revealed himself to be quite an accomplished liar, so it was just possible that when he said he'd got "a hole in one", he was referring to something entirely different.

Chloë was sitting happily in Postman Pat's van, even though it wasn't moving as The Ex hadn't put any money in it. *Once a tight arse always a tight arse.* He stood and read some messages on his iPhone before eventually ordering Chloë out of the van. The inevitable happened and she started screaming in protest. Looking very uncomfortable as people stared at them, he dragged her out of the van and led her away. Even when they were out of sight I could still hear her distressed howls. God, it was so weird seeing him like that; someone so familiar to me but who now lived a completely different life and had a child to care for. Was he happy? He certainly didn't look it, but then everyone has an off day now and then. I couldn't imagine he enjoyed having a kid in his life but was it worth it to be with her, The FT? Was he happier than he had been with me? Did she threaten to stuff his dirty socks in his big gob if he didn't pick them up from the bedroom floor? Did she have to force the hoover into his hands, turn it on and push him up and down the hall, or did she accept him as he was, warts and all? Did he love her? Would he actually be with her if Paul hadn't found out about their affair and turfed her out?

I sighed inwardly as I finished my coffee. I was going to have to get in touch with him soon to sort out the divorce. I hadn't yet decided what I was going to do about my surname. I liked King; it was plain and simple and no one ever asked "You what?" and suppressed a giggle as they did when they heard my maiden name, Widger. There was no way I wanted to go back to that. I slipped off the stool, feeling my stomach bloat from the onslaught of caffeine. Oh sod it - no point in continuing to look for jeans now. I'd just have to hack off the straggly bits from the hems of my old pair and make them do for another couple of months. I'll have lost lots of weight by then.

Sunday

The sound of the phone ringing sliced through my rather yummy dream. I was being questioned by Sergeant Hathaway, who then proceeded to give me mouth-to-mouth (even though I was fully conscious) following the discovery of a mysterious white powder in my attic. My initial fury at the interruption to the dream was quickly replaced by a huge sense of foreboding - who the hell phones at eight thirty on a Sunday morning? It must be bad news, my mum, perhaps, gone missing, or my dad, in hospital, a slug-rage induced heart attack. Or my brother, a kitchen knife in his back, having asked his wife "What's up with you today?"

I whipped back the covers and careered down the stairs but the answerphone cut in before I got there. I heard a man's voice leave a short, excited message. Had someone got the wrong number? I played it back.

"Kate, old girl, are you there? Put that poor man down and get out of bed! You've got to go and buy the Stun on Sunday - *now*. I'll call your mobile too. Bye." It was Big Andy. What on earth was that all about? I turned my mobile on and several messages pinged in. I opened one which had been sent from Hissing Cyn: "Have u seen the papers?" What was going on? Probably just another hatchet-job article on Perypils. That was nothing new.

I decided there was no point going back to bed now; it was never possible to re-enter dreams at the point you left them, more's the pity. I showered and dressed and applied a layer of make-up. I was only nipping up the shop but I didn't want to scare the crows from the trees. I had once gone through an ill-advised 'bare faced chic' phase of make-up application, in an attempt to look fresh and natural. This look had, unfortunately, coincided with a tendency to wear floaty white dresses, which I thought terribly bohemian. As I'd walked through town one day, a little girl squealed: "Ooh look mummy, a ghost!" I never got things quite right.

Mervyn was in his front garden, poking around in a border. There was no hope of sneaking past him unnoticed so I called out a cheery "Morning!"

"Ah, morning!" *Honk* "I was just checking for overnight slug activity; I've declared war on the little blighters!" *Honk honk.*

"I've got slug pellets if you want some," I offered, "and my father always sets beer traps; that's if you can bear to part with your beer, of course!" *Honk.* Oh no! Now I'd started honking!

"Oh, I always use hair," said Mervyn, blinking at me. "They find it impossible to slide over hair, you know. I put it round my plants, works every time." He held out his hand to show me a matted mass of dark, grey hair. "I got this little lot out of the plug-hole this morning. Amazing how much collects there, isn't it? You should see it on the first of the month after Sissy has had her bath!"

Ugh! I backed away, muttering about being in a hurry. I passed Ernie and Doris, Mervyn's neighbours, who were clearing out their garage. Why did the oldies always get up so early? Did it become more difficult to sleep in as you aged? I was obviously bucking the trend; The Ex used to call me the Lie-in King.

I reached the paper shop and perused the Sunday papers piled up on the floor. There was nothing obvious on the front pages. I looked again, more closely, then did a double-take. On the front of one of the tabloids, underneath a huge headline of 'I slept with 200 men in one term!' was a smaller caption: 'Insurance Boss Sex Shock!' There was a picture of a hunched, grotty-looking man leaving the Co-op carrying a plastic bag, through which a packet of Marlboro and a bottle of Smirnoff were clearly visible. No, it couldn't be ... it was! It was Brett! Oh my God, what was he doing on the front page of a Sunday tabloid? And he looked *terrible*. A small paragraph underneath the picture read: 'Callous Perypils boss sacks employee after making her pregnant. Full story page seven.'

Stunned, I paid for the paper, then sat down on the low wall outside to read it. I turned to page seven and couldn't believe what I was looking at. It was a large photo of Cruella. But it wasn't the thin-lipped, evil-eyed Cruella that I recognised from the past. Her angular face was softly framed by fluffy, honey-brown hair that had been expertly blow-dried. Her baby pink glossy lips were slightly parted and there was a sorrowful expression in her eyes as she gazed mournfully into the distance. Her hands were folded protectively across her enormous baby bump. The whole photo looked like it had been shot through a hazy mist of marshmallows.

My head swam as I read the story:

Lovely Clare Ratched seemed to have it all. A rewarding career, financial security and a loving man at her side. Delighted to discover she was pregnant with her first child, she told her lover and boss, Brett Norcross, expecting him to share in her joy.

Sadly for Clare, she could not have been more wrong. Sickeningly, Norcross told her he wanted nothing more to do with her or the baby and turned his back on her and his unborn child. He broke off all contact with his pregnant lover and in a final shocking act of betrayal, he coldly sacked her from her prestigious management role at Perypils Insurance.

Broken-hearted Clare has bravely spoken out against her callous ex-partner: "I can't believe he has treated me like this. I never intended to start a relationship with my boss, but you can't help who you fall in love with, can you? I thought he would be overjoyed when I told him about the baby, but instead he dumped me! It was terrible to be so cruelly rejected. And then just a few weeks later, completely out of the blue, he sacked me and gave my job to a second-rate, inferior colleague." *That was me! You bitch.* "He's destroyed my world; I'll never forgive him."

This is not the first time senior managers at Perypils have been exposed as bullying philanderers; autocratic and cold. Clare described the culture at the company as "soulless; completely unsupportive of family values and concerned only with profit".

We also tracked down Norcross's long-suffering ex-wife, who he abandoned, along with their two young children. She told us: "This doesn't surprise me in the least. Brett's always been a selfish, self-centred womaniser..."

The article ended with another picture of The Boss. He was still outside the Co-op, but had obviously spotted the photographer, as he was holding a copy of Nuts magazine over his face. The caption read: 'Insurance Boss Covers Up'. I walked home in a daze, made a pot of coffee on autopilot and phoned Big Andy.

"You've seen it then, Kato?"

"Bloody hell, Andy, I just can't believe it. Cruella's baby is Brett's? *No way!* Did you know there was something going on between them?"

"No! And Brett used to tell me everything after a couple of pints! He never once mentioned Cruella. Mind you, you wouldn't, would you? I mean, that's hardly a conquest to brag about, is it? And knocking her up! The careless idiot. What do think their child's going to look like? A cross between Ted and Chuckie, I reckon! I bet she thought she would save her job by sleeping with him or perhaps she was just after a performance-related bonus!"

I shuddered. "What do you think is going to happen? At work, I mean. Surely he can't stay on? He'll be a laughing stock."

"I should imagine he'll have to go. Or take a discreet secondment somewhere until it all blows over, I just don't know. What a total bloody embarrassment. The Chief Exec must have choked on his black pudding this morning!"

I was surprised we hadn't heard his Mancunian roar reverberating down the M6. I said goodbye to Andy and ignored the phone when it immediately rang after the receiver was replaced. I turned my mobile off, too. It was all so sad and seedy and anyway, I was still smarting from Cruella's words - *second-rate, inferior.* Everyone would know she was referring to me. Is that really what people thought of me? Well, at least I hadn't shagged my boss. Or slept with two hundred men in one term, like the student on the front page. How many men had I slept with? Certainly not enough to cover the inside of a tent with all their names, Tracy Emin-style. Perhaps a very small cloche.

I sipped my coffee and flicked through the rest of the paper. There was a very sad story about a young boy, Michael Moore, who had a rare brain condition and his family were trying to raise enough money to take him to the States for treatment. It was the only hope to save his life. All their friends and neighbours were rallying round, organising sponsored walks, fetes, quizzes - anything to raise some cash. The boy had three brothers who were all giving up their weekly pocket money to the cause. They'd also sold their PlayStations and Xboxes. It contrasted sharply to the Perypils Shagged & Shafted exposé that had been positioned on the adjoining page.

I really should do more for other people; perhaps I could volunteer for something? Help the community, support those less fortunate. I flipped open the iPad and found a volunteering website which displayed all the local opportunities when I entered my post code. Most of them appeared to be for the bloody scouts! Outdoor helper, sport's instructor, fundraiser - 'from Donkey Derby races to Cream Cracker eating contests and Apple Dunking, there are plenty of ways to fundraise for the scouts!' It wasn't quite what I had in mind. You wouldn't catch me Dob Dob Dobbing, or whatever else it was they did. Or was that the Brownies?

Still, I did have a great big pile of clothes to donate to charity, so that would help others to dress nicely. I wondered if I'd see some tramp sitting outside Tesco's in my Karen Millen hairy black gilet. Probably not; even the most undiscerning tramp would run screaming from that disaster. I bagged up the clothes and flung them into the boot of the car, along with several hundred empty wine bottles, ready for a dump-run. I noticed that Ernie and Doris had left an old battered crate on their drive, so I scooped that up too and chucked it into the boot. Might as well get rid of it for them. I resolved to do at least one act of kindness for somebody each day.

Karen came round in the afternoon, bringing with her some plants for my garden - peppers, chillies and courgettes. She was supposed to help me clear a space in the jungle for them, but she said she was just going to "direct" and sat down in one of my dodgy deck chairs with a glass of wine, watching me toil. The pink camellia, still bravely flowering, eyed her apprehensively.

"You've got to get yourself out and about, Kate," she urged, flapping her free hand around. She took a swig of wine. "You can't sit around in, in..." *In what? In this crappy dump?* "in Pensioner's Row, discussing fifty ways to kill a slug whilst waiting for a hip replacement. You'll become pot-bound. Or depressed." She pointed her wine glass at me. "You probably are depressed and you don't even realise it. Let's see." She Googled 'signs of depression' on her smartphone.

"Right," she muttered, scrolling up and down. "Christ, get this! It says a sign of depression in women is a depressed mood! No shit! Ok, hang on, right then, here goes: do you feel sad, apathetic and worthless?"

"Er, well-"

"Do you feel anxious and scared all the time? Do you blame yourself for everything?"

"Um, perhaps, but-"

"Do you have trouble sleeping? You said you weren't sleeping well!"

"Yes, but that's because the cistern is so bloody noisy and there's all this scuffling-"

"Appetite and weight changes?" She looked me up and down. "Hmmm. You have filled out a bit."

"What? No I haven't!" *Oh yes I have.* "I'm probably just at a bad angle, or it's these trousers-"

"Do you have trouble setting boundaries? Do you have feelings of hopelessness?"

"I certainly have now..."

"Loss of interest in activities that you used to enjoy?" She looked at me triumphantly. "There you are, you see! You used to love going out, socialising with friends. You've got to make the effort Kate, don't crawl away under the nearest flower pot. Give your roots a shake and go spread 'em! Get out and meet some new people."

I put down my spade and sighed. "You mean meet a man, don't you? I'm not ready Kazza; I can't face it and I haven't the energy to fake a smile let alone an orgasm. I didn't even hold my stomach in when a fire engine went past me the other day, that's how little effort I'm making. But I have been thinking about doing some voluntary work, or something useful like that."

She lit up. "Ooh yes, what a great idea! You could join a group!"

A group? What did she mean? She scrolled down her phone. "It says that a good cure for depression is to keep up with social activities, as being around other people will make you feel less depressed. It suggests joining a group is one of the very best things you can do."

"Really?" I was suddenly suspicious. "Show me that." She promptly flicked her phone off, saying, "Would you look at that, it's run out of charge." She tucked it into the pocket of her baggy trousers and beamed at me. "I've got just the thing."

"Yes, I thought you might," I said warily. "You've got some ghastly group you want me to join, haven't you?"

"It's not ghastly at all!" Karen cried indignantly. "I was thinking of the school committee. It's great fun and you could help arrange fund-raising events, such as the summer ball or help out at the fete. You'll get to know lots of people, mainly mums of course, but there are dads too. And some of them are single. Well, they say they are."

"But I'm not a teacher and I don't have children at the

school. Well, I don't have children full stop. How could I be on the committee?"

"Oh, that doesn't matter!" exclaimed Karen, not in the mood for excuses. "We're grateful for any help we can get. And what's more, the committee meets at The Crown! You like it in there, don't you? They've got a wonderful selection of wines."

She was right, I did like The Crown and I was actually quite taken with the idea of being linked to fund-raising or the kudos of organising a classy summer ball. I'd never considered being on a school committee, or any kind of committee come to that, unless you counted the college debating society. That had all ended very badly. The first (and only) debate had been: "Animal rights are a load of sentimental rubbish". One of the debaters bought in their pet rabbit, I assume to demonstrate how innocent and harmless animals are and it had gnawed right through the OHP cable, fusing the entire college.

"You're tempted, aren't you?" Karen waved her empty glass towards me. "Brilliant! Pour me another and I'll tell you all about it. Next meeting's on Thursday night; you're really going to love it!"

Later, as I helped an unsteady Karen into James' car and waved them off, I saw an anxious-looking Doris talking to Mervyn over the fence. I heard her say: "You haven't seen Gonzales, our tortoise have you, Mervyn? We left him here in his box when we were unloading the wheelbarrow round the back." *Oh shiiiiiit.*

CHAPTER EIGHT

It was a very surreal feeling, walking into an office that had been so publicly shamed in a national newspaper. I had been intending to sit in the Property department, but I went straight round to Concerns, Cruella's old haunting ground. It was also where any difficult customer calls were likely to come into. I thought there would be some guidance from the Chief Executive's office on how to handle queries from staff and customers, but - what a shocker - there was nothing in my inbox.

Although it was early, some wag had already been round the office and pinned up a drawing of a cartoon Cruella carrying a baby. The baby, who was swaddled in black Grim Reaper robes, had Brett's face. It was clutching a scythe in one hand and a can of lager in the other. A fag dangled from its mouth. I had to admit it was rather a good drawing, but I hurried round and collected up as many of the photocopies I could find before the office filled up.

A distressed-looking Blubber arrived with The MC. She sat at her desk, mopping her eyes while The MC fetched her a cup of tea. I gave them a few minutes, then ventured over.

"Are you ok, Pat?" *Daft question.*

She blew her nose noisily on the paper napkin that had been supplied with her bacon sandwich. "It's just so awful. Poor, poor Clare. Used by a man like that, then shamelessly cast aside. Pure evil. I can't bear to think about it. It's simply wicked."

The MC nodded her head. "I always knew there had to be a reason why they got rid of Clare when she was clearly the best person for the job." *I am stood here, you know!* "I'd always been suspicious. To think she's had to go through all that alone. Poor Clare."

"Clare was very much a woman who knew her own mind," I said. "She's always been strong. You know, impregnable." *Aargh! Very bad choice of words!*

"But how will she live?" wailed The Blubber, a dribble of tomato ketchup on her chin. "A single parent! No job, no partner! What will become of her?"

"Well, don't forget she'll have been well paid by the newspaper. I'm sure that will keep her going for a bit."

"She must have been desperate to sell her story to a tabloid," muttered The MC. "This company drove her to it."

Someone was hovering. "What is it Carol?"

"Um, I've got a customer on the phone who wants to know if Perypils are going to apologise publicly for what's happened and if the manager concerned has been sacked. He's going to cancel his policy if not."

They all looked at me. *Oh God.* "Nothing official has come through yet, so we'll have to say to customers that we're obviously very disappointed in the article and the company will be making a statement later today." *Would it?* Who knew.

I went back to my desk to email this message round to the teams. Hissing Cyn slithered over, eyes glinting greedily. "I shouldn't tell you this, Kate, but I thought you ought to know, as you're the manager." She glanced over her shoulder to make sure she wasn't overheard. "The rumour is that Brett's resigned! Jackie, who works at head office, saw him go into the Chief Executive's office this morning. She tagged him on Facebook. When he came out, he was really white and shaking and apparently, he left the building and started to walk towards the train station. You see? He had to leave his company car behind! Jackie said it's parked in one of the visitors' spaces. She knows it's his because it's still got her footprints on the windscreen. So he must have gone, mustn't he? I'm not gossiping, you understand. I just thought you ought to know."

"Cynthia, how many times have we had this conversation? Rumours of this kind are not helpful, you know that. When I get something official through, you'll be the first to hear. Now please, no more of this speculation. It's difficult enough for everyone as it is." She slid off in a huff, only to be replaced by Big Andy.

"The Brett-meister's gone then!" he boomed, sitting down so heavily on my desk I feared it would collapse. "He's resigned, but as the Chief Exec would have sacked him anyway, he didn't have much choice in the matter."

"I've just told my staff off for spreading rumours, Andy!"

"Oh, it's not a rumour. Jenny at head office phoned to tell me. She sits outside the office and heard the whole exchange. As did most of Greater Manchester, by the sound of it. So we're going to get a new boss! Wonder who it will be? Just be careful not to shag him, Kate, or you'll be the next one to go! Ha ha!"

"It might be a her, you never know."

"That's about as likely as me having a bunk-up with Pippa Middleton!" He roared this parting shot, causing most of the department to look up in bemusement.

Thursday evening

I wasn't sure how to dress for a committee meeting. I considered keeping my work suit on but this was a school group; teachers tended to be casually dressed, didn't they? The committee was probably full of left-wing hippy types, like Karen. I didn't want to alienate myself by turning up looking like a private sector Nazi. I wiped off some of my make-up and perused the wardrobe to find the closest thing I had to a corduroy jacket with velvet elbow patches. I settled on an old cream denim jacket and put it over a grey T-shirt and my frayed blue boyfriend jeans. A pair of purple All Star trainers completed the look. I examined myself in the long mirror, putting my hands in the pockets of my jeans and pulling a slouchy pose, hoping I looked a little bit like a grungy student. Albeit an extremely mature one.

I set off for The Crown, a pub on the edge of Cheltenham. It used to be a dingy den of a place, full of old men and smelly dogs (and old dogs and smelly men) but it had undergone a radical transformation and now fancied itself as a bit of a pub slash trendy bistro. I saw Karen at the bar and gave her a wave.

"Hi Kate," she said, looking me up and down. "What on earth are you wearing? You look like one of those poor sad creatures on a before and after make-over show, you know, before Gok introduces them to Monsoon and gives them a reason to live."

"But I didn't want to look too corporate," I said, wounded. "It is a school committee, after all."

"Yes, well," Karen looked doubtful. "Come and meet the others."

"Has the meeting started already?" I asked, following her

under a wooden beam and through into a small side room. A raucous screech of laughter rang out from one of the alcoves. Karen stopped at a table and beckoned me over. "This is Kate everyone!" she announced brightly, pushing me forwards. I found myself facing four women, all around my age and all beautifully attired in an array of Boden wrap dresses, Hermès scarves and lots of expensive-looking chunky jewellery. They were immaculately made-up with every strand of hair teased and sprayed into perfect place.

"Kate, this is Jane, Belinda, Melanie and Gwen," Karen introduced me, but I immediately forgot every name. All I could think of was Snobby, Snooty, Tory and Haughty. I nodded "Hello" to their inquisitive stares and slid into a seat, wanting to hide my faded jeans and scruffy trainers as soon as I could. I felt like I'd been on my way to Poundland but had accidentally stumbled into Gucci.

"Glass of wine, Kate?" Snobby asked, pulling a bottle of Pinot Grigio out of the cooler in the middle of the table.

"Yes thanks, but just a drop, I'm driving," I replied, nostrils twitching from a sudden blast of overpowering Chanel.

"Ah, rookie error!" exclaimed Snobby the wine pourer. "She'll soon learn the commandments, won't she girls! *Thou shalt not drive to a committee meeting!*" They all rocked with laughter.

Karen suddenly whipped out her smartphone and examined the screen, even though I hadn't heard it make a noise. "Oh no!" she exclaimed. "My mother's not well, I'm going to have to go." I stared at her. Hadn't she told me her parents were on holiday in Alicante for three weeks?

"It's nothing serious, I'm sure," Karen said to the others

who were all clucking in concern. "Her back plays up from time to time and er, her hips too sometimes, she's such a martyr to her ailments, really she is!" *What ailments? Hadn't she been skiing at Christmas?* "I'd better go and check up on her, you know, dutiful daughter and all that..."

I fixed her with pleading eyes but she didn't look at me as she scurried off. *You traitor.* I couldn't believe she'd left me.

"Ah well, all the more for us!" Tory hoiked out the bottle and topped up her glass.

"You'll get used to us, Kate," Haughty patted my arm, then looked as if she wanted to wipe her hand on something. "We don't get out much so we really like to cut loose when we do!"

"Are you all teachers at the school?" I asked, thinking teaching must pay more than I realised.

There was a short silence as they all gaped at me in shock-horror. "*Teachers?*" Snooty repeated with an involuntary shudder. "Good God no, what on earth made you think that? We take charge of all the social events and fund raising for the school; we certainly couldn't leave it to the teachers! We asked one of them to organise the egg and spoon race at the fete last year and she forgot the bloody eggs! You should have seen it - people running up and down clutching spoons... who's ever heard of a spoon race? I ask you. Ridiculous. Quite ridiculous."

"Do you all work together, then?" I asked. They looked at me blankly. "Perhaps you have children at the school?" I was confused. It was an infant school; surely they were all a bit too old to have children of that age?

"We used to," replied Snooty and swiftly changed the subject. "Melanie, how is your daughter doing? I saw her in town the other day and I thought she was looking just *fabulous*."

Tory-Melanie nodded as she took a sip of wine. "Yes, the diet's going so well, I'm so terribly proud of her." *Pause, sip.* "She had another fitting for her bridesmaid dress and it very nearly did up this time." *Sip.* "She looked utterly ravishing in it; if she's not careful she's going to upstage the bride, you know!" They all tittered with laughter.

"Who's she wearing, Mel darling?" asked Haughty.

Tory-Melanie sipped more slowly so she could create a dramatic pause. "Vera Wang," she announced, looking smugly round the table.

"Ahhhh," they all sighed, as if climaxing.

"And I'll be wearing Alexander McQueen," Tory-Melanie continued to more sex-murmurs of approval. "But I will be taking my Issa with me, I mean, one can't be dressed in Alexander McQueen all day, can one?"

"Oh God no, of course not," Snooty helped herself to the last of the wine and slung the empty bottle back into the cooler upside down. "You're both going to look absolutely divine Mel darling, you must take lots of lovely pictures to show us."

"Oh, there's a very famous photographer who's going, so I don't think my snaps will compare to his!" Tory-Melanie laughed and reached for her handbag. "I'm just popping out for a ciggie. Shall I order us another bottle on my way?"

"Ooh yes, lovely," they all replied.

Tory-Melanie disappeared into the bar and the mood at the table changed abruptly.

"God, her daughter looked an absolute state when I saw her in town," hissed Snooty. "She looked bigger than ever,

Mel's totally deluded. Her daughter shouldn't be seen in Vera Wang, it's an insult."

"Yes, I saw her the other day too," whispered Haughty. "She was wearing a tunic top but honestly, it looked like a tent. You can't disguise these things you know, no matter what you wear. This famous photographer is going to have to be an absolute magician if he's to stop her looking utterly hideous in the photos. If I was the bride I wouldn't let her anywhere near my wedding."

The others nodded. "And just how much is Melanie drinking these days?" sniped Snobby, gulping her wine. "I mean, we can't keep up with her, can we? I think she's got a problem and you can see it's beginning to take its toll on her skin; her face looks really dull and she just appears so much, well, *older.*"

They all shuddered at hearing this heinous word uttered out loud. Huddled in the small alcove around the sacred bottle of Pinot Grigio, the three of them suddenly put me in mind of Macbeth.

Haughty caught herself and touched my arm again. "Oh Kate, you must think we're the most dreadful bitches!" When I didn't deny it, she continued quickly, "We're just concerned for Melanie, aren't we girls?" Snobby and Snooty nodded, looking all sincere. "We've been friends for such a long time," *friends?* "And it's so easy to be in denial about these sort of things, isn't it?" Haughty looked at me through narrowed eyes as she took a large sip from her glass.

"Well, I really wouldn't know," I forced a smile, beginning to need a wee but not wanting to move from the table in case they starting slating me while I was gone.

Tory-Melanie returned with another bottle of Pinot

Grigio to cries of "Oh thank you Melanie darling", "Oh, what a trooper", "Oh, you are fabulous darling". I caught Haughty's eye and she looked away. *What a bunch of phoneys.*

"Are there any other committee members coming tonight?" I asked, covering my glass with my hand to ensure it wasn't topped up.

"No, it's just us tonight," replied Snobby. "And I suppose we'd better get down to business, hadn't we girls? You'll have to keep us in check Kate, that's going to be your first role!"

They all laughed and I gave a weak smile. "So, what's first on the agenda, then?" I prompted, keen to get on with it.

"Well, the summer fete and the ball," said Snooty. "They're the school's biggest fund-raisers. Terribly popular."

"Gosh, that's a lot to organise," I said, crossing my legs. "Where do we start?"

"Oh, we'll just do the same as last year," slurred Tory-Melanie. "Who's sorting the catering for the ball?"

"The headmaster," replied Snobby.

"What about the band?"

"The headmaster's wife."

"The table decorations?"

"Headmaster's wife's sister."

"Trestle tables for the fete?"

"The caretaker."

"What about the raffle prizes?"

"Headmaster's wife."

"P A system?"

"Caretaker."

"What about posters?"

Silence. "Oh, that's just typical," snapped Snooty. "They

never think about anything; we'll have to do that, I suppose." They all tutted.

"I could get my son to do the poster on his computer," offered Tory-Melanie. "He's simply wonderful at that sort of thing, so creative. He's awfully talented."

"Right, that's settled then," said Snobby. "Mel will sort the posters. I think that's everything, isn't it?"

That's it? "Er, is there anything I could be doing?" I asked.

They all looked at me. "Um, well, you could run one of the stalls if you like-" began Snobby.

"But not the Pimms tent, I'm afraid," cut in Haughty quickly. "We already have plenty of willing and well, *suitable* volunteers." I saw her looking down at my frayed denim cuffs and I tucked my wrists under the table. She continued, "You could man one of the farmer's stalls perhaps, or how about the hog roast?" *You bitch.*

"Balloons!" exclaimed Tory-Melanie loudly, making us all jump. "We're doing a balloon release thingy. You could run that."

"That sounds great," I lied. "What do I need to-"

"Just give the headmaster a call," said Snooty airily. "He'll give you all the details. Oh look, there's Guy!"

All four of them suddenly sat up a little straighter; Snobby flicked her hair, Haughty smoothed her dress down and stuck her chest out. A handsome man with slicked-back blonde hair and wearing a smart navy blazer over sand-coloured chinos approached the alcove.

"Hello ladies!" he purred. "Don't you all look lovely. Your husbands must be mad letting you out alone like this!"

They all giggled and Haughty simpered, "Won't you

come and have a drink with us, Guy?"

Four pairs of glazed eyes gazed at him beseechingly. "Unfortunately I can't, ladies," replied Guy, looking very sad. "I've got a bit of business to attend to, you know, got to see a man about a dog." He tapped his nose with his finger, causing another fit of giggles at the table. He fixed his hazel eyes on me. "Hello there, a new girl I see!" He put out his hand. "I'm Guy."

"Kate," I replied, shaking his hand quickly, hoping he wouldn't notice my tatty cuffs.

"As in Kiss Me Kate?" he grinned.

Haughty shot me a filthy look. "Kate's just recovering from a very messy separation," she announced. I glared at her. What the hell had Karen told them about me?

"Ah well, bad luck," Guy sympathised, "but don't let this lot lead you astray! Your life could get a whole lot messier!"

They all howled with laughter as he waved goodbye, disappearing into the bar.

"Guy is a local hotshot businessman," explained Snobby. "He sometimes attends our meetings because he's one of the school's benefactors. He's terribly generous."

"And terribly gorgeous!" shrieked Tory-Melanie. They fell about laughing again, although I noticed Haughty didn't join in. When Snobby picked up a menu I realised they were intending to make a night of it. I made my excuses, saying very pointedly I had get up early *for work* and headed off, making a relieved dive into the toilets before I left.

Guy was standing outside, smoking a cigarette. "Hello Kiss Me Kate," he said smoothly. "Escaped from their evil clutches, have you?"

"Yes, I fancied some fresh air," I said, waving my hand

about in a big exaggerated motion to fan away the smoke from his cigarette. "But clearly it's not my lucky night."

He laughed good-naturedly. "Are you going to be a regular attendee at these meetings?" he asked. "I do hope so. I might even turn up to some myself." He took a drag on his cigarette and looked straight into my eyes. My legs felt wobbly. I hadn't the least intention to go to any more, but now perhaps...

"Maybe," I said, forcing my legs to start walking towards my car. "But not when there's a full moon."

I shot him a look over my shoulder and saw him grinning broadly. God, he really was incredibly good looking. Bloody typical - stumble across the world's most gorgeous man and I'm dressed like a lesbian.

CHAPTER NINE

I found an email from the Perypils Communications team waiting for me on Friday morning. They had been eerily silent all week, presumably trying to figure out how to spin the Brett/Cruella sex scandal into a positive message for the company. I half-expected to see a joyous good news story on how two Perypils managers had formed a successful merger and created 'Insurance Baby', a new super race. Their email was actually headed: "Cycle for Michael".

Perypils is proud and delighted to announce the Cycle for Michael campaign. You may have read about the Moore family's heart-rending predicament in the papers this Sunday. As a devoted family man himself, our Chief Executive was enormously moved when he read about Michael's plight. He is making it his own personal mission to raise sufficient funds for Michael to go to the States to receive the treatment he needs to save his life. *Giving up his bonus then, is he? No? Didn't think so.*

Kevin says: "This is an opportunity for all the staff at Perypils to be involved in something amazing by helping to save the life of this little lad. As a father myself, I can think of no worthier cause. I expect every Perypils colleague will jump at the chance to support a family in need." *Participation is compulsory, in other words.* "This family need our help. We will answer their call."

Excitingly, there will be a sponsored bicycle ride linking every Perypils site and a twenty-four hour cycling marathon, where everyone will be able to participate. So even if you're more Biggins than Wiggins you can still do your bit! Together, we can save Michael's life - let's Cycle for Michael! More exciting details of the day will follow shortly.

There was a picture of The Big Cheese standing with the Moore family. He had his huge, meat-hook hands on the thin shoulders of Michael as the little lad's brothers and parents formed a tight knot around them. The publicity machine certainly hadn't wasted any time; the story only came out at the weekend. There was also an 'action shot' of the Chief Exec on a racing bike, head down, looking serious and competitive. His yellow lycra cycling top still had the sales label hanging down from the back of his neck and his cycling shorts were a little on the small side. I wouldn't be eating turkey giblets ever again.

I phoned Karen at lunchtime. "Thanks a lot *mate*."

"What do you mean?"

"You bloody well know what I mean! Leaving me with the Witches of Eastwick while you did a runner. How is your poor sick mother, by the way? What was wrong with her - her back wasn't it? Lying awkwardly on a sun bed, was she? Or was it those dodgy hips again? I don't know how she manages to do all that skiing and hill walking and dancing the carlos bleeding fandango..."

"Oh alright, I'm sorry Kate," Karen sounded genuinely contrite. "But I just couldn't face them. I'd had the day from hell at school; I got landed with class 3C all afternoon and you know I can't stand those little shits. They ran me ragged. If it wasn't for bloody Childline ... anyway, the meeting wasn't that bad, was it?"

"Oh no, not bad at all for a Pinot Grigio convention.

But rather pointless for a school committee meeting. Who are they anyway? They're not teachers and their kids don't even go to the school anymore. What have they got to do with anything?"

"Everything I'm afraid," groaned Karen. "They're known as the school mafia; they control everything that goes on. The headmaster's terrified of them, he just does what they tell him. I keep in with them for a quiet life."

"Well, I think they're a ghastly bunch."

"Was Guy there?"

"Guy? Oh, er, there was someone called Guy. I only met him very briefly-"

"Gorgeous isn't he?" said Karen triumphantly. "I knew you'd like him! He's single at the moment, can you believe it? You should get in there, he's lush."

"For God's sake Kazza, he's a hotshot business man, he wouldn't be interested in me! No, stop it, I don't want to hear it. And, by the way, forty-something year old women do not say *lush*. Now, I've volunteered to run a balloon stall at the fete so can you find out about it for me and let me know what I need to do?"

"Alright, I'll let you know when the next meeting is. If you promise to come I'll buy you drinks all night. And you never know, Guy might be there again."

"Shut up."

I was munching my way through a plastic carton of listeria when another email from the Communications team arrived. I opened it up, chewing thoughtfully, wondering how the canteen managed to get its lettuce so gritty.

Kevin is delighted to announce Roger Fitzall's appointment as the new Senior Manager. Roger has many years experience with Perypils, working most recently within process design, where he was instrumental in shaping the future of the company's sales strategies. Roger lives in Stratford, with his devoted wife of twenty years and their two sons. Roger's priorities are first and foremost his family, followed closely by fishing, a passion he shares with his delightful boys. A teetotaller, Roger spends much of his own time working tirelessly for his community where he is president of the local scouts group. His mission is to "support the development of our people to achieve their full potential." *Sales potential, presumably.*

There was a picture of Roger. He had a long face, sandy hair brushed down into a side parting and a big, bushy ginger moustache. I was immediately put in mind of a German porn star. He may have worked at Perypils for many years, but I'd never heard of him. However, he was a family man; a non-drinker with harmless hobbies and most importantly, with that moustache, no one was ever going to want to shag him. He was clearly the perfect candidate for the role.

I received a short email from The German Porn Star, saying he would be in Cheltenham on Monday and would like a meeting with me to discuss our 'priorities'. I felt disappointed that he hadn't picked up the phone to say "hi" and to introduce himself. Disappointed, but not surprised. No one seemed to like talking anymore. TLS George frequently emailed me even though he was sat twenty feet away. I was guilty of it, too. Once, I had been lying in bed, badly hung-over and I'd found the Husband's iPhone in the covers. Knowing he was downstairs looking at emails on the laptop, I sent him one asking him to bring me up some Alka-Seltzer. He got his own back by bringing up a glass of water and a sachet of flower food. Blurry-eyed, I didn't notice. He dined out on that story for months. "Do you think Kate looks blooming?" and "Better give Kate some water before her head wilts!" How I laughed.

The weekend didn't start particularly well. I had slept badly, kept awake by scuffling sounds that seemed to be all around me. I'd sit up and put the lamp on, but there was nothing in the room. "Bloody pigeons, I expect," my Dad said when I called him. "They've probably got into the loft. Take a bloody shot gun up there, that should do the trick." I didn't mind the thought of pigeons so much; it was squirrels that freaked me out. Horrid great bushy tails, always twitching... I shuddered, opening the cupboard to get some porridge. About a ton of Quaker Oats fell out onto me. What the heck? Oh great - the packaging had a big hole in it. I dusted myself off, swept up the mess and made myself a much-needed coffee. When I opened the fridge to get some milk, the door all but came off its hinges. I managed to close it again but it looked as if it could collapse at any time. I really was going to have to get someone in. The shower never got warm enough and the bathroom door probably needed planing, as it didn't shut properly. Perhaps I could ask my brother, he was a builder, after all. But then again, he always had enough problems of his own so I'd feel a bit guilty asking.

I planted Karen's peppers and courgettes into a tiny patch I'd cleared in the jungle and put the chilli plants in little pots. I sprinkled slug pellets all around and ripped some bindweed away from the camellia. Its iron-like tentacles had begun creeping up the pot towards the plant, which had shed all its blooms in terror. Apart from my father and the woman in Sainsbury's who'd told me I'd saved nineteen pence by shopping there today, I didn't speak to anyone else all weekend. No one called and no one texted. Not even O2. Karen was right; I did need to get out more. When you find yourself saying to a potted plant: "Ah, there you go sweetie, that's better, isn't it?" it's time to take some serious action.

It was Monday morning misery on the roads. I crawled to a halt on the A42 and didn't move an inch for forty minutes. The driver next to me picked his nose sixteen times. Not just a delicate, discreet flick which could have passed for a scratch, but a real deep rooting around, as if he was trying to get his finger up into his hairline. *Gross.* The bumper sticker on the Polo in front of me read: "I had a life ... but my job ate it!" *Hilarious.* When a Katie Melua song played on the radio I felt I might do a Michael Douglas - abandon the car on the carriageway and go on the rampage with my blusher brush.

It was ten past nine when I eventually made it to work, two full hours after I'd set off and with a bladder at bursting point. Stalin Stan tried to stop me at reception. "Seen what those little gits have been up to now, have you? Bogeys on the banisters! Bogeys! I ask you. What is this, a bleeding kindergarten? It's a disgrace; poor Gladys, the cleaning lady, they know she's partially sighted and has to cling to the banisters when she goes up and down the stairs-"

"Can't stop, Stan! Need the loo!"

"Well, you can't use those ones! Blocked. Again. Empty

vodka bottle this time..."

God, what sort of people were working here? I walked at top speed to the toilets by the canteen, just making it in time. *The relief.* I didn't think I would ever stop weeing. When I was confident the last trickle had stopped, I made my way to the canteen, picked up a cappuccino from Grinding Greta and finally walked into the department at 9.30. I didn't recall ever being late for work before. There were thirty calls queuing, which wasn't particularly unusual for a Monday morning. I wasn't convinced all the staff were busy on calls, but they soon whipped their headsets on as my gaze swept round the teams. There was a tall man stood with his back to the room, reading the team statistics on George's whiteboard. Who was that? He turned at my approach - woah! Very big ginger moustache! It was The German Porn Star.

"Roger!" I said, putting down my coffee to shake his hand. "I didn't expect you to be here so early."

"No," he replied, with a pointed look at the clock and then at my cappuccino.

"Accident on the A42, been held up for hours." Even to me it sounded like a made-up excuse. "How was your journey?"

"Fine - I made sure I left in good time. Shall we make a start?"

"Yes, of course. Would you like a coffee?"

"Never mind about coffee, I don't want to waste anymore time." *Ouch!* Bugger me, he's a humourless bastard. Well, that's just great; why couldn't it be someone jovial and cheery, someone who at least pretended to be human and showed a bit of interest in me as a person, perhaps ask me where I lived, how long I'd worked here, if I liked to do it doggy-doggy ...

The GPS sat at the table next to my desk and watched in silence as I put my bags down, struggled out of my coat, frantically searched for my desk keys, finally unlocked my drawers, more frenzied searching for a notepad, then a pen, until finally, I joined him at the table, flushed with embarrassment at the first impression I was making. Even my bum was sweating. I thought I should try and redeem myself.

"Look Roger, I'm sorry I'm not better prepared for you. I want you to know that I've rarely been late for work and this morning was a very unfortunate one-off. I'm no shirker. I always put in a significant number of hours; I believe I worked at least sixty last week, possibly more."

Bushy red-squirrel eyebrows shot up. "Why aren't you managing to perform the duties of your role within the appropriate timescales? That doesn't sound very efficient."

Shit. "Isn't it the same for everyone?"

"No. I suggest you show me your daily task list and we'll go through it, see if we can establish where you're going wrong." *I don't have a daily task list!* "But first, we need to talk about performance." He produced my teams' monthly sales reports from a folder. I could see many of the figures had been circled or underlined several times with a red pen. "Do you understand what your target is?"

"Of course. It increased to 110% in April."

"Why aren't you achieving that?"

"We are getting there, you can see we're improving each month. But it was such a sudden and significant increase; the most we'd ever achieved before was 103% and that was when attrition was at its lowest. I've had a few leavers and I'm not able to replace them because I can't recruit." *And I'm not Paul bleeding Daniels; I can't just magic an extra 10% up out of my arse.*

His thin lips all but disappeared behind his carroty lip rug. "It's not an acceptable level of performance."

"Well, it's not exactly easy when I have a higher target but fewer people." *You do the maths.*

"You don't need more people, Kate, you just need to manage the existing ones more efficiently. How many of your staff are on performance progress plans?"

"Um, I'd have to check if you want the exact number. About ten at the moment, I think."

"Only ten? What would you say if I told you I've undertaken an in depth analysis of your figures over the weekend?" *I'd say get a fucking life* "And from these figures, you should have at least sixty-five on plans and that's just in your Property teams."

I gaped at him. "*Sixty-five?* But, but surely-"

"Sixty-five are clearly under-performing, so your team managers need to set plans immediately for these individuals." He pushed the report towards me. "Improvement must be evidenced; and quickly."

"But over half the department will be on progress plans! It's just not achievable, I mean, that's all the team managers will have time to do-"

"Good. That's all they should be doing. If they're spending time on things other than performance you need to find out what it is and put a stop to it. It's about priorities, Kate."

In my head I could already hear the cries of horror from my team managers. Progress plans were horrible great hairy things, demanding a huge amount of mind-numbing form filling followed by endless tracking and reviewing. I took a deep breath. "It was always my understanding that progress plans should be used for the minority, not the majority. Surely if over half the team aren't able to reach the target, it suggests that the target might be unrealistic."

He tucked his pen into his folder with careful deliberation and I got the feeling I'd walked into a trap. "Well Kate, let's see, shall we? When I arrived this morning, I found staff chatting whilst calls were queuing, endless group trips to the drinks machine and agents surfing the Internet as a team manager sat there, seemingly oblivious. A team manager, I might add, who has a black eye." *For God's sake George, you bloody chav.* "That's as well as time-keeping issues, of course. There appears to be significant room for improvement, wouldn't you agree?"

I couldn't really disagree. He stood up. "I've got a teleconference now, but when I come back I'd like to talk about the sales results in your Concerns teams." *Well, that won't take long.* "That and an explanation for why you haven't got any Cycle for Michael posters displayed. It's a big initiative for Perypils; the Chief Executive is expecting everyone's full support. Absolutely everyone's. There must be no exceptions, Kate."

That went well. He was right about one thing though, standards had slipped. The teams had become too big for the team managers and some of the staff were beginning to take advantage. It was all the team managers could do to pat the performers on the head while they begged the Muppets to do better. I called them together to share The GPS's feedback and to break the joyous news about the progress plans. I included the Customer Concerns team managers so they'd know what was heading their way too.

The Lazy Shit: "It's impossible. Can't be done, it's schtoopid, we can't possibly do all that, we don't have the time. Is it okay if I leave early tonight? I'm playing pool."

The Snake: "The staff won't like it all, I wouldn't be surprised if lots of them leave. They'll probably just walk out."

The Drain: "What's it matter? We're all slowly dying."

The MC: "Clare would never have allowed this. We shouldn't have a sales target in complaints, it's unethical."

The Blubber: "It's a calamity, a total calamity! Whatever will become of us?"

The Rock: "I think I might retire after all."

I think it was fair to say they were languishing at the bottom of the change curve. I gave them my most positive spiel about how we were all in it together and everything would be fine, but I couldn't even convince myself.

I met Big Andy by the drinks machine. "Have you met Magnum P.I?" he boomed.

"Mmm, there is a touch of the movie star about him."

"I've seen him somewhere before, I know I have," said Big Andy, stabbing the hot chocolate button. "I just can't recall where."

"Starring role in one of your dodgy films, perhaps? Debbie Does Dusseldorf?"

"Don't think so. It'll come to me. He's going to be trouble though, Kate, I can tell you that. He spent about three minutes in my departments before telling me I'm over-staffed. Over-staffed! I ask you! We had to work over a hundred hours of overtime last month to keep up with demand, but according to him, that's because we're inefficient. He wants us to record absolutely everything we're doing, down to the very last detail. If you pause to scratch your arse he wants to know about it so he can time it on his stopwatch. It's going to be hell."

"Yes, it is," I replied, gloomily. "He's already told me my performance is unacceptable."

"Bloody hell Kate, I thought I told you *not* to sleep with him! That's a sure-fire way to get yourself demoted! Ha ha!"

CHAPTER TEN

As if the week wasn't torturous enough, I faced another committee meeting on Thursday evening. I'd told Karen I was only staying for half an hour and then I was off. I had hundreds of unread emails that needed deleting. I met her in the bar at The Crown and even as we were ordering our drinks I could hear raucous shrieking coming from the side room, indicating that the committee 'meeting' was underway. I'd decided to keep my work suit on this time. We carried our glasses through and found the four women seated at a long table with their cauldron of Pinot Grigio. There were three men there too; Gorgeous Guy was at the far end of the table, deep in conversation with a chubby, red-faced man in a pinstriped suit and there was a thin, nervous-looking man wedged between Snooty and Snobby. We were greeted with cries of "Oh super, here are the troops, how marvellous!" as we sat ourselves down at the end of the table. I noticed, with disappointment, that Guy hardly glanced in our direction.

"That's Eddie, the headmaster," said Karen under her breath, nodding at the thin, squashed man.

"Ed the head?" I whispered back and we both giggled, receiving a black look from Haughty.

"Kate," she said, "you look quite different from the last time we met you. You look more, well, what's the word-"

"Professional," finished Tory-Melanie, beaming at me over the rim of her wine glass, a little boss-eyed.

"Yes, unless you've just been appearing in court or

something!" Haughty peeled with laughter. "What was the charge? Crimes against glamour? Possession of an offensive outfit?" *Ouch. You cow.* She laughed loudly to make everyone think she was only joking. Karen saw my face clouding over and quickly stepped in.

"I'm afraid Kate can only stay for half an hour," she said, "she's got some work to catch up on. So perhaps we could start by discussing the fete and the balloon stall, in particular."

"And I can't stay for long either," chipped in Snobby. "I'm helping out at the scouts hall this evening, the beavers are doing some outdoor events for their activities badge. Although it looks as if it's going to pour with rain; there's nothing worse than wet beavers!"

I couldn't believe she'd just said that. I looked round the table in delight but no one else was laughing. I buried my face in my glass and pursed my lips hard. Next to me, Karen made a strangled sound and reached down to fumble with her bag, hiding her face. I looked down, cheeks aching with the effort of not laughing. I felt someone's eyes on me and when I glanced up, I saw Guy watching me with amusement. I had to quickly look down again.

Ed the Head managed to negotiate a way between two prominent pairs of bosoms and leant forwards. "For the balloon stall, I've ordered three hundred balloons and a canister of helium. I thought people could pay a pound and write their name and address on a tag, which we'll tie to the balloon. We'll release all the balloons at the end of the fete and there'll be a prize for the balloon which ends up travelling the furthest."

"How will we track them all?" slurred Tory-Melanie.

"Er, what?"

"How will we know which one has travelled the furthest? Will we have people in cars following them or-"

Snobby interrupted with a snort of contempt. "For goodness sake, Mel! It's the same as last year. The tag has the telephone number of the school printed on it. There are instructions for whoever finds the balloon to call in with the name and address and where they found it. That's how we know whose went the furthest."

"Oh yes, I see," Tory-Melanie still looked perplexed.

"Do you think a pound is enough, Headmaster?" asked Snooty. "I mean, by the time you've bought the prize as well there won't be much profit in this stall. Shouldn't we charge more, say five pounds for each balloon?"

Five quid to release a balloon? You're having a laugh.

"Er, well, five pounds might be a bit much," said Ed the Head nervously. "Perhaps two pounds, maybe-"

"Nonsense," Snooty talked right over him. "Five pounds it is. We've got to think big this year Headmaster, squeeze out every penny we can."

Ed the Head shot a defeated look in my direction. I shrugged. I couldn't believe anyone would stump up a fiver so it looked as if my stall would be rather quiet. "Do you need me to prepare anything, Eddie?" I asked him. "Shall I bring some pens or-"

"Oh, the Headmaster will see to all that ... detail," Haughty flapped her hand dismissively. "These meetings are aimed at a much higher level Kate, you know, strategies and pricing and such. How did you get on with the posters, Mel darling?"

"Ooh yes, let's see the posters!" cried Snobby excitedly.

Tory-Melanie produced an A4 poster with a dramatic flourish from a large leather pouch that looked brand new. Had she brought it specially? "My son's done an *amazing* job," she said, proudly holding up the poster. "He's so artistic, so talented. I just don't know how he does it!"

The poster said 'Summer Fete and Ball 7.30' as the headline banner and had an explosion of colourful fireworks in the background. There was an outburst of admiring exclamations: "That's super Mel darling", "What wonderful colours, how tasteful", "Your son is so clever, Mel", "Simply fabulous, darling".

I looked closely at the poster. "You don't think that the time is a bit misleading?" I asked. Horrified faces swung round to glare into mine. Had I dared to criticise?

"It's just that it says fete and ball at 7.30," I ploughed on. "Doesn't the fete start at eleven in the morning - won't people be confused?"

"Only if they're incredibly stupid!" laughed Karen, trying to cover my faux pas.

"I think it's perfectly obvious to anyone that the 7.30 refers to the ball," sniffed Tory-Melanie. "Perfectly obvious."

"W-ell, ok," I said doubtfully. "And will there be any fireworks on the night?"

They all looked at the headmaster. He shook his head. "Not after the incident last year with the Roman candle and the vicar's robes," he said, shuddering at the memory.

"I'm just not sure that there should be fireworks on the poster, then," I said. "I mean, if there aren't actually going to be any. Again, it could be misleading."

There was a short silence. "Well, if you don't like my poster I suggest you make a better one yourself," Tory-

Melanie snapped, in a huff. "My son has spent a lot of his own time on this design, you know. It wouldn't hurt for you to show a bit of gratitude."

"You've not printed many have you, Mel?" asked Ed the Head, who clearly agreed with me.

There was a short pause. "One hundred and fifty," she replied, adding defensively "And I've already sent some to all the local parish magazines."

"Shouldn't the committee have agreed the design first?" I asked.

"Oh, I think the posters will be absolutely fine," chipped in Karen, shooting me a look which said "Shut the fuck up!"

I couldn't stop myself. "Well, I suppose if you're all happy with them," I continued. "I just thought that posters advertising events would usually have the date of the event on them. But it's up to you, of course."

They all looked at the poster. Tory-Melanie suddenly slammed her glass down on the table, burst into tears and rushed out of the room. As Snobby and Snooty hurried after her, Haughty stood up slowly and addressed a weary Ed. "It seems our happy little group has been infiltrated with a rather negative presence, headmaster," she announced, without looking at me. "I think we need to seriously rethink the quality of our attendees, don't you agree?" She didn't wait for an answer and stalked out after the others.

"For God's sake, Kate," Karen hissed angrily. "Why did you have to be so pernickety? You've upset Mel."

"*Pernickety?*" I was incredulous. "What's the point of advertising the fete if you don't actually tell people when it is? Her son may well be the arty-farty type but he's hardly Einstein, is he?"

"All you need to do at these meetings is nod and smile," hissed Karen. "How hard is that? You're in management, for Christ's sake, that's what you do all day long. My life's going to be hell now, absolute hell. They'll see to that. You've tarred me with your brush."

"You really are a bad girl Kate, aren't you?" called Guy from the other end of the table, eyes twinkling. "Quite the little trouble maker. Someone needs to take you in hand!"

"If only I could find someone man enough!" I shot back. He laughed and his pin-striped friend gave a dirty chuckle. I turned back to Karen. "I think I'd better go Kazza, I'm sorry about, well, telling the truth and upsetting everyone. Nice to meet you Ed, I'll see you at the fete. Bye guys."

I felt Guy watching me as I picked up my bag and left the room. I could see the others outside stood around Tory-Melanie, who was drawing on a cigarette between exaggerated sobs. My ears should be in flames. I backed up and used another exit, walking briskly around the pub to reach my car. I was thinking about Guy's amused hazel eyes looking into mine. *Stop it.* He was miles out of my league; he was just a flirty tease. It started to rain quite heavily. There would definitely be some wet beavers about tonight.

The Rock and I were working our painstaking way through the team's rotas and attempting to match them to the forecasted volumes for next month. Even David Blaine would have struggled with this illusion; there simply wasn't sufficient resource to cope with the number of complaints. "Can't we recruit more people?" sighed The Rock, already knowing the answer.

"There's a freeze on recruitment. And before you ask, I

don't know if this means Cheltenham is closing. I've no idea if it's a short-term thing or a long-term strategy." Although the use of the word "strategy" suggested that the company had some sort of plan in place; a hopeless fantasy. "I don't suppose there's any way we can fit in some sales training?"

The Rock pursed her lips. "Um, yes, look - there's a quiet spell Friday fortnight at three thirty. We should be able to squeeze half an hour in there."

"Oh, that's great! At this rate, we should have everyone trained within twenty years or so."

"I have been giving my guys some coaching on sales," said The Rock. "The youngsters are really quite keen because they want the extra money. The trouble is, their approach is a bit gung-ho. One customer called us, devastated, after all his worldly possessions were destroyed when his house flooded and he was complaining bitterly because we could no longer cover him for flood damage. The advisor said to him: 'Well, never mind! I expect you need a good holiday now! Shall I quote you for some travel insurance?' They've no idea of tact or diplomacy."

I groaned. "We're just creating more complaints for ourselves - I'm going to need Facilities to start answering calls if this carries on. I may as well use the canteen staff, their diplomacy skills are almost as good as ours; just this morning one of them said to me: 'Wouldn't you prefer decaffeinated? It might make you less bloated'."

The Rock sniffed. "Well, we'll just have to get on with it and do the best with what we've got. You do know Cycle for Michael's coming up, don't you? We've got half the team out with activities and whatnot; it's going to blow us out of the water. There's the 24-hour cyclothon, the Olympic-themed fancy dress competition and the canteen are organising a barbeque on the grassy bank in the car park."

"Oh great, so sickness will go through the roof."

"I'm more worried about the fancy dress! Can you imagine what some of the outfits are going to look like? There will be loads dressed in cycling gear and someone's bound to come in Speedos ... can I take the day off? I'm too old for all this."

"No, you can't! I'm going to have to ban holidays all together, I think. And sickness. Talking of sickness, is Andrea back yet? She's making my absence figures look terrible."

I didn't miss the smirk that fluttered across The Rock's face even though she tried desperately to suppress it. "Yes, she's back."

"Why did you smile? What's so funny?"

"Nothing! I didn't smile-"

"Yes you did! Come on, what's the joke?"

The Rock gave in to a huge grin. "It's Andrea and her, er, lunchtime activities."

I raised my eyebrows and waited for her to continue. "She meets a friend. A male friend. I think he works for Insight Health, on the first floor and I'm pretty sure he's married. Anyway, they go off in his car at lunchtime, for, um, well, you know what. Apparently, Dennis the Dip from Finance went for a walk one lunchtime - he has to walk two miles a day for his sciatica - and he stumbled across them in Fenham Woods! He was traumatised, poor chap: he's only just had his eye laser surgery so unfortunately for him, he saw everything very, very clearly! He said he was thinking about getting the procedure reversed now and actually, he wished he was blind!"

I was shocked. Andrea! Moist, moaning, bog brush-headed Andrea had a lover and by the sounds of it, a very active sex life. When had I last had a tryst with anyone? How had she managed to attract a man but I couldn't? Or did frustrated married men just do it with anyone that offered? Is that what my husband had done? The Rock was still talking: "... she's organised an ice cream van to come to the site next week for the Cycle for Michael day, and the team want to know if she's going to ask for a ninety-nine or a sixty-nine!"

We shrieked with childish laughter, resorting to constrained snorts when the teams shot disapproving glances in our direction, not impressed by the sight of two managers having fun. They needn't have worried; it was unlikely to ever happen again.

CHAPTER ELEVEN

I'd risen bright and early, well, early, to drive to the Birmingham site to undertake a disciplinary hearing for them. It was a sexual harassment case, so it had the potential to be a lot juicier than the usual run-of-the mill disciplinary i.e. lateness, sickness or the good old 'my manager is a bell-end' on Facebook. The journey into the city had, as always, been a total nightmare and I had, as always, got completely lost in the swirling, cesspools of hell that are the roundabouts of central Birmingham. I'd eventually seen a beacon of divine light in the form of a jumping fish which, on its brown sign, pointed the way to the Sea Life Centre. I knew I could park there and walk to the site.

I was met by one of the team managers, Jackie, who was short and plump, with really small black beady eyes. She was one of those women whose age was indeterminable, however she chatted away about her daughter who was just about to start working for Perypils too (poor thing, more work for the Samaritans) so I placed her age at around thirty to fifty. We made a quick pit stop at the canteen and then went to a tiny cupboard of a meeting room where a large personnel file was waiting for me.

'Royston Pembleton' was the name on the file, which sounded rather flamboyant, as if he lived in a grand country house and drifted around in a Noel Coward dressing gown, chatting to his petunias...

"Creepy pervert." Jackie savagely crushed that image. "Disgusting little man. We've wanted to get rid of him for years but no one's had the nerve to do it. Well, we've got him this time; grabbed one of the girls' breasts he did, the dirty swine. Blatant as you like. It's all in the file." She sniffed. "We were glad to hear it was you doing the hearing."

I was surprised. "Why?"

"Because you always sack people at a hearing."

"No I don't! Do I? No, I can't possibly-"

"Yes! Your nickname is The Hatchet King, didn't you know?"

No, I bloody well didn't! That's an awful reputation to have and surely it wasn't true? I tried to recall a hearing when I'd just given someone a warning ... there must be one, I just couldn't think of it at this moment. Oh God, what did that say about me? Why didn't I ever give anyone the benefit of the doubt? Is that why my husband was drawn to someone more tolerant, more patient? If he wanted someone malleable, perhaps he should have married Morph.

"Anyway," Jackie was still talking, "it should be pretty straight forward really, being that it's gross misconduct. He can't stay, can he? Not after he's groped someone."

"I never pre-empt the outcome of a hearing, Jackie," I said, a touch sanctimoniously. "It wouldn't be professional. Let me read through the file and I'll expect Royston in here at eleven to see what he has to say for himself."

This clearly wasn't the response she'd been expecting from a notorious Muppet slayer and she pursed her lips disapprovingly as she left the room. I opened the file and started to read through the numerous file notes, which documented several incidents of inappropriate behaviour. I made a summary on my pad:

1. Grabbed Sarah Heaney's breast whilst they were both filing in the storage cupboard.

2. Crept up behind Louise Banting when she was alone at her desk, put his arm round her and whispered in her ear, making her feel very uncomfortable and scared.

3. Accused of stalking by Mary Newman, after he 'hounded' her for her new address. He eventually obtained it by 'other means' and she is now terrified he'll turn up at her house.

4. Seen 'lurking' in the bushes by the car park, apparently seeming to 'fiddle with himself'.

I felt rather grubby after I'd been through the file. It was all rather damning and each incident had a witness statement, although they were rather brief and lacking in substantial detail. I was surprised HR hadn't insisted on more thorough notes, but it must be difficult to read things properly when you're sat in the dark covered in cobwebs. I wasn't looking forward to meeting Royston one little bit. I went to find Jackie to arrange someone to sit in with me, under the guise of note-taker, so I wouldn't be on my own with him. She wanted to do it herself, but I gently suggested someone neutral would be more appropriate, and after treating me to the lemon lips again, she sent me Andrew, one of her team coaches. He was a very nervous-looking young man, tall and thin, with ginger hair. I guessed Jackie had chosen him as she would be able to bully all the details out of him later. There wasn't really enough space for three people in the meeting room and poor Andrew had to sit hunched up in the corner, trying to balance his jotter pad across his long legs.

On the stroke of eleven o'clock, there was a knock on

the meeting room door and a portly balding man in a white-grey shirt and horrid brown floral tie came hesitantly into the room. I eyed him with distaste. "Sit down please."

He slid with difficulty into the vacant chair, having to edge it out further from the desk to fit his stomach into the gap and forcing Andrew's knees to all but touch his chin. "My name is Kate King and I'm the hearing manager. Andrew will be taking the notes. Do you understand the purpose of this formal meeting?"

He nodded.

"And can you confirm that you have chosen not to have any representation and that you are happy to continue?"

Another nod.

"Good. Well, let's make a start. There are four particular areas I need to discuss with you, but I want to focus first on the incident with Sarah Heaney." He looked blank.

"In the storage cupboard," I prompted. He stared back at me.

"I, I don't know what you mean," he stuttered. So that was his game, was it? He was going to pretend he didn't know anything about it. What a slime ball.

"You mean, you don't remember grabbing Sarah's breast?" I asked, coldly. "I'm afraid I find that very hard to believe. Are you denying that it happened? Because I should remind you that there were several witnesses."

He turned white. "I haven't grabbed anyone's breasts! I haven't been anywhere near the storage cupboard!"

"Come on Royston, you're not doing yourself any favours. This is a very serious charge and you need to tell me what happened. For your own sake."

"But, I'm not Royston."

"Sorry?"

"My name's Steven; Steven Jones. I'm here about the Systems Analyst role. My interview invite said room twelve, at eleven o'clock."

"This is room eleven," said Andrew.

"Oh, sorry." He got up, looking hugely relieved and scuttled from the room. *Well, good luck with that interview!* A bloody systems analyst who suffered from numbers dyslexia! That explained a lot – I often received a self-congratulatory company email heralding our IT 'triumph' whilst all around me systems crashed, customers raged and colleagues openly wept. Andrew calmly flipped the page over on his note pad and pretended to be absorbed in a doodle, not wanting to make eye contact, perhaps sensing I was fuming and also, I suspected, trying to disguise a smirk.

"Andrew, why the hell didn't you tell me that wasn't Royston?"

"I didn't know the meeting was with Royston! Jackie never said who it was, just that it was a hearing to dismiss someone."

"We're not necessarily going to dismiss... oh, it doesn't matter. So where is he?" I got up and looked into the corridor. A man was sitting by the water cooler, anxiously wringing his hands.

"Royston?" I called. His head shot up and he came rushing over. He was slightly built, with thin greying hair and large, rectangular framed glasses. Beads of sweat glistened on his brow and top lip.

"I hope you don't think I'm late," he gushed, "but I saw you had someone else in here so I thought I'd better wait. Was that the right thing to do?"

"Yes, yes," I muttered, ushering him into the room with a shudder. He really was an odious-looking thing.

I went through the formalities all over again as he perched nervously on the edge of his seat, leaning forward over the desk and staring at me unblinkingly through his serial-killer glasses. I asked him to comment on the accusation that he'd grabbed Sarah Heaney's breast.

"I didn't! I know they say I did, but I didn't! I didn't!"

"But why would several of your colleagues say that you did?"

"I don't know! I was standing on the small ladder, taking a box down from the top shelf and when I stepped down I accidentally brushed Sarah, who was at the bottom of the ladder. There's not much room in there, you know, it's all very awkward and I always go up the ladder because I don't think the ladies should have to. Not in their high heels, it's too dangerous. But I didn't mean to touch her, I just couldn't help it."

"The statements say you grabbed her breast-"

"I didn't! I just brushed past her when I stepped off the ladder. I couldn't help it."

He was sweating quite profusely now; it was trickling down his face and I could see dark patches emerging through his grey tank top. I took a packet of tissues out of my handbag and passed them over to him.

"Let's talk about the second incident, Royston, with Louise Banting. She said you approached her when she was on her own and that you put your arm round her. Can I have your comments on that?"

Royston mopped his brow and blew his nose loudly. Behind him, Andrew's nose wrinkled in disgust.

"Yes, I did go over to Louise. The poor thing was sat on her own as the rest of her team had gone off to a meeting, or something. I think they left her behind to cover the phones. I only went to see if she wanted me to get her a cup of tea! I felt bad for her because she'd been left behind."

"And did you put your arm round her?"

"No! I didn't touch her!"

"Are you quite certain, Royston? Think back, please."

"I'm one hundred percent certain! I didn't touch her! I wouldn't!"

"And did you whisper in her ear?"

"No! I asked her if she wanted a cup of tea, that's all. I didn't go near her ears."

In his anxiety, he was leaning further and further forward and I found myself straining my lower back to push as far away from him as possible. I pressed on. "Well, tell me about Mary Newman. Why were you so keen to obtain her new address?"

He looked surprised. "Because I'd heard she'd moved to Cloverton and I know the buses through there are most unreliable, so I thought I would offer her a lift to work in the mornings. She doesn't drive, you know, not with her spasms and her short leg syndrome and Cloverton is on my way."

"I see. So you asked her for her address?"

"Yes. She said she'd write it down for me, but she must have forgotten about it, so I asked Patricia if she knew Mary's address and she gave it to me."

"Right." This wasn't going quite the way I thought it would and his vehement denials had rather taken me by surprise. I knew I had to tackle the fourth accusation but I wasn't sure how to word it. "The last issue for you to comment on Royston, is rather, er, sensitive, shall we say? You were, apparently, seen in the bushes by the car park. Can you tell me what you were doing there?"

Andrew stopped scribbling and looked up with great interest. Royston stared at me in bewilderment.

"In the bushes? I, I don't recall that ... when was it?"

I referred to my notes. "Tuesday the third. At lunch time."

He scratched his head, causing flakes of dandruff to drift down onto his shoulders and made an attempt to push his glasses back up his sweaty nose. They immediately slid down again.

"I can't think. Why would I be in the bushes? There's no logical reason ... oh, yes! I do know! It must have been when I saw a pigeon in the car par; the poor thing had a broken wing and couldn't fly. I went to help it but it scooted away into the bushes. I went after it, but it had gone right into the undergrowth, so I had to give up in the end."

Was this guy a raging pervert or Mother sodding Teresa? I hadn't the faintest idea but I knew I had to ask him the next, excruciating, toe-curling question. I clenched my buttocks.

"The witness statement suggests that you were, er, touching yourself Royston, when you came out of the bushes." It was my turn for moist armpits now and I saw Andrew quickly put his head back down, his face the same colour as his hair.

"Touching myself? Whatever do you mean?"

I squirmed in my chair. "I mean," Christ, how could I put this delicately? Were you engaging in a little hand to gland combat, Royston? Getting to know Pamela *Handerson*, perhaps? Whacking the one-eyed weasel?

"Were you fiddling with your, er, you know, trouser area?" *Trouser area! Anyone would think his hems had come down!*

"My, my trouser area?" The penny dropped and Royston looked aghast. "Oh my God! You mean ... no! *No!* Of course not! That's disgusting! Who would say that? Who? Why would they?"

Unable to bear it any longer, he dissolved into distressed sobs, fumbling blindly on the desk for the packet of tissues. I sent Andrew to get him a cup of tea, the young lad leaving the room with much relief. I was always pretty hopeless with tears but it was especially awkward when men broke down in front of me.

"Come on Royston, please calm down," I urged. He was sobbing so vigorously he could hardly catch his breath.

"You must calm down, Royston, I don't know CPR! I won't be able to resuscitate you!" *And I'm buggered if I'll be giving you the kiss of life.* He managed a half-smile at my feeble attempt at humour and slowly began to gather himself together, gratefully accepting the plastic cup of scolding muddy water offered by Andrew.

I considered him as he noisily slurped his tea and mopped his nose. There was no denying he was a creepy-looking guy, but he had explanations for all the incidents and he had defended himself with so much gusto, it seemed entirely genuine. However, the witness statements completely contradicted him; something wasn't quite right.

"I'm going to call a time out here, Royston, ok? So you go and get something to eat and take a breather for a while and I'm going to go through these witness statements again. I'll call you back in later this afternoon to let you know what the next steps will be. Are you alright? Good. Off you go, then." I had to add "Not you" when Andrew attempted to escape too.

"Andrew, I need you to round up these people for me." I gave him the list of names. "We'll start with Sarah Heaney if possible, so can you find her and send her in. I'll need you to make a note of everything she says. Ok? Thanks. Oh, and leave the door open, would you? Let some fresh air in."

I read through all the statements again whilst Andrew was gone. They were short and to the point and on the face of it, Royston was dead meat. Which was exactly how the room smelt. I fetched myself some water and nipped to the loo, returning to find Andrew and a young slip of a girl in the room.

"This is Louise Banting," explained Andrew. "Sarah's at lunch, but I've left a message for her to come as soon as she gets back."

I smiled at Louise who looked nervously back with eyes as large as saucers. "I just wanted to run through your statement please, Louise," I said. "Nothing to worry about. Now, you said Royston approached you and put his arm round you, is that right?"

"Yes, that's right."

"He definitely put his arm round you?"

"Um, well, I think he did."

"I need you to be very sure, Louise, it is important. Did he actually put his arm round you?"

"Um, I'm not sure now. I thought he had, at the time, but now I think back, I don't think he did."

"Right, so he didn't actually touch you. And did he whisper in your ear?"

"Well, yes, he spoke really quietly."

"Where was he standing when he spoke to you?"

"Um, just to the side of me, I think."

"And did he actually bend down and whisper in your ear?"

"Er, well, not really."

I sat back in my chair and looked at her. "So he didn't touch you in anyway, or get closer than could be considered necessary? Why does your statement say he did?"

She fidgeted in her chair, looking uncomfortable. "I only mentioned to Jackie that I was left alone and creepy Royston had come over to me. She insisted on a statement and I got a bit confused, I think. Jackie typed it all up; I didn't really look at what I was signing. I won't get into trouble, will I? I mean, he really is very pervy."

I felt like saying yes, you bloody well deserve a bollocking you empty-headed little rash of wind, but I could see she was no match for Jackie; she'd been bludgeoned into making something out of nothing. I told her she'd need to sign a revised statement and said she could go. As she was leaving, an older lady came to the door of the meeting room and looked in, her thin pointed face framed by wispy strands of mousy hair. "This is Barbara," said Andrew, and when I looked blank he muttered, with much embarrassment, "You know, bushes Barbara."

"Oh, right. Take a seat please Barbara, I'm just going through everyone's statements. You saw Royston in the bushes on the afternoon of the third? Can you describe exactly what you saw please?"

"He's a pervert, everyone knows it. He's never had a conversation with my face you know, only ever speaks to my chest. It's about time someone did something, it's not-"

"The bushes please, Barbara. What did you see?"

"I saw him coming out of them, looking very shifty, very sly. He'd definitely been up to something."

"What else?"

"I saw him touch himself."

Andrew gave an involuntarily cringe. I took a deep breath. "I'm afraid I need a bit more than that, Barbara. I know this isn't easy," *trust me, I know,* "So please take your time. Where did he touch himself?"

"You know. Around his groin."

"Could you actually see his groin?"

"Well, no, not exactly."

Not exactly? What do you mean; you only saw a bit of it? Which bit? How long was it, for Christ's sake? "So he wasn't exposed?"

"No."

"And when you say he touched himself," *shit, I'm sweating again* "did he, you know, I mean was he, er, rubbing himself?"

"Well, I couldn't see very clearly, of course, but he definitely touched that area."

He was scratching his balls. I sighed. "Men often touch that area, Barbara. It's not very pleasant, I know, but there's a world of difference between a quick scratch and something much more inappropriate. Do you think it could have been a quick scratch?"

She sniffed. "Possibly. But I really don't see what difference it makes when he's the way he is, with that horrible, dirty mac of his ... you know he wears elasticated trousers, don't you? It doesn't take a genius to work out why. None of the women want to work with him you know and-"

"Thank you Barbara, I've got all I need for now. There'll

be a revised statement for you to sign shortly. You can go."

She stood up in a huff, appeared to be about to say something, but thought better of it and left the room, not quite slamming the door but closing it very, very firmly. Andrew looked up with a sudden grin. "This is quite exciting, isn't it? It's like that film, that really old one, when most of the jury think the suspect's guilty, but one of them doesn't and he has to break them all down one by one. What was it called?"

"Oh yes, Twelve Angry Men, you mean? Great film, but I preferred the Simpson's version when Homer votes against the rest of the jury just so he can have a night in a hotel with room service and free cable TV."

"We should try that!" laughed Andrew. "Oh, but I didn't mean together, you know, you and me, I wasn't, er-"

"For God's sake!" I got an attack of the giggles at the sight of his stricken, crimson face and he couldn't help but join in; a welcome release of tension. We were still laughing when the door opened and a young stocky blonde girl came into the room, eyeing us disapprovingly.

"This is Sarah Heaney," Andrew said, recovering himself and eagerly picking up his pad again.

"Hi Sarah." She looked back at me defiantly, arms folded across her stomach, below an absolutely enormous bosom. *Yay Gods!* I tried not to look at her chest, but it was so difficult not to. She was wearing an extremely tight white T-shirt and her breasts simply dominated the entire room. She slid into the hot seat and rested them on the desk.

"I need you to clarify a few things for me please, Sarah. I appreciate it's rather personal; are you ok for Andrew to remain in the room? Ok, thanks. In your statement, you say that Royston grabbed your breast?" I looked across at her, desperately keeping my eyes fixed on hers so they wouldn't slip downwards.

"Yes, he did and I was very upset about it. And distressed."

"He actually grabbed you? Do you think you could describe exactly how?"

"Like this." She made a quick movement with her hand, like a fish darting.

"So, did he take hold of your breast?"

"Well, no, he didn't exactly take hold of it." *Here we go.*

"Would you say he brushed it? Or did you feel him actually squeeze it?" I noticed Andrew was crimson again.

"Well," she thought for a moment then stuck her chin out. "He definitely touched it."

"I believe you were in a very small room and that Royston was stepping down from a ladder. Could it possibly have been accidental?"

"He touched me and I'm very upset about it. I don't think we should have to do the filing with him, in that confined space. It's not right; he's a total creep."

"No, it's not right that this has happened to you, but I do need to know please, Sarah; could it have occurred accidentally?

"He definitely touched me so I don't see what difference it makes; it shouldn't have happened at all, should it? We shouldn't be put in that position in the first place. Not with him."

I inadvertently glanced down at her breasts again; I wasn't sure there was anyway Royston could have avoided touching them. "Please answer my question, Sarah. Could it have been accidental? Yes or no?"

There was a long, sulky silence. "I suppose so. Maybe."

Behind her, Andrew did a quick air punch as if to say "Result!" I let her go, feeling extremely weary. "That just leaves Mary Newman, the lady who said he was stalking her. Did you manage to find her, Andrew?"

"No, I'm afraid Mad Mary's off sick today."

I stared at him. "*Mad* Mary, did you say? Why do you call her that?"

"Oh, she's barking!" he replied, cheerfully. "Completely gaga! She's got a framed picture of Roger Federer on her desk; says they're in a relationship and wildly in love. She even pretends to take calls from him during the Wimbledon fortnight - everyone takes the piss and there's always cries of "Mary's being Rogered again!" or "New balls please!". She's as mad as cheese!"

Oh God. "Right, well in that case, I think I'll discount her statement, especially since Royston has given me a plausible explanation for wanting her address."

"What happens now?" asked Andrew, with great interest.

"I'm going to tell Royston he's got no case to answer. As all the statements have been discredited, there's simply no other outcome."

"Jackie will go spare! She's wanted him out for ages."

"Yes, well, there clearly are issues with Royston but I'm afraid exaggerating things isn't the answer. I'm going to suggest she sits down with him and has a proper heart to heart, take things from there. Thanks for all your help today Andrew; you've got quite a bit of typing to do now! Are you ok with it all?"

"Oh yes, no problem, I'll get it to you pronto." He

hesitated at the door, face firing up again. "I thought you were great today, I mean, really fair and stuff. All the girls have got it in for poor old Royston but he's not a bad bloke, he just tries too hard to please people and ends up giving everyone the creeps. I'm glad he's not getting the sack."

I gathered up all the empty plastic cups and took them to the bin in the corridor. As I did so, I saw Sarah Heaney walk past sharing a laugh with a group of others, one of whom, a very good-looking lad, slapped her playfully on the arse. She squealed with laughter, exclaiming, "Ooh yes, spank me, spank me!" Hmmm. She didn't seem too upset or distressed about that. Double standards? Almost certainly. I was guilty of this too, sometimes. I recalled raging at an overweight, slobbery colleague who had brushed his hand against my thigh once, but when a gorgeous young man had plunged his hand down my top during a works night out, I laughed it off. I think I felt flattered that someone so good-looking should want to drunkenly grope me. Had I really had such low self-esteem? That was probably why I'd agreed to a second date with a bloke who'd nodded off whilst we were making out on our first. I only paused to sit up and wipe the steam from my glasses and when I turned back he'd fallen asleep on the sofa with his tongue still hanging out.

I returned to my prison cell where I found a thundery-faced Jackie waiting for me. "I understand Royston's getting away with it?" She must have pounced on poor Andrew the minute he put his nose outside the door. I looked into her angry, beady little eyes, trying to suppress a rising urge to scream in her face.

"Getting away with it? That's an interesting choice of phrase, Jackie. Getting away with what, exactly? Asking someone if they wanted a cup of tea? Helping an injured pigeon? Not grabbing someone's breast?"

She bridled. "Well, I can see he's managed to pull the wool over *your* eyes-"

"Don't even go there, Jackie!" My voice was rising, but I couldn't help it, I was pissed off now. "I've never come across such a shambles of a hearing, with these so-called witness statements that, I noticed, were all produced by you. I'll put them away in a folder named Bullshit Productions whilst I type up all the correct ones, shall I? Exaggeration, inconsistencies, downright untruths ... you'd better pray that Royston doesn't want to raise a grievance case against *you*. Christ knows, he'd have every right."

Her blackbirdy eyes opened wide in alarm. "He can't do that! I only wrote what people told me had happened-"

"Why can't he? I bloody well would if malicious lies were spread about me! This is your influence Jackie, you've encouraged this witch hunt behaviour by your attitude towards him. But, I will do my best to discourage him, for your sake and I'll see if he'll accept an apology as an end to the matter."

"An apology? I'm not apologising to that creep, I'd, I'd rather, I'd-"

"You'd rather what? Invent another crock of crap and waste everyone's time again? Tut tut Jackie; you really are going to get yourself into serious trouble if you carry on down this path. It's not the answer, is it? Now, would you please let Royston know I want to see him? Thank you."

She hesitated at the door and looked back at me. "He really is a pervert - he's not safe to be around. I want you to know that."

I gathered up my notes as I waited for Royston to re-appear, Jackie's words running through my head over and over again. Was I about to let a dangerous predator get away scot-free? Had I been so determined not to live up to my reputation as The Hatchet King that I'd morphed into a pussy cat? What if next time he really did assault someone? I'd never forgive myself.

A feeble tap at the door and a shiny-faced Royston slid into the room carrying a coffee that had been purchased from the canteen. "I thought you might need this," he said, pushing it over to me. "Trapped in here all day! I don't suppose you've managed to get any lunch either, have you?"

He sat down and stared at me through his Harold Shipman glasses as I told him he was off the hook. He beamed with delight and said there was absolutely no need for an apology, he quite understood how "these things happen" and was more than happy for the case to be closed. He told me he was leaving work early today as he was doing a clothes bin collection round in the Rowan Hospice charity van. Was he a genuinely misunderstood good guy or the Childcatcher? I really didn't know.

CHAPTER TWELVE

Saturday

I awoke to a grey blustery day. I'd had visions of drifting around the summer fete in a pastel-coloured tea dress and matching cardy, nibbling on a piece of Victoria sponge, sipping Pimms and exchanging pleasantries with the other stall holders. As it was, the forecast had said it was unlikely to get above sixteen degrees, with a chilly north-easterly, so I dressed in boring old jeans and a jumper.

I arrived at the school playing fields just after ten. There was a large marquee in the distance for tonight's ball. I wasn't going to that, despite Karen's nagging. I didn't own a ball gown and the tickets alone were forty quid. I couldn't justify it, not when I'd just forked out for a new tortoise. Jesus, the cost of it! It had been over a hundred quid!

The stalls were all in the process of being set up, but it was not proving easy with the gusty wind. Table cloths were flapping madly and posters were being torn off, with several already whirling around the field. Ed the Head approached, looking wild-eyed and harassed. "Ah Kate, this way, your stall's just over here. I'm afraid you're going to have the devil's own job controlling the balloons in this awful wind, but I've pegged the net down as tight as I can, so it should hold them all in."

"Don't worry Eddie, at five quid a pop I shouldn't think there's going to be that many to worry about!"

"No, you're probably right about that." He peeled a

poster away from his shin as we walked to the stall. There were two cardboard boxes on a trestle table; one contained balloons, the other labels. There was a helium canister stood next to the stall, on the grass.

"Reverend Kelly will be here to release the balloons at four o'clock. The prize for the balloon found furthest away is a meal for four at the Pizza Palace. Now, don't leave the stall unattended when we're open, not even for a minute. Helium's a bloody magnet for the kids - we had hoards of them roaming the fete last year, like gangs of Munchkins. If you need a break, get one of the others to mind the stall. Okay?"

Great. No wonder there weren't any other takers for this stall. Was helium poisonous? I didn't think so, but knowing my luck I'd turn my back and some kid would inhale a lungful and collapse; why couldn't I run the cake stall instead? Oh my God no - nut allergies! The cake stall was even deadlier! Bugger me, this whole field was a death-trap.

Karen came over to join us, tugging at her tasselled scarf as it flew up over her face. "Morning all. What a shitty old day! Sorry Ed, but I think you might be wanted over at the tombola. Sid's got his prosthetic arm caught in it again."

"For Christ's sake!" The headmaster hurried off.

I pulled a face at Karen. "What stall have you got?"

"Bloody Bric-A-Brac. I was scheduled to have the plant stall, until, well, you know."

"Until you got tarred with my brush."

"Exactly."

"Where are Double, Double, Toil and Trouble?"

"Oh, it's a bit early for them, daylight makes them crisp up. They'll be along later to make sure someone's polished the pea shingle in front of the marquee."

"Karen?"

"Yes?"

"What is Bric-A-Brac?"

"Stuff you're too embarrassed to take to the dump. Fly tipping, basically."

The fete opened at eleven. I was amazed how many people were turning up, even in this weather. Most made a bee-line for the food stalls - the hog roast already smelt amazing - and a queue for the bouncy castle quickly formed. The plant stall was proving very popular, too. As I watched people pass my stall, I couldn't help noticing that the majority of the mothers fell into one of three categories:

Smug Mum: stepped straight out of a Joules catalogue, all pristine Hunter wellies and matching padded gilet: "Yes, of course we're going to the gymkhana, Fifi darling, straight after you've won the best organic kumquat cupcake competition..."

Psycho Mum: clearly had too many children in too short a space of time, head twitching and eyes bulging: "Oh God Freddy, look hold Sophie's hand, will you? Just hold it while I help Ollie, he's got his head stuck again... No, don't do that Freddy, it's unhygienic, oh my God, where's Benjy? Where the hell is Benjy! Oh, you're Benjy, aren't you? Are you? So who's missing? Oscar! Oh God, where's Oscar-"

And finally, Chav Mum: flesh bulging out of leggings following a traditional family Bargain Bucket breakfast, greasy hair scraped back with a stained scrunchy: "You 'it me with that catapult again, yer little shit and you'll get my fist, you 'ear me? Yer little gobshite-"

My stall wasn't proving very popular, with typical

comments such as:

"Can I have a balloon, Mummy?"

"How much are the balloons?"

"They're five pounds. But they're not for taking away, they're-"

"Oh, that's ridiculous! No you can't have one, darling. Mummy's not going to be ripped off."

"Waaaaaaahhhhhhhhhhh!"

Or

"Can I have a balloon, Daddy?"

"Yes, if you promise to be very good today."

"Er, you don't get to keep the balloon, I'm afraid. We put them here, under this net and then we let them go, into the sky."

"Waaaaaaahhhhhhhhhhh!"

By twelve thirty, I had a meagre five balloons trapped forlornly beneath the net - and the headmaster's wife had bought two of those. Snobby and Tory-Melanie had tripped past several times on their way in and out of the Pimms tent but they'd very pointedly ignored me. I'd seen Haughty visiting several stalls brandishing a clip-board but she didn't come near mine. I was cold and very, very bored. Bugger it, I couldn't stand here like an ice sculpture all afternoon, I was going to slash the price. That's what Alan Sugar would do. I changed the £5 to £2 and decided I would let people buy the balloons to take away, if that's what they wanted. People started to drift over. Then some more. As kids started to walk around the fete waving their balloons more were attracted and a queue started to form; suddenly it was all very stressful. I was trying to take the money, write the tags and inflate the balloons whilst the wind gave me a savage whipping and constantly covered my face with my hair. A couple of kids started to tug at the net to get at the balloons and I yelled, "Oi! Leave that alone, you little sods!" earning myself a stiff reprimand from a shocked parent.

Karen noticed the scrum and came to help out. "You won't believe the sort of crap I've had to take on that ghastly Shit-A-Brick stall," she hissed under her breath. "Some old bag actually haggled over the price of a decrepit toy rabbit with one eye - it was only 30p! People have been chucking the stuff around too, they don't care, the grasping bastards."

Together, we transformed the melee into an organised conveyor belt and worked tirelessly until, by three thirty, the balloon net was bulging. Things only calmed down when the food stalls started to discount and the crowds flocked in that direction. Karen heaved a sigh of relief. "Phew, well done us – this stall may actually turn in a profit! Right then Kate, I'm off. Got to get to the stocks whilst the head of department is trapped in them. I've been practising my right hook for weeks! Teach the bastard to keep giving me 3C..."

As I tidied the stall, someone said "Hi Kate!" I looked up, having to peer through my windswept horse's hair.

"Oh, Kieron! Hello there. What brings you here?"

What a stupid question. He was holding the hand of a small sulky-looking boy, who had a mop of thick blonde hair.

"Max goes to this school. Don't you Max? Say hello to Kate."

Max stared at me sullenly. Most kids did that. "Where's Mum?" he demanded, tugging at his dad's hand.

"She's still in the Pimms tent, isn't she? Sorry Kate, it's been a bit of a long day. He's very tired."

"That's ok," I replied cheerfully. "Do you want a

balloon, Max? You'll have to be careful, mind, or the wind will carry you away on the end of it!"

His face brightened and he nodded enthusiastically. I stopped Kieron as he fumbled for some money.

"No, no, this is on me. The last time we met you bought me two drinks and rescued me from the Rocky Horror Show. It's the least I can do. Tell you what, I'll buy you a balloon to release, too. You might win a meal for four at the Listeria Palace if you're really unlucky. What's your address?"

"I'll tell you mine if you tell me yours!"

I laughed. It was sweet of him to pretend to flirt with me when I looked like Stig of the Dump. I gave him a label to complete while I inflated a balloon for Max.

"There you go. Are you going to show it to Mummy?"

He nodded and started to run around in circles with his balloon. He didn't look the least bit tired now.

"We're not together," Kieron said quietly, glancing up at me as he wrote his address on the label. "His mum and me, I mean. We split up some time ago."

"Oh." I wasn't sure what to say and anyway, I was distracted by the advancing figure of Haughty. Her black woollen cape billowed around her, giving her the appearance of a demented bat. She didn't look too happy.

"What's going on here, Kate? Who gave you permission to reduce the price of the balloons?"

Oh crap. "They weren't selling, so I decided to take action. Now, as you can see, we've practically sold out." I stared at her defiantly. Kieron looked nervously from one of us to the other.

"Well, I'm going to have to report this *breach* to the committee. It's completely unacceptable. And what's this I hear about you swearing at the children?"

Kieron muttered something and backed away, grabbing Max's hand and leading him towards the sandpit. I felt my hackles rise.

"I did, unfortunately, let a naughty word slip out, but it was completely accidental and I apologised immediately. Now, I've been stood out here for five hours without a break and I've made hundreds of pounds on this stall. What, exactly, have you been doing? Apart from swanning around on your fake fucking Jimmy Choos, dressed like the Scottish Widow, moaning and whining and throwing your considerable weight about? So, either you have the decency to say thank you very much, or I'm going to shove this helium canister right up your arse and you'll be farting like a chipmunk for the rest of your-"

Too late, I realised the headmaster and Reverend Kelly were standing behind me. There was a short, horrified silence. Haughty's jaw flapped in the wind.

"Er, Gwen," the headmaster stepped in. "We really need you at the cake stall; the Rock cake competition is showing signs of turning ugly - we don't want broken windows again, do we? Could you come and supervise, please?"

He took hold of Haughty's arm and led her away. I could hear her wailing loudly, even above the howling wind and the crackly PA system. Reverend Kelly and I looked at each other. He appeared rather alarmed to be left alone with me.

"I'm sorry you heard that, Reverend, I don't know what came over me."

"Yes, well, never mind, I'd better get these balloons released. I've got to judge the fancy dress in a minute and then justify my decision to swarms of exhausted, disappointed parents who were up all night making paper mache heads."

"But I don't think it's been announced on the PA yet. There's no one here to watch-"

"It can't be helped, we'll just have to get on with it. Let's get this net up."

We tugged at the iron pegs that had been beaten well into the ground. Huffing and puffing, we managed to raise them sufficiently to lift the net and the red balloons started to swirl up into the sky. It was a wonderful sight. A sudden strong gust of wind blew a large number into an oak tree and there were several loud bangs but at least most managed to avoid the power cables.

Thank God. My bit was done - I could go home for a nice hot bath and a warming brandy. I packed up the stall and went to find Karen to say goodbye. I thought I ought to tell her about my run-in with Haughty too, although she'd probably heard about it already. She might never speak to me again. Why had I sounded off like that? I should have just held my tongue. As I walked across the field, Ed the Head came rushing over. *Here we go.*

"Look, I'm sorry Eddie, I just couldn't-"

"No, never mind all that, Kate. What are you doing now?"

"I'm going home. Aren't I?"

"I'm desperate for some help. Those pissed-up idiots at the Pimms tent haven't been washing up the glasses and we need them for the ball tonight. It starts in a couple of hours and there's no clean glasses. None at all! Could you help us out, Kate? I know you've had a long day and er, a trying one, but I'd be so grateful to you."

You've got be kidding me. I looked into his beaten, bloodshot eyes. "Yes, of course I'll help." *Why did I say that? Why?*

"Oh, that's fantastic." I thought he was about to cry with relief. "I've got someone lugging the crates of glasses over to the school kitchen. Can you make your way there?" *Crates* of glasses? Just how many were there?

As I was nodding, an anxious-looking woman ran over. "Oh, headmaster! Can you come to the sandpit? It's little Tommy Lane, he's eaten a dog poo, he thought it was chocolate. Mrs Lane says she's going to sue the school."

"Oh, for Christ's-". Ed was gone.

I couldn't see Karen, so I made my way into the school and found the kitchen. Crates of dirty glasses full of bits of mint and strawberries were piled up around the sink. Some grumpy teenagers preparing vegetables for tonight's ball acknowledged me with a grunt. I filled the sink with warm soapy water and got started on the glasses. I thought others would be along to help me, but no one came. When I ran out of space at the side of the sink, I had to start drying up the glasses too. It took hours to get through them all and my back was killing me. I wasn't used to being on my feet all day, but hey, I must have burnt up thousands of calories! Every cloud.

The kitchen filled up with catering staff and stress levels rose as the start time for the ball approached. I realised I hadn't eaten or drunk anything all day. My hands were sore and pruny and my jumper had dribbles of Pimms down it. The kitchen had become very hot and my Worzel Gummidge hair was plastered to my head. I went outside to breathe in some fresh air, relieved that the wind had dropped at last. It had turned into a reasonable evening and guests were arriving for the ball; the women a riot of colourful ball-gowns, freshly washed hair expertly swept up into classy knots, beautifully applied make-up and sparkling with jewellery. Their partners, penguin-smart and proud, darting eyes seeking the bar. It all looked so twinkly and lovely. I kept well back, watching from behind a tree, like a grubby urchin spying on the landed gentry.

A sudden flicker of light next to me made me jump. Someone else was stood in the trees. I saw the top of a fair head as it dipped to light a cigarette and then I was looking into a pair of familiar amused eyes above a wolfish grin. It was Guy.

"Well, if it isn't Cinders, lurking in the woods! What's the matter, Cinders? Can't you go to the ball?"

He looked just *edible* in his white dinner jacket, with his bow tie hanging loose around his unbuttoned collar. I wondered if he was going to bother doing it up, he looked so sexy the way he was.

"I don't want to bump into the ugly sisters."

He gave an easy laugh. "Yes, I heard you'd upset one of them again. The headmaster hasn't stopped laughing about it. You really do have a wild side, don't you Cinders?"

I gave him a knowing smile, fervently wishing that I did have a wild side. I didn't, of course. The closest to wild I ever came was wearing a leopard print blouse. And even that felt a bit too racy.

"Why don't you come in with me? I'll protect you from their evil clutches. Come on, I'll finish my ciggie and then I'll buy you a drink."

"Well, you may fancy yourself as a dashing Prince

Charming, but I'd say your eyesight's started to fail. I'm hardly dressed for a ball."

He came closer and looked me up and down. "You look perfectly good to me."

He stared straight into my eyes. I thought my legs were going to buckle.

"Could you do my tie up for me? That's the only reason I regret divorcing my wife, you know! She was always such a dab hand with my dickie."

I chuckled as I started to do up his tie. He looked into my eyes the whole time, a teasing grin playing across his lips. I wasn't brilliant with bow ties; The Ex used to have a ghastly clip-on one. In fact, our first date had been to a black tie dinner. I'd been quite shocked when, half way through the evening, he plucked off his bow tie and chucked it onto the table, next to his calculator. I should have known then really; never trust a man with a detachable dickie.

By some miracle, I managed to form quite a decent-looking bow around Guy's neck. "There you go, you do look smart. I mean, it's a shame you're so ugly and all that, but at least you're dressed nicely."

"Mmm," he purred, not moving away. He edged his face even closer to mine. "Do you ever take anything seriously?"

His eyes were fixed on my lips as he moved closer again. He smelt absolutely gorgeous, of summer-meadows and limes. That definitely wasn't Lynx he was wearing. What was happening, was he going to kiss me? Giddy from a sudden rush of hot hormones, I thought I might pass out. Then I remembered my Kate Bush hair, my stained jumper, my pruny fingers - and my breath! It must be rank; I'd only sucked on a couple of strawberry bits all day. I took a step backwards. "Right, well, have a great evening, won't you? I'm sure it will be good fun." He looked momentarily confused. Either he wasn't accustomed to women slipping through his grasp or he couldn't understand what I was saying because my hand was covering my mouth. He recovered himself and smiled broadly.

"Alright then Cinders, have it your way. But look; why don't you let me take you out for dinner sometime? Go on, it will be fun; I know some great places. You might even enjoy yourself! What do you think?"

What did I think? That you can't possibly want to go out with me! What am I, your bit of rough? Where would you take me, somewhere really fancy probably and I'd be totally bedazzled by the array of cutlery to choose from, or drink from the finger-bowl and you'd tell all your hoity-toity friends about it so you could all have a good old laugh at my expense...

"Yes, ok then, I mean, I suppose I could, as a favour to you. I'd hate to think of you dining all alone."

"Great! That's settled then. I'll give you a call."

"You don't know my number."

"I'll find it. I'm very resourceful, you know." He winked as he ground out his cigarette and headed towards the marquee. He looked back over his shoulder to flash me a cheeky, white-toothed grin and my knees went all wobbly again.

I was physically exhausted by the time I got home and crawled into bed. But I couldn't sleep. I was wide awake, thinking about Guy. Replaying the scene under the tree over and over. Had he really asked me out or was he just teasing? Did he fancy me? Would he bother to find out my number and call me? A little devil kept popping up by the side of the bed to say "You're punching well above your weight there, love!" but I ignored it. Someone found me attractive enough to want to have dinner with me. And they weren't even from an institution. The day hadn't been so bad after all.

CHAPTER THIRTEEN

On Sunday, I was fuzzy-headed and gritty-eyed from lack of sleep. It was a warm, dry day so I should have been outside tackling the jungle, but I found myself pacing around the house, surreptitiously checking my mobile for messages every ten minutes or so. I knew I was being an idiot - as if he'd call the very next day! He was a businessman; no doubt he was putting together some high level deals or schmoozing with clients, even on a Sunday. Or busy counting his cash. He'd probably call during the week. That's if he called at all.

As I was checking my emails in the afternoon, one pinged in from Karen entitled 'Before and After'. I opened it up and there were two pictures of her. In the first, she was stood posing at the entrance to the marquee, a radiant smile, wearing a midnight blue ball gown with her hair elegantly clipped up and a silver tiara holding it all perfectly in place. In the second, she was slumped over a toilet bowl, hugging the porcelain surround, her hair flopping all over the place and the tiara looking as if it was just about to fall into the pan. Oh dear! She'd written:

Hi Kate

I know you're not on Facebook, so I thought I'd send you these! Great night (I think) but Huey, Spuey, Pooey and Mooey were shooting me daggers all evening. Think I must have upset them somehow, but don't remember doing so. But then, I wouldn't, would I!

Anyway - hot news! You'll never guess who asked me for your number? Only Oily Oliver! You know, he didn't look too bad - some of his acne has cleared up, and his hair transplant was definitely showing signs of life. At least, there were a few tufts at the front. Or that may have been horns, of course...

No, only joking! It was gorgeous Guy! Well, I nearly fell off my wedges! He wanted to know all about you – what you did, where you lived, if you had a family - he was very, very interested! I didn't know if you'd be happy with me giving him your number, so let me know if you are and I can text it to him. I just knew you two would hit it off! I should be a professional matchmaker!

Anyway, let me know. I'm off back to bed now.

Kazza aka Cilla

xxx

Ugh! Here I was waiting for his call and he didn't even have my number! I hit 'reply' and typed:

YES YES YES! For Christ's sake woman, give him my bloody number!!!!!!!!

Fortunately, I stopped myself from pressing 'send'. *Calm down dear.* I deleted it and wrote:

Hi Karen

I think you looked better in the 'after' picture - can't see your face! Ha ha.

I did bump into Guy last night and he asked me to have dinner with him sometime. I don't think he was pissed. He may have been stoned, of course. Anyway, I thought it might be fun, so please do pass on my number.

Love to James.

Kate xxx

I didn't fess up to upsetting Haughty yesterday just in case she was angry with me and didn't pass on my number to Guy. Oh well, he wouldn't be calling me today, so there was nothing for it now; time to brave the jungle. I went to inspect my plants. Slimy silver trails circled all around them. The courgette's leaves were in tatters and the peppers and the chillies had also been nibbled. These pellets were absolutely useless! Just like the 'How green is my grass' feed I'd put on the lawn, which was now brown. I'd have to try setting a beer trap for the slugs, as my father had suggested. At least they'd die happy.

I went inside to the kitchen and took an illy coffee tin out of the cupboard. I emptied it of teabags - the days of being able to afford illy coffee were long gone. I found some cans of lager at the back of the fridge, purchased in the unrealistic hope of luring a man back to the house, and poured some into the tin, taking it outside to bury into the ground next to the courgette. *Take that, you bastards.* The camellia was ok; it had a thick ring of pellets around it that didn't seem to have been breached. It looked at me hopefully, as if to say "Can I go back to that nice garden centre now?" I told it no, it was stuck here with me. Its leaves seemed to droop a little.

Monday

The GPS was on site again; he'd come to listen to some

calls, which was extremely nerve-wracking. I'd tried to get him to sit with our best advisor but he hadn't fallen for that one and instead had plugged himself into the online call monitoring system where he could sample calls at random. I was furiously attempting to delete as many Muppets from the system as possible before he came across them, while out of the corner of my eye, I could see him scribbling away furiously in his black book. Would the feedback be good or bad? My tummy felt very uneasy, but that could have been because I was still waiting for Guy to call me. I found myself checking my mobile every five seconds in case I'd missed a call, even taking it into the loos with me. This was ridiculous! I was behaving like a love-struck teenager - he probably wasn't even going to call. Why would he? Why would someone like that be even the slightest bit interested in me?

I was just starting to re-type Andrew's notes from the harassment hearing when a dark shadow was cast over my desk. The GPS was stood in front of me. I looked up with a bright smile. "How have you got on, Roger?"

Dead-eyed stare. "Perhaps you would listen to this call yourself and let me have your thoughts?"

Uh-oh. That didn't sound too good. With a feeling of dread, I put my headset on and clicked into the call monitoring system, trying to look unconcerned as The GPS lurked, watching me closely. I entered the reference number he'd given me and located the call. The recording was an outbound call made from The MC's team and after several rings, a rather creepy male voice answered "Hel-lo?"

"Hi, is that my racy, racy rabbit? How is my naughty bunny-wunny this morning?" *Oh God, no.* It was Andrea.

"Mmmm, feeling very naughty indeed. I think I might

need to be taken in hand and punished."

"Oooh, you bad rabbit! What am I going to do with you? I think someone deserves the leash this lunchtime, don't you?"

"Oh yes, yes, I've been so bad, I do deserve the leash; you must pull it tighter and tighter, harder and harder, until I literally explode in your..."

Ugh! I whipped my headset off abruptly. "Well, Roger," I fiddled with my fringe, unable to look him in the eye. "Our guys are allowed to make the occasional, quick personal call-"

"It was over fifteen minutes long."

"And it is not our policy to listen in to personal calls; should we happen to come across one in the course of our quality checking we stop immediately and move on."

Thin lips pursed. "You mean, you turn a blind eye? How is it possible that your customer advisors can spend so long on a personal call - a totally inappropriate personal call - and it go completely unnoticed by your team managers? How?"

It was a good question. Had he listened to the whole call, the perv? Perhaps he was considering signing Andrea up for his latest home movie.

"I accept it's very unfortunate and I'll deal with it. However, why don't we focus on the positive things you must have heard? I'd be very grateful for some *constructive* feedback."

He considered me for a moment and I realised I was holding my breath. "My call listening has uncovered a number of areas we need to discuss." *Oh shit.* "And I understand from Birmingham that you have been rather lenient on a persistent offender, which was very disappointing to hear. Perypils doesn't accept that sort of behaviour and I expect our managers to deal with it very firmly, not let them off the hook with weak decision making."

"Now just a minute!" I was stung by the injustice. "I undertook a perfectly fair hearing-"

"I think the way forward is to formalise your performance issues into an action plan, so that improvement can be properly tracked and maintained. I'll arrange a meeting so we can make a start on this."

I looked at him in alarm. "What do you mean by formalise? You mean a formal progress plan?"

"There's no need to put a label on it; it's all about working together to recover and improve performance. My PA will send you an invite, along with my observations from today. I'll speak to you tomorrow."

I watched his tall straight back getting smaller as he strode towards the door. The bastard was putting me on a progress plan! I'd never been on the receiving end of one before, I'd never under-performed! He wanted me out, I could sense it. *Jesus, I might lose my job.* My bowels felt icy and a wave of nausea swept over me. Keep calm. He couldn't just kick me out on the basis of a few dodgy observations. Still, I'd better call the union. I'd paid my subscription for thirteen years and never called on them for anything; well, it was pay-back time. Fear began to turn to anger, and I decided the healthiest thing to do was let my feelings out. I went to find Andrea.

Wednesday

I was on my way to a meeting when I bumped into Big Andy. I told him that The GPS was putting me on a progress plan, fully expecting him to dismiss my fears and take the mickey like he normally would. However, he suddenly looked extremely apprehensive. "You need to be careful, Kato - there are rumours that Cheltenham's days are numbered, especially as they've stopped recruitment. They won't want to fork out on large redundancy payments, so if they can get us out some other way then they will. Bonking Brett handed it to them on a plate, of course. Don't you go giving them any ammunition."

"I thought I should ask the union for some support."

He snorted. "You'd better start practising your 'Big Issues' then. Lap dancing's out of course, unless you're collecting two pence pieces ... oh, I think Ann Summers are recruiting, that's worth a try; dusting the vibrators is probably the closest you're going to get to the real thing now."

"Cheers for that."

My mind was in a whirl. What would happen if I lost my job? Would I get another one? The economy was so flat; not even clever-dick BA MA double-hons-with-knobs-on graduates could find work. I couldn't concentrate on the meeting's agenda, which appeared to be about holding some sort of stapler amnesty. After half an hour, I wanted to staple the agenda into my head. When my mobile rang, I excused myself, saying self-importantly "I have to take this one" and left the room, grateful to escape for a bit. "Hello, Kate King."

"Hello. Is that Kiss Me Kate King?" It was Guy! He'd called me! He'd actually called me! Play it cool, play it cool...

"Oh dear, not another obscene phone call."

He laughed. "It's Guy. From under the tree. I don't usually make obscene phone calls, but I can turn this into one if you'd like me to."

Hell yes, I'd like that. "That might not be entirely appropriate for the office."

"Well, why don't we discuss it away from the office? Over dinner? I know it's short notice, but I was calling to see if you were free on Friday night?"

Aah! What should I say? If I say yes, I'd look like I had no social life at all, a saddo, a friendless loser. But if I said no, he might think I wasn't interested; he might not ask me again.

"Um, just let me check a minute." I was near the water cooler which had a paper towel dispenser above it. I grabbed a towel, held it to the phone and scrunched it up, hoping he'd think I was rustling through a busy diary. Two girls passing by stared at me as if I was mad.

"Well, I don't have anything I can't re-arrange."

He laughed again. "Don't appear too keen, will you! I'm going to translate that as yes, you'd like to have dinner with me. Do you know the Mucky Duck? It's next to the Silhouette club in town."

"The Silhouette club? Isn't that-"

"A disgusting den of iniquity? Yes, it certainly is. But don't worry, the Mucky Duck's a fabulous restaurant and the owner's one of my clients, so he'll look after us really well. And they often have a jazz band there on a Friday."

Oh no. "Sounds great," I lied. "Shall I meet you there?"

"No, no, text me your address and I'll come and pick you up. About seven? We can get a drink first. Look, I've got to go, I'm due at a client's. See you Friday?"

"Yes, see you."

Oh my God, oh my God, oh my God! I had a date! With a totally drop-dead gorgeous, smart, funny, successful business man. Woo-hoo! Had I just nodded off in the meeting and dreamt that conversation? Things like this never happened to me! I strutted back into the meeting room, tossing my hair as I sat down. They could stick their staplers up their arses! *I had a date.* I may be facing financial ruin, repossession and the inevitable drug-addled decline into prostitution and a wolf fleece - but I had a date!

I phoned Karen to tell her about Friday.

"*What?* This Friday?"

"Yes, what's wrong with that?"

"How the hell are you going to fit in a Brazilian before Friday? And a moustache wax? Some men may prefer the Mediterranean look but I'll swear Guy's not one of them; he wasn't even keen on a furry gilet I wore once. Kept joking that I looked like a silverback. And what about a pedicure? You can't go on a date with crusty-looking hobbit feet. There's a huge amount of plucking and exfoliating to be done - you haven't thought this through, Kate."

"I haven't got a bloody moustache! Or hobbit feet. And as for everything else, it doesn't matter, I'll be covered up. It's not as if I'm going to be jumping into bed with him."

"Why ever not? Because it's your first date? You're not a teenager, Kate, if you feel like doing it you should go for it. And I would, before bits of you seize up completely! You ought to be prepared for the eventuality, at least."

She was right. What if the mood took us and we did end up sleeping together? It would be a bit of a slutty way to behave on a first date, but why shouldn't we if we really wanted to? As I undressed for bed, I examined my naked form in the long mirror. I saw a pot belly, dejected breasts and a double chin. Jesus, was my neck showing signs of crepiness? It was! No, no - stop. What would Gok say? He'd tell me to be positive and to find the bits I did like. Um, well, my toes are quite pretty and painted a nice coral colour. But my feet looked like two frozen fillets of cod. *No, be positive.* Er, my fingernails are quite nice. That's about it. So; I have to find a sexual position in which he is only able to view my toes and my fingers. I picked up the iPad to Google it, but stopped myself. God knows what sites that search would direct me to. I didn't want the house suddenly surrounded by flashing blue lights.

I lay in bed, stroking my stomach as if that would flatten it down. Perhaps I was worrying too much. The most important thing is that you both enjoy the experience and I wouldn't be able to do that if I was constantly concerned with trying to stop bits from wobbling into view. The Husband had never seemed to mind what I looked like in bed, or even if I was fully conscious, although he didn't much care for my British bull-dog nightie - he said it reminded him too much of his mother.

I'd nip to M&S tomorrow and invest in some sexy undies. Maybe a new outfit if the credit card would stretch that far. At least if I could make my top layers look half decent, he might want to peel them away to see what was underneath...

CHAPTER FOURTEEN

Friday night

I was almost ready. Trussed up in my new pencil skirt from Per Una, I could barely move my legs more than two inches apart. The skirt was grey with big black flowers on it and I had eventually teamed it with a black short-sleeved jumper with a very low neckline. Even with the benefit of a Wonderbra, there was only the merest hint of cleavage on display. Talk about low-hanging fruit. Why was everything getting lower down? I'd even found a pube growing on my knee the other day. My whole body was an avalanche; no wonder I had such hairy toes, they were growing a bloody beard!

My legs were the biggest dilemma. They were too white to be let out uncovered, but my forgiving black 60 denier tights looked far too wintry and the barely black 10 denier looked really dated. I'd never risk hold-ups again, not since that dreadful Christmas party where a pair had ended up around my ankles and I'd danced around like Coco the Clown for hours until someone took pity on me and pointed it out.

In the end, I had to plump for a pair of 'nude' tights, which were basically a light version of American Tan. Totally unsexy, but at least they toned down the moonshine coming from my legs. I decided that if things did heat up between us, I could always try and whip them off in the bathroom beforehand. A pair of black suede high heels and I was ready.

I turned myself this way and that in the long mirror and did a beaver impression to make sure there was no food stuck in my teeth. I looked ok. A tad too much mascara but nothing I could do about that now. Right, I must think of topics of conversation for the dinner table; make sure there are no long, awkward silences. Steer clear of politics and religion. What did that leave? How was your day? Good journey? Come here often? Dull, dull, dull! He was a smart, eloquent entrepreneur, for God's sake! He'd expect witty banter, with meaningful observations on life, or the economy. No, I can't do this, I'm way too unsophisticated for him. My tits are too saggy. My house is too woebegone. My car has four doors. What on earth was I thinking? *Laughing stock.*

Deep breath. Calm down. What would Gok do? I Googled: How to get the man of your dreams, even when you know he's totally out of your league, times a million. I found a four step process:

1. Catch his attention - show him you're available without throwing yourself at him. A little smile, a glance, a friendly touch - sexy but subtle. *Yes, I could do that, as long as I didn't get too pissed and attempt to straddle him.*

2. The chase: make him suspect you're interested without knowing for sure. Men love a chase! *Really? Is that true? At the end of our first date The Husband had said to me: "Are you up for it or not, then?" I'd admired his pragmatic approach at the time.*

3. Don't forget who you are. Men want an independent woman who has a life of her own. No man wants a girl that doubles as a shadow; it's suffocating. *Again, is that true? Aren't men scared of independent women? Mrs Thatcher, Joan of Arc, Arlene Phillips ... James once said that he only had to hear the name Esther Rantzen and his penis would shrink in terror.*

4. Together forever - men want a woman who is positive, upbeat and a blast to be around. *So - don't nag.*

I picked up my mobile and was about to pop it into my handbag when I noticed I had a text message. It was from Guy. *Nooooo!* Don't tell me he was cancelling!

"Sorry Kate meeting running late. Can you meet me there? Very sorry. Promise to make it up to you!"

Oh. Still, that wasn't the worst thing. At least now he wouldn't see Pensioner's Row in the daylight. These things happen when you are running a business, I guess. I texted back:

"No probs! See you there." That was positive and upbeat, as per step four. I took the opportunity to check the slug beer trap before I left. Ugh! The illy tin was completely filled with dead slugs! It was disgusting. Another was teetering on the edge, about to topple in. What the hell was I going to do with the tin now? I couldn't very well put it out with the rubbish. Perhaps I should leave it there as a warning to others. I watched the teeteror fall over the edge onto his dead drunken mates. He hadn't heeded the warning.

I drove to the Mucky Duck and parked in the large car park that it shared with the Silhouette Club. There were plenty of spaces. I checked my nose was clean in the rear view mirror then walked towards the entrance, taking tiny, tottery steps in my restrictive new skirt. I found myself in a small bar, which felt a bit like a library, with its bookcases and leather furniture. There was nobody else in there. I approached the bar and perched self-consciously on a barstool. Where was Guy? Still in his meeting? Or had he decided not to come? A door behind the bar opened and a plump middle-aged woman appeared carrying a pile of menus.

"Oh!" she exclaimed, as if someone waiting at the bar to be served was an unusual occurrence. "Can I help you?"

"Can I have a vodka and tonic please?" I half expected her to say "what on earth for?" but she put down her menus and started to put ice and lemon into a glass. Another door opened behind me and the sound of a hand dryer filled the room.

"Ah, Kiss Me Kate! You made it."

Thank goodness. He was here; I hadn't been stood up. I turned to greet Guy, who was dressed in dark blue chinos and a white open-necked shirt. He looked rather casual to have been at a business meeting, but then not all clients were formal and stuffy. He gave me a kiss on the cheek and I immediately felt myself colouring up. *Get a grip.* "Glass of shiraz please, Ruth and put these on my tab. Shall we have a seat, Kate?" I attempted an elegant dismount and joined him at a table in the corner, sinking down into a squashy, leather armchair that forced my knees almost up to my chin.

"You look rather lovely," he purred.

"Thank you. You look, well, the same as usual."

He laughed. "I'm sorry I couldn't pick you up. I'd reached a seriously tricky negotiation point - it really could have gone either way."

Ruth brought our drinks over and placed them wordlessly on our table before retreating back behind the bar.

"What is it you do, Guy?"

"Ah, no work talk tonight! We want to enjoy ourselves, don't we? Cheers."

"Cheers." I could have kicked myself. Why had my first

question been to ask him what he did? I may just as well have asked to see his bank statements. Now he would think I was a gold-digger. From where I was sitting I could see through to the restaurant, a large square room. The tables looked half-full, with mainly silver-haired diners. I was a bit surprised, I was expecting something swankier. Still, it wasn't always about glitz and glamour; no doubt the food was top-notch.

"Have you eaten here before?" asked Guy, as if reading my thoughts. "They do an excellent chateaubriand. Ruthie, what special treats have you got lined up for us tonight?"

"You'll have to ask the waiter," she growled. I thought her customer service skills were appalling, especially towards an important client such as Guy. He didn't seem to notice and started to talk about some of the fabulous places he had eaten at. I hadn't heard of any of them. I'd bought fish and chips from Rick Stein's in Padstow once, and had to eat them hunched and cowering behind a wall, fearful of the Alsatian-sized seagulls. I didn't offer that information up. When we'd finished our drinks, we went through to the restaurant. I felt very proud to walk in with such a handsome man; if only The Ex had been there to see it. In the ideal fantasy, he would be sitting miserably opposite The FT, to whom he'd have absolutely nothing to talk about and he would look up from slurping his leak and potato to see me sashay in, slinkily dressed in my hot new pencil skirt, about to have dinner (followed by amazing sex) with a gorgeous, charming man.

We were seated by Marco, a tall, dapper waiter, who pulled my chair back for me. I glanced around and saw a bearded man playing plinky-plonky elevator music on a grand piano in the corner. There was no sign of a jazz band setting up, *thank Christ.*

"Right, wine list first, I think Marco, dear Chap." Guy perused the choices, although I had the feeling he knew them all off by heart. "Are you a full-bodied sort of girl, Kate or something fruitier?" He winked at Marco who remained poker-faced.

Ah, this was awkward. How would I get home if I had another drink? I thought Guy would be driving me, but he clearly wasn't intending to, so I'd have to get a taxi home. Unless I'd be going back to Guy's? But it was far too early to say. A taxi would cost a small fortune. My credit card was already groaning from the pencil skirt and the Elle MacPherson faux silk French knickers.

"Um, well, as I'm driving, I'd better just have a mineral water. Sparkling."

"Oh, we can't have that!" Guy protested. "I'll get you safely home, don't you worry. Now that's settled, how about you let me spoil you and I'll get us a nice bottle of Barolo as a treat?"

I glanced at the wine list – the Barolo was £40! "Lovely," I smiled, apprehensively. Guy was clearly used to the finer things in life; he was bound to be able to tell the difference between real silk and faux. I really was trailer-trash.

"Well, what are you going to have to eat, Kiss Me? See anything you fancy?"

"Mmm, not really, everything seems a bit cheesy, doesn't it?"

He chuckled as Marco poured us enormous glasses of red wine. I resolved to sip it very slowly so he'd think I was savouring his excellent choice, as befitted a demure connoisseur, not a philistine glugger. I eventually chose chicken liver pâté as a starter and then the rump of lamb with buttered new potatoes, although I wouldn't eat the potatoes in case of bloating and a wind-during-sex disaster. Guy, having quizzed Marco at length on their origin, decided against the scallops and ordered the baked camembert followed by a sirloin steak, medium-rare.

"So, is it the owner you know here, Guy, or the chef?"

"I've actually done a bit of bizzo with both of them. But I don't want to talk about me! Tell me all about yourself. You intrigue me! Come on, what makes Kate King tick?"

Not talking about myself in the third person, for a start. I told him a bit about Perypils, trying to make my role sound interesting, which wasn't easy, skated over the whole husband-cheating-bastard-wanker thing and said I spent most of my spare time "renovating my new home, it's quite a project". I thought that sounded more impressively Sarah-Beanie than "patching up the hovel, it's quite a shit hole". He really was an excellent listener, asking lots of questions, genuinely interested in my life. He didn't look at his iPhone once! A true gentleman.

Over our starters, he told me he was "Drawn to people who take a chance in life. Do you know the sort I mean? They're original, unique in some way. They don't follow others like a flock of sheep. That's what I like about you, Kiss Me. You're different, you don't run with the herd. I think we could be very good for one another."

Blimey! Was he thinking about "us" in a longer term sense already? This was really going amazingly well.

"I mean, I'm sure you enjoy your job and everything," *No, I lied about that* "but, is all the hard work really worth the reward? Insurance is highly competitive, isn't it? Must be a constant battle to keep afloat, pretty damn exhausting, I should imagine. What does one earn, in insurance these days?"

I blinked at the direct question. "Well-"

"Thirty thousand a year? Thirty five?"

"A little bit more than that-"

"Well, say forty, then. I mean, how far does that go these days? I bet once you've covered your mortgage payment, all the household expenses, credit card, food and everything else, you've got nothing left! Or less than nothing! Am I right?"

"Yes, but-"

"So don't you ever wonder what it's all about? What's it all for? You're working flat out day in day out and just managing to scrape by; that's not a life, is it? Not really. It's just an existence."

I squashed some pâté onto a piece of toast. The toast was a bit stale.

"There's good money to be made out there, Kate, very good indeed. Especially for those who aren't afraid to take a chance in life. Spirited individuals who have a bit of something about them, as well as good connections. People like you, Kate."

"I don't think I'm very well-connected."

"Of course you are! Working for a large insurance company? You must mix with hundreds of like-minded people every day." *Like-minded? I should hope not.*

"That's the great thing about my business, Kate. It's minimum effort for maximum reward. It's wonderful. Genius, even. You literally sit back and watch the money roll in."

"Really? How?"

Guy, clearly making up for my tiny sips, was on his third

glass of Barolo and I noticed his eyes had gone a bit goggly. He obviously felt very passionately about his business.

"It's so, so simple. All you have to do is make a one off payment, say £1000 for example and find six others who'll do the same. And that's it! Ker-ching! Sit back, relax and watch the pounds roll in."

I looked at him in surprise. "You mean, a pyramid scheme?"

He almost spat out his wine in disgust. "*No!*" Several heads swivelled in our direction. "That's such a crass way to describe it, that's an *insult*. My business is an extremely sophisticated, multi-layered marketing model. I've had to describe it to you in very simplistic terms, of course."

I felt incredibly stupid. Someone as smart as him would never be involved in pyramid selling; what a total buffoon I was.

Marco placed his steak in front of him. "What's that?"

"Sirloin steak, sir. Medium rare."

"I asked for rare. Take it back." I cringed at his rudeness and looked down at my lamb. There was a short silence, in which I thought Marco was going to tell Guy that he did bloody well ask for medium-rare, but he merely said, "Yes, of course, sir," and removed the offending dish. There was an awkward pause in conversation. I tried to be positive and upbeat again.

"Are all the others involved in your, er, business? You know, the ugly sisters, the ones I manage to upset all the time!"

Guy nodded. "Some of them. The smart ones. Things got a bit tricky with Gwen, of course, but it's always difficult mixing business with pleasure. I should have known better."

Woah! My fork stopped halfway to my mouth and a piece of dry lamb dropped back onto my plate into a watery jus. Marco returned with Guy's steak and then left to fetch another bottle of wine when Guy pointedly tapped the empty one.

"You and Haught-, I mean, Gwen?" I tried to sound casual and disinterested.

"Yes. A mistake, of course. I thought we were just having a bit of fun, but she seemed to think it was more than that. It all got a bit sticky."

"But, she's married, isn't she?"

"Oh lighten up, Kate! Her husband never knew a thing. We were very discreet the whole time. No harm done."

He started on the second bottle, but his nonchalant attitude to the affair had rattled me. 'No harm done' - how did he know that? I bet Haughty's husband had been suspicious, just like I'd been when The Husband was cheating on me and I really thought I was going mad. It had been an awful period in my life; I wouldn't wish it on my worst enemy. Guy pointed his bloodied fork at me. "I've shocked you! Ha ha! Who'd have thought you were such a puritan! Or are you the jealous type?"

I struggled to find anything to say. He took a noisy slurp of wine and looked serious.

"But down to business, Kiss Me. Do you think you'll have any difficulties recruiting six others?"

Down to *business?* Did he think this was a business meeting? A huge cold tidal wave reared up in front me.

"You shouldn't have any problems, should you? There must be lots of managers like yourself at Perypils who'd jump at this opportunity. And what about your family? Karen said you had a brother, I think, in the building trade? He must have some great connections too."

The tidal wave smashed down on my head and left me floundering in its surf. I put my knife and fork down; I didn't feel like eating anymore. Guy was still talking, but I wasn't taking it in. When he'd cleared his plate, he excused himself and stumbled towards the Gents. I caught Marco's eye and asked him for the bill. He arrived back at the table with it at the same time as Guy, who reeked of cigarette smoke.

"Ah, I see you've got the bad news already. Shall we just split it straight down the middle? I expect a modern girl like you is into equality and all that!"

Split it? But you invited me out for dinner, didn't you? And you've had two bottles of wine!

"Fine," I said, too embarrassed to argue in front of Marco. I handed him my poor exhausted credit card.

"That's ninety-eight pounds, please."

"No, I'm just paying half on this card."

"That is half, Madam."

I examined the bill. As well as our meal, there was an additional bar charge for forty-three pounds.

"This is a mistake." I showed Marco. "This isn't ours."

"Yes, Mr Wiseman bought two rounds of drinks at the bar before your meal."

We both looked at Guy. "Oh yes," he said vaguely. "For my clients."

I waited for him to say "but I'll pay for those, of course." He didn't. People were already looking over at us, so I told Marco to charge the £98 to my card. Guy was fumbling in his wallet. "Oh, I haven't quite got enough cash to cover my half, Carol old bean. I tell you what, I'll give you these two twenties. Would you be a love and sub me the difference? I'll pay you back pronto."

"Why don't you just put it on a card?"

"Er, d'you know what, I don't seem to have brought any out with me. They must all be in my other wallet, in my other jacket..."

I looked at Marco and with eyebrows raised, he added the rest of the bill to my 'half'. I realised Guy was now trying to locate his car keys.

"Can you call my friend a cab please, Marco."

"Call your friend a what, Madam?"

I almost managed a smile for him as I gathered up my handbag. Guy slurred, "Could you give me a lift home, Cathy, I mean, er, Katie?"

"No. Marco's calling you a cab."

"But, I haven't any money for a cab."

He really was taking the piss now. I took one of his twenties back out of my purse and slid it over to him. "Oh, I'm not sure that will cover it-"

Hot with humiliation, I slapped the other twenty pound note down on the table and stalked off, hearing him call: "Righto, I'll give you a call then, shall I, Carol, er, Cathy? Alright?"

I wasn't sure I'd ever felt as low as I did on the drive home. *What a fool I was.* What a poor, sad, deluded fool. Had I really thought that Guy was interested in me, that he'd wanted to date me? Yes, I'm afraid I really had. The only thing he'd wanted me to put out was cash. Although he hadn't turned out to be quite what I'd expected - *all that glitters is not gold.* I fought back tears of self-pity; I mustn't cry, my mascara was so thick any moisture would glue my eyes permanently shut.

As I arrived home, I started to turn into my drive, but there was a van parked in it! What the hell? I got out of the car with the engine still running and peered into the small white van. The driver was slumped in the front seat, asleep. It was my brother! What on earth was he doing here? I knocked on the window. "Stu! Wake up! What are you doing?" He jolted awake and let the window down.

"Oh Sis, I'm sorry just to turn up, but Kirsty's chucked me out again. I usually go to Dave's to crash, but he's on a promise tonight with the waitress from the Pizza Palace and he didn't want me there. I can't go to Mum and Dad's, they ask too many questions and they've never got any booze in the house. Could I sleep here?"

"Sure, I'll fetch you a blanket! Only joking. Of course you can. I must warn you though, the spare bedroom is more of a cupboard. Well, a coffin, really. I hope you're not claustrophobic."

"I'm sure it's bigger than the van - I've slept in here enough times!"

I parked my car in the road and let us into the house. I got Stu a beer and poured myself a massive glass of white wine. We sat in the lounge with a bag of Doritos. "So what did you and Kirsty argue about this time?"

"Christ." He gave a big sigh and rubbed his forehead. "It's not good, Sis, something terrible's happened. Georgia's pregnant."

I gaped at him. "B-but, why has Kirsty chucked *you* out? What have you-"

"Oh bloody hell, Sis! No, no! Jesus. I'm not responsible. Georgia only told us tonight, after school. Her father frog-marched her round to ours and made her tell Kirsty. She's almost four months gone! She's only sixteen."

"What do you think she's going to do? Will she keep it?"

"God knows. She was saving up for a tattoo."

"How did Kirsty react?"

He took a swig of beer. "Very badly. But I'm not sure what upset her more, Georgia's news or her ex-husband yelling at her. It was all very Dallas; he actually called her a tramp, a drunk and an unfit mother. Blamed her entirely for Georgia's behaviour. I had to ask him to leave in the end, even though he's Georgia's dad and they all really needed to talk about it together."

"I still don't understand why Kirsty threw you out?"

"All I said was that I was going for a pizza with Dave and she went ballistic. Absolutely berserk. Said I was an uncaring jerk, a total dic... well, you get the picture. The usual stuff."

"Mmm, perhaps, in the circumstances, you should have stayed in-"

"But I wanted to give her and Georgia time alone! You know, for mother and daughter stuff. I'm no good at all that. But she didn't give me the chance to explain. Just went mental."

"Does Georgia know who the father is? Sorry, that sounded really insulting. I didn't mean it quite like that."

Stu looked at me. "She says it's that bloody George. Your George."

Oh crap. How typical of The Lazy Shit not to bother with contraception. Clearly his sperm wasn't as sluggish as the rest of him.

"That's not good. I mean, he's not a bad bloke, but I'm

not sure he's ready for that kind of responsibility." Knowing him, he'd delegate it to someone else. Plus, there was every possibility I'd have to sack him in the not too distant future. His prospects didn't look rosy.

"Kirsty hates him," said Stu, miserably. "It's all such a mess."

I got him another beer and tried to cheer him up by telling him all about my evening and my "business-meeting-date" disaster. It sounded quite funny when told out loud and he roared with laughter. We cheerfully concluded that we were a couple of sad losers and then watched a repeat episode of Fred Dibnah's Industrial Age, thus making it official.

For the first time since I moved in, I fell asleep straight away. It must have been because Stu was staying and I felt safe for once, not trying to sleep with one ear open, listening for windows being forced open, footsteps on the stairs, axes being sharpened...

A piercing scream ripped through the house. I shot bolt upright in bed. The landing light went on and Stu stood illuminated in the bedroom doorway, his hair standing on end.

"Sis! Sis! There's something in that room! B-bloody w-wildlife!"

Wildlife? In my befuddled state I thought he meant a tiger was roaming the house. "What is it, Stu? What have you seen?"

I stumbled to the landing. He pointed a shaking hand into the spare room. "I turned over and it was there! Right by my head! Its eyes were glowing-"

"You what? What the hell was it?"

"It was on the bedside table. Inches from my face.

Staring at me."

My head began to clear. "It was on the table? So it was quite small, then?"

"It had huge eyes! Its nose was twitching and it had these whiskery-things-"

"It was a mouse?"

"Yes! A mouse! Right by my head!"

"Jesus Stu, I thought there was a monster under your bed or something." I tiptoed cautiously into the spare room, my brother staying behind me. There was a chocolate candle on the bedside table that had little teeth marks in it.

"Look! It must have been after the candle."

"But I thought they liked cheese?"

"Dunno. Perhaps your socks attracted it." I removed the candle, took it downstairs and put it outside the front door. We checked all round the spare room and then the rest of the house but there was no sign of the mouse. Reluctantly, we went back to bed, leaving the landing light on in the hope that mice only ventured out in the dark. I pulled the covers up to my ears, knowing I wouldn't get back to sleep now. Poor Stu - I bet he was wishing he'd slept in his van.

CHAPTER FIFTEEN

When I got up on Saturday morning I found a note by the kettle.

"Sis - gone to work. Then will go home to see how Kirsty is. Hopefully all will be good now, so thanks very much for putting me up. If things not good, I'll see you tonight! Stu x

PS I have asked Kieron to call round later to sort out your mouse problem. Hope that's ok!"

I thought Kieron did general maintenance, not pest control, but still, I was grateful for any help at all. Karen was on the phone before I'd even finished my marmite fingers, desperate for details of last night. She was incredulous when I recounted the story.

"Are you sure you read it right, Kate? I mean, you've never been great with signals, have you? Remember the time when that poor chap from Halfords changed one of your bulbs and he said your headlights could do with a good buffing? You slapped him round the face! You're making Gorgeous Guy sound like a, well, a cross between Del Boy and Oliver Reed."

"Let's just say, my credit card got the message all right. I'm going to be living on Spam fritters for the rest of the month."

We chatted for a good hour, making the most of Karen's free weekend calls with BT. We were eventually interrupted when I heard a loud thud outside the front door. I told Karen I'd call her back and went to investigate. A reddish-grey tile lay in pieces on the drive. Where had that come from? Had someone thrown it? I looked around and then squinted anxiously up at the roof. Yep - I could make out a gap where the tile had been. Thank God my car was still parked in the road; it would have gone right through the windscreen. Mervyn appeared at the fence. "I wondered what that noise was! Made me jump out of my skin; lucky I'd just finished cutting the last of Sissy's corns. Come off the roof, has it?"

"Yes, I think so." The bloody house was literally falling to pieces around me.

"Good thing you've got a builder friend staying with you, then! Saw his van parked in the drive, *all night.*" Honk! "Will he be staying again tonight, your *friend?*"

"Depends on his wife," I said, distractedly. Why did roof tiles just fall off? Did the whole shitty roof need replacing? I said goodbye to Mervyn, who seemed to have been struck dumb for a change. Probably worried about his roof too.

I spent the rest of the day attempting to catch up with work emails as old war films banged and crashed in the background. The doorbell rang just after four and I got up to answer it with a bad-tempered groan.

It was Kieron. "Hi Kate! Stu said you had some furry tenants you wanted to evict!"

I laughed, standing back to let him into the house. "Thanks for coming round Kieron, I didn't know you did pest control. We had a mouse in the spare room last night; scared my poor brother half to death, but there's been no sign of it today. It's probably moved on."

"Mmm." He seemed unconvinced. "I'll have a look round, shall I?"

I left him to it while I made some coffee. I heard him

moving around upstairs and then he joined me in the kitchen. "Seen any signs in here?"

"Er, no, I don't think so." A sudden thought struck me. "Well, actually, a heap of breakfast cereal fell out on me not so long ago, when I opened a cupboard door. I assumed the box was damaged." I showed him the cupboard. He peered inside, then reached right to the back and pulled out a long-forgotten Thornton's Easter Egg that my mum had given me. The box had been partially destroyed and there was only the tiniest piece of chocolate left inside the foil wrapping.

"Bugger me!" I was horrified. "How the hell did it get inside the cupboard? Can mice open doors?"

"They get in down the back; probably come down the pipes or the wires and squeeze in through any gap. Amazing really, how they can get through the tiniest hole."

"Does this one have a sweet tooth? He tried to nosh a chocolate candle last night."

"Oh, mice love chocolate. If you set traps you should use Milk Tray, not cheddar. And I'm afraid you'll find there's more than one of them. There usually is."

I shuddered. "I hear a lot of scuffling at night, above my head. I thought it was pigeons in the loft. Do you think it's mice?"

"Yep. I'll go up there and put some poison down. Unless you'd rather I set up some humane traps? Then you can release them unharmed."

What a dilemma. I could no more handle a trapped mouse than I could fondle The Drain's itchy parts. But what would Kieron think of me if I said I wanted to kill the mice? Animal cruelty; you couldn't sink much lower.

"It will have to be the poison I'm afraid, Kieron," I said

eventually. "I mean, if I let them go they'll just get back in again, won't they? So it would be pointless." *Pathetic attempt to justify it.* "Oh God, do you think I'm an evil mouse murderer now?"

"There's worse things to be!" he said cheerfully. "Your brother told me he'd killed his pet hamster once; fed it a hot cross bun and the raisins swelled up inside its little belly. The poor thing dropped dead!"

I stared at him. "Do you mean Buster?"

"Yes, that was the one."

"Buster was *my* hamster. And my brother told me it had escaped its cage and the cat had eaten it. I'd always blamed myself for not closing the cage door properly."

"Ah. Er, right, I'd better just get on with this then..."

Kieron had no sooner left when I saw my brother's van pull up outside. Very downcast, he came into the house muttering, "A few more nights, I think, Sis." I went to fetch him a beer, intending to get him very drunk and force a full, exploding-Buster confession from him.

Monday

I wanted to headbutt the desk. My progress plan meeting with The GPS was due tomorrow so I'd put in a call to the union. Forty minutes later, I was still waiting to speak to someone. Every twenty seconds an irritatingly cheerful woman told me my call was important to them but they were they were experiencing a "higher than expected" volume of calls. *Why?* Why was everyone suddenly calling the union? Perhaps the Samaritans were refusing to take any more calls from Perypils staff; we probably caused too many of them to commit suicide.

I gave it another five minutes, then pressed hash three to request a call back. I was actually at home watching the end of Corrie when they finally called. A stressed-out sounding man bellowed "Hello? Is that Catherine?"

"It's Kate, actually."

"Sorry Catherine, can hardly hear you, the station's very noisy."

I could hear train announcements in the background. "IT'S KATE. I wanted to discuss a meeting I'm facing with my line manager. It's about my performance."

"Right. Is it a formal meeting?"

"Well, he said it was to formalise an action plan."

"What?"

"IT'S TO FORMALISE AN ACTION PLAN!"

"Right. The union only supports colleagues with formal meetings."

"But it is a formal meeting!"

"No, it's just to draw up an action plan. It will only become formal if you fail the plan, so call us then."

"No, that's not right! Hello? *Hello?*"

He'd gone, the useless dollop of shite. That was just brilliant advice - call them back when I'd failed the plan? I'd have been sacked by then! Perhaps they'd prefer me to call them directly from the job centre? Or a hostel for the homeless? Bloody hell - I really was on my own. Prickly tears of self-pity welled up again so I quickly channel-hopped to Eastenders - that was guaranteed to make my own life seem like Brigadoon.

The meeting was scheduled for eleven o'clock. Sweaty and anxious, I had armed myself with reams of target-hitting statistics and previous good reports. I was also wearing my lucky pink pants; they were a bit torn around the edges but the elastic looked like it should hold up. Which was a miracle really; I was so nervous the pants had been hoisted up and down all morning. At the appointed hour, I made my way to the meeting room where The GPS was waiting and without any pleasantries, he produced a neatly typed document from his black folder.

"This is your *recovery* plan, Kate. I've detailed each area that requires improvement, the actions needed and the standard of performance that must be achieved. I've also included a section which covers the consequences of your continued under-performance so that your expectations are completely clear."

I stared at the massive plan and my head swam. I rubbed my temples and tried to assert some control.

"Roger, this is most irregular. Any type of improvement plan should involve a detailed discussion between you and me with the areas jointly agreed upon. You don't just present someone with actions you've already decided."

"But we have agreed upon these areas, Kate," said Roger, sounding astonished. "There's nothing in here we haven't already discussed. Together. Can you see anything in there that we haven't talked about?"

I read down the list. Sales targets, colleague behaviours, time-keeping, progress plans, complaint reduction, supporting Perypils initiatives; he was right, there wasn't anything he hadn't already brought to my attention. Although you could hardly call his constant barrage of criticisms 'a discussion'. "I can't see anything about support for me," I said, aware I sounded like a sulky child.

"There it is." He tapped a paragraph of small print. I peered at it closely and read: "I agree to request the support of my line manager should I require it to complete this plan." I looked up at him. "That's a bit vague, isn't it?"

"Not at all. Remember, this is your job, Kate. You've been performing it for some years now, so it's difficult to understand why you would suddenly require a great deal of support. However, just ask if you feel you need to."

"I do need support! I need to recruit more staff, for starters! We're running on fumes at the moment and the guys are knackered."

"And like I've told you before, there needs to be a significant improvement in staff behaviours; that in turn will lead to greater productivity and efficiencies. You don't need any more people."

I wasn't listening to him. I was reading the section annotated 'Outcomes' which stated that failure to complete the plan successfully could lead to my dismissal. I swallowed. Hard.

"This really isn't right, Roger. HR policy states that there is a three month informal plan before a formal plan is instigated. I haven't been on an informal plan - ever. It seems as if you've jumped straight in at the formal stage."

Icy eyes burned deep into my soul. "It is my opinion that you have been under-performing *informally* for three months, Kate. All your statistics demonstrate that, along with my findings and observations, so the informal part has already been completed. And as you have failed to evidence improvement, we are now starting the formal part. I should also draw your attention to this wording," he tapped another area of ant's print. "It states if there is insufficient improvement it may be necessary to bring forward the final review date."

I gaped at him. "So I may not even get three months to improve? But that's so unfair! Have HR seen this plan? I can't believe they would approve it." Of course I could believe it. They probably wouldn't have understood it; not with all those long words.

"It's all been through HR," Roger was drawing the meeting to a close. "You must focus on the improvements you need to make now, Kate, they're clearly documented in the plan. Would you sign it, please?"

"No," I snapped. "I'm not signing it; I'm not happy with it. I want to show it to the union first - I'd like to know what they've got to say about this."

"As you like," he said, getting up. "But I should draw your attention to the last paragraph which states that even if you don't sign the plan, you will still be considered to have accepted it." *You steaming great turd of a bastard.* A progress plan! Why didn't he just have the honesty and decency to call it 'Kate's Exit Plan'? He didn't want me to make any progress; he wanted me to fail so he could boot me out at no cost to the company.

I sat in the room, gazing at the reams of carefully typed impossibilities. I couldn't believe that after all my years of meticulously dotting i's, crossing t's and jumping through bloody great hoops to ensure that Perypils policies were applied to the letter, he could just ride roughshod over everything and do whatever the hell he wanted. Wasn't I entitled to the same treatment as my colleagues? Why were managers different? I gave a hollow laugh as I recalled threatening him with the union. That was about as scary as being savaged by a woolly sheep. What on earth was I going to do? The job centre was beckoning. But who would employ me with "dismissed" on my reference? No one reputable. I doubted I would even make an effective prostitute - I'd probably get more complaints than I would satisfied punters. But the enormity of my situation crept over me like The Drain's Blue Stratos. If I was going to be forced to walk the plank, it might be time to jump ship.

Chapter Sixteen

I thought the best way to make a positive start on my 'progress' plan was to take some holiday. That way, I couldn't be accused of doing anything wrong for at least a week. Not to my face, anyway. Now was a perfect time to take some leave because I could get my CV up straight and apply for jobs, if there were any out there to apply for. Plus, I was worn out. Since my meeting with The GPS, I hadn't been able to sleep properly and kept having the most disturbing dreams about sharks. Last night, I dreamt I had been walking along a beautiful river bank, thinking about taking a dip in the sparkling blue water and then all kinds of sharks started to drift past just under the surface - Tigers, Great Whites, Hammerheads ... they all looked up at me through their dead eyes, waiting for me to step into the water. I Googled a 'dreams means' website and discovered that sharks represented: "Unseen danger; you are dwelling on doubts and uncertainties, trouble is brewing but you are not sure from which direction or from where." Hmmm. It was hardly an unseen danger that was keeping me awake. I was surprised the sharks didn't all have ginger moustaches and bushy eyebrows.

I had to find another job. In the advert break during Lewis, there was one for an employment website which featured a very smug actor whose name I couldn't recall, but I knew he was a friend of Robbie Williams so he must be okay. He said you just upload your CV and they find you a fabulous job! As easy as that! How marvellous. I opened my laptop and pulled up a copy of my CV. It was reasonably up to date, as I'd had to re-apply for my own shitty job last year, so with just a few tweaks it would be ready to go.

I registered my details on the site then undertook a job search by entering the word 'management' and my post code. Only two came up. One was for an Engineering Manager at Gatwick airport, a round trip of two hundred and twenty six miles (what on earth was the point of putting in my post code?) and the other, slightly closer to home in Swindon was for a Client Services Value Stream Manager. Even after I'd read the lengthy job description several times, I still had no idea what the role actually entailed. "You will develop the client services value stream into a stand-alone revenue and margin generating business" - what the buggery bollocks did that mean? Anyway, I'd uploaded my CV now - I just had to wait for the offers to roll in.

I ironed the bedding from the spare room and put it all back on the bed, ready for my brother's next visit. I didn't think it would be too long; Georgia had decided to keep the baby but her father had told her she couldn't stay with him anymore. He already had a baby with his second wife and said there wasn't room for another. According to Stu, Kirsty was "flipping out" at the thought of her daughter living with them. "It will be like living in the middle of a catfight, Sis," he'd said gloomily. "The fur's gonna fly." Poor sod. I resolved to keep the fridge stocked with beer.

Settling down with another glass of red wine, I flicked into my work emails. *What the hell was I doing?* It was supposed to be a holiday, not parole. *Come on woman, live a little.* Was I brave enough to do something frivolous and take a holiday

on my own? Emboldened by half a bottle of Merlot, I
Googled 'singles holidays'. There were hundreds! Cruises,
trekking, cycling; I followed the first link to JustYou Holidays
and read a section which told me it was natural to feel a little
nervous taking your first holiday on your own and that age
didn't matter as people of all ages come along. This was
followed by several pictures of sixty-something couples -
women with tightly permed grey hair stood next to suave
Nigel Havers lookalikes. Hmmm, perhaps I was a little too
young for this site, although I wouldn't say no to Nigel
Havers, should he ever be desperate enough to ask. If he
could fall for Audrey Roberts, then maybe, just maybe...

I clicked on another called Solo Adventures. A healthy,
bronze-limbed young woman was quoted: "We were a
fantastic group and got on like a house on fire! We spent the
whole week laughing and joking and I've made lots of great
new friends!" That sounded promising. I read a bit more of
the blurb which told me I would make life-long friends as I
would always be travelling with like-minded people. It
sounded good; I read on. We would share a great many new
experiences - and a tent. Woah! What sort of holiday was
that, for Christ's sake? Camping with a bunch of strangers?
Were these people background-checked beforehand? What if
they were psychopaths, rapists, murderers - members of
UKIP?

I picked up the bottle of Merlot and screwed the cap
firmly back on. *No more of that.* I didn't want to wake up to
find myself zipped into a sleeping bag with Norman Bates.
No, it would be a staycation for me this year.

The next morning dawned gloriously bright and sunny
and it looked as if my week off would be blessed with several

days of lovely weather. How lucky was I? It had been raining seemingly non-stop for months. I got up ready to tackle the nettle patch but with a distinct lack of enthusiasm. Bugger it! Why didn't I do something spontaneous for once in my life and spend the day at the seaside? Just grab a beach bag and bikini, get in the car and go! Yes! I was going to do it!

With a sudden spring in my step, I rummaged around in the bottom of my chest of drawers to find a matching bikini top and bottom. I found an old halterneck one from Next, in a dark red leopard print. Would it still fit? The pants looked reasonably roomy and the bra was padded, so I decided to risk it. When had I last shaved my legs? Or other parts? Oh my God, I was practically Chewbacca! Why hadn't I paid any attention to those patronising "are you beach-ready?" adverts instead of burping "feck off" at the telly? *Stop panicking.* I remembered I was in possession of the beach equivalent of a fat suit - a maxi dress. All I had to do was stick it on and all my sins would be covered. Hoorah! Admittedly, it wouldn't cover my moustache or those random disturbingly long chin hairs, but still, I'd just have to keep my head down. Sun lotion, sun hat, bottle of water and a book and I was good to go. I'd started the car before I remembered I'd forgotten a towel, then had to go back into the house a second time to fetch my sunglasses.

At last, I spontaneously set off towards Brean Sands, having looked up the directions on Google maps and written them all down, even though I already knew the way. It was a good hour's drive but I hoped it would be a little quieter than its hugely popular neighbour, Weston-super-NightMare. It was a beautiful morning; even the sheep looked like they were smiling at me as I whizzed past them along the motorway. It

felt like I was embarking on an exciting adventure, like Enid
Blyton's Famous Five, just without the other four; another
milestone in my new, independent life. If only I could stop
worrying about whether I'd be able to park, or the dangers of
UV rays and rip tides, or treading on spiny weaver fish and
there might be quick sand, of course.

I reached the coast in good time and headed to Brean
Down, parking in the large National Trust car park before
making my way along the path to the beach. The bay was
absolutely stunning; golden sands were sandwiched between
emerald green downs and a sparkling sapphire sea. There
wasn't a cloud in the sky. The beach was already busy and
family groups had marked out their territories on the sand
with colourful windbreaks and miniature tents. I picked my
way somewhat self-consciously towards a space near the front
of the beach. I felt totally overdressed in my voluminous navy
maxi; everyone else was in swimwear, shamelessly displaying
acres of flesh. The tide appeared to be going out so I selected
a spot close to the shoreline. That meant I could sit with my
back to the crowds; I felt extremely exposed on my own. I
unfolded my towel and sat down, wishing I had a windbreak
to hide behind or at least an umbrella. I glanced around the
bay but I couldn't see anyone else on their own; it was all
couples and families. Oh well. *Just relax for once.* Why the hell
hadn't I put my bikini on at home? Now I was going to have
to try and wriggle into it surreptitiously.

Swapping the knickers wasn't too bad under the
protection of my billowing dress but the bra was a nightmare.
I had to hoik up my dress, undo my bra then wriggle one arm
out of the strap, almost dislocating my shoulder. I eventually
got it off, then did up the bikini bra and stepped into it. As I

pulled it up, my dress fell away, leaving someone's poor old grandad looking directly at my naked breasts as he took an innocent stroll to the water's edge. I don't know who was the more traumatised.

I folded my clothes carefully away in the beach bag and applied a generous coating of factor thirty to my pasty skin. I was so white, I'd probably get mistaken for a giant cuttlefish if I lay down flat. Annoyingly, a group of noisy youngsters arrived and set up camp quite close to me. There were seven of them, four lads and three girls who looked like college students. Skipping lessons, no doubt. The girls stripped down to teeny weeny bikinis and ran shrieking into the sea, a whirl of slender, golden limbs flailing around in the surf. Did they know how gorgeous they looked? Or did they have the same body hang-ups as everyone else? I hoped not. I wished nobody cared at all about how they looked. Unless, of course, you'd reached the point where you were about to be winched out of your home by a crane into a specially reinforced ambulance. Then it was probably time to cut out the Custard Creams.

I sighed and took out my book, Captain Corelli's Mandolin. I was determined to get past page twelve this time. I'd always had my nose in a novel when I was younger but all I read now was meaningless wankily-worded emails or the subtitles on Inspector Montalbano. My aunt had phoned me recently and asked if I thought she should read Fifty Shades of Grey, because it was so popular. Embarrassed, I asked her if she knew what it was about. She'd replied "Oh yes, it's all whips and bum beads isn't it, dear?" *Ugh!* She's eighty-one!

I lay back on my towel and opened my book, holding it up in front on my face to shield my eyes from the sun. I finally found myself beginning to relax. I was aware of the sound of waves breaking, gulls calling, children laughing ... gosh, it was hot. Really very hot indeed.

Oh my God! What was happening? Someone had emptied a bucket of cold water over me! I was immersed in icy, salty wetness; *what the hell?* The bloody tide had come in! A wave had run right up the beach and covered me; I thought the tide was going out! Gasping for breath, I floundered in the sludge just managing to grab my flip flops before they floated away on the retreating wave to Barry Island. I was completely drenched. My beach bag was sodden and my book, which I was still clutching, open at page ten, was reduced to a soggy, tissuey mass. I could hear hoots of laughter. I glanced around me as I scooped up my wet things; everyone else had moved themselves back. There were lots of people grinning in my direction and the skiving college students were openly laughing out loud. *Bastards.* I must have nodded off; why hadn't anyone woken me when they saw the waves creeping closer?

Scarlet with humiliation, I moved back up the beach, wanting to leave but unwilling to show defeat. I sat down miserably on my horrid wet towel and examined the contents of my beach bag. My clothes were soaking, so I shook them out and lay them in the sun but I knew that even if I stayed there all day they were never going to dry out. My purse was full of sand and water and both my ten pound notes were soaked. *What an absolute mess.* Two young girls skipped past me, stopping to nudge each other and giggle. *Yes, I'm wet - get over it.* They returned two minutes later with a little boy and pointed towards me. He bent double with laughter and then they all ran off. What was so funny? I looked down and saw that I had a large piece of seaweed stuck between my legs. It looked like a huge mass of pubic hair.

I sat, shivering, for what I thought was the best part of an hour. I couldn't be sure of the time, my watch was no longer working. When I thought I'd left it long enough for people to have hopefully forgotten the incident, I put my wet sandy towel round me like a sarong and trudged back to the car. I drove home, getting some very strange looks from other drivers, unaccustomed to seeing a woman driving up the M5 in a bikini. I thought I might get some appreciative honks. I didn't.

The next morning, I peered at the alarm clock through bleary eyes. It was almost ten o'clock! My head felt fuzzy from the bottle of white wine I had downed last night and my stomach was swollen and acidic. When I'd got home from the beach, I decided I needed to lose some weight (again). My resolve had lasted precisely two hours and twenty-five minutes, when I discovered the freezer had wet itself all over the kitchen floor. To cope with the demise of my beloved Ben and Jerry, I had succumbed to buttered toast with lashings of Philly, followed by a family sized bag of Doritos and then the entire contents of a pot of chocolate sprinkles, purchased in the wild fantasy that I would be indulging in some form of home baking. I'd imagined myself as Doris Day, resplendent in a vintage gingham dress, inviting visitors into my pristine home so they could sample my large squidgy buns.

I heaved my disgusting turgid body out of bed and into the bathroom. Aerosmith peered back at me from the mirror - I *must* get my hair cut. I pulled it apart to reveal red-rimmed puffy eyes, jowls like a basset hound ... God, what a mess. Doris Day? Calamity Sodding Jane, more like. Right, that really was it. I had to start today, in earnest. No more eating crap, no more bottles of wine, no more slumping for hours in front of the TV or over the laptop. Think posture, think healthy body, healthy mind - eat lots of fruit and veg, read a quality newspaper and exercise. That was the key. Wasn't exercise supposed to release those endorphins that fill you with a sense of well-being? Or was that an orgasm? Well, look at me, for Christ's sake; an orgasm wasn't on the cards anytime soon. Even a dildo would insist I put a bag over my head first.

I braced myself and splashed ice-cold water into my face, gasping as it hit me. I scraped back my horse's hair and secured it with an old scrunchie. I was only going to be gardening, I didn't need make-up. What if I had to answer the door, though, or decided to walk into the village? I applied a layer of BB cream to my face, as it was supposed to be a good 'multi-tasker'. Perhaps it could do the ironing while reading a novel. It did have UV protection, so I convinced myself that I was being very sensible, rather than unbelievably vain. I unlocked the wobbly French doors and stepped outside into brilliant sunshine, flipping my sunglasses down from my head to cover my eyes. I still felt a bit ropey but that would pass when the endorphins kicked in. I surveyed the jungle and all the junk that I had piled up there, yet to sort through. Bits of mismatched garden furniture, a broken water butt, numerous buckets, plant pots, a large chiminea that had seemed like a good idea at the time but we'd only ever lit once - what was I going to do with it all? What did other people do with their relationship debris? The dump or Fleabay, I suppose. I'd get round to it at some stage.

I went to see how my plants were doing. Eight stalks stood where the peppers and chillies had been. The courgette had disappeared completely. I wanted to cry. So much for my vision of a spicy courgette and pepper stir fry. One of the chilli stalks had a miniscule green leaf still growing on it - I saw a slug positively hurtling towards it. *You slimy little bastards.* The camellia was as yet untouched but it was only a matter of time. Neither the pellets nor the beer trap had made any difference; oh God, I was going to have to do as Mervyn suggested and put some hair down. I was buggered if I was going to poke around in the plug holes but there might be some caught in my hair brush. I went to get it and then knelt down by the camellia, pulling the hair from the brush and laying it around the earth in the pot. "There you go," I muttered. "I'm doing my best to protect you." As I patted the hair down, I suddenly became aware of a pair of brown deck shoes on the patio. Where had they come from? I followed them upwards and saw they were attached to sandy chinos, a brown checked shirt and a round face, which was half-hidden behind a ridiculous pair of Aviator sunglasses.

"Kate? What on earth are you doing?"

Who the hell was it? I squinted up into the sun. The figure removed his sunglasses. Good grief, it was The Ex! What was he doing here, in my garden ... did I have sunstroke?

"When did you start wearing deck shoes?"

"What? Are you ok?" He peered down at me anxiously. "You're not pissed, are you? You're brushing a potted plant."

"Er, no I wasn't," I started to recover from the shock and stood up to face him. "I'm putting some hair round it. Slugs can't slide over it, you see and the beer trap didn't work-"

"What did you give them beer for? It just makes them hungry!"

For a moment, it was like being back in our marriage; always in the wrong and constantly criticised. I folded my arms defiantly. "Thank you, Alan Titchmarsh, for that advice. Now, do you mind telling me what the hell you're doing here?"

"I wanted to see you. To talk about things." *What things?* "I called your office but they said you had the week off, so I thought I'd call round on the off chance that you'd be in. I knew you lived in this area so I drove around until I spotted your car." He looked back at the house. "It's not what I was expecting."

"Where did you think I'd be living, Downton Abbey? What do you want to talk to me about?"

"Could we go inside?"

I didn't want him to see inside the house but neither did I want him to know that I didn't want him to see it, so I nodded, sulkily. I saw him take in the precariously balanced French windows that creaked and groaned in protest as I forced them open. There was a big fat slug half way up the glass. The lounge was in its usual gloom and I banged my leg on the side of the coffee table, not seeing it clearly because I still had my sunglasses on. I couldn't take them off as I wasn't wearing any eye make-up. I realised what an absolute state I must look - frizzy-haired, bloated stomach, a horrid pair of too-tight denim shorts stretched to bursting across my enormous arse - what a time for The Ex to turn up. Just typical of my bloody luck.

"Heavy night?" he asked, a touch sarcastically, nodding

towards the empty wine bottle. "He's not still here, is he?"

"What? Who?"

"Whoever you shared the wine with. Is he upstairs, exhausted, or did he just slip out the front?"

I saw there were two wine glasses on the coffee table (one was last night's and one was from the night before, what a slattern) and he could have been forgiven for thinking that I had shared a family-sized bag of Doritos with someone else, instead of scoffing them all myself.

"What's it to you, anyway?" I snapped, embarrassment making me irritated. "Even if I've had the whole of Cheltenham Town FC trooping in and out, it's none of your business. And I really don't appreciate you just turning up like this; what is it you want?"

"Depends what you're offering," he attempted to soften his manner with humour, giving me one of his gut-churning, trying-to-look-suggestive smiles. "A coffee would be great, though. I've come to talk to you about the divorce."

Ah, the D word. Of course. Well, it did need to be addressed at some point. He followed me into the kitchen, his eyes darting everywhere.

"Aren't you working today?" I asked him, standing by the kettle with my stomach pulled in as much as possible. I kept my jaw slack so my jowls weren't so noticeable.

"Er, no, not today. I've got a few days off."

"Do you still take milk and sugar?"

"Do you have soya?"

"Er, let me see ... oh yes, here it is, between the mung beans and the joss sticks - no, of course I haven't got any bloody soya! Semi-skimmed or Coffee Mate?"

"Oh, right. I'll just have it black, then."

We sat at the kitchen table, both clutching our mugs defensively. I kept my sunglasses on. "How's your family?" he asked.

I sighed. "Mum and Dad are as mad as ever; Dad's still obsessed with the neighbours. He's convinced they're chucking snails over the fence into his garden because they know he hates the French. He's spent hours hidden behind the net curtains trying to catch them; that's when he's not chasing cats. I bought him one of those pest alarm things that are supposed to keep cats out of the garden, but on the very first day a steaming pile of poo was deposited right in front of it. And Stu and Kirsty, well, you probably know better than me, being such good Facebook buddies."

"Yes, well," he took a sip of coffee and rubbed his forehead. "I'm sorry about turning up at Stu's fortieth with, er, with Debs, we shouldn't have gone." Hold the bus! Had I just heard him apologise for something? He never apologised! He didn't have to; he never thought he was in the wrong. "Stu did say you weren't going to be there, though, I did check, but even so..." He took another sip, shooting me a quick glance. *What was he up to?* Why was he being all smarmy?

"Why are you here?" I asked him, pointedly. "Yes, I know you want to talk about the divorce, but we could have done that over the phone, or via email. Why have you come round?"

"I'm just trying to do the right thing!" He threw his hands in the air, mask slipping as he fell naturally back into the injured party role. "Christ, I thought it was the decent thing to do, you know, after twelve years of marriage, to come round and speak to you face to face, not just have a solicitor's letter drop on your doormat. And, well, I wanted to see how you were doing, you know."

Yes, I do know. You wanted to see what my life was like without you in it.

"Do you like living here?" he asked, innocently.

I took a sip of coffee so I could consider my response. What was there to like? It was dark and dreary, full of things that scuttled or scampered, bits of it fell off at regular intervals, every appliance either groaned, creaked or spluttered and there was probably a family of travellers living at the bottom of the garden, trapped behind the tangle of nettles and bindweed.

"It's fine," I said, looking at him defiantly. "Do you like living in your flat? Must be a bit of a squeeze, for the three of you, I mean, children have so many toys these days, don't they? Where does Chloë keep her voodoo doll collection - in her toy coffin? And what with Debbie's thighs, well, I doubt you've got room to swing a premature kitten, let alone a cat."

His face darkened at the cheap shots, but, disappointingly, refused to take the bait. "I didn't come round to rake over the past or to start a row. If you want to know, I bumped into your brother and he said you were finding things quite tough at the moment. I genuinely wanted to know how you were. I felt concerned."

"You felt guilty, you mean." *What had Stu said about me? Surely he hadn't told him about my humiliation with Guy?* "Or perhaps you've just come round for a gloat?"

"Jesus Kate, you don't need to be so defensive, no one's gloating. And maybe I do feel a bit guilty, but I should remind you that it was you who wanted us to split up, I never did. When your brother said you were struggling a bit, I was worried about how you might react to the divorce."

"I'm not struggling."

"Well, I did find you talking to a potted plant-"

"I wasn't!"

"And as for your appearance, well, I wouldn't have dreamt you'd ever let your personal hygiene standards slip, but I've never seen you look quite so, so, *ragged*." I should have been offended, but that was actually a fair point.

He got up to go. "I thought coming round was the best thing to do and that we could at least be adult about this, but I've obviously got that wrong. I'll go ahead and instruct my solicitors; you'll be hearing from them soon."

I followed him to the front door, feeling churlish. I knew I should thank him for coming to tell me to my face but I wasn't able to bring myself to; I just didn't trust him. Why should I trust him? After all, this was the man who would, even if caught stark naked in bed with someone's legs wrapped round his neck, say, as he pumped away: "What, her? Oh, we're just good friends..."

He turned on the doorstep and looked back at me with a hurt expression. "Kate," he pleaded, "it's such a shame to leave things like this, after all our years together. I really did want to see you today; see how you're doing. You can't just switch everything off like that, I mean, I miss, well, I ... look, can't we move forward now? Come on, why don't we get together for a coffee in town sometime soon? It will make the whole divorce thing easier for both of us if we can try to be friends and talk about it. What do you think?"

I hesitated, torn. Behind him, I could see a dark green Mazda MX5 parked in the road. He'd always wanted a sports car. "I don't think *she* would like that very much, would she?"

I ventured, meaning The FT. He gave a shrug.

"This isn't about her, it's about you and me." *So, are you going to tell her?* "It's only a coffee; just a chance for us to keep in touch after all we've been through." *You mean, after all you put us through?* He gave me a brave smile and flipped his Aviators down over his eyes. What a wally.

"Let's see, shall we?" I replied, softened by a sudden unexpected surge of pity. "Perhaps we could. I mean, maybe."

"Oh, that's great! Really great! I'll give you a call then, shall I?"

I noticed, too late, that Mervyn was in his front garden, wearing his most striking, multi-coloured tank top. Perhaps he wouldn't notice us-

"Oh, look at that! Found yourself one with a sports car, eh?" *Honk honk.* "You should be in St Tropez!" *Honk.* "Is it a, er, a porch?"

"No, it's not a Porsche Mervyn, it's a mid-life crisis."

Nervous honking. "Well, you are very popular aren't you, all these young men coming and going!" *Honk honk.* "How do you do it? Sissy will be most envious! I'll tell her you've hooked another one, shall I? Another *friend* who'll be here all night, no doubt!" *Honk snort honk.*

The Ex was staring at me open-mouthed. I gave my head a quick tap to demonstrate that Mervyn was a sausage short of a fry up and said goodbye. He took several attempts to start the Mazda and as I was closing the front door, I heard its throaty roar as he drove away. What had that visit really been about? Why had he wanted to see me and why had he been so pleased when I'd (sort of) agreed to meet him for a coffee? We'd already divided up our worldly goods; we'd done all the hard stuff, the actual divorce was just a formality. *What did he want?* I sat on the sofa and fiddled distractedly with the iPad, eventually Googling "Why is my ex being nice to me". The top answers were:

1. He realises he behaved badly and is trying to apologise/make up for it. *Unlikely. That would mean he'd had a complete personality transformation.*

2. He is being civil so that you can both move on with your lives. *But we have already moved on with our lives. Haven't we?*

3. He has nothing else in his life and you are a convenient back-up. *Again, unlikely. I was an inconvenience even when we were married.*

4. He is not getting any at the moment so he's trying his luck with you. *Extremely unlikely. Even John Terry would have thought twice if he'd seen me in those shorts.*

I phoned Karen when the schools were out.

"How did he look?" she asked.

"Well, like a bit of a prat, actually. He was dressed in some ghastly Man from M&S lumberjack outfit, with those idiotic Top Twat glasses and he was driving a sports car. Well, it was a car without a roof, it didn't sound very sporty. He kept trying to be nice, but couldn't help the odd sarcastic remark from slipping out. What do you think is going on, Kazza?"

"Hmm, I don't know, it's difficult to say. Sounds like he's up to something, so I'd tread very carefully if I were you."

"That's what I thought, but I really don't know what he can be up to; everything's done and dusted apart from the actual divorce. What does he want?"

"Well, whatever he's after you can bet The FT's put him

up to it, the scheming cow. Perhaps they're scared you'll name and shame her and that will make the whole process more lengthy and expensive. Either that or he's come into some money and they want to make sure you can't get your hands on any of it. So he's being all nice to make sure the divorce goes through smoothly."

"Well, I suppose I could meet him for a coffee; there's no harm in being civil. And they do say to keep your enemies close."

"They also say once a knobhead always a knobhead. You watch yourself, Kate."

CHAPTER SEVENTEEN

First day back from my holiday and it was time to review The Lazy Shit's dismal lack of progress. He'd failed the informal part of his performance plan in March, thus triggering the formal stage and his three months were now up. He hadn't mentioned his impending fatherhood at all so I hadn't either. It was none of my business, after all. I sat in the meeting room with a copy of his plan, his team's sales and quality statistics for the last quarter, which I'd carefully analysed, his attendance records and an assortment of file notes. He arrived with just his iPhone.

"Take a seat, George," I said, trying to keep the weariness out of my voice. "Haven't you brought any notes with you?"

"No, I haven't." He seemed astonished by the question.

"George, what's your understanding of the purpose of this meeting?"

"It's a review, innit?"

"What are we reviewing?"

"My progress plan, I fink. Aren't we?"

"Yes, that's right, your *formal* progress plan, to review your performance against the targets we agreed. I'm not sure you appreciate how serious this meeting is, as you don't seem to have prepared for it-"

"I have prepared! I don't need no notes or nuffin'; it's all in my head." *It must be bloody lonely then.*

"Okay." I produced a copy of his plan and held it up in

front of me. "So, for the first objective, tell me how you've performed against the target." I looked at him expectantly.

"Um..." he wriggled in his seat, pretending to think whilst he surreptitiously tried to see through the paper at what the first objective was.

"Something wrong with your neck, George?"

"No, no. Er, what was the first objective again?"

"Planning. Would you like me to remind you of the targets we set? Ok. Firstly, you agreed to read and action all emails by close of day two of receipt and secondly, you agreed to arrive on time for all meetings, be fully prepared and make an active and valuable contribution." I shuffled the papers to give him some thinking time. "So, how have you done?"

"Yeah, good. I always do my emails on time now and I haven't been late to any meetings, well, apart from the complaints review, but that's because the meeting room had changed and no one told me."

I pushed a piece of paper towards him, which he eyed with suspicion. "What's that?"

"It's a print-out from your email inbox, George, which I took this morning. You have 189 unread emails, the oldest being twelve days ago and funnily enough, is the one which informed you of the change of room for the complaints review."

George's iPhone emitted a loud clang. He remained silent. "Why do you think you haven't been able to meet these standards, George?"

"There isn't time to do it all! There's just too much of everything now, we've got bigger teams and the targets keep going up and-" he broke off as he saw me studying another print out, which he guessed, correctly, was about to sink him.

I placed it in front of him so he could read an email chain entitled "Lauren B - shag, marry or off the cliff?" and so he could view the twenty or so times he had contributed to the inappropriate discussion. He folded his arms, unable to think of anything to say. I'd read it with great interest; the conclusion had been, somewhat predictably, 'shag'. Lauren had seemingly ruled herself out of marriage material when she'd agreed to take part in a line-up behind the recycling bins at Asda. I wasn't entirely sure what that meant but Lauren was now known as 7 Up, so I could take an educated guess.

"We've been here before, haven't we, George? Several times, actually and there's just no improvement, none at all." I couldn't stop myself from heaving a big sigh. "Let's move on. The second objective is attendance and the agreed standard was to reduce your absence to 5%, with no further occurrences of lateness. So, how have you done?"

"Alright, I fink."

Clang! "Your absence was 8% during the target period because you had three further occasions of absence, which were for an upset stomach," *a hangover* "a dizzy spell which was caused by getting kicked in the head at football," *got beaten up* "and a severe headache." *Attempted a crossword.*

"You've also had three further occasions of lateness that I've recorded; once when you forgot to put your clocks forward, once when your road was blocked by an overturned milk float and you couldn't drive round it. Or reverse. And once when you phoned to tell me you were a lizard and you couldn't find your tail. Here are all the file notes. So I'm afraid you haven't met the required standards of this objective either; do you agree?"

I looked up to see if he was going to respond, but as I was getting the sulky mutinous face now, I ploughed on.

"Third objective: your teams' quality figures to be at 95%." Clang! "Last month you achieved 89%, which was actually a deterioration from the previous month-" Clang, clang, clang! "Can't you turn that bloody thing off, George?" *I could always shove it somewhere, of course. Then you would quite literally be buggered.*

He fiddled disconsolately with his iPhone, unbelievably pausing to scroll through a text before reluctantly switching it off. What was wrong with him? Didn't he care about his piss poor performance at all? Was he really so ignorant he thought he would keep his job no matter what? I tried to prompt him into some sort of defence: "Have you got anything you'd like to say, or add to this review of your performance? Anything at all?"

Head down, surly shrug. "Not much point, is there?"

"There's every point, George! Pride, for one thing. But you just don't seem to care."

Another shrug. I let the silence hang for as long as I could stand it, but eventually had to give up. "Well then, I'm sorry George, but as you've not managed to meet any of the targets we agreed back in March, or offer suitable explanations, it means you'll now be required to attend a formal performance hearing-"

"I won't lose my job, will I?"

"It won't be my decision, George, as the hearing will be with an impartial manager," *shame there's no such thing* "but you need to be aware that dismissal could be one of the potential outcomes. You'll receive a letter inviting you to the hearing over the next few days. Are you in the union?"

"No." *Not that it would make any difference; they're about as much use as a blind lifeguard.*

"Well, the letter will contain contact details of where you can get some advice and guidance, so please make sure you seek some support before the hearing; you've got to help yourself now, George. Do you understand?"

He nodded and I noticed he had gone pale under his man-tan; perhaps reality was sinking in at last. He left the room and as I was despondently gathering up my notes, Big Andy popped his head round the door.

"Kate! I've had a thought!"

"Well, could you lend it to George?"

"Ah; how did his review go?"

"Like firing at ducks on a rifle range; he kept on lining himself up. I tried to give him an opportunity to defend himself but he just didn't take it. You can lead a horse to water I suppose, but you can't make it drink."

"No, but you can hold its head under and force it to take a fucking great gulp! If he had any sense, he'd cut his losses and resign. Anyway, do you want to hear my thought?"

"Do I have any choice?"

"I thought we could hire one of those two-seater bicycles and do a tandem ride round Cheltenham for Cycle for Michael. If you wear a really short skirt, perhaps one of those little frilly tennis ones, people will pay us to stop. We'll make a fortune! What do you think?"

"You're a sick man."

I was sitting on the sofa with my laptop, typing up the notes from my meeting with George, as Jeremy Paxman raged at some poor, female politician as she stuttered and stammered out her apologies for being alive. She'd foolishly attempted to express an opinion that wasn't his; how could she possibly have got it so wrong? The phone rang, making my heart race. It was late - was someone calling with bad news?

"Hello?"

"Er, hi Sis." It was Stu, sounding very awkward. Did he need somewhere to stay again? "I'm sorry it's a bit late, Sis, but Kirsty's asked me to call you ... what? Ow! Sorry, I mean, I wanted to call you, because of the, er, the situation with George."

"What do you mean?"

"He's told Georgia you're going to sack him and she's dreadfully upset; she's terrified that if he loses his job he won't be able to support her and the baby. She's in a right old state, Sis! You can't let this happen to her."

I was speechless. What on earth did he expect me to do? This was so unfair! I wasn't responsible for Georgia's well being ... but, actually, I was responsible for George's performance; that *was* down to me. "I'm not really sure what to say, Stu," I managed, eventually. My voice sounded echoey and I realised he must have put me on speakerphone so The Bunny Boiler could listen in too. I could hear some deep raspy breathing so she must be stood right at his shoulder. "I can't discuss George's position with you, it wouldn't be right. But I can tell you that the decision to dismiss him or not is out of my hands now, as it-"

"But you have a say in it, surely? You're his boss. Please Sis, can't you do something? Georgia's planning to move in with him when this term finishes and what if he can't pay the rent on his flat? What will happen then?"

Ah, so, that was the real panic; they didn't want Georgia and the baby moving in with them.

"I'm sorry Stu, but I really can't do anything now. He might not be dismissed, you know, there are several other-"

"Oh, that's just bloody typical of your family, isn't it? They couldn't give a toss about me and my daughter! They're obviously happy to let the bloody baby starve to death, or perhaps they'd rather Georgia sold it on Ebay, or swapped it, perhaps, for a Kenwood fucking sandwich toaster-"

"Er, sorry about that, Sis, but Kirsty's a bit upset, as you can imagine-"

"*A bit fucking upset?* Yes, I fucking well am! And don't you apologise to her, she's got no idea what it's like to bring up a child, she only cares about her twatty job, she don't give a shit about me or you, not one shit-"

There was a large crash in the background. "Are you alright Stu?" I asked anxiously.

"Yes, yes, I'd better call you back, Sis." *Smash!* He swiftly hung up. Christ. I replaced the handset feeling a mixture of injustice and guilt. I couldn't possibly have taken into account George's personal circumstances when I'd reviewed and failed his progress plan, could I? Or should I have done? After all, Georgia was almost family and if you don't support your own family then doesn't that make you the worse kind of shit? Should I have turned a blind eye to George's staggering lack of progress in order to protect him and made sure his job was safe? I looked at my laptop and the half-finished notes. Nothing had been sent off yet; it wasn't too late, I could still alter the figures to make it look like George had successfully passed the plan. No, stop - copies of all the individual file notes had already been sent to HR; details of every time he'd been late, or absent, or more stupendously gormless than usual had all been meticulously recorded, documented and submitted. It *was* too late.

I waited up for another hour in case my brother called me back, but when he didn't, I went to bed. I lay awake, tossing and turning, my mind racing with a million thoughts and thinking of my brother spending another night in his van. When I did fall into a fitful sleep, I dreamt I was sitting on the loo in a toilet cubicle and all the walls suddenly fell down, leaving me exposed, knickers round my ankles, to hundreds of staring shoppers on a busy street. A guilt-dream if ever there was one.

I was at my desk when my mobile rang. It was Maddie at Regis Resourcing who said she wanted to discuss an exciting opportunity with me. She had a strong South African accent, brusque and clipped, which was rather intimidating. I asked her how she'd got my details and she said I'd entered them into their website. I knew I hadn't and assumed my details had been sold on to them by Robbie Williams' friend but still, I wasn't about to throw a hissy-fit in case she had a shit-hot job lined up for me. Perhaps it would be rubbing down James Martin with a cold flannel after his hot messy stint on Saturday Kitchen; no doubt he'd be covered all over in splashes of gravy or smearings of butter-

"It's a major insurance brand; they're looking for a manager to help run their operation during a period of significant change."

"Oh, that sounds interesting." *Does it buggery.*

"Yes. The contract is for one year and has the potential to be extended further."

"Great."

"I see from your CV that you have a great deal of experience in managing insurance operations?"

"Yes, that's right. I've worked-"

"And why are you leaving your current role?"

"I, er, I feel I've taken it as far as I can and I'm ready for a new challenge-"

"Have you any CCJ's?"

"What? Er, no-"

"Have you any criminal convictions?"

"No."

"Any disabilities?"

"No."

"Oh. Well, never mind. I can still put you forward for an interview with the company's directors. They're based in Birmingham."

"Right." Birmingham was a bit further than I would have liked but it was do-able. "Could I ask what rate of pay they're offering?"

"It's nine hundred."

"Nine hundred what?"

"A day."

I gasped. *Nine hundred pounds a day?* "But, that's, gosh that's about two hundred grand a year, isn't it? Look, I really don't think I'm a suitable candidate-"

"But with all your experience you should be seeking that sort of salary. If you say things like you don't think you're suitable because the pay is too high then you're seriously undervaluing yourself. Companies will think you haven't got the skills they want."

Well, they'd find out soon enough when they met me. "Maddie,

I'm really not comfortable with this role. That sort of salary makes me think they're expecting a senior executive and that's not me. I'm seeking more of a middle management position."

She sniffed. "You shouldn't undersell yourself, it's the worst thing you can do. You need to talk yourself up; you should be commanding this sort of salary with all your experience and expertise. I'll put you forward for an interview."

I said I'd call her back. Should I go for the interview? Did I really have the required skills for that sort of salary or was she just bullshitting me in order to get someone in front of their clients to fulfil their order? It might be worth a punt, after all, anyone with half a brain could be considered gifted in the insurance industry. I eventually decided against it; my confidence had taken a bit of a battering lately - perhaps I should limit my job search to trolley-pusher. And I bet that's harder than it looks.

No sooner had I finished speaking to Maddie, when Karen called me. "Jesus, Kate, what have you done to your brother's wife?"

I felt sick. "What do you mean?"

"Facebook. She's given you a right slating. Do you want me to read what she's put?"

"No, I don't think I do!"

"Her spelling's absolutely atrocious, isn't it? She's spelt cucumber with a Q and arse a-s-s."

"Oh God. Has it got any likes?"

"Just your mother. Only Joking! Two likes so far; Georgia of course and that dipshit you work with, George."

I shuddered. "They want me to stop George getting the

sack but I've said I can't. Do you think I've got it wrong, Kazza?"

"Well, no, but let's face it Kate, she's a total skitzo. I wouldn't want to make an enemy of her, so unless you've got a particular desire to re-enact the final scenes from Carrie and end up covered in pig's blood, I'd do what she wants."

"Thanks mate, that's helpful."

"Anytime!"

CHAPTER EIGHTEEN

I was dreading today's Cycle for Michael events. I'm not uncharitable but I am unsporty. I think it stemmed from the trauma of having to do PE in my pants and vest at school and the evil Sarah Fox had pulled my knickers down in front of all the boys in the gym. What is Sarah Fox doing now, I wonder? Head of cavity searches at Heathrow, perhaps? Mammographer?

I'd had to purchase a pair of grey jogging bottoms especially for the occasion, which have to be the most unflattering garment I've ever worn, with the exception of a voluminous smock-top from Dotty P's. This had prompted several people to ask me when my baby was due. My huge rhinoceros arse and I were taking part in the Perypils twenty-four hour cyclothon, where colleagues at each site were to cycle around the clock - on an exercise bike. We were doing thirty minute sessions each and I'd put myself down for three, which was rather ambitious but I was keen to do my bit so I could prove to The GPS that I was a real team player, devoted to each and every one of the company's pseudo-initiatives.

I arrived at work just after seven so I could get a good head start on the day and was just parking up when my mobile rang. *Bloody hell, who was calling me at this time of the morning?* "Hello?"

"Is that Kate? Oh, thank God. This is Jenny, Kevin's PA. I urgently need your help." She sounded panicked but that's how everyone who worked for The Big Cheese sounded.

"What's up Jenny?" I jabbed my iPod off as it was difficult to hear her while Celine Dion was wailing her head off.

"Kate, it's a disaster. The plan for Kevin today was for him to officially start the cyclothon then he was due to meet Michael Moore and his family here in Manchester, at head office. He's invited the press, too. But I've just found out that the bloody Moore family aren't going to be in Manchester; they're about to be on breakfast telly this morning in sodding Bristol!"

"O-kay." My stomach lurched.

"So, we're going to try and re-arrange everything from Cheltenham." *Shit a brick!* "Kevin's already on his way down, he should be there by about nine thirty, I reckon." *Oh Christ - hide everything, gag the staff, shred the stats – no, better to hide the stats and shred the staff -* "I'm going to get the Moores to go to Cheltenham when they've finished in Bristol and see if I can re-organise the press coverage. Are you still there, Kate?"

"Yes," I squeaked.

"Great. Kevin will want to start the cyclothon and take part, so make sure you get lots of pictures of him plus any other activities you've got going on. Are you doing the Olympic-themed fancy dress competition? Good. Get him to judge that and hand out the prizes; remember, lots of photos, Kate and make sure there's always plenty of happy smiling colleagues around." *How the fuck was I going to achieve that?*

"Right, ok Jenny," I recovered myself. "Will Kevin be bringing anyone with him?" He usually travelled with a huge entourage of brown-nosed cling-ons.

"You'll be inundated later in the day, but just now he's with Amanda Fisher, his executive assistant." The Climber! Back in Cheltenham. The day was getting better and better. The way Jenny spat her name out I guessed she was still about as popular as a smear test. "There were lots of others due in Manchester, of course, so I'm going to be contacting them all to see if they can divert to Cheltenham. I've got to go Kate; I'll call you again as soon as I know what's happening."

Stunned, I climbed out of the car and walked in a daze towards reception. The Cheltenham site always tried to keep its head down for fear of it being blown clean off and we weren't accustomed to being thrust into the spotlight. And it would all be down to me today; Big Andy had booked a last minute holiday to Fuengirola, the sneaky sod. It could be a very positive thing for the site of course, if the day went well but if it didn't...

In reception, a bleary-eyed young man in white shorts and T-shirt was half-heartedly pedalling away on an exercise bike while scrolling through his iPhone. Another sprawled on the sofa, seemingly asleep as he waited his turn. A black plastic bucket sat on the floor next to a crudely scribbled sign: "Doh-n8 Cycle 4 Micheal". So the cyclothon had already started - well, we'd just have to pretend to re-start it when The Big Cheese arrived; no one would know. We might have to put a bit more oomph into it, though.

Congratulating myself on arriving so early, I set about tidying up the departments as best I could, ripping down anything that was out of date from the walls or that looked a bit tatty and rubbing off 'Ben's a knob jockey' and the marker-penned penises that always appeared on the white boards following the late shift. As colleagues started to arrive, I got them to tidy their desk areas, aware that my eye had developed its stress twitch that always made the boys uneasy because they thought I was winking at them.

It was all very well tarting up the departments but I realised it was the staff that were the real problem. *Bloody dress down day, what a collection of horrors.* Many had opted for football or rugby shirts over jeans, which was fine but some of the girls; *oh my God.* One walked past me in a denim mini skirt that was so short you could actually see the beginnings of her bum cheeks. Another was wearing a vest top with tiny spaghetti straps, which were struggling to contain her ample bosom; it looked ready to leap out and smother somebody to death. Why did they bother with clothes? They might just as well walk round naked. I set The Rock on them; she was the motherly sort, hopefully she could persuade them to cover up. I couldn't have our Chief Executive wondering round with a massive erection.

Jenny phoned me several times sounding shriller and more fraught with each call. The Moores were due to arrive at around 2pm, along with several members of the press and the Perypils publicity team. She said Kevin had stopped at MacDonald's for breakfast so he would probably arrive nearer to ten. That was fine by me; the later the better. As I finished a call I heard a ripple of murmuring running through the department and looked up to see that The Drain had come into work in casual clothes. This was unheard of - the Drain never dressed down! He wouldn't pay the required pound, even though it was for charity. He was dressed in jeans that were just a little too short, finishing at his ankles, exposing grey socks and black canvas plimsolls. He had a white track suit top on which was unzipped far enough to expose a flash of gold chunky necklace and a white baseball cap with the Nike logo on the front.

As he removed his DairyLea Dunkers from his Asda bag, I could see his team were all hiding their faces, shoulders shaking as they attempted not to explode with laughter. I thought I heard one of them say, "Dizzee's in da house, innit!" followed by several suppressed snorts and chortles. I went over to say well done for entering into the spirit of the day and to tell him that I wanted to see all the team managers at nine o'clock sharp. I came away chewing on a thick cloud of TCP; the gold-looking necklace was apparently playing havoc with his heat rash.

The Drain's appearance did not stay headline news for very long. On the stroke of nine o'clock, there was uproar. Loud shrieks of laughter and cries of "Oh my God!" filled the department. *What the hell was going on now?* I looked up to see Ben and Danny making their way to their desks, both wearing sparkling green mankinis with bright orange tans, glittering hair scraped up and faces plastered in garish make up. They sashayed through their squealing colleagues, stopping to do lunges or simulating the breast stroke. TLS George looked across at me in horror but I just shook my head helplessly; words failed me.

It was almost nine thirty before I'd managed to round up all the team managers; it was proving impossible to get the teams to focus on their work. As it was, I had to start the meeting without The Drain who had last been seen heading towards the Gents to "drop the kids off at the pool" as TLS George so indelicately put it.

"Right guys, here we go. This is a big day for us. You

know that the Chief Exec is on his way here and we're going to have to pull out all the stops to ensure today's Cycle for Michael activities are a great success, as well as keeping today's work on track. Not an easy juggling act, I know, but we've really got to make this work. I'm going to stay with Kevin and, er, his assistant so I really need your support to keep things running smoothly."

"His assistant?" The Snake spat some venom. "Do you mean Amanda Fisher?"

"Yes, that's right, Cynthia and I'm sure you'll be joining me in welcoming her back to the site." *Not a chance in hell.* "I need you all on the ball today; make sure you send your teams to the activities in good time and keep those left in the department heads down and cracking on with their work."

"Are the Moore family really coming here?" asked The Blubber excitedly. "Can I meet them? I've never met real-life celebrities before!"

They're not the Kardashians. "If there's that opportunity Pat, I'll let you know. I'm sure they'll be really appreciative of everyone's efforts today."

"Are Ben and Danny going to stay dressed like that all day?" The Snake addressed TLS George. "It's not hygienic; their chairs will need cleaning and they've already covered their handsets with fake tan-"

"Just until the fancy dress competition," replied George. "At least I've got them to take their nose clips off when they're talking to customers."

The Drain arrived and pulled up a chair. I noticed he was no longer wearing his baseball cap. "Where's your cap, Martin?" I asked him. "Was it making your head too hot?"

"It met with an accident," he replied mysteriously, sitting

down rather gingerly and not making eye contact. I looked round at the others; they were as intrigued as I was.

"What sort of an accident?" asked TLS George. "What's happened to it?"

The Drain placed his pen on the table very deliberately and studied it, clearly undecided whether he should tell us or not.

"Come on Martin!" I urged. "Put us out of our misery - what's happened to your cool baseball cap?"

He looked uncomfortable. "It happened when I went to the toilet. I took my cap off and put it on the cistern behind me."

"Yes?"

"I turned round to, er, well, you know, unbuckle and I think the cap must have fallen down into the toilet bowl without me realising."

We all looked at each other in delight.

"You mean you...." started TLS George.

The Drain nodded, concentrating hard on his pen.

"You crapped in your hat!" shrieked The Blubber.

We all screamed with laughter, causing the whole department to look over at us in bewilderment as we howled and clutched our sides. We tried to pull ourselves together but when George asked, "How come you took your hat off to have a dump?" we fell apart again. I eventually let them go, remembering, just in time, to ask The Rock to quickly knock up a new sign for the cyclothon donations and replace the dyslexic version.

At ten o'clock, I hovered at reception, ready to greet The Big Cheese. Thankfully, Stalin Stan was on holiday and the lovely smiley Annie was there instead. A girl I recognised from Big Andy's Finance team was pumping away vigorously on the exercise bike and two of her friends were shouting encouragement. This was more like it! With perfect timing, a black Mercedes swept up outside and the driver got out to open the rear passenger door, revealing an angry-looking John Prescott. *What on earth was he doing here?* Ignoring his driver, he strode towards reception bellowing into his mobile: "Who do those fucking shitheads think they are? You fucking well tell them to get their sorry fucking arses down here! I've got half the country's press descending on me this afternoon; what sort of limp dick am I going to look like if they're not here? So you bloody well get them here and you tell those little shits that they'd better look *fucking grateful* or so help me God-"

My mistake; it was undeniably the Chief Executive. "Hi Kevin! Welcome to Cheltenham!" I did a stupid jazz hands movement; *why, why?* What an absolute Muppet.

"Oh, aye, hello, er-?"

"It's Kate. Kate King. Great to see you again! How was your journey?"

"Bloody shite; morons and dickheads clogging up every road, bloody farce ... oh, what have we got here, then?" Suddenly, he was all smiles, having spotted the girls around the exercise bike and leaving me rooted to the spot, went over to introduce himself, resulting in much nervous giggling. I was obviously wearing my invisibility cloak again; I seemed to have acquired it sometime in my mid thirties and now, in my forties, I wore it more and more. A familiar, annoying laugh rang out behind me and I turned to see The Climber. She was talking into her BlackBerry and flicking her long brown hair around. "Got to go, Rupert darling, work to do!

You wouldn't know about that of course!" Another peel of irritating fake laughter. "Kate! You're still here then!" *Where else would I be? What did she know that I didn't?*

"Hello Amanda," I said warily. "How are you?"

"I'm really good, super in fact, everything's been going so well for me. I expect you heard me chatting to Rupert just then; he's head of marketing you know and such a naughty thing! I do move in very different circles these days, of course; best thing I ever did, getting away from this place!" She looked me up and down. "You're looking very well, Kate, I must say! A bit of extra weight can be quite flattering, can't it?" *You what? These bloody sweatpants!* "Oh, I wasn't being rude or anything - I think it really suits you!"

The old urge to grab her by the hair, swing her round and toss her through the revolving doors came rushing back. I gritted my teeth.

"Well, you look great too, Amanda and gosh, look at that! Your skirts have got even shorter! Who'd have thought that possible? Or perhaps your legs have stretched?" I quickly turned back to The Big Cheese, who was about to take his turn on the bike. He removed his jacket, flinging it at The Climber who saw it coming just a fraction too late and wasn't able to prevent it briefly covering her head completely. She yanked it off, glancing furiously at my grinning face as hers turned flame red.

Kevin was starting to pedal, so I positioned the girls and Smiley Annie around him and took some photographs. When my mobile rang, I handed the camera to The Climber so I could answer it.

"Kate, it's Jenny again." She sounded a bit tearful. "I need a really big favour. The Moores are being driven to

Asda; they've been promised a free trolley load of food by the manager of a store just outside Cheltenham. I really need to make sure they get to the Cheltenham site or I may as well end my life now; could you go and fetch them later? I can't ask Kevin's driver, he's had to go and collect some big knobs from the airport."

Argh! Me - pick up important celebrities in my Ford Focus? When had I last washed it? Or hoovered it out? It had horrid flakes of skin round the gear stick, a One Direction CD in the centre console-

"It will probably be about midday, I should think. I'll call you and tell you when but we must make sure that we get them to the site or Kevin's going to, well, you don't want to know. Please can you do it?"

I could hardly say no. I ended the call and watched the exercise bike buckling under the weight of The Big Cheese as he made a huge show of manly pedalling and smiling inanely for the camera. When he'd had enough, The Climber announced she was going to take him on a tour of the building before the fancy dress competition so he could "say hello to everyone".

"No need for you to come, Kate," she said, abruptly. "I know my way round and I'm sure you've got lots to do!"

Uh-oh. Still, I couldn't very well insist in accompanying them, it might look as if I had something to hide. They were going to start on the third floor with the Ops guys, provided they could cut their way through the cobwebs and skeletons, so I returned to the fourth to see how things were going in my teams. Not very well, was the answer. There were over forty calls queuing in Property.

"It's bedlam," The Drain announced, clutching his

stomach. "We've got people getting ready for the fancy dress, others helping set up the barbeque-"

"Oh my God, what's happened to Craig? Don't tell me we've got another outbreak of mumps?"

"He's taking part in a sponsored marshmallow eating competition."

"And, what is *that*? A boiled egg? It looks a bit like Lizzie, but it can't be-"

"Sponsored head shave."

"Oh."

"Don't worry, I called a halt to the sponsored soggy biscuit."

Jesus.

Things weren't much better in Concerns. The Rock was on the phone to a customer and I heard her say as I walked past: "I'm sorry the cartoon characters on our TV adverts freak you, Mr Lewis but I really don't think we'll be able to make their noses any smaller..."

I asked The Blubber why her admin team weren't on calls when there were customers queuing and she replied: "Sponsored silence." I was just considering battering her to death with a hole punch when my mobile rang. It was Hissing Cyn, informing me that the Chief Exec had arrived in the Property department. I hurried back round there just in time to hear The Climber exclaim, very loudly, "Oh, dear me! Look at all those calls waiting! That would never have happened when I was here."

Bitch. I always knew she'd be my downfall. "Ah, here's Kate. Come on Kate, fess up! What have you hidden away, out of sight? Kate always hides things, Kevin, when she has visitors, either that or she throws everything out! I bet if I looked in the bins they'd be stuffed full of things she doesn't want us to see! Ha ha!" *Shit - the bins were absolutely crammed.* "Oh no, look, there's Martin! Didn't you have time to chuck him in the bin, Kate?" She peeled with laughter and The Drain, clocking the situation, swiftly turned back in the direction of the toilets.

This was turning into a nightmare. Fortunately, The Big Cheese was distracted by Carla (young, blonde, busty) who was writing some figures up on the whiteboard and he went to quiz her on them. "What are you playing at, Amanda?" I hissed. "I expect a little more loyalty from you and so do your colleagues; we do all work for the same company, you know."

"Oh, I'm only joking! Goodness me, lighten up Kate! Ah, there's George, on his iPhone again, I see! Nothing changes, does it?"

I knew George was only pretending to speak earnestly into his phone because it rang while he was talking. Carla anxiously called me over. "Er, Kate, Kevin's asked me why our colleague satisfaction survey increased so much in quarter one, but I don't know the answer. Do you?"

"I do," The Snake jumped in. "It was due to the Sales team's results, they shot up significantly."

"Shall we move on?" The Climber suggested quickly.

"That's a bloody good jump that is. Aye, a bloody great jump." The Big Cheese nodded his approval. "What happened in the Sales team to make it increase like that? Why was morale so much better in quarter one?"

"We've got lots more to see!" The Climber squealed.

"Their team manager left," stated The Snake, with great relish. "It made a huge difference to their morale and the satisfaction score shot up."

"Aye, well, they must have been a bloody crap team manager, then. Good work Kate, that's what I like to see - get rid of the rubbish, we don't need their sort at Perypils."

The Climber looked desperately at me to save her but I didn't feel inclined to rob The Snake of her moment of triumph.

"Oh, but the team manager still works for Perypils! Don't you, Amanda?"

Everyone looked at The Climber who stood there with her jaw flapping and her face crimson.

"Aye, well, that's very disappointing to hear Amanda, very disappointing indeed." The Big Cheese jabbed a sausagy finger in her face. "If you want to be a great leader in this company you've got to bring your people with you; I had to get shot of my last assistant because he couldn't lead his dick out of his trousers without pissing down his leg. I can't be doing with those arrogant anal types who can't get on with anyone else; can't be doing with 'em at all."

I didn't think I'd ever seen The Snake look so happy. Perhaps the time when George had dropped his wallet containing his £300 Gold Cup winnings down the toilet came the closest. Shame-faced, The Climber led her boss on through the department as quickly as she could and round the corner to the Concerns teams. I knew he wouldn't stay there long - nobody did without sufficient protection - so I scampered down four flights of stairs to make sure things were in place for the Olympic-themed fancy dress competition, which was being held in the canteen.

I found a gaggle of contestants beginning to line up excitedly, everyone trying to avert their eyes from the disturbing sight of Ben and Danny who were parading around in their mankinis and nose clips. At least they had made an effort; one man had strapped a candle to his head as the Olympic flame, Horsey Helen had turned up in her jodhpurs to represent Equestrianism, two girls were in their tennis gear and what on earth? One guy had dressed up as Ali G! *Why?* What was he thinking?

The door to the canteen whipped open and The GPS appeared. *Great.* I wondered how long it would be before the weeny pilot fish congregated around the big fat shark. He was momentarily nonplussed when he saw Ben and Danny, who were now lying face down on the floor doing the front crawl, their bare buttocks wriggling from side to side, but he quickly recovered himself to launch another attack on me. "Kate - there's no one at the cyclothon! What the hell's going on? Need I remind you that it's a *continuous* twenty-four hour event and that a number of very high profile visitors are due here any minute. What on earth are they going to think? Why isn't there anyone on the bike?"

What time was it? Oh buggeration; it was one of my stints! Why hadn't anyone phoned me? "Right, don't panic, I'll go and jump on the bike myself," I declared, heroically and made a dash for the door, leaving him awkwardly facing the fancy dress crackpots who beamed expectantly back. All apart from Ben and Danny; they were busy doing synchronised squat thrusts. I reached reception and sprang onto the bike just as a group of expensively-suited alpha male types marched in. I pedalled away furiously and they said things like "Oh, well done you!" and "Super effort!" while they, somewhat reluctantly, dropped a few coins into the bucket. Smiley Annie led them all off to the canteen and I reduced my pedal power before I had a coronary.

The Big Cheese strode past with The Climber tagging along at his heels and soon I could hear shrieks of laughter emanating from the canteen, suggesting that the fancy dress competition was in full swing. Outside in the car park, stalls were in the process of being set up and the barbeque was beginning to send up smoke signals, probably warning Cheltenham's Red Indian population: "You no come here. Food shite." My mobile rang. Jenny again.

"Hi Kate. The Moores will be ready to pick up at one o'clock from Asda. Is that OK? It's just Mister and Missus and poor little Michael, of course, the other brothers are all at school. And you'll have to put their shopping in your boot."

"No problem," I panted. "How are they getting home?"

Silence. Then "Shit. I suppose I'll have to order a taxi for them. It's going to cost a bloody fortune; he's going to go absolutely-"

The line went dead. I pedalled gamely on, feeling extremely relieved when TLS George eventually came to take over. He told me that Horsey Helen had won the fancy dress competition; apparently the Chief Exec had been rather taken with her whip and that he had also awarded an additional prize for "bravery" to Ben and Danny. He'd made The GPS present them with a bottle of wine each and on receipt, the boys had leapt on The GPS, smothering him with kisses. How I wished I'd been there to see that! Priceless.

I had to get going if I was to reach Asda by one o'clock. I took a few minutes to try and make the inside of my car look respectable but as it was pretty much a lost cause, I set off. I gave myself a good talking to on the way there:

Don't go all dopey and star struck.
Don't ask them if they've met James Martin.

Don't say "I bet you're dying for a cup of tea!"
Ditto "You must be dead on your feet!"

My heart was racing by the time I pulled into the car park at Asda and swung round to the front of the store. A grossly overweight, sportswear-clad couple with two trolleys piled high were having a heated argument outside the front door but there was no sign of the Moore family. I switched the engine off and went inside to the customer services desk, where I told the assistant I was here to collect the Moores. A tall thin man in a grey suit immediately appeared at my side. He looked drained.

"Are you from Perypils?" he asked wearily. "*Thank Christ.* The Moores are outside."

"Oh! I didn't see them."

His eyebrows shot up. "Really? How the hell did you miss them?"

I followed him to the front doors and he pointed wordlessly towards the squabbling couple.

"That's them?" I whispered. They didn't look a bit like they did in the papers or on the telly.

"One fucking trolley load I said, as a gesture of goodwill," the manager hissed in my ear. "And the greedy bastards loaded one with food and another with booze. I could hardly say anything, could I? Had the bloody press here, taking pictures, so I had to smile and pretend all was fine. Head office is going to go spare when they see the bill - it's a frigging monster. Anyway, they're all yours now, thank fuck. And best of bloody luck."

I approached the couple apprehensively. How the hell was I going to get that lot in my boot? And where was Michael? As I got closer, I saw him; he'd been completely hidden behind boxes of Carling. I swallowed hard and plunged in. "Hi! Mr and Mrs Moore, is it? I'm Kate, your driver! No peaked cap, I'm afraid!" *High pitched, fake, nervous laugh.* Mrs Moore, face like thunder, looked me up and down.

"Bout time an' all. Starvin' we are." I looked at the food trolley, bulging with biscuits, cakes and crisps.

"I'm not going to be able to get all that in my boot-"

"You'll 'ave to make two trips then-"

"So I was going to suggest I phone a colleague and get them to come out too. Could you take the, er, the drinks trolley back inside and leave it at customer services for now?"

"Go on Mikey," his father ordered. The poor little lad put all his weight behind the trolley and tried to get it to move while his parents turned back to their bickering. I gave him a hand to push it, having to steady the beer boxes so they didn't fall off. "How are you Michael?" *Doh! You idiot! How do you think he is? He's bloody dying, isn't he!*

"Fine thanks," he said in a small voice and my heart went out to him. Poor lad; I bet he was hating all this fuss - TV appearances, trolley dashes, corporate events bollocks - he should be at home resting. I phoned The Rock and asked her to come and pick up the booze. A nice young man on the customer service desk said he would get someone to help her load up. We just about managed to squeeze all of the food into the boot of my Focus and then they climbed in the back seats because Mrs Moore said, "That looks posher, dunnit?" She continued the argument with her husband the whole way; as far as I could ascertain, it was because she couldn't get any Häagen Dazs, and blamed him for not insisting they be allowed to do the shop on the Internet, so they could have stocked up their freezer.

It was not without an enormous amount of relief that I pulled up outside the Perypils building, where a beaming Big Cheese and a group of suits were waiting to welcome their much-prized guests. The Moores didn't move until I got out and opened the rear door for them and then they were all smiles, apart from Michael, who looked pale and anxious. The GPS sidled over to me. I thought he was going to say "well done" for getting them here but instead he snarled, "Where have you been Kate, we've been waiting here for ages. And move your car; we don't want *that* in the photos." I felt like revving it up and ploughing straight over him.

As I was driving around to the car park, I saw that the Moores were being taken in the direction of the barbeque. That poor little sod Michael; now he'd have dysentery to add to all his woes. I locked the car and had started to walk back to the building when I noticed The Drain sitting in his little red Noddy car with his head on the steering wheel. I knocked on the window and he lifted his head and wound the window down. "Are you ok, Martin?" I asked anxiously. "Is it your heat rash?"

He shook his head. "I've seen him. It's so awful, so *horrible*. I'm in shock."

"You mean the Chief Exec? Yes, he is a bit of a disturbing sight, isn't he-"

"No! That poor little Michael! He looks scared, so pale and sickly; makes me think of my own son. It's difficult to bear."

"Yes, it is." I could hear The Manic Street Preachers on his car radio, "like a cat in a bag, waiting to drown-". "Why don't you come inside, Martin?" I said quickly. "Get a nice cup of tea. It's supposed to be good for shock."

He shuddered. "Don't make me go back in there. The quotation system's gone down, hundreds of calls are queuing, customers are screaming, Ben and Danny are playing leapfrog-" Suddenly, the tinny chimes of an ice cream van rang out behind us and we both stared in astonishment as Sergio's Ices swept into the car park playing Greensleeves. It stopped right in front of The Drain's car. Of course! Andrea had arranged an ice cream van for today.

"Do you want to join me in a sixty-nine?" I asked The Drain, cheerfully. "I'll treat you – I'm sure it's just what you need to cheer you up!" His eyes widened and he scrambled to turn his keys in the ignition. I leapt out of the way as he slammed the car into reverse and shot out of the car park. The poor thing; it must be his irritable bowel again.

I fumbled for some change and went to beat the stampede to Sergio, stepping over The Drain's skid marks.

I didn't have a particularly big part to play in the rest of the afternoon, as the Perypils publicity machine took over events and all I was required to do was ensure there were always enough suitably-attired, grinning staff around to appear in the press photos and interviews. There were lots of 'fun' competitions, such as horseshoe throwing and a boob-busting sack race which I gallantly took part in, smiling broadly whilst hating every single second. At one point, I stumbled across Mrs Moore in the Ladies toilets applying face powder to an embarrassed-looking Michael. "Just want 'im to look a bit elfier for the pictures," she said, quickly. I felt like pointing out she was actually making the poor thing look even paler but I decided against it; she was a rather formidable woman and I didn't want my head flushed down the bog. She was exactly how I'd imagined the evil Sarah Fox had turned out. Perhaps they were related to one another.

At the end of the afternoon, I helped a taxi driver load up the Moore's shopping and the family left. I noticed they didn't get much of a send off; presumably we'd got all the publicity we needed out of them. Wearily, I took another turn on the exercise bike, having to pedal like mad each time groups of big wigs passed through reception on their way out. The Big Cheese shook my hand as he left with The Climber and The GPS, who were practically glued to either side of him. "Well done Cathy!" he boomed. "Bloody great effort today! Aye, bloody great!" I didn't have the energy to correct him.

"Bye *Cathy!*" called The Climber, with a smirk. *Bye Bitch. Mind the road, won't you?*

"We'll talk tomorrow, Kate," growled The GPS, threateningly. What was wrong now? I thought the day had been salvaged pretty well. Oh, who cares. Only a few hours to go and then I could reward myself by opening a bottle of wine and a bag of Revels, slouch in front of Emmerdale and have a dribble over Cain. I'd earned it.

CHAPTER NINETEEN

The MC was hovering. "There's something funny going on, Kate."

"Could you define funny?" I knew she couldn't. Even during a meeting when The Blubber had kindly tried to remove a strand of hair from Hissing Cyn's chin, only to find it was attached and half tugged The Snake across the table, The Miserable Cow had remained dry-eyed.

"Well, we've had a couple of complaints where customers have phoned us for a quote, but when they receive the quote in the post, it's different to what we said."

"That's odd; you'd better show me." I followed The MC back to her desk so I could examine the evidence. She showed me a screen shot, which clearly quoted a monthly premium of £27.33 for Eileen Murray's car insurance. Eileen's letter showed the premium quoted as £33.27.

"That's the second one today," said the MC. "Do you think it's the Pox?"

The Perypils Online Quotation System had been beset by problems since it was introduced last year. It really was a piece of crap and it looked like it had produced yet another turd.

"What should I tell Mrs Murray?" asked the MC anxiously. "I've got to call her back and she's not very happy. And she's Scottish."

"I wish I could say give her the lower amount but I don't know what her policy documents are going to show, so you'll have to tell her we're doing some urgent investigations. I'll phone IT to see what they suggest."

"Oh, you can't phone them anymore; you have to complete an online report form and submit that."

"And get a response in six weeks time? And that will probably be 'Oh, I'm afraid I don't know my arse from my elbow, have you tried turning it off and turning it on again?' No, this is urgent, I'm phoning them."

Despite my bravado, I got completely stonewalled by a Dalek-sounding IT service manager, who told me it wasn't a priority and refused to do anything with my problem until I'd submitted the online report. Fuming, I punched the details into the online tool, which took almost half an hour. The Rock had tentatively approached, but on witnessing the vicious stabbing of the keyboard she simply slid a note under my nose and scurried away. It was details of another similar complaint.

I left a message on The GPS's voicemail so that he was aware of the issue.

I phoned IT for an update at 11.30am, 12.15 pm, 1pm, 2pm and 2.30 pm. Was told each time: "We're looking into it."

The GPS phoned. "Have you resolved this one, Kate?"

Am I in charge of IT now? "No. The number of complaints is rising and I can't get anything out of the IT guys."

"Why not?" he snapped. "You need to be more persistent; get some answers."

"But I've tried-"

"You should have escalated the issue, Kate; a lot of time's been wasted. *I'll* phone the Head of IT; try and get some traction on this one."

He'd gone. I couldn't do anything right. I told the guys they'd just have to apologise to the affected customers and tell them we'd call back as soon as we could. If the customer asked when that would be, throw a coughing fit.

A 'Special Edition Newsletter' popped up in my inbox, sent from the Communications team. I was quite excited at the prospect of seeing how the Cycle for Michael photos had turned out; it should give the Cheltenham site some great PR. I opened the newsletter to reveal numerous colourful shiny pictures of The Big Cheese: grinning like a loon on the exercise bike, arms around Mr and Mrs Moore, hugging little Michael, groping Horsey Helen, pretending to flip burgers ... weren't there any of me? Was that me? *Oh no.* It had been taken close to the horseshoe throwing competition and I was bending down ready to take my turn ... those bloody jogging bottoms! My arse looked ridiculously huge! Had the photographer used an extra wide-angled lens, for Christ's sake? Surely he must have deliberately stretched it on Photoshop? *No way* was it as ginormous as that. I looked at the distribution list; the newsletter had been sent to every single employee at Perypils. True to form, an email pinged in from Big Andy, entitled 'Solar Eclipse blacks out horseshoe competition!'. He wasn't even in the country! I didn't bother to read it.

On Saturday, I drove to my Mum and Dad's to help them sort through some boxes in the loft. I came across a diary I'd kept when I was fourteen. It was full of football results and a detailed analysis of my latest ice-skating movements. God, I was dull, even back then. Shouldn't I have been experimenting with herbal cigarettes or practising French kissing on my Kajagoogoo poster? What would my diary read now? Went to work, it was shite. Removed forty-seven slugs from the garden. Had marmite on toast. And a Crunchie. Said goodnight to a potted plant. Dreamt I was savaged by a Great White (shark that is, not Barry). Woke up, went to work. It was shite ...

My mother said, "Your brother's very worried, you know, about the baby."

"I know, Mum. But there's nothing I can do about George and it's not fair of them to ask me to."

"What about your husband, can't he do anything?"

"My husband?"

"Yes, Cedric." *Who the hell is Cedric?* "He knows all about babies, doesn't he? He used to like wearing a nappy."

I looked helplessly at my father who simply shook his head and gently persuaded my mother to go and make a pot of tea.

"That bloody brother of yours," he grumbled, when she'd left the room. "Nothing but trouble that lot he's married into. Bloody idiots, all of them."

"Kirsty's very angry with me, Dad, and I know Georgia's really upset but I can't do anything, I really can't."

"Can't or won't? I'm sure this bloke is bloody useless, Kate but can't you find him something else to do? There must be some sweeping up or something? What about shredding? Getting rid of all those complaints you lot are always hiding."

Yes, ha ha. Even my Dad thought I was in the wrong. Perhaps I was. What the hell was I going to do about George?

On Sunday, the national press actually carried positive articles about Perypils! It was the first time I'd ever witnessed this phenomenon. Admittedly, they weren't the massive spreads they usually devoted to our financial misdemeanours and moral transgressions but there were some good-sized articles under headlines such as "Insurance Company does its best to protect our Michael" and "Corporate greed set aside for day of generosity". There were pictures of The Big Cheese with the Moores, who were smiling gratefully at the camera. I scoured all the papers, both in print version and online, to make sure there weren't any pictures of my arse, but thankfully there weren't. Probably not enough room, even in a broadsheet. There were various descriptions of the Cycle for Michael events held "up and down the country" by Perypils, with Big Cheese quotes, typically: "We've pulled out all the stops to help this wonderful little lad and his devoted family receive the support they need. I have a son myself and I live and breathe family values, as does every member of the Perypils management team. We just hope and pray that together, this country can do enough to save little Michael's life."

I noticed that one paper wished the Moores well, as apparently they had been suffering from a 'mysterious' stomach bug. I bet they were regretting eating their own bodyweight in free burgers at the botulism barby.

I examined the jobs section but couldn't see anything remotely suitable. On the Internet, I searched 'vacant managerial positions' and found an advertisement for an assistant branch manager at Blacks the Chemist in Cheltenham. The annual salary was just £14k! *Are you kidding me?* That was less than half what I currently earned. I'd have to get an evening job too if I was going to cover all my outgoings. Well, I wasn't afraid of hard work and I was rapidly reaching the stage when I'd take anything I could. The minimum-effort job site that magically matched you to your perfect role hadn't quite worked out that way. I'd received a string of calls from various recruitment agencies that all started:

"I've got an exciting opportunity that's just become available! I think you'll be absolutely perfect!"

And usually ended:

"Have you actually read my CV? I haven't got any experience in arranging mortgages/refunding PPI/selling bathroom appliances/engineering/interpreting Polish-"

I spent the rest of my Sunday completing an online application for the assistant manager position at Blacks the Chemist. If I was successful at least I would never run short of facial hair remover.

It was a bit of a bollocks of a Monday. The weather was wet and windy, guaranteeing a surge of calls for flood damage, holes in roofs and from idiots who'd driven their cars into fords while saying to themselves: "I've never seen that stick thingy say five feet before."

Complaints were still coming in from customers whose premiums were incorrect and some of those who were waiting for us to call them back were beginning to phone in for a second time. Even a roasting from The GPS hadn't produced a response from IT, at least not one that was decipherable. The root cause appeared to be the server, which kept "falling over". Someone told me the server "does a dump every Saturday", which was undeniably true.

The poor guys on the phones, or the punchbags as The Rock referred to them, were fed up listening to complaints they could do nothing about. Morale was on the floor. Even the promise of an additional free dress down day this month did little to rally spirits. One exception was TLS George, who for a man possibly about to lose his job, seemed positively chipper. Someone from Bridgend was coming to do his hearing tomorrow. I'd dropped several unsubtle hints such as "Are you sure you've considered *all* your options, George?" in the hope that he would resign with his references intact, thus avoiding screwing up the rest of his life, but he'd simply replied, "Yep, fink so."

I arrived home late to find a message from Big Andy on my voicemail. "Bloody hell, Kate, have you seen the news? If not, switch the telly on or go online. Now!"

Mystified, I turned on the BBC news channel. They were discussing high street sales. I was about to try the Internet, when a white headline ran across the bottom of the screen: "Michael Moore's parents arrested for shameful scam". Noooooooo! No no no! Surely not?

I sunk down onto the sofa and called Big Andy. "Oh Andy, please don't tell me the Moores have done something stupid with all the money that's been raised for Michael's treatment? They can't have."

"It's worse than that, old girl," Big Andy sounded unusually gloomy. "There's nothing wrong with Michael. Never has been."

"*What?*" My head swam as the news article changed to show two bulky figures with track suit tops covering their heads being led into a police station through a howling pack of jostling reporters, flash bulbs popping all around them.

"They made the whole thing up. They reckon Mrs Moore saw a similar story on Lorraine and thought she'd try her luck. Paid someone to produce a bunch of fake medical documents as proof, moved areas so they wouldn't be recognised and probably promised all the kids a trip to Disneyland if they played along..." he tailed off, too depressed to even finish his sentence.

"But how could they possibly think they'd get away with it?" I was incredulous. "The truth was bound to come out."

"I don't suppose they figured on it getting this big. I bet they thought they'd raise a bit of cash, have a nice trip to the States, stuff themselves with nachos at Planet Hollywood then come back and tell everyone Michael was cured."

"*Jesus.* What the hell is the Chief Exec going to say?"

"Nothing a lady like you would want to hear, that's for sure. Another bloody calamitous error of judgement; I think he's staring down the barrel of the gun this time. And after the scandal with Brett the Bonking Bronco, well, shareholders are getting twitchy."

"But who could ever replace him? Are either of the Krays still alive?"

"Only Jeremy Clarkson comes close."

We said our goodbyes and I sat for a while on the sofa, trying to take in the news. I saw I had another message; it was from The Ex.

"Hi Kate, it's me. I expect you're working late as usual! Some things never change, do they! I wondered if you were around on Saturday morning for a cup of coffee? It would be really great to catch up. How about Costa's? About eleven-ish? I really hope you can make it. Let me know. Bye."

What should I do? Did I want to 'catch up' with him?

Part of me was curious about his life and what he'd been up to but is it really healthy to know too much about your ex? Isn't it better just to make a clean break? I'd stopped hacking into his Facebook account months ago. It wouldn't hurt to go for a quick coffee; at least we could get the divorce sorted. I'd tell him yes. I wandered to the French windows and peered out into the dusk. The camellia had blown over. It looked back at me as if to say "Forget it. Just let me lie here."

David, a manager from Bridgend, arrived to undertake TLS George's hearing. He was short and dark, with thick round glasses that gave him an endearingly owlish expression. I was glad to escape from the department and the uproar over Michael Moore and his family. Everyone, somewhat understandably, wanted their donations back and no one seemed at all relieved that little Michael wasn't actually going to die. There was no guidance from the Communications team, so I just had to bat all their questions away. David said one of the other managers at Bridgend had taken part in a sponsored waxing where you could pay to literally tear a strip off him. They'd done his entire body. "What, even his-"

"Every single nook and crevice! He was in absolute agony all day. Bet he feels a bit of a tit now."

I provided David with George's file and a short summary of the action I had taken to date, which he absorbed with cheerful competence.

"Thanks Kate, it all looks very thorough. What were your own thoughts on the potential outcome?"

He blinked at me, clearly asking without actually asking: "What do *you* want to do with him?"

I swallowed, hard. This was my chance to save George. I

could say that I thought he should be given another chance; that if you scraped away the badly applied St Tropez tan and fought a path through the fug of Hugo Boss, there lurked a hopeful little glimmer of talent and that if he would only take his mind off his todger for five minutes, he could actually turn his performance around.

But, regretfully, it simply wouldn't be true. George was so dense light bent around him, and in all honesty, he should have been turfed out long ago. I sighed. "I'd rather just let the hearing run its course, David; I've every confidence you'll reach the right conclusion."

I went to see how George was feeling about the impending meeting and to check that he had actually prepared for it, but I couldn't find him anywhere. Hissing Cyn told me, eyes glinting, that she thought he'd gone out to the car park to have a look at his mate's new "wheels". She added, pointedly, that had been at least half an hour ago. *Hmmm.* I looked on his desk, but it was the usual hotchpotch of reports, file notes, crushed Red Bull cans, crisp packets, Pac Man stress ball (stress! ha ha!) and apart from some Listerine breath strips, there were no obvious signs of preparation for an imminent, life-changing meeting. He *had* remembered it was today, hadn't he?

I returned to my desk to tackle my ever-expanding inbox and was halfway through deleting the 'Your mailbox is full' ones when I saw George saunter into the department, happily chatting away on his iPhone, which he knew wasn't allowed. The boy really was unbelievable. At the appointed hour of eleven o'clock, I went to collect him from his desk, interrupting his viewing of the BBC News. He smoothed his hair down, tucked his shirt in and picked up his iPhone, jumping when I snapped, "Leave that bloody thing alone George!" I felt a small flicker of hope when he picked up a pink cardboard folder but that was extinguished when I realised it was far too thin to hold anything remotely useful in the way of his defence. In fact, I would say it was empty.

I walked with George to the meeting room and introduced him to David, who couldn't help expressing surprise that George didn't have anyone to represent him. He really was a hearing manager's dream - unaccompanied, unprepared and as thick as a brick. I closed the door and, with a massive feeling of doom, left them to it.

This was always a horrid time, waiting for the outcome of a formal meeting, knowing that one of your colleagues may be about to take the walk of shame. In full sight of everyone, they'd have to pack up all their belongings, sign out of their systems, hand over their keys and be escorted from the building. It was a cringing, ground-swallow-me-up few minutes that seemed to last for hours. Just after midday, my mobile rang.

"Kate? It's David. I've adjourned the hearing and sent George to lunch. Could you come to the meeting room?"

I arrived to find him looking dishevelled; he'd loosened his tie and tufts of hair were sticking up. "You'd better sit down," he said wearily when he saw me. I sat opposite him, the chair still warm from George's buttocks.

"How did it go?"

"Hmmm," he removed his glasses and rubbed his eyes before putting them back on and picking up his notes. "Did you know George suffers from OCD?"

"*What?*"

"Yes, he says he has an obsessive compulsive disorder

which affects his ability to manage his time and perform some of his duties effectively."

He looked across at me. "Your mouth is open."

"But, he's never mentioned that before! Never ever! What is this disorder?"

"He says he has to do tasks several times over, such as checking he's turned the gas off or locked his front door - he has to do everything five times-"

"He can't even count to five!"

"And it's the same at work, where it takes him five times as long to complete some of his tasks than the other managers. He has to read everything five times, apparently and that affects his performance. He says he can't work extra hours to catch up as he has to leave on the stroke of five o'clock every night; it's part of his disorder."

It was my turn to rub my eyes now - in sheer disbelief. "David, this is utter bullshit!"

"Yes," he sighed, "but I'm afraid I couldn't break him down and get him to admit that. I tried my best, but he stood firm. So now, I've got to go through the occupational health team and that will mean reports, assessments ... well, you know the drill. It's going to take a while."

"Jesus Christ, what a load of bloody hairy buggery bollocks! *That lying little shit.*"

David couldn't resist a grin. "You're not suffering from Tourette's, are you? That's covered by the DDA too, you know! Don't worry Kate, I'm absolutely certain George's doctor won't support his claims, so we will nail him, but I'm afraid it won't be very quick."

I saw David to the canteen as he was desperate for a bacon sandwich before he tackled the M4 and on my way back to the department, I saw George emerging from the Gents toilets. I nearly called, "Have you wiped your arse five times, George?" but I just managed to stop myself. He was no longer The Lazy Shit. He was now The Lazy Crafty Shit. And he wasn't quite as stupid as he made out.

CHAPTER TWENTY

I felt incredibly uneasy. I was sitting in Costa Coffee, waiting for The Ex, trying to sip a frothy cappuccino without disturbing my carefully applied lipstick. I'd had another restless night, unsure if this meeting was really such a good idea and as a result I'd had to plaster on a significant amount of make-up to cover the dark circles and pasty complexion. What was I doing here? Having coffee with a man who'd cheated on me, lied to me and made me feel useless and worthless - would Hillary Clinton be sitting here, wasting a morning on someone like that? Maybe that was a bad example. Michelle Obama, then. I ought to be strong like her – I should have more respect for myself, after all, I didn't need him in my life anymore. I was supposed to be Robust Woman! I started to get up to leave but it was too late, he was here, striding towards me with a big beaming smile. "Hi! No, no, don't get up, I'll get them in, shall I? Are you having your usual?"

I smiled weakly and nodded, sinking back down into my chair. I watched him as he stood in the queue. He was wearing those sandy chinos again but this time he'd teamed them with a pale blue shirt and there was no sign of those hideous deck shoes. Meeting up with him was like putting on a really old unfashionable outfit; it felt like I still had yesterday's knickers on. Were people looking at me? I really thought they were. I was put in mind of the time when, as a teenager, I'd gone into town dressed as Dexy's Midnight

Runners. I was wearing dungarees over a moth-eaten, baggy jumper with a rag tied around my head and I had crimped and back-combed my hair to within an inch of its life. I can still recall my friend begging me not to go out in public like that but I ignored her. I shuddered, remembering the staring, nudging, pointing, howls of laughter... I never got things quite right. And then there was that Adam Ant Tippex disaster...

Enough. Why do I spend so much time dwelling on the negative aspects of my life? I lifted my chin up and forced a bright smile as he returned with the coffees. "I got you a Biscotti to dunk," he said, waving it at me. "I know how much you like them." He'd clearly forgotten I'd broken a tooth on the last one he'd bought me.

"Cheers."

He took a sip of his Americano, watching me over the rim of his cup. "You look very well." *Did he mean fat?* "Glowing, in fact."

So would you be after five coatings of bronzing powder. "I'm fine," I said airily. "I've been taking care to eat very healthily and have started this exercise regime, you know, jogging and er, er yoga. It's made me feel like a new person."

"Yoga? Really? Well, I'm very impressed, I must say. It's supposed to be good for your spiritual well being, isn't it? I've been thinking about it myself actually; where do you go for your yoga?"

"The village hall," I said, anxious to change the subject very quickly. "Are you playing much golf?"

His face clouded. "No, not as much as I'd like. And I need a new set of clubs now, after Chloë discovered the storm drain outside the flats by the river. She liked to put things down it..." he broke off, shaking his head sadly.

"It can't be easy," I said, swallowing a smirk. "Not in a small flat with a toddler. Have you thought about getting somewhere bigger?"

He stirred his coffee, not looking at me. "No. There's no need now, anyway. Debbie and I, well, it's over." There was an uncomfortable silence. I didn't know how to respond. He glanced up. "I told her I'd been to see you and we had this huge row; she accused me of still having feelings for you. And, when I didn't deny it, we decided there wasn't much point in going on. She's fearfully upset, of course and I feel like a prize bastard, but what could I do?"

He waited for me to say something but I was trying to absorb the fact that he still had feelings for me. What sort of feelings did he still have? Pity? Guilt? Nausea?

"I really have fucked everything up, haven't I?" He looked up at me again but I wasn't about to disagree. "Life's not turned out to be at all how I'd imagined it would be."

I still didn't know what to say so I kept quiet. "How about you?" he realised he was going to have to ask me a direct question to get a response. "Are you happy?"

Ah, the killer question. How to answer? Truthfully? Or a yoga-filled crock of shite? I shrugged. "I didn't expect my life to be like this, no. I thought I'd be living in a lovely house, basking in financial security, with my only dilemma being having to choose red or white. But there's no point in looking backwards and feeling sorry for yourself, is there? You've only to turn on the news to realise how lucky you are. If you've got a roof over your head and you're not rummaging around in bins at the back of Asda then you're blessed."

He raised his eyebrows. "Wow. I think all that yoga must be filling you with positive energy! Perhaps I really should give it a go." I nodded innocently as he returned to his studious stirring. "Do you ever think about what it would be like to go back? You know, going back to how things were?"

Warning! Danger! Alert, alert! "Like I said; there's no point in looking backwards."

"Isn't there?" He held my eyes in a sad, sincere stare. "Don't you ever feel we gave up on things too quickly?"

Maybe. I had slung him out the moment I'd become aware he'd done the dirty on me. "I mean," he continued, "we've never even talked about it, have we? Not properly."

Was he expecting us to talk about it now? In Costa Coffee? I noted that the middle-aged, poker-faced couple seated at the next table, less than two feet away, had fallen silent. Were they listening? "I'm not sure what we'd gain by raking over it all now. But it wasn't just your affair, was it? You weren't happy with the way things were, you weren't happy with me. You know you weren't."

"No, that's not true." He said this with some passion but I noticed he wasn't looking me in the eye. "I think we just drifted apart a bit; stopped communicating. We should have made more effort to spend time together - we hardly ever went out just the two of us, did we? It was always with others."

That was a fair comment. I shifted uncomfortably in my seat. "I really don't understand why you're saying all this. We've done all the hard stuff and we've gone our separate ways. It's too late to go back. We've just got the formality of the divorce and then-"

"About that," he said. "Are you sure you still want to? Get divorced, I mean? Because I don't."

"It's too late," I repeated, feebly.

"It's not! I never wanted us to split up in the first place. Can't we put the brakes on for a bit? Say you'll at least think about it? You want to be sure it's what you really want. And I'm not convinced that it is."

He looked at me anxiously, trying to read my face. "What do you think?"

I didn't know what to think! I turned to the ear-wigging couple next to us. "What do *you* think?"

The man buried his face in his cup leaving his wife to stutter that she didn't know what I meant as her face turned crimson. They gulped down their coffees and scurried out. The Ex was chuckling. "You don't change, do you? But maybe we should discuss this in private. Perhaps I could come round to yours one evening?"

He could tell from my wary look that he'd pushed things a bit too far. "No, no, that might be a bit much. But how about dinner? We could go for a nice meal and have a proper talk. What about Chives? We've always liked it there, haven't we?"

I loved Chives, especially their house speciality, spicy meatballs. I hadn't been there for ages. It was tempting. I was trying to think how I should respond when he exclaimed, "Oh, I nearly forgot! I picked up this leaflet when I was at the doctors; it's all about dementia and support groups for family members. It's written in a really positive manner so I thought you might find it useful. Or your Dad might. It tells you what benefits are available and where you can go to get help and advice."

"Thank you." I was genuinely touched. Was this a new, more considerate him? I tucked the leaflet into my handbag. "I've never known you visit the doctors! Why were you there?"

He fiddled with his spoon. "It's a bit difficult to talk about to be honest, but I don't mind telling you, I know you'll keep it to yourself. I've been feeling pretty down and it got to the point where I needed to talk to someone about it. My doctor prescribed me with anti-depressants."

"Gosh." That was shocking news; he'd never so much as taken an aspirin before. "Well, if it's any consolation, you don't come across as being depressed; in fact, you seem quite chipper."

"I always was a good actor!" *Ain't that the truth!* He realised the irony of that statement and swiftly moved on to talk about his work, which was the usual stories of lunatics and gorps whose homes he turned up to in the hope of terrifying them into some life cover or bamboozling them into placing their life savings into intricate 'goodbye money' unit trust funds. He said things were going really well, despite the recession. He didn't ask about my work; he never had shown any interest in it. I suspected he blamed my long working hours for driving us apart, conveniently overlooking the fact that he'd chosen to commit adultery while I was working the long hours. Or it may have been because whenever he'd asked me "How's work?" I would simply reply "Shit" so that hadn't exactly encouraged further exploration or discussion.

I accepted a third cup of coffee and we found ourselves having a chuckle over 'old times', which consisted primarily of Karen and James' drunken exploits, the barking mad members of our families and the neighbours at our old property, who were extremely reserved and religious but hadn't done anything to deserve the monstrous Pope snowman we built in their front garden when they'd gone out, complete with a mitre made from a Cornflakes box and a 'For Sale' sign for a cross. I had to call a halt when I saw that my car parking time was about to expire. We both stood up and he looked at me anxiously. "So what about Chives, Kate? Please say yes; it's been so nice to see you and talk properly without bickering. I feel so much better about everything."

Did I want to? I just wasn't sure. But this hadn't been too bad, in fact, it had turned out to be quite fun. And there were spicy meatballs to consider ... "Yes, okay," I said, carefully. "But let's leave it a couple of weeks, shall we? I don't want to go rushing into things."

"Good idea." Had he just agreed with me for once in his life? His happy pills were working wonders! "I know it's a lot to take in. I'll give you a call, then? We'll arrange something?"

I nodded, taking a large gulp of fresh air as we stepped outside and squinted up at the blue sky. "Ah brilliant, the sun's come out!"

"It's about time! That reminds me, I've got to get some new sunglasses."

"Oh, what's happened to your Aviators?"

"Storm drain," he replied, gloomily. Clearly the Devil Child had taste.

I was reading the Sunday papers in my M&S sleep suit of pink cotton shorts and vest top, with James Martin propped up on my iPad as I half-watched Saturday Kitchen on BBC iPlayer. James was doing his clever drizzly thing with sugar syrup and a rolling pin. I had tried to do it once; two years later I was still having to scratch brown bits off the utensils.

I finally reached the financial pages and there was

another article on Perypils. The headline read:

Mis-quoting, mis-selling – customers give Perypils a miss!

Beleaguered insurance company, Perypils, have hit another low note with their customers. It seems the company have been mis-quoting their premiums, making customers believe their insurance is cheaper than it actually is. Andrew Byrne from Reading told us: "I phoned Perypils for a quote to insure my Volvo and was quoted a monthly premium of £24 which I thought was a really good deal and I accepted it. When I received my documents, a premium of £42 was quoted! I immediately called Perypils but had to wait 45 minutes for my call to be answered. When I finally got through to somebody, they told me the first quote was the correct one, then they said "Oh no, hang on, I think it's the second one." When I asked why I'd been given an incorrect quote over the telephone, they replied "Well, the telephone quote was more of an estimate." They haven't a clue what they're doing and I've decided to cancel the policy. I'm still waiting for the premium to be refunded and compensation for wasting my time. I've written to their complaints department but they haven't even acknowledged my letter."

We have received several letters from other customers, all telling a similar story. Is this a cynical attempt to exploit their long-suffering customers or yet another example of poor managerial controls at Perypils?

Ouch. This was all IT's bloody fault but I knew it was going to fall at my door on Monday morning. *Beleaguered* company? That didn't sound good. The Communications team were always telling us how well we were doing; even

when the papers announced our annual losses, the team
would point out that if you looked at the pre-tax forecasted
figures and deducted the provisions set aside for refunds of
mis-sold policies, then added them all back in again and
multiplied by the first number you thought of, Perypils had
actually made a healthy profit. Surely they wouldn't have got
it so wrong?

Monday

I received a voicemail message from The GPS saying he
would be down first thing to discuss Sunday's newspaper
article and the meeting was a 'diary crash'. He also said he
would be bringing someone from the executive team with
him. Oh great, the heavy mob. I could expect a horse's head
in my bed tonight, then.

I took The Rock and The MC with me to the meeting
room, hoping for safety in numbers. We were armed with
masses of data that showed the increase in calls and
correspondence and had numerous examples of customers'
complaints. The GPS was already there, sitting next to a very
stern, robust-looking woman who was in the mid-thirty
range. She had short dark hair, cropped into a helmet shape
and she was wearing an oversized black trouser suit. The GPS
introduced her as "Sandra from the executive team", as if that
were some sort of job title. I smiled at her but she just stared
stonily back. *Brilliant. Another one straight out of the Perypils
charisma gene pool.* The GPS said Sandra would be working in
Cheltenham over the next couple of months to help us
overcome the problems with the Online Quotation system. I
nearly said she should block out the next twenty years but I
bit my tongue.

"Now." The GPS produced a report from his black folder of doom. Here we go - another set of figures he's spent all weekend analysing and which will prove beyond any reasonable doubt that I am totally shit at my job. Why not just put a black cap on as well? "The Chief Executive is extremely concerned by the sharp increase in the number of concerns that are being recorded."

We looked at each other. "But that's because of the quotation issue," ventured The Rock.

The GPS shook his head. "No. Those aren't concerns and shouldn't be recorded as such."

"But they are concerns," said The MC in bewilderment. "The customers are extremely unhappy about it and they're complaining, I mean, they're concerning, no, I mean they're concerned."

"No," The GPS spoke very slowly, as if he was talking to the infirm. "They are *comments*, not concerns. The customers are simply advising us that their telephone quote is different to their written quote."

"Well, they're certainly advising us in no uncertain terms, Roger," I said. "Surely the definition of a concern is when a customer tells us they are unhappy."

"No, not always, the customer can make a comment about a product or service; it doesn't necessarily mean they're unhappy."

I glanced over at Sandra to see if she had an opinion, but she was scribbling away on a note-pad and didn't look up. I noticed she had extremely large hands. Strangler's hands...

"So, are you saying that we shouldn't be recording concerns about the quotation issue as complaints?" The MC asked, sounding confused.

"They're not complaints," The GPS corrected her. "They're comments."

"Would it help to look at an example, do you think?" I plucked a customer's letter from the top of the pile and read it aloud:

Dear Cretins

You are either a bunch of lying bastards or a shower of useless wankers. First you told me my premium was £24.45 and now you tell me it's £45.24! Which is it? Why don't you just pick any number you bloody well like? Tried to call but no bugger answered. Doubt you'll read this as you're too busy ignoring all your other customers. I'm going back to Norwich Union. They were completely shit but you've made them look fucking fantastic.

Yours sincerely
Steven Price

I looked up at The GPS. "I don't know about you, but Mr Price's *comment* seems a little on the negative side to me. Maybe it's just the way I've interpreted his letter, but I get the impression he's a little unhappy with us."

Oh no, the lips had thinned! *Not the lips, not the lips!* "The decision's been taken, Kate and I expect your full support. They are not to be recorded in the department's concerns data and I need you to go through last month's figures and remove every comment on the quotation issue. I'll need the revised set by tomorrow morning as the figures have to be re-submitted to head office."

I eyed him with huge dislike. He knew full well that exercise would take me hours.

"I'll help you with that, Kate," said The Rock quickly, sensing trouble. "Luckily I've nothing else planned for this evening!"

I smiled at her gratefully but I felt like screaming. This was ridiculous; a total farce. We were deliberately fudging the figures, making it look like the number of complaints to Perypils hadn't increased. But they had! What was the point in trying to hide it? Surely the fact that customers were complaining should be a serious call to action? A lever to force IT up off their arses or their elbows and do something about it. In the meantime, my poor guys had no choice but to absorb all the blows being rained down on them.

I turned to Sandra again. "So what are your plans to support us with this one then, Sandra? I expect you read the article in the newspaper so you'll know the issue is causing us a great deal of pain; we're struggling to answer calls quickly because of the increase in volume and a backlog of complaint letters has built up. It's a really poor customer experience."

The GPS swiftly stepped in. "Sandra will be making a full assessment of the situation and implementing an action plan on the back of her findings." She nodded fiercely but looked down at her flat, ugly shoes. Was she mute? "I've told her she can expect the full co-operation of the management team." He shot me a black, warning look. What had he told Sandra about me? "Kate's days are numbered so just dig out a bit more shit on her, could you, so I can bury her even quicker." I was more than capable of digging my own grave. I couldn't seem to stop shovelling.

Chapter Twenty-One

I found Sandra a desk as far away from mine as possible but within earshot of The Rock, who promised me she would listen in to all her conversations. I was deeply suspicious; why was she really here? To spy on the site? Was she one of the evil flying monkeys whose job it was to recommend closures or force hundreds of redundancies? Or was it to replace me? Quite possibly The GPS was warming her up to step into my shoes so she could see the site through to closure. She was dressed a little like the grim reaper; she had probably culled thousands of sites before us. I asked her where she wanted to start.

"Um, I'm not really sure..."

"Well, do you want to listen into some calls or have a look at some complaint letters?"

"Oh yes."

"Which?"

"S-sorry?"

"Which one do you want to do? Listen to calls or look at letters?"

"Oh yes."

Jesus, was she being deliberately moronic or was it all part of the act to catch me out? Break me down, make me lose my temper so that I'd lash out and she could report back to The GPS that I was, as he suspected, becoming unhinged? Perhaps she could sense I was close to taking out the whole department with an AK-47 before turning it on myself. At least she could claim she'd reduced the headcount.

After I'd deposited her with The MC, I returned to my desk to find a text from my brother.

"Hi Sis wud u lik to cum 4 t on Sun? Kirstys bday. She agreed make efort & b nice"

Oh God. First Boudica descends on me and now I have to face Carrie.

When I saw Sandra leave the department, I whipped over to The MC. "How's Sandra been getting on?" I hissed.

"She's hardly said a word," she whispered back, glancing fearfully over her shoulder. "She seems to be reading every letter really carefully and making lots of notes. She sat for a while, too, and just stared at everyone from behind her fringe; the team feel quite intimidated by her. They've already nicknamed her Darth Vader."

Hmmm. Was she making notes on the complaints or on the team? I walked nonchalantly over to her desk and was just trying to read what she'd written on her note-pad when she appeared at my side.

"Oh, Sandra, there you are!" I beamed a huge smile trying to cover up my awkwardness at being caught red-handed. "I was just wondering how you've been getting on."

She seemed taken aback by my over-friendly tone. "Oh yes, good thanks. Making progress. Lots of progress. Um, I was just about to go for a coffee; would you like to join me?"

So that was her game, was it? Pretend to be my friend and lull me into a false sense of security in the hope that I'd confide in her about what a ghastly tool The GPS was or utter some teeny weeny indiscretion about the company being a bunch of bastards. *They were good these head office vultures.* Well, she'd have to get up earlier than this to catch me out. I accompanied her down to the canteen where the staff were busy getting ready to serve the lunches and weren't impressed at having to stop to make two cappuccinos. As Sandra was paying, I ordered a large one. I wouldn't normally do that but bugger her - she was trying to screw me so I was going to screw her. *Small victories.*

We sat down at a table by the window that overlooked the car park. It was raining again. She stirred her coffee very slowly but as she didn't say anything, I attempted to strike up a non-work related conversation.

"Whereabouts do you live, Sandra? Near here?"

"No, Nantwich."

"Oh, nice. That's a bit of a trek every day though, isn't it?"

"They're putting me up in a hotel during the week."

I bet they are. I couldn't even order a box of staples without getting it signed off by twenty different accountants but there was no expense spared when the company sensed a kill. She was probably staying somewhere lovely, like the Ellenborough Park, all beams and sumptuous bed linen and wrought iron baths. I bet their sheets didn't need scraping nor the soap de-pubing. I'd had to stay in a Travelodge when I'd been up to Manchester for a two-day course. It was about forty miles from the site and right on the M6. A more depressing place I cannot describe. Apart from, perhaps, the Shitall Chef next door with its legendary scrambled eggshells.

"Do you live alone or have you got a partner?" I asked, desperately trying to keep the conversation going.

"I used to live with my mother." More concentrated stirring of the coffee. "But she died." To my horror, she started to cry, flapping her chunky hands in front of her face saying, "I'm sorry, I'm sorry, I didn't mean to do this."

I fumbled up my sleeve and produced a tissue. "Here you go, it's clean. I'm so sorry about your mum."

Sandra dabbed at her eyes. I noticed, too late, that the tissue wasn't clean. I'd forgotten I'd used it this morning to wipe red lipstick off The Drain's nose after he'd left his glasses lying around unattended again. When Sandra put the tissue down, her eyes were smudged with bright red rings. I couldn't bring myself to tell her.

"I'm so sorry about this, I just can't seem to get over it. It's this time of year, I think. It brings it all back."

"Oh, I see. When did you lose your mother?"

"It's been eleven years now."

Eleven years? "Oh, right. Well, I guess there are some things that you never really get over."

"My father was a very cruel man, you know."

"Was he?" *Why are you telling me this?*

"Yes. She had a terrible life with him, just terrible. When he left we were so happy; it was just the three of us, me, my mum and my sister. The Three Musketeers we called ourselves! Of course, he left my mother penniless; we never had holidays or treats like the other children did and our clothes were always covered in patches and we had to stand in the queue for free school dinners which was just so *humiliating*."

She was crying again. I looked round in despair. Big Andy was picking up a sandwich so I tried to wave him over but he noted the tears and gave us a wide berth, disappearing rapidly through the swing doors. *Git.* I patted Sandra's meaty hand whilst she told me, between sobs, how she was horribly bullied at school. I had no idea how to respond. Why would someone you'd known for about five seconds want to tell you such deeply personal things? Why? It must be a ploy, a way of drawing someone in by confiding in them; she wanted me to feel flattered that she'd chosen to share something so personal in the hope that I would then confide in her. She was good, I give her that. The tears were real too; she wasn't even peeling an onion.

I had so much I needed to be getting on with but I could hardly chirp "Oh well, hey ho, must crack on!" I was trapped. I watched the raindrops hit the window and roll down, imagining myself somewhere miles away, outside in the fresh air, running across wild, open countryside with nothing around me, perhaps stopping for a quick roll-around with Cain Dingle, the modern day Heathcliff. I wouldn't even moan about getting covered in mud and twigs. It was over an hour before she ran out of steam, and realising I wasn't going to break, she agreed we should return to the department. She told me how grateful she was to me and thanked me for being such a great listener. I nearly said "Sorry, what was that?" but stopped myself. I could match her acting skills. I did suggest she visit the Ladies to "fix her eyes"; I couldn't leave her looking like a vampire for the rest of the day, tempting though it was.

Bridgend David emailed to let me know that he had sent George's medical request forms through to Occupational Health and they would be seeking a doctor's report. I'd been keeping a close eye on TLCS George, but he seemed the same as ever. I still hadn't mentioned the baby and neither had he; I wasn't sure if anyone knew he was going to be a father. His team's performance showed little sign of improvement and although he hadn't had any further absences, he was frequently AWOL from the department. When challenged about where he'd been it was always, "I had to see someone in Concerns" or "there was a customer at reception". Where did he really go? Was there genuinely something wrong with him?

Saturday

I was sitting with Karen at her breakfast bar, as we munched our way through a batch of slightly burnt Welsh cakes she'd made for Tom Jones day at school. James was out playing golf. She shrieked when I relayed my conversation with The Ex.

"The bloody cheek of him! Saying he wants you back after what he did to you; has he no shame at all?"

"It wasn't all his fault, you know. There's no excuse for what he did, but I knew things weren't right between us and I chose to ignore them. I chose to ignore *him* most of the time."

"*Kate!* I can't believe you're even considering getting back with him-"

"I'm not! But, he said he still had feelings for me-"

"The only feeling he should be getting is your boot up his backside! You can't be that desperate, Kate. Is it because you're lonely? Can't work the broadband? Sexually frustrated? I could lend you James if you like, we're going through a dry spell. He'd shag a plank of wood if you drilled a hole in it."

"It's not about sex! It's about, well, *familiarity*, I suppose." I saw Karen pull a face. "It's just so damned difficult on your own, Kazza, you don't appreciate it when you're inside a nice safe relationship bubble. I didn't know how hard it was going to be. And it's not just the scary one salary thing, although that's terrifying enough when you think you're about to get the bullet. There's no one to share your day with; if you see something on the news there's no one to slag the Government off to or moan about how shit The One Show is."

"But there is! There's Facebook! It's wonderful, you can say how you're feeling or what you're doing and all your friends will comment right back. Why won't you use it? What are you so afraid of?"

"Because it's full of banal crap! I'd find it too annoying, I don't want to know what someone had for breakfast or if they didn't sleep very well."

"But that's what people's lives are like! Anyway, it's so much more than that; it keeps you in touch with friends so you can share in their good times and they can support you through the shite times. Look at my page." She flipped open the cover on her iPad and logged in. I peered over her shoulder at her news feed.

First post: "My new clothes line arrives today! I am soooo excited!"

Second post: "Feeling very lonely I miss my gawjus boyfriend so much!"

Third post: "Sometimes those who fly solo have the strongest wings."

Fourth post: "Andrew Hopkins likes Andrex".

Fifth post: "You can't put limits on your goals, the more you dream the further you will get."

Sixth post: "OMG, I can't believe that just happened!"

The feed updated as Simon Budden 'checked himself in' at a service station on the M40, letting us know he was getting petrol.

"Bugger me Kazza, how do you keep from running straight into the traffic? I couldn't wade through that drivel every day. And those twattish sanctimonious quotes! What do they even mean?"

"Hmmm," she tapped her fingernails on the breakfast bar. "You might be right. Perhaps Twitter would suit you more."

"No!"

"But you're going to become so isolated, Kate! You'll lose all your confidence and ability to interact with other people - you're going to turn into Rainman. Well, if you're determined not to do the social media thing, at least let's try online dating."

"Not this again," I groaned. "I don't want to! It's so embarrassing; what if some of my team saw me on there? I'll be an absolute laughing stock at work."

"Nonsense." To my horror, Karen started to search for online dating sites. "Everyone does it these days, it's how many people meet their partners and no one bats an eyelid. Here's one - it's called Shagaholic.com. Cuts straight to the chase, doesn't it? No? What about this one, then; it's one of the most popular and it says it's free to register."

"But I don't want to!"

She grinned at me. "Come on; let's go and have a liquid lunch and then we'll come back and give it a whirl. Nothing ventured nothing gained! Even a blind pig finds an acorn once in a while. If you don't meet the love of your life you can go back to counting toothpicks and I'll never mention it again. What do you say?"

"Oh crap."

Two bottles of Chardonnay later and giggling stupidly, we swayed precariously on our bar stools in the kitchen as Karen attempted to register my details on the site 'eDates.com'. She was having difficulties focussing on the iPad and kept pressing the wrong things, so it took an absolute age and the air turned blue.

"Right, profile - let's go." She tapped away. "I am outgoing, fun-loving and have a very bubbly personality."

"You're making me sound like an air-head!"

"Men can't stand a grumpy boots, Kate, you've got to pretend to be frivolous." She continued to type. "I have a G-S-O-H and my interests include..." She looked up at me, pursing her lips, then "salsa dancing-"

"I've never been salsa dancing!"

"Alright, I'll just put dancing, then; they'll think you're all bendy. I know, I'll put *double-jointed*, that should do the trick. Also, wine tasting - that will filter out the bearded real ale saddos - musical theatre-"

"Musical theatre?"

"It will make you seem intellectual! Anyway, it's true, you love the Wizard of Oz. And cooking-"

"I can't stand cooking!"

"Yes, but men love home cooking, it reminds them of their mothers. Finally, I'm B-N-W-O-T-S."

I stared at her. "What the hell does that stand for?"

Karen rubbed her chin thoughtfully. "I'm not sure, but it's written on all the lonely hearts ads so it must be important."

We waded through questions on my social dependency, self-confidence, family orientation ... Karen finally snapped, declaring, "I've no time for this psycho-babble bollocks! All anyone needs to know is woman, forty-three, not great at parties but good tits." She scrolled through her Flickr site to find a suitable photo of me to upload, eventually settling on one of me clutching a glass of wine and laughing drunkenly into the camera. It wasn't great, but it was the only one where I didn't have at least three chins and she did manage to Photoshop out the piece of lettuce that was stuck in my front teeth.

We thought that once we'd completed the registration, we would finally be able to view the available 'matches', but for some reason we weren't able to, so with much frustration, we decided to call it a day and when James returned from golf, we made him drive us back to the wine bar.

Another Sunday, another fuzzy head, wine-bloated stomach and self-loathing seizure. A semi-cold shower had done its best to revive me and as I was standing by the kettle in a trance, wondering whether or not a piece of toast would stay down, I felt a cold drip on my head. *What the heck was that?* I looked up just as another drip hit me in the eye. Blinking it away, I saw that water was dripping from the light fitting and a round, damp patch had appeared on the ceiling. Oh God, what now? I figured I was immediately below the shower, so it must be leaking. *Bloody hell.* I trudged despondently up to the bathroom and peered into the narrow shower cubicle but there was nothing immediately obvious. Would it be something small and simple or something big and hairy - and terminally expensive? Was it even safe, or if I took another shower would I plunge straight through the ceiling? Would the dripping water bugger up all the electrics and burn the house to the ground? I'd better put the batteries back in the smoke alarm.

I went downstairs to make a coffee and waited in the kitchen until the dripping had stopped. I knew I was feeling hung-over and grotty, and low blood sugar turned me into a pathetic, self-pitying wretch, but I'd had about enough of the new independent me; it was just too bloody hard. I wanted someone else to share the burden; I wanted someone to look after me, put their arms around me, give me a big hug and say everything would be alright. Then they'd sort out the damp patch so I didn't have to. And maybe give the car a quick wash. I didn't want to be on my own anymore. Had I been too hasty in booting out The Ex the minute I found out about his affair? Many couples managed to weather the storm; perhaps I should have tried harder to get over it. Had I simply taken the easy option? Well, it wasn't very easy now.

I remembered, with a sudden stomach-lurch, that an inebriated Karen had registered me onto an online dating site. I doubted very much that anyone would have responded to my profile, but perhaps I should check, just in case. With great trepidation, I logged into the site. My profile popped up and goodness me! It said I had thirty-three messages waiting! *Thirty-three!* I must be an absolute goddess - I was smoking hot! Thirty-three men wanted to date me and I'd only registered yesterday. They couldn't all be munters and lunatics, could they? Any of them could be The One, my next true love! Or even better - a plumber!

Heart racing, I attempted to open the first message but instead, I was directed to another page which told me in order to view my inbox I had to 'complete my registration'. Confused, I clicked forwards a page and was asked for a payment of £47.99. Woah! The site had said registration was free. I read through the joining instructions again and discovered it was free to register, but if you wanted to actually use the site you had to pay. *What a flipping con.* I knew I should simply delete my profile in protest but there were thirty-three men willing and ready to date me! I was totally torn: was I really going to let the potential perfect partner get away for the sake of £47.99? He who dares ... I fetched my credit card and tapped in the number. When it had been accepted, another button appeared that said "publish profile". I hit it and was told "Congratulations! Your profile is now live on e-Dates.com - your perfect match is just one click away!"

As I was excitedly returning to my inbox, a thought struck me. If I'd only just published my profile, how the hell could thirty-three men have already seen it and messaged me? The answer was, of course, they couldn't. I knew, even as I clicked on the first message, I'd been had. It read "Welcome to e-Dates.com!" The second read "Important information about your registration". And so on. All thirty-three messages were from the company itself. What a stupid, naïve, pea-brained klutz. A red-hot goddess? What a joke. "I'm so sorry," I said to my Mastercard. Oh well, as I'd just kissed goodbye to the best part of fifty quid I may as well have a look at my potential matches. I was about to click on them when a little red love heart started to flash at the bottom of the screen. It said "Live chat! Your match David Zeller wants to chat with you now!" Jesus, was he luring me into one of those Internet chat rooms that you always heard such dreadful things about on the news? I clicked on David Zeller's profile and almost leapt back from the screen. The first thing I saw was his picture and it was such a close-up of his face it was like he was in the room. Unsmiling, dead eyes, long nose - he had restraining order written all over him. I didn't know how to make the red heart stop flashing so I ignored it. He'd been bloody quick off the mark, or did he lurk on the site all day waiting for someone new and unsuspecting to log on?

It seemed I had hundreds of matches. Hmmm. Perhaps I should try some of the filtering options; I'd remove any that didn't provide a phone number, as they were obviously married. Let's try filtering by distance. Here goes - blimey! I was matched to someone less than one mile away! That could be extremely convenient and just think of the saving on fuel costs. I clicked on their profile and up sprung a picture of a young Mexican-looking guy. He had jet black hair, a bushy moustache and was wearing a dazzling yellow waistcoat. His name was Mervyn Antonio Dudman. I looked more closely. Roll forwards thirty years and it could almost be ... it was! It was next door Mervyn. *Oh no.* He would see that I had looked at his profile and he would therefore look at mine and we would both know ... *Christ.* Why was he using such an out of date picture? His profile said he was an 'exotic horticulturist'. He wasn't! He used to work at the Post Office and did a bit of gardening now and then. His middle name wasn't Antonio, it was Arthur. I'd seen it written enough times on his Steam Railway News magazine that always seemed to end up on my doormat. Did everyone lie and exaggerate on these sites? It was hardly a sound foundation on which to build a new relationship. David Zeller was now requesting a video chat with me. I logged out.

I returned from Sainsbury's to find a message from Karen on my answerphone. "Kate! You have to change your dating profile! I've remembered what B-N-W-O-T-S stands for - it's Brand New Without Tags. It's an eBay thing; nothing to do with dating. Sorry."

Great. Any potential dates probably think I'm an inflatable.

I had to be at Stu and Kirsty's for five o'clock. I knew this was Stu's attempt to make the peace and I was grateful to him for trying, but I was extremely apprehensive. What sort of welcome was I going to get from The Bunny Boiler? Was she going to make an effort to be civil or had she already slaughtered a Gloucester Old Spot in preparation?

I'd gone a bit OTT on a present, although I could ill afford to; I'd bought her a silver necklace with a fairy pendant which I thought would match her most recent tattoo and a bottle of pink champagne. I had briefly considered the "To a wonderful sister-in-law" birthday cards but they'd made me feel nauseous so I'd gone for one that had a picture of a smug-looking man doing up his tie, saying, "You know me dear, I always call a spade a sp..." whilst behind him a demented woman is about to crack him over the head with a shovel.

I pulled up outside their mews house with my heart pounding. My Dad's car was parked in the road; that was good. Surely The Bunny Boiler wouldn't kick off in front of my parents? I picked up the sparkly gift bag from the passenger seat and approached the front door, pressing the doorbell. I could hear chatter coming from inside and then I saw my brother's figure approaching.

"Sis!" he exclaimed over-cheerfully. "Come on in."

I stepped into the narrow hallway and stood awkwardly in the doorway to the lounge where everyone was gathered.

My Mum and Dad were sitting on the brown leather sofa with cups of tea and Georgia was seated opposite them on a footstall. She was wearing a purple vest top that was stretched to bursting over her very large bump. She scowled up at me as my parents said their 'Hello's, how are you's'.

"Kirsty's in the kitchen," my brother prompted, sounding anxious. "She's just checking on the quiches."

"Oh, has she been cooking? That's nice."

"No, she's defrosting. Look who's here, love."

As we entered the kitchen, a furious-looking Bunny Boiler swung round from the microwave. "This really is a piece of fucking shit, Stu, we've got to get another one. You know every time I turn it on my ears get really hot? That's not fucking right, is it?" She saw me cowering behind my brother and tried to adjust her demeanour.

"Oh, hello Kate. I didn't know you were here."

"Yes, well, I like to take people unawares!" I gave a nervous snort of laughter. "Happy birthday, Kirsty. Thanks for inviting me round, I really do appreciate it."

She had no option but to soften as I thrust her presents into her arms. She carried them into the lounge to open them and seemed genuinely pleased, putting the necklace on straight away. The card made her roar with laughter, although I saw Stu read it and visibly wince. I squeezed onto the sofa next to my Dad, who muttered far too loudly, "Real bloody leather, this is! How can they afford it? Bloody idiots, spending that sort of money on a settee. Nothing wrong with that old one they had, nothing at all."

"How's work, dear?" asked my mother.

Everything went quiet. I could sense Georgia glaring at me. "Um, well, rubbish as usual!" I stuttered. "My new boss is giving me a hard time and he has this really horrid ginger moustache - he actually looks like a German porn star!"

"Oh, we've suffered enough under the Germans, haven't we dear?"

"Er, yes, I suppose so-"

"Let's eat!" my brother clapped his hands together, making us all jump. "And I'll open some wine, shall I?"

Nooo! Don't give your wife any alcohol! I calculated it would be two glasses before she turned psycho and fetched the pig's blood. We all trooped into the kitchen and helped ourselves to the spread on the table. It was like an Iceland advert; I'd never seen a prawn ring in real life before. My Dad said he "just wanted a bleeding sandwich not this farty foreign rubbish", so I kept him quiet by piling up his plate with a few dozen sausage rolls. I spread some strange-smelling brown paste onto a cracker.

"Georgia made the pâté," Kirsty announced proudly.

"Oh great." I took a bite. It had the most unusually strong taste. "Mmm, lovely," I lied, trying not to retch. "How did you make it?"

Georgia edged over to me. "Squeezed it out of the cat," she hissed, eyes gleaming with spite.

I forced a smile, unsure if she was actually joking or not. "Let me get you some," I said loudly.

"Oh no, you can't eat pâté when you're pregnant," she sounded shocked. "You wouldn't know that, of course. Didn't you ever want children? It's a bit late now though, isn't it? Shame. I expect your mum and dad would have loved grandchildren."

Ouch. A direct hit on my Achilles' heel. Yes, they certainly would have loved them and I'd let them down with my unnatural, unmaternal ways.

"Lucky they've got you as their step-grandchild!" My brother moved in, giving her a big hug. She pulled a puke face. "You and baby bump, of course. So you'd better be nice to them! You never know, they might just be up for a bit of babysitting!" By the look of absolute horror on my father's face, I guessed there was more chance of him applying for French citizenship then there was of him looking after Georgia's baby.

"Do you know what you're having?" my Mum asked her. *The Omen, probably.*

"No, I want it to be a surprise."

"Oh." My mother looked confused. She turned to Kirsty. "Could you get Georgia some food, dear? But don't show her what it is, she wants to be surprised."

"Georgia's got this app on her phone, it lets her track what the baby should look like each day of its development," said Kirsty, picking up a soggy piece of quiche. "It's ever so clever."

"What's an app?" asked my father.

"It's what athletes always want, isn't it?" replied my mother. "They have to do hundreds of sit-ups to get them."

"Wine, anyone?" my brother asked, wearily.

"YES PLEASE!" a chorus answered.

The rest of the evening didn't pass off too badly, despite Georgia glowering at me constantly and making barbed comments such as, "I'm eating for two, while I still can" and "Got work tomorrow, Kate? Still got *your* job, then; lucky you" and "Ever seen a cockroach, Kate? Do you think they'll be many in the mother and baby homeless hostel?"

Stu surprised his wife with a birthday cake in the shape

of a squashed pig, or it could have been a pink elephant, it was impossible to say and we all sang "Happy birthday" before she blew out the candles. I wondered what she had wished for and was surprised when I didn't turn into a toad. I remembered to ask Stu if he'd take a look at my leaking ceiling and he said he'd call round during the week. He opened some Cava and put the Antiques Roadshow on for Mum and Dad. I kept a wary eye on The Bunny Boiler; she had consumed two large glasses of red and was now knocking back the Cava. An angry rash was beginning to creep up her neck - this was one of the danger signs and I started to think I should make tracks. There was only going to be one person in her firing line if she suddenly flipped, and there was a bloody great carving knife next to the cake plate.

Georgia's iPhone emitted a honk. She examined it and said, "Dad's here to collect me. He's outside." She struggled up out of her armchair.

"He's too early," snapped The Bunny Boiler. "He can bloody well wait."

"He can't, he's got Lauren and Megan in the car."

The Bunny Boiler flushed dark red. "He's bought them *here*?" she spat. "To my home? That, that evil, marriage-wrecking bitch and the Munchkin child?"

"Calm down, love," my brother begged, trying to take her hand. "They're not coming in, they're just waiting in the car."

"Trust you to take their side!" she wrenched her hand away and made for the front door. "Why can't you ever stick up for me? What about my feelings? No one ever cares about me, not even on my birthday! Well, I'm not having this, I'm gonna make them wish they'd never-"

She flounced out and from the window I could see her bearing down on the unsuspecting Volkswagen Passat as it sat innocently by the kerb, exhaust pipe lightly smoking. Stu shot after her with a waddling Georgia taking up the rear.

"Time to go!" my Dad stood up, tugging at my bemused mother's arm.

"Yep, good idea." I jumped up too and fetched their coats from the banisters. As we exited the house, we saw Kirsty struggling to get inside the car through the driver's window whilst Stu clung onto her waist, trying to pull her out. A woman's arm was lashing out at her from the back window and Georgia was stood screaming at her from the passenger's side of the car. A baby was howling. A number of anxious-looking neighbours had come out into the street to witness the rumpus. It didn't feel right to be leaving without thanking our hosts but my Dad and I felt that a hasty retreat was for the best.

Mum said "Are those friends of Kirsty's?"

I thought I'd better make up the spare bed for Stu, just in case.

CHAPTER TWENTY-TWO

I was slumped at my desk gazing in despair at my inbox - I'd cleared all my emails on Saturday but now it was full again and it was only 9.30 on Monday. I looked up with a start; I hadn't noticed Sandra approaching. "Morning!" she said, brightly and placed a tin of Roses on my desk. *Woo hoo - chocolates!* "I baked you a cake. It's a banana cake," she explained, as I prised the lid off.

"Oh, you shouldn't have." I peered at the doorstop-looking sponge cake adorned with dried banana chips. *You really shouldn't have.* "That's, um, so kind of you. Er, thank you."

"It's just to say thank you for listening and being such a good friend." *A good friend?* She was attempting to lure me in again. Baking a cake indeed! Trying to make out she was the comfy, homely, floury baps type. "I was wondering if you're free for lunch today?"

I'd rather prise my own fingernails off with a Swiss army knife! Unable to think up an excuse quickly enough, I heard my voice answering, "Yes, that would be great! Bout twelve thirty-ish? Fab!" I was so bloody slow on my feet.

I emailed Big Andy to see if he wanted to meet me for lunch so I wouldn't be alone with her. He replied:

Kate

Please stop chasing me, I'm way out of your league. Have you asked Smelly Barry from the boiler room? He's quite lonely too, I believe. He can't eat much now he's had his gastric band fitted, but he might be able to keep some soup down, although the pea and ham plays havoc with his flatulence so you might want to check with the canteen first...

Sorry, can't do lunch today old girl. I'm off to Manchester shortly to hear a disciplinary. One of their advisers called a customer a "dopey, flat-capped whippet-worrier". I thought that passed for a compliment up north! Don't know whether to fire him or promote him! Catch you later

Andy

Crap. Who else could I ask? I picked up the tin and took it over to The Rock. "I know it's only ten o'clock Jan, but would you like a piece of banana cake?" I waved it under her nose and she eyed it with suspicion.

"Did you make it?"

"It's home made."

"Is it a bribe?"

"No!"

"Because I'm already being as creative as I can be with the stats," she whispered "I don't think I can squeeze them anymore-"

"Honestly Jan," I said crossly, "Just because I offer you a piece of cake you think I'm after something. I'm disappointed in you."

I couldn't ask her to lunch after that but I left the cake with her anyway, knowing she wouldn't be able to resist it for long. And it would be a good test to see if it had been poisoned. So it was going to be just the two of us for lunch, then. Oh God. What was she going to try now? More sob stories perhaps, but what was left? A dead pet, a long lost child? Better have the canteen remove all the sharp knives and get Oprah on speed-dial.

We sat at the same table as before, me with my lukewarm, tinny-tasting tomato soup and Sandra with her jumbo sausage roll and 25% extra Yorkie Bar. She had changed tack by trying a different approach today, appearing all bright and cheerful. I managed to keep the conversation light and fluffy, steering clear of the topics of dead mothers, abusive fathers and vicious bullies. I asked her what her sister did.

"Oh, she doesn't need to work. Her husband's extremely well paid."

"The lucky thing! What does her husband do?"

"He's the Chief Executive."

"Wow. Who for?"

She blinked at me. "For us. For Perypils."

My spoon stopped half way to my mouth. "You mean he's the Big, the er, I mean, your sister's married to Kevin Goddard?"

"Yes. They've got an amazing house with an indoor swimming pool and lots of staff. She doesn't have to lift a finger. Money hasn't changed her, though, not one bit, she's still my lovely big sister!" *Is she bigger than you? Your poor mother must have been walking round the maternity unit like John Wayne.*

She prattled on about her sister's life of luxury but I was only half-listening. My mind was whirring; I couldn't believe I was working with the Chief Exec's sister-in-law! They really had sent in the heavy mob. Thank God I was on my guard and hadn't said anything incriminating. Did she report back to him on everything that went on in Cheltenham? What was she telling him? Did she talk about me? What was she saying? Had she witnessed me attempting to strangle Ben this morning when he'd spilt hot chocolate in his telephone turret again? Had she seen the picture of the photocopied buttocks that had been doing the rounds? Had she heard me ask that irritating woman from HR to call back once she'd taught her arse to speak some sense?

I smiled and nodded while she was talking, pretending to look enthralled at her tedious family stories, knowing she was attempting to destroy my resolve through vapidity. Little did she know, when I was laid up with flu over Christmas, I'd sat through Sex and the City, films 1 *and* 2 – what doesn't kill you makes you stronger. When we took our trays over to the trolley, she heaved a big sigh and said; "It's so nice to have someone to talk to. Of course, it gets very lonely staying in a hotel on your own. I know I live on my own, but a hotel room is so impersonal. A bit depressing, really. I start thinking about things, you know? Dark things." *Ah, here we go, the depressed and lonely card; trying to make me feel sorry for you now.* I nodded sympathetically. "I don't suppose you're free for dinner one evening?" she asked hopefully, eyes all shiny. "It would give me something to look forward to, instead of another evening trapped in that room on my own. The only person I speak to is the girl who delivers the room service and she can't get away quickly enough."

I know exactly how she feels. "Yes, great," I heard my voice say again, "that would be really nice." How could I say no? She was The Big Cheese's sister-in-law! What if she told him I'd been mean to her; I'd get the most almighty hoof up the arse. I'd end up face down in Cherbourg with a size-twelve imprint on my derriere.

"Oh, brilliant! How about Wednesday?"

So soon? "Yes, that's fine," I replied, weakly. "Are you staying at the Ellenborough Park?"

She looked puzzled. "No, the Premier Inn."

I was surprised, but still, times were tight and the company probably didn't want to be seen giving luxurious perks to their executives. We arranged to meet in town, Sandra exclaiming very excitedly, "It's a date!"

I'd never felt quite so dispirited in all my life. I'd even faced the school trip to the brass-rubbing museum with more eager anticipation. But I wasn't going to let her break me. *No way.*

"Karen, pleeeeease come with me."

"I can't, Kate, it's parents evening on Wednesday. I have to lie to a bunch of sycophantic parents about how much I love teaching their snot-nosed, bratty little half-wits."

"Do you actually enjoy teaching, Kazza?"

"About as much as you enjoy managing."

"Oh dear."

When I was home, I couldn't stop myself from logging into eDates.com. But did I really want to date someone who had been stupid enough to fall for the £47.99 payment scam? Someone who was as stupid as me?

I had twelve messages in my inbox, seven of which were from the company but five looked like genuine contacts. I clicked onto my 'stats' and saw that my profile had been viewed sixty-eight times! Wow! But how come only five had made contact? What had put the other sixty-three off? Was it my photo? I did look a bit cross-eyed, but at least my fringe was hiding the crow's feet. Perhaps it was my description - bloody musical theatre! That must be it. Made me sound like I was part of the Edinburgh Woollen Mill brigade.

On examining the stats more closely, I saw that David Zeller had viewed my profile forty-four times! Oh my God, I was being cyber-stalked! But on the positive side, that did improve my hit rate. One of the messages was from him so I deleted that one without reading it. I opened another entitled "Contact from Sean Moyes":

Dear Kate

I'm not very good at this sort of thing, but having seen your profile I felt I really wanted to contact you to say hi!

I have recently come out of a long-term relationship and friends thought I should give online dating a try. It's all a little daunting and I didn't think anything would come of it but you do sound like exactly the sort of person I would really love to get to know.

I work for a national newspaper but it's nothing too grand! I support the editing process and am lucky enough to be able to work from home most of the time.

This is the first contact message I've sent so I really hope you will be kind to me and reply!

Yours (nervously!)

Sean

Aw, he sounded really sweet and genuine, and more importantly, he could spell. I clicked onto his profile and saw a photo of a clean-shaven, bright-eyed man, aged around forty, brown hair swept back into a small trendy quiff. He looked friendly and well, *normal.* I read his description; he lived just outside Cheltenham and liked rugby, pub lunches and long country walks. I liked the sound of him very much, apart from the long walks of course, and it was quite endearing the way he was new to this process too and yet he had been brave enough to contact me.

This was really quite exciting - was it possible I had found someone special already? I would definitely reply to him. While I was thinking of a suitable response, I clicked on the next message. It read:

Dear Lesley

I'm not very good at this sort of thing, but having seen your profile, I felt I really wanted to contact you to say hi!

I have recently come out of a long-term relationship and friends thought I should give online dating a try. It's all a little daunting and I didn't think anything would come of it but you do sound like exactly the sort of person I would really love to get to know.

I work for a national newspaper but it's nothing too grand! I support the editing process and am lucky enough to be able to work from home most of the time.

This is the first contact message I've sent so I really hope you will be kind to me and reply!

Yours (nervously!)

Sean

What a little weasel! He was just cutting and pasting to anyone he could find!

Dear Sean

I thought I'd let you know that Lesley did not receive her "unique"

introductory email from you, because you sent it to me straight after you
sent me mine.

How is the job in editing going? Or do you keep sending your work
to the wrong newspaper?

Yours (as in up)

Kate

This online dating was a minefield! I had to wise up and
stop being so bloody naïve. The rules were different on the
Internet; people were able to pretend to be whatever they
wanted to be. I had to assume that nobody told the truth
about anything. I read through the interests listed on the
profiles of some of my other 'matches' and translated them:

Art = pornography
Photography = pornography
Wildlife photography = bestiality
Military history = firearms
Entertaining = swinging
Gazing at sunsets = arson

I opened the third message warily. It was from Jamie
Weston and was very short and to the point.

Hi Kate.

I saw your profile and thought I would contact you. If you like my
profile, too, then please reply. If you don't then have a nice life anyway!

Cheers

Jamie

Hmmm. I didn't mind the direct approach, but surely

you should put a little more effort into an initial contact? I clicked on Jamie's profile. The photo showed Jamie leaning against a bar, a square-jawed face set above a thick-set neck and shoulders, a diamond studded ear-lobe - was Jamie really a man? I looked very closely but I wasn't completely convinced. What if Jamie was a woman? I hadn't considered lesbianism. Perhaps I shouldn't rule it out, not at my age when the buckshot approach might be more advisable. I may actually be a lesbian, I just didn't know it yet and after all, I did really like Clare Balding. I Googled her and flicked through several pictures waiting to feel some sort of urge or longing. Not a thing. There were no seismic Saturday Kitchen surges; not even a Cain Dingle tingle. I deleted the message in the end. Sorry Jamie, but I do hope you have a nice life too. There was one message left to read but suddenly the red heart started flashing, letting me know that David Zeller was requesting a live chat. I logged out.

Wednesday evening

Well, here I was in the wine bar again. I'd dressed casually in white shirt and skinny jeans, which were digging uncomfortably into my stomach and had cut off all circulation to my crotch. The seams might survive the night provided I didn't eat, breathe or attempt to move. I had my tan Kurt Geiger knee-length boots on but even their zips wouldn't go all the way up now. I'd have to keep my knees pressed together so no one noticed. Why the hell hadn't I worn my fat uniform of tunic top and leggings? At least I wouldn't be sat here worrying about bursting out of my clothes like the Incredible Hulk.

Oh no, she'd arrived. The bar was busy but I noticed people rapidly moving out of Sandra's way. She'd abandoned her usual black suit in favour of grey trousers and a bright yellow hairy jumper. All I could think was 'Where's the honey, Mummy?' I stood up to get her a drink but to my astonishment, she gathered me up in a huge hug. My tits were completely squashed and I thought a rib was about to pop.

"Great to see you!" she exclaimed, as if we hadn't just seen each other an hour and a half ago.

"You too," I gasped, extracting myself as gently as I could and pulling a yellow hair out of my mouth. "What can I get you to drink?"

"Oh, let me!" I let her. I couldn't be bothered with the usual "No, let me!" "No, I insist!" wrestling. I asked for a vodka and tonic and she ordered herself an apple and mango J2O.

"Do you drink, Sandra?"

"Not anymore. Not after the incident at the barbeque, with the shears ... alcohol affects me you see. And not in a good way."

"Oh, right." I knew I should ask more but that would be like driving up a long cul-de-sac of doom. *Quick - think of a different subject ...* "Did you manage to park alright?" *Lame! So lame!*

We took our drinks downstairs to the bistro when I pretended I was hungry, hoping we would eat a quick meal and then the evening would be over. Sandra spent an absolute age perusing the menu, even though the choices were very limited. The tall, dark Cary Grant waiter came over a couple of times with his pen poised hopefully but she kept sending him away.

"I just can't decide between the crab cakes and the

calamari." *Bugger, she was having a starter.* "I haven't had crab cakes in a long time, but then, you see, I do so love calamari..."

The waiter came over a third time, looking determined. "I'll have the soup and the chicken, please," I said quickly, handing him my menu. We both looked at Sandra who panicked under the pressure.

"I'll have the calamari, no, I mean the crab cakes! Yes, definitely the crab cakes! And then, um, let me see..." *Just fucking choose something!* "I'll have the carbonara. No, no I won't, hang on, oh well, yes I will. Yes, the carbonara. I think. And could we have some water please?"

"Still or sparkling?"

"Er, um..."

"Tap please," I said "Unless you actually *want* to be here all night?" I winked at Sandra as the waiter returned to the kitchen, letting her know I didn't buy her dithering idiot act. She smiled back.

"I'm sorry to be so indecisive. My therapist says it's all to do with what I've been through."

A gaping black hole opened up before me; a swirling cesspool waiting to suck me down into its hellish depths and drown me in its misery.

"I have issues with control, apparently." *Too late. I was going down.* "You know, with my father and the bullies. I've never been in control of anything in my life and while my mother was alive she protected me from that. She put me in control, if you see what I mean. But when she died, well..." Tears sprang up in her eyes. "All the issues came rushing to the surface."

"How long have you been seeing your therapist?"

"Since mum died." *But that was eleven years ago! He must be an absolute quack! Or imaginary.*

"Look, don't go upsetting yourself, Sandra." *Because you're wasting your time! I'm not caving in.* "Your mum would be very proud of everything you've achieved in your life. You know she would."

"Do you really think so?" she looked at me with glistening eyes.

"Yes, I really do. I mean, just think of everything you're doing for us in Cheltenham." I made a valiant attempt to steer the conversation towards work. "Supporting us with those awful system issues. How is all that going, by the way?"

"Good. All good."

"Any thoughts on actions we should be taking? Have you got a plan of attack yet?"

"Yes, yes." She produced a tissue and trumpeted into it. I waited for her to finish and to expand on her thoughts but none were forthcoming. Damn, she played things close to her chest. Clearly she wasn't prepared to share her findings with me while she was feeding everything back to The GPS and her brother-in-law. It was like having the sword of Damocles hanging over me. Christ, why couldn't they just put me out of my misery with a shot to the head? A nice quick kill.

The starters arrived and although I wasn't in the least bit hungry I sipped my scolding broccoli and stilton as quickly as I could. Sandra declared her crab cakes "delicious" and offered me a piece on her fork. I tried to say no, but she persisted, virtually forcing the morsel into my mouth. Being fed by her was a toe-curlingly intimate experience, not to mention unhygienic. I saw a couple of people at other tables glance over. Did they think we were together? As in, an item?

As if I'd choose someone as intimidating as Sandra to have my first lesbian experience with! I'd go for a pretty, delicate sort of lesbian, like, um.... well, never mind. Sandra didn't appear to notice my discomfort and forgetting her surfacing issues, chatted away about her cat and its many whacky exploits. She was trying to drive me insane with banality, and she was doing a bloody good job. When she'd finished a very lengthy tale about Nutmeg and its riveting night trapped in next door's garage, she launched into another about the ornamental pond escapade. I felt like lying face down in one myself.

Over her sizeable shoulders, I watched the waiter flirting with two young women seated at the table behind us. His face was all lit up and there was lots of smiling and giggling. When he came to our table he didn't so much as glance at us. I was wearing that invisibility cloak again. I hated being in my forties; I wanted a gorgeous waiter to giggle and flirt with me! This one couldn't even bring himself to look in my direction. Around the bistro, everyone seemed to be having fun, enjoying themselves eating a meal with someone they presumably wanted to be eating a meal with. I wondered if I'd ever before felt quite so low. Could I be depressed? Or was it perfectly normal to want to stab your fork repeatedly into your own thigh? If their plan was to have me sectioned, it was working.

As I started on my main course, I feared my waistband was actually going to cut me in half. I badly wanted to undo the button on my jeans but there was no way I could do this without it being obvious and I couldn't get up to go the loo in the middle of the meal. Sandra tried to feed me again with some pasta but I told her very firmly that cream disagreed with me and she backed off. Embarrassingly, my mobile rang, causing several disapproving heads to swivel our way. Full of apologies, I was fumbling to turn it off when I saw that it was my parent's number. They never called my mobile! Had something happened?

"I'm so sorry Sandra, but I've got to take this." I hit the green button. "Hello?"

"Kate? It's Dad. You haven't seen your mother have you?"

"*What?* Isn't she at home with you?"

"Would I be bloody phoning you if she was? She went out to close the greenhouse but that was an hour ago. I just wondered if she'd turned up at yours?"

"But I live twenty miles away, Dad! How could she get to mine?"

"On the bloody bus, of course. She's done it a couple of times now; got on the bus and forgotten where's she going. I drive around the route until I find her, somewhere."

"Bloody hell Dad! It's cold and dark; what if she's lost? I'm coming over to help you-"

"No! Don't make such a fuss! She won't have gone far. I'll call you when I've found her."

I stared at my phone in disbelief. My mother had gone missing and I wasn't to make a fuss!

"Everything ok?" asked Sandra.

"Er, no, not really." I didn't want to go into details with her or give her anything she could use against me. "I'm really sorry to do this Sandra, but I think I'm going to have to go. Bit of a family crisis."

She nodded understandingly. "That's quite alright, you go. Family comes first! I'll sort the bill, don't you worry about a thing."

"Thank you." I snatched up my handbag and swept past her as she half-stood and leant forwards in a failed attempt to kiss me goodbye. I ran all the way to my car, which was agony in my skin-tight boots and just as I sank into the driver's seat, my mobile rang. "Dad?"

"I've got her. She was having a cup of tea at Jean's over the road. I'd called there once already but they thought it was Jean's hearing aid that was ringing."

Thank Christ. I said a weary goodnight to my father, took a deep breath and undid the button on my jeans so I could exhale. I knew I should do the decent thing and go back to Sandra but why look a gift horse in the mouth? I fired up the car and turned on the radio. 'Mad World' was playing, the Gary Jules version. I didn't know whether to head for home or make straight for the suspension bridge.

CHAPTER TWENTY-THREE

I received an email from Blacks the Chemist inviting me to attend an interview for the assistant manager position with the shitty slave's salary - hooray! I'd forgotten all about the application, it had been so long ago. I'd had to complete an online 'personality' test, so it hadn't surprised me when I'd heard nothing further. I'd have to do lots of prep, but there was no time to think about that now, it was too bloody hectic. I was just getting up to find out why so many calls were queuing, when the big, black-suited figure of Sandra reared up in front of me, blocking my path to The Snake. "Kate!" she exclaimed, holding out her arms to gather me into another bear-hug. Too late to dodge her, I stood, mortified, with my arms pinned to my side as she crushed the air from me. I noticed, at very close proximity, that she was wearing a blue tie with her white shirt, the collar of which now had my Angel Pink lipstick on it. Some of the team were staring over at us, no doubt intrigued at our sudden close bond or perhaps marvelling that someone was brave enough to hug me. The last time anyone had attempted to make physical contact with me in the office (The Drain had tapped me on the shoulder to say "excuse me"), I'd screamed "Don't touch me!"

"Morning Sandra," I wheezed as she released me. "I've just got to check on the queue-"

"I've got something for you!" she declared, excitedly. "I really hope you like it! I bet you're intrigued now, aren't you?

Admit it! You're dying to know what it is!" *No, I'm not, I'm working and there are customers waiting. Was this a test? What should I do? Ignore her or the customers? She's related to the Chief Exec-*

"Yes of course, a surprise, how lovely." I led her back to my desk to get away from all the inquisitive eyes and she handed me a carrier bag, watching me with a beaming smile. I put my hand inside and pulled out a bright yellow shaggy bath mat.

"Oh! Er, right, well, thanks-"

"Do you like it?"

"Well, yes, I mean, it will certainly cheer up my bathroom."

She shrieked with laughter. "You are funny! Always the joker! I couldn't get you the sweater so I had to get the cardigan version instead. It's just as nice though, don't you think? Now we're jumper buddies!"

I shook out the bath mat; three brown leather buttons revealed it was, indeed, a cardigan. I had, after all, pretended to admire her ghastly Furby jumper, so I'd only got myself to blame.

"Gosh, how nice of you, Sandra. But I must pay you for it-"

"No, I wouldn't hear of it! It's a gift, to say thank you for all you've done for me. You can wear it when we go out to dinner again; we'll match! How are you fixed this week?"

Think of an excuse, think of an excuse "I'll have to let you know." *Put sad face on.* "It's a bit tricky, with my mother and everything so I'll have to play it by ear this week."

She nodded empathetically. How shitty of me to use my mother's condition as an excuse, but I just couldn't face another evening being tortured by her. She finally left me alone after forcing me to commit to going for a coffee with her later. I gazed gloomily at the custard monstrosity in front of me. What the hell was I going to do with that? Its label read 'Ogo Paris', which wasn't a name I recognised. I couldn't tell if the garment was from a market or a boutique, but it felt good quality. Was it expensive? Why was she buying me expensive gifts? She'd claim it back on expenses no doubt, but how did this fit into her plan? Perhaps if I wore it, my insanity was proven beyond any reasonable doubt and she had the men in white coats standing by.

"That's nice, old girl!" Big Andy's voice boomed around the office. I hadn't seen him approaching. "Where the hell did you get that? You're not thinking of wearing it, are you? You'll look like an emu with yellow fever!"

Bridgend David emailed a report headed 'Strictly Confidential'. I opened it up to discover it was TLCS George's occupational health report. About time! I started to read with great interest. The report confirmed that George was indeed suffering from an obsessive compulsive disorder that had a significant impact on his personal and working life. It described, in detail, the difficulties he faced when trying to complete routine tasks, and certain things such as leaving the house were fraught with problems. The report concluded that adjustments should be made to his working conditions and these should cover flexible working hours and tolerance with deadlines and task completion.

I phoned David. "What do you think of this report, Dai?"

Big sigh. "It's ridiculous, Kate. All Ock Health has done is a telephone interview with George, so their conclusions are only based on what he's told them."

"But what about his doctor's report?"

"They haven't even requested one! Told me it wasn't necessary! Can you bloody well believe it?"

Nothing surprised me anymore. "What happens now?"

"I've told them I want to see a doctor's report and I wasn't taking no for an answer. They moaned like buggery, all to do with costs apparently, but I couldn't give a flying f-, I mean, I don't care. George could have told them anything he liked! It's absurd. This bloody company, Kate, it's going to the dogs. They expect us to manage people robustly but provide us with this sort of shite! It's like being sent into the scrum without your jockstrap on!"

I cringed at the image. "Makes you wonder why we do this job, doesn't it?" I said, sympathetically. "It's certainly not the money. Although, I suppose the benefits are okay-"

"Benefits are just sugar on shit as far as I'm concerned," he said, gloomily. "I really don't think I can do this for much longer. You know, the other day, I had to do a hearing in Birmingham about a serious sexual allegation that had been made. I mean, we're not qualified for that sort of thing, are we? Why the hell don't HR do these hearings? It's ridiculous."

My blood ran cold. Oh no. Was it Royston? I'd let him off. I'd got it wrong. What had he done? Had he attacked someone?

"Birmingham, you say? Um, it, it wasn't Royston Pembleton, was it?" I asked, dreading the answer.

"Yes! Do you know him? He was accused of serious sexual harassment. There were thirty-seven witness statements testifying that he'd exposed himself in the office."

"Oh my God! That's *terrible*. Oh David, I feel just awful, I mean it was me that-"

"Turns out the poor sod got his foreskin stuck in his zip and had to run round begging for help with his knob hanging out."

"Oh, right. Did you believe him?"

"He showed me the damage." I could sense David give a shudder. "Trust me, you couldn't make that up."

The GPS called. He sounded stressed. "Kate, I'm in Manchester for the monthly executive board meeting. The Chief Exec wants an update on the quotation issues and your remedial actions, specifically detailing your plans to reduce our customers' concerns. I mean, comments. So you'll have to join us via video conference at twelve o'clock. I'll need you to walk us through Sandra's action plan. Can you forward it to me please?"

Oh heck! I hadn't seen her action plan yet; I'd no idea what was in it. "Um, do you think it would be more appropriate for Sandra to take the executive team through her plan?" I asked, "I wouldn't want to tread on her toes."

"No, I don't. You're the manager so you have responsibility for the plan and its implementation."

I didn't know what to say. "Problem?" he snapped.

"Er, no. I'll send you the action plan."

"Straight away please, Kate and make sure you're ready for the video conference at midday sharp."

Buggery buggery bollocks. I shot over to Sandra's desk and she looked up with a big smile. "Hi Kate! Is it coffee time?"

"No, it's not. Roger needs to see your action plan straight away, Sandra and so do I. I've got a video conference with the Chief Exec and his team at twelve o'clock today and I've got to take them through the actions."

Her smile faded away. "Oh. Right. Yes, of course. I'll send you both the plan." I expected her to immediately flick into her emails to do this but she didn't move.

"I need it now, Sandra," I urged. "I haven't read it yet and I need to get myself prepared for this meeting." *Or I may as well drive straight to Beachy Head.*

"Yes, of course. Shall we discuss it over a coffee?"

"NO!" I caught myself. "I mean, no thank you, I don't have time for coffee, Sandra. I need to see your action plan. Now."

"No problem, Kate. I'll send it to you. Just give me a moment to check over it and I'll forward it to you."

"And to Roger."

"Yes, ok."

I heaved a sigh of relief and was just returning to my desk when The MC grabbed me. "Kate, it's Pat. She's in a terrible state in the meeting room, she wants to go home. I've done my best to console her but I really think you should see her."

I haven't got time for this! The MC was looking at me anxiously; I didn't have much choice. I couldn't ignore a colleague in a distressed state, as much as I wanted to. "Right, yes of course I'll see her." I swung round and marched to the meeting room where I found The Blubber sobbing.

"Oh Kate, it's just so terrible. I need to go home, something awful's happened."

"Whatever is it?"

"It's, it's my hairdresser."

Mmm, yes, well, I'd be seriously upset if mine had cut

my fringe that badly. "Never mind Pat; it will grow out, you know. You've just got to be a bit patient. Perhaps you could wear a nice hat."

"What? I mean, it's my hairdresser's daughter. She's got leukaemia; I just found out. Isn't it awful? Awful. Why is life so hateful and cruel to people?"

I patted her hand as she strangled her tissue to a flaky death and tried to surreptitiously view the time on her watch. "I'm so sorry, Pat. Are you very close to your hairdresser?"

"Oh yes, yes, I've been going to her for some time."

Resist the urge to ask her why. "And how old is her daughter?"

"Um, school age, I think. It's just terrible; I can't get over it. I've got to go home."

"Do you mean infants school or is she older than that?"

"I'm not really sure."

"Er, have you ever met her daughter?"

"We're friends on Facebook! That's how I found out. The poor, poor thing."

"And how often do you see your hairdresser, Pat?"

"I go a couple of times a year. Well, usually. Sometimes I can just get away with the one trim at Christmas." *Trust me - you can't.* "Do you see her at any other times?"

She mopped her eyes, looking puzzled at the question. "I see her in Asda occasionally."

I took a deep breath. "Forgive me Pat, but I thought you said you were close and although it's very shocking news, I-"

She threw her hands up in the air, wailing loudly. "You managers don't understand anything! You don't have feelings at all; you don't care about real people! I've just told you that a little girl might be dying and you don't seem to be moved at all! Oh, you are just terrible, just, just *wicked*; how can you sleep at night?"

I'm surprised you haven't said that Clare would have let you go home-

"Clare would have understood." *Spoke too soon.* "She was such a compassionate woman; she had such warmth." *That would be from the flames when she exhaled.*

"I'm sorry Pat. You can stay in this room until you feel a bit better and perhaps give your hairdresser a call if you want to let her know you're thinking of her. But then I expect you back at your desk, please. Would you like a cup of tea?"

Realising that was the best she was going to get, she nodded her head, sniffing loudly. Had I handled that fairly? I thought I had, so why did I feel like a prize bitch? I couldn't have team managers going home willy-nilly, not when everyone was under so much pressure - it was all hands to the pump. Did I care more about my job than a child with leukaemia? *Yes, I did!* Oh my God, I was inhuman! I was practically Vulcan, I was ... *Christ, it was half past ten.* I fetched Pat her tea and hurried back to my desk to view Sandra's report. The MC tried to stop me yet again but I side-stepped her, screeching, "Not now Joy! I'm having a crisis!" I clicked on my emails, expecting to find one from Sandra. There didn't seem to be one. I checked again. No, nothing. I saw that I'd missed three calls from Roger on my mobile; he must be chasing it too. *Bloody hell.* I looked over at Sandra's desk but she wasn't there. I strode over towards it - her desk was empty! Where the hell was she? "Has anyone seen Sandra?" I bellowed, wide-eyed with panic.

"That's what I was trying to tell you if only you'd let me," said The MC, sniffily. "She's had to go. Said Nutmeg had been taken ill – is that her daughter? She said to give you this." The MC handed me a large manila folder; thank God, it must be the action plan. I opened it up and found hundreds of pages of notes stuffed inside. What the-? I pulled a couple of pages out. They were just transcripts of complaints calls. I pulled out a few more. They were the same. Where was the sodding plan? I tipped the whole lot out onto the desk and rifled frantically through them. No plan. The cold realisation swept over me; she'd left me in the bloody lurch. She and The GPS must have set this up between them; I should have been more vigilant! *They'd got me.*

My mobile rang. The GPS. I swallowed and answered "Hi Roger."

"What the hell's going on, Kate? Why haven't I received the action plan?"

Think, think "Sorry, but everything's gone down here; emails, systems, the lot."

"Oh. Well, send it through as soon as you're back up and I'll see you on the conference at twelve. *That* had better be working."

What was I going to do? I phoned Sandra's mobile number but it went straight to voicemail, of course. I had to face the entire executive team in just over an hour and I didn't have the first clue what I was going to tell them. Should I go and sabotage the video conferencing equipment so it couldn't be used? No, that wouldn't work, they'd just phone me instead. Could I feign a sudden illness or make up some dubious sick relative story? Perhaps I could faint before I had to speak. There was a fair chance I wouldn't even have to fake that.

I collected myself and tried to calmly sort through

Sandra's notes to see if I could pick out her key findings and suggested actions. There was absolutely reams of stuff, but nothing at all coherent; she seemed to have just been copying down customers' comments verbatim. There were no summaries, no corrective actions, nothing useful at all. I took a blank piece of paper and picked up a pen, noticing my hands were trembling. *Think logically.* What would the executives be expecting? A quick, high level update, that was all. Chuck in a few meaningless wank words like "gap analysis", "strategic fit" and "bandwidth" and it would be fine; after all, that's all they ever did. I'd never heard an executive say anything of actual substance. I'd be ok. It was a shame I was wearing my shapeless old grey suit and not something tartier, but there was no way I'd get to Next and back before twelve. Bonmarche was in striking distance but a red velour twin set wasn't really going to be much of an improvement.

I phoned Sandra again, thinking I could throw myself at her mercy but it was still voicemail. My bowels were lurching alarmingly but someone was in the toilets each time I dashed in and I couldn't bring myself to sit down next to them in case I blew the doors off the cubicles. Just before midday, I made my way down to the video conferencing room on the ground floor. There were leads and wires trailing everywhere, so I picked my way cautiously across the carpet to a small table that faced an enormous television screen. Should I be sitting down or standing? I stood awkwardly for a moment before deciding to sit down, then changed my mind and stood up then changed it back and sat down again. I glanced out of the window and saw one of the groundsmen staring in at me with an amused grin. It must look like I was playing some kind of demented game of musical chairs with myself.

It was twelve o'clock. *Here goes.* I picked up the remote control, sat up straight, buttocks clenched, stomach sucked in, jaw relaxed to make face look thinner - I hit the button. The screen flickered into life and there, as large as life, sat the executive team. *Jesus, there were loads of them!* There were at least thirty sat around a very long table and they were all looking at me. Perypils didn't have that many executives, did it? No doubt most of them were cling-ons; those sycophantic butt-lickers that preened and ponced around the Bigwigs - "Would you like me to wipe your arse, for you Chief Executive? No? What about a blow job, then? You'd like me to knock my front teeth out first? No problem!" I spotted The GPS in the middle of them. They were all men; that very nearly surprised me, the Communications team were constantly reminding us what a diverse company we are.

The Big Cheese was sitting at the head of the table. He didn't look particularly happy. "Right, this is Kate from the team at Cheltenham," he growled to the others. "Let's hope she's got some good news for us because this meeting has been an absolute shower of shit so far." Everyone looked down at their hands, notes, laps, hooves ... "Kate's going to give us an update on the online quotation issues. Kate, bring some common fucking sense to this meeting, for Christ's sake."

I gave a nervous laugh. "Well, if it's common sense you want perhaps you should have some women in your team!" I paused, expecting an appreciative titter but none came. I saw a few of them glancing towards a stout looking man seated near the end of the table. Oh no! It was Sherman Sheila, Head of Finance. I hadn't spotted her. Flustered, I quickly pressed on. "The situation with the online quotation system is proving to be an extremely challenging one for my guys and our customers," I started, "and of course, we are all hoping that IT can address the root cause as quickly as possible." *Good start - blame IT.*

"Aye, we've just been discussing that," thundered The Big Cheese, glaring across the table at a pinch-faced, nervous-looking man in glasses, who flinched. The Head of IT, I assumed.

"Until that time," I continued, "we've had to think outside the box on this one, to try and er, you know, stretch the envelope, as it were." They were all staring at me. I could feel my face getting hot. "S-so, having undertaken a great deal of gap analysis, we've concluded that..." *what the hell had we concluded?* "that we should empower our colleagues to, er, to explain to our customers that when they call us for a quote, it might not be the correct one."

Incredulous stares all round. That was obviously the wrong thing to have said. "W-what I mean is, we have to be extremely client-focussed and manage their expectations accordingly." Still staring. "Because we have no way of telling which customer is affected by this issue." *Another dig at IT - throw the focus back at nervy rat-boy.* "We only know when the customer contacts us to complain, I mean, to make a comment and then they're already very upset. Can't get the toothpaste back in the tube, can we?" My laughter hung in the silence. *Had I really just said that? Please kill me.*

The Big Cheese was perplexed. "Are you seriously telling me that we're saying to every bloody customer that calls 'here's your quote, it might be right but then again, it might not'?"

Yes. "Er, well, you could say we're being proactive instead of reactive." Every single part of me was sweating now. "And this approach has really reduced the number of complaints, sorry, concerns, no sorry, I mean comments." *Quick - throw in a number to make it look authentic* "They're down by 8%, which is really quite significant."

I shuffled my notes around to make it appear I had evidence to support this claim. Everyone on screen winced.

"Kate, try not to cover the microphone," said one of the faceless suits at the front. "It causes a lot of disturbance at this end."

"Right. Sorry." I moved my notes and they all winced again. "Sorry." I looked up and smiled with what I hope looked like confidence into the screen. "Any questions for me?"

They all looked round at each other. The Big Cheese appeared lost for words; that had to be a first.

"Um, yes, I have," piped up Alan, head of Human Remains. "How are your colleagues feeling about all this? What's morale like down there?"

Oh, it's just peachy! We're all turning bloody cartwheels up and down the office, you knob. "We've got a very resilient team in Cheltenham," I replied, cheerfully. They all waited, clearly expecting a bit more. I switched to my serious face. "But, it is difficult, you know, what with all the bandwidth issues and everything."

Silence. The Big Cheese cleared his throat and said "Right, thank you, Kate. We'll take a break there, I think." I thought I caught "because I fucking well need one" but I couldn't be sure.

The screen went blank. My ordeal was over. One word,

as Craig Revel Horwood would say - *Dis-as-ter*. What the hell was The GPS going to say? He'd kept very quiet; well, what had I expected? That he'd jump in and save me from drowning in my own dribble? That was never going to happen. I returned to my desk via the canteen, picking up a giant-sized cappuccino with two squirts of gingerbread syrup and a Twix. May as well overdose on sugar.

I spent the remainder of the afternoon fidgeting nervously and perspiring freely, waiting for The GPS to call me. It was almost six o'clock before it came. Gulp. *As I walk through the valley* ... "Hello Roger."

"Kate." How come he managed to make even my name sound threatening? "I thought we should discuss your contribution to the executive meeting."

"Look, I'm sorry Roger, I know I was a little unprepared, but it was sprung on me very last minute and-"

"That's no excuse, Kate. All you had to do was walk us through the action plan. That shouldn't have been too difficult, should it? That doesn't require much preparation. I notice you still haven't sent it to me."

"I'm afraid I couldn't find one," I replied, cringing in anticipation of his response. "From Sandra's files, I think she was still at the research stage-"

"You *think*? Don't you know? She's been working with you for weeks and you don't know what's she been doing? I'm beginning to wonder if you've any idea what actually goes on in your department, Kate."

I bristled. "I've got two departments to manage, Roger, not just the one. And Sandra has only been here for a couple of weeks, you bought her in to support me, remember? I didn't know I was expected to manage her on top of everything else."

There was a short silence. There often is just before a bomb goes off. "What I expected, *Kate*, was for you to work closely with Sandra and be fully involved in all her findings and recommendations." His voice was thin and icy and I shivered. "I consider two weeks to be more than enough time to have undertaken sufficient research and produced a highly innovative plan. But, obviously, that was asking too much. Now you've placed me in an extremely embarrassing position with the Chief Executive and I can tell you he's not impressed at all. I'm sure I don't need to remind you, Kate that you are currently on a formal plan to improve your performance, so this sort of incident is really very disappointing, isn't it?"

I'm a gonna. "Do you want me to explain to the Chief Exec? Or Sandra could, perhaps?" She was family, after all, surely she could smooth things over with him?

"No, I do not. But I want that action plan first thing tomorrow morning; no excuses."

He didn't say goodbye. I felt like a tent peg, constantly being hammered into the ground, deeper and deeper. It wasn't so long ago that I used to be the hammer! What the hell was happening? I was being driven so far into the earth I'd never be able to claw my way back up. I looked at my phone. There was a text from Sandra:

Soz K8 my pussy is still not right. Having to stay home for lots of stroking! Got 2 tickets 4 KD Lang next Wed do u fancy goin?

Was that some kind of a joke? She was laughing at me! And clearly having a dig about my sexuality. I *knew* I should have found time for a moustache wax.

I staggered into the office like a zombie. I'd worked all through the night, trying to make sense of Sandra's notes so I could come up with something coherent for the action plan. I had accidentally nodded off around three thirty only to dream I was doing the doggy-paddle in a swimming pool full of sharks and jolted awake in a cold sweat and with a pounding heart. I felt strangely light-headed and my eyes were sore and gritty. I met Big Andy at the coffee machine.

"Morning Kato - Christ, you look rough! Night on the tiles again? You must have worn the poor bugger out, whoever he was!"

"No such luck. Me and my mate Lenny the Lap Top had another all-nighter."

"Oh, that sucks. How's Big Bird getting on?"

"Who?"

"Sandra. Don't worry, I expect they'll shunt her on somewhere else soon."

I stared at him. "What do you mean?"

"Well, she's bloody useless, isn't she! They had to find her a job as a favour to the Chief Exec's wife after she got sacked from Confused dot com, but she can't do a bloody thing. Roger got saddled with her so he's dumped her on you until he can bin her off elsewhere. She's absolutely clueless."

I was stunned. "But, she's a member of the exec team, isn't she?"

"Is she buggery! The Chief Exec just wanted to keep his wife happy so he found a job for her sister. His PA told me he'd said: 'She's about as much use as tits on a bull. Don't let her near the customers for fuck's sake; just get her to sit with her arse in a dike, well away from any sharp edges'."

"But, but I've been so careful around her! And so *nice.*

I've spent hours listening to all her hang-ups, her family history, her dreary bloody cat stories-"

"Ha ha! You utter creep! Well, you needn't have bothered, old girl; she's even more unpopular at Head Office than you are!"

That bastard GPS. He'd stitched me up like a kipper. He knew Sandra would cock up and he'd planned to blame me for it all along. Why hadn't I been more assertive with her? Why hadn't I insisted she told me what progress she was making and asked to have seen evidence? That's what I would have done with anyone else. But no; I'd been too paranoid about her intentions and what she might say about me to her relatives. Well, that had backfired big time. The lid of the career coffin was beginning to close on me.

David called me from Bridgend. "Hiya Kate. Bit of progress; George has finally agreed to a doctor's report, so I've made the request. Shouldn't be too long now."

"Thanks for letting me know. How are things over the bridge?"

"Grim. Roger the Dodger's just sent in his pack of blood hounds to help us sniff out *efficiencies* in our claims processes. Efficiencies he calls it! Redundancies is what he means. One of them is a big scary woman, hands like Evander Holyfield. Said she's just been working with you." Uh-oh. I wondered what poor Welsh bastard was currently listening to the cat stories, dressed in a bright yellow bath mat and wondering just how much hand-sanitiser you needed to swallow in order to end it all.

CHAPTER TWENTY-FOUR

I was preparing for the Blacks interview by making a list of my key achievements in life on a Post-it note, when I received a text from The Ex. "Hi Kate, how are things? Shall we go to Chives one night like we said? Let me know when you are free and I will book us a table."

What should I do? Did I want to have dinner with him at our favourite restaurant that held so many happy memories? Well, apart from that one time I'd been laughing so hard I'd regurgitated an oyster. Was it possible to go back and start again in a relationship? I could tell he was really making an effort because he'd tried to send a grammatically correct message and hadn't used any of that text talk that he knew I couldn't decipher. If only we could go back to how it used to be when we were first married; it was fun, we were happy, we didn't argue and bicker or have sex with other people. I couldn't remember how or why it had changed. Could we start over? But I hadn't really given this online dating a proper chance yet. I logged into the dating website. There were eleven messages waiting for me. I opened up one from a Mike Steadman. It read:

Dear Kate
I read your profile and thought I would contact you. I recently registered with eDates and almost didn't continue with it when I got stung for £47.99! However, I'm a strong believer in fate and that everything happens for a reason so when I saw your profile I felt that just

maybe something great could happen! You never know, you could be my
soul mate!

    I really hope to hear from you.
    Regards
    Mike

I didn't believe in fate or soul mates. Was he some sort
of hippy? I clicked on his profile picture and was pleasantly
surprised. He had fair wavy hair, pale blue eyes and he was
smiling nervously at the camera. He looked like an older
version of Luke Skywalker; with any luck, he might have a
very large lightsabre. His description said he was forty-four
and worked in recruitment. *What a result!* He might be able to
help me find another job! Apparently he enjoyed golf, good
conversation and romantic walks. Why was everyone
obsessed with walking? Probably it was just something to fill
up your profile and it couldn't be proven either way. Would
he be dreadfully dull? Although being dull wasn't necessarily a
bad thing; all I wanted was someone who didn't shave their
palms or howl at the moon. I would reply to him. What
should I put? It was important to be positive and concise.

    Hi Mike
    Sorry to take a little while to respond to you. I'm new to this online
dating lark so I'm finding it all a little scary!
    Thank you for contacting me. I too got stung by the 'free'
registration but decided to carry on; you've got to take a chance in life
sometimes, haven't you?
    I see from your profile that you work in recruitment; that must be a
very rewarding job. I work in insurance (please don't judge me!) which is
quite demanding on my time.

I haven't contacted any other "dates" on this site so I'm not sure what happens now! But it would be very nice to hear from you.
Regards
Kate

Was that ok? It contained lots of honesty, some feeble attempts at humour and a bit of flattery. I thought I'd let him know upfront that my job took up a great deal of my time; may as well manage his expectations from the word go. Would he reply? Or had he got a better offer from another of his matches? I left the screen open on the sofa and started to hoover around the lounge so I could keep checking for his reply. David Zeller was flashing me again; he was a bit slow today! After I'd practically hoovered a hole in the carpet, I gave up and went to empty another truckload of dead slugs from the illy tin beer trap. I'd been burying them in the jungle, which was fast becoming a gastropod graveyard. When I came back inside, there was a reply from Mike Skywalker! I opened it excitedly.

Hi Kate, how great to hear from you! I'm new to this lark too and agree with you - it is all rather scary! Of course I won't judge you for working in insurance. I'm hardly in a position to, I used to be a banker! And that's not rhyming slang, before you ask!

Look, I hope you don't think I'm being too forward but do you fancy trying a web chat? I've not attempted it before but you never know, it might be quite fun! I'll log on at eight o'clock tonight and request a chat with you. If you don't want to, I'll quite understand and please don't let it stop you replying to me!

Hope to see you later!
Mike x

I read his message several times. There were a few too many exclamation marks and he'd put a kiss after his name - was that appropriate when we'd not even met? But he did seem nice and normal. Was I brave enough to try the web chat? The Ex was always using 'Facetime' and I'd often find him sitting in the study chatting away to a head on his laptop, but I'd never done anything like that. I called Karen for advice.

"That's brilliant, Kate! Go for it! That way you'll be able to tell how out of date his picture is."

"What should I talk to him about, Kazza?"

"Not your job. Or your damp spots. Actually, make sure he can't see anything of your house in the background, so keep your head really close to the screen. Have you shaved today? Definitely don't talk about the slugs. Best to avoid any mention of your family. And don't tell him about those shark dreams you keep having; there's nothing more boring than other people's dreams."

"But I'm always telling you about my dreams!"

"I know. And do I ever respond? No. That's because I'm watching the telly until you've finished."

"Oh." I said, crushed. "You haven't left me with many topics, have you? Is my life really that tragic?"

"Yes. Now, if he asks you to take your clothes off for him, don't go all the way. Perhaps just down to your bra and pants and only if he really begs. And make sure you're wearing something sexy, not those baggy grey willy-shrivellers I saw hanging on your radiator."

"I won't be taking my bloody clothes off!"

Karen sighed. "We're never going to get you into the twenty-first century, are we?"

Eight o'clock was fast approaching and my feet were getting decidedly cold inside my black suede stilettos. Why had I put my best shoes on? He was only going to see my head and shoulders! This was going to be another train-wreck, I just knew it. Karen was right; my life was tragic, why would anyone want me in theirs?

My heart was beating faster and my hands were getting clammy. I didn't have to do this. All I had to do was ignore the laptop - easy. But, interestingly, I found that I didn't want to ignore it; I must actually want to speak to Mike. That was a good sign. I just had to be brave. "Screw your courage to the sticking place" - who had said that? Shakespeare? Yes, it was Lady Macbeth. Oh Christ, look what happened to her! I can't do this. Come on, it's eight o'clock. It's now or never.

I opened the laptop and logged into the site. The red flashing heart told me that Mike was requesting a web chat. Good, he was punctual, I liked that. Here goes. I fumbled my way around the keyboard and suddenly there he was! His head was in my lap!

"Oh! Hello there!" I actually waved at him. *What a dork.*

"Hi!" To my relief, he looked just like his profile picture. He was sitting on his sofa too, I could see butch brown leather behind him. "I didn't know if you'd be up for this! I had second thoughts after I'd sent the message, worried I'd scared you off!"

I laughed, trying to surreptitiously slide a cushion under the lap top to raise it after realising I was looking down on him and talking out of quadruple chins. He'd think he was communicating with a pancake stack.

"Well, I nearly whimped out but I really wanted to meet you!" We grinned at each other.

"So what would you usually be doing at eight o'clock on a Thursday evening?" he asked.

"Truthfully? Ploughing through hundreds of tedious work emails whilst munching on a Marmite sandwich and wringing the last drops out of a bottle of Chardonnay." *May as well be honest.* "What about you?"

It was his turn to laugh. "Pretty much the same! Although I'm more of a Merlot man. Did you know you can get Marmite chocolate now?"

He was so nice! What on earth had I been worried about? We chatted away, completely at ease. He was so natural and unassuming that I found myself telling him all sorts of things about my life, even the break-up, in fact, just about everything that Karen had warned me to avoid. Mike divorced two years ago and he had managed to stay on good terms with his ex-wife even though she had cheated on him. He said he had started to feel ready for a relationship again and friends had persuaded him to give online dating a go. We talked and talked, breaking off for twenty minutes so we could get ready for bed and then I continued to chat to him sitting up in bed in my pyjamas. I hadn't removed my make-up, of course, I didn't want him to have nightmares, but I was so relaxed in his 'company' that I forgot all about sucking my cheeks in or keeping my eyebrows raised to smooth out the crow's feet. It was almost three in the morning before we eventually said goodbye after arranging to meet up for a drink. Hooray! My head hadn't scared him off - he wanted to meet the rest of me!

Interview

I took the day as holiday; I never had been able to pull a

sickie. I was due to meet the branch manager, Kim Walsh at the Cheltenham branch of Blacks the Chemist at ten o'clock. I arrived a few minutes early. It was a cold drizzly morning and there weren't many customers in the store. A small knot of women, dressed in their black Blacks' uniforms, stood gossiping around the perfume counter. I asked a blonde one with a face like a sultana if she could let Kim Walsh know I was here for an interview. She gave me an unsmiling, quick up-and-down, clearly disapproved of what she saw because her wrinkles deepened and begrudgingly went to summon her manager. The others ignored me and carried on their conversation slagging off some poor unfortunate called Trisha. Didn't anyone have social graces these days? If I'd heard someone say they were here for an interview I'd at least have said "Oh, good luck!" or "Don't worry, she doesn't bite!" or something of that nature. It didn't appear to be the friendliest working environment.

I looked around the capacious store at the bewildering array of brightly coloured products filling the shelves. There would be a lot to learn; what if I gave the wrong advice to a customer? What if I gave them Deep Heat for their itchy bum? What if I killed someone? Killed a child? Oh my God, I'd be vilified, trolled on the Internet, doggy doos through my letterbox ... I turned to flee back through the automatic doors when I heard "Kate King? Nice to meet you."

I swung round and beamed into the face of a teenager. She had short shiny black hair, a freckly nose and a deep tan that almost looked real. She was probably here on work experience and had been sent to fetch me. I shook her outstretched hand and followed her towards a corner at the back of the store where there was a staircase. We went up to a small dusty office at the top where I sat down in a chair next to a desk and to my surprise, the teenager sat down at the desk.

"Right, I'll just find the forms we need to fill in," she muttered, half-heartedly searching through several piles of paper. "I'm a bit disorganised, I'm afraid! Just got back from holiday."

"Where did you go?" I asked, confused. Was she going to be taking the interview for Kim or was she just doing the initial form-filling?

"Gran Canaria," she sighed. "It was lovely. I really didn't want to come back to work today." She finally located the forms she needed in a box file and after another flurry of rustling, produced my application and personality test results. Another big sigh as she picked up a name badge from the desk and pinned it onto her uniform. It said "Kim Walsh Branch Manager". Bloody hell! She looked like she should be down the local youth club, taking swigs from a bottle of illegally-bought cider while a spotty boyfriend fumbled at her bra fastening and tried to give her a love bite.

"Ok, so..." she glanced down at my application and rubbed her eyes. "Rather than me read all this about you, why don't you tell me about yourself? That's better, isn't it?"

Better than what? Better than you having done me the courtesy of preparing for my interview? "Well, I've been working for Perypils Insurance for thirteen years," *and sticking pencils up my nose for at least ten of those* "but now I feel really ready for a new challenge! I've always wanted to work within retail," *big lie* "because I love serving customers," *even bigger lie* "and I want to be right at the front end of, er, of customer service." *God, what a load of waffly old bollocks.* Kim had her head down so I ploughed on. "I'd love to work for Blacks as they have such a fantastic reputation on the High Street for quality products and excellent service and I really feel I could bring a great deal to this role as I have so much experience in management positions." That sounded a bit up myself; I didn't want to appear like I knew more than she did. "But I would be equally happy working on the shop floor, or, um, well, any position, really." Even missionary, if that would help. All fours might be a bit of a challenge; my knees hadn't recovered from copious weeding.

Kim's head stayed down; was she still conscious? Surely she was going to challenge me about why I wanted to leave a fairly well-paid role for a very piss-poorly paid one slap bang in the middle of a recession?

"Mmm, well, there's a lot of forms to fill in, I'm afraid. I hate all these bloody forms, don't you? I've got to ask you some questions based on your personality test results."

"Oh, how did I do on that?"

"Um…" shuffle rustle shuffle "Wow! You got 90%! That's fantastic."

Yes! This train is calling at Bullshit central!

Kim produced a pink glittery pen ready for my first question. "This is all about building relationships, because that was by far your lowest score on the test." *Ouch!* "So, how would you help a new person who joins your team?" She blinked at me. I blinked at her. Surely that was a question for a simpleton?

"Well, I'd try and get to know them," I said slowly, wondering if it was a trick question. "You know, ask them about themselves, where they live, what things they like doing and then, er, make sure they are involved in the team. So, ensure they are well trained, that they know what they are doing and checking regularly on how they are feeling about things." I trailed off as Kim nodded. She hadn't written much down. "Good, good. Next question. If a colleague was struggling with personal problems, what would the signs be and what action would you take?"

"I never bring my troubles into the office with me, so I expect others to behave in the same way. It's just a matter of choosing your attitude, isn't it? I can't stand those moaning Minnies who wake up in the morning and decide they're going to be miserable all day long!" I emitted a snort of laughter. "So unless they're actually teetering on the window ledge-" I broke off as I realised Kim was expecting something a little more compassionate.

"What I mean is, apart from appearing sad, and er, suicidal, another sign could be that their work deteriorates, or they could perhaps become a bit snappy and tense." *Or emit a lot of squeaky farts, like The Drain.* "I'd take them to one side for a quiet chat and try to discover if there was anything wrong. Then, depending on what they told me, I'd take it from there and try to understand how I could support them." *And then go out of my way to avoid them.*

Kim's eyes watered as she attempted to stifle a yawn. "Great. Sorry about all these questions! I do so hate all this, don't you? Ok. Can you give me an example of a time you've helped a colleague?"

I made up an answer about supporting another manager with their workload when I noticed how stressed they'd become. Kim jotted down a few notes, the pink fluff on the end of her pen waving about madly. I noticed she crossed through several other questions then informed me we would be going down to the shop floor to undertake some exercises. I was a bit nervous at this; would it be some sort of practical test? Would she ask me the difference between an adenoid and a haemorrhoid? I had no idea!

I trotted nervously at Kim's ankles as she led me back down into the store. "This first exercise is all about helping customers. So have a good look round at all the customers on the shop floor. Can you tell me if there are any that you *wouldn't* approach?"

Well, definitely not the guy in the raincoat masturbating by the feminine hygiene counter. I looked around at a little old lady peering at skin creams and an orange middle-aged woman fondling the fake tans. *Step away now madam!*

"I wouldn't approach anyone who looked like they were in a hurry; you know, someone who comes in and heads straight for a particular aisle. They know what they want and probably wouldn't appreciate an interruption."

"Yes, good." Kim nodded, pink fluff bobbing. "Are there any products where you think people might not want to be approached?"

I felt myself get slightly hot. "Oh, um, well, I suppose there might be some medical products, like, er ..." *Lubricants? Ointment for scrot rot?* "oh, er ... condoms!" I blurted out, slightly too loudly. *Idiot!* I should have said the sexual health aisle! Too late now; Kim was moving on. "The next scenario is a female customer who asks you for help. She says she has been using the same shampoo for ten years but feels her hair isn't as shiny as it used to be and wants your advice."

"Right." We were stood in the expansive Hair Care isle. "I'd show her some products which are for shiny hair." Kim nodded but was clearly expecting more. "Um, so that would be, these shine hairsprays perhaps, or..." *Shit, what else was there? Crack an egg on your head love, save yourself some money.* "There's shiny hair gels, of course," *aren't there?* "And special shiny shampoos."

Kim scribbled something down. "O-kay; the customer tells you she doesn't use conditioner. What would you do then?"

Of course! Bloody conditioner! Why didn't you think of that, you utter dip shit. Face hot with embarrassment, I effused about the wonders of conditioner, believing this was probably all in vain now. When I ran out of steam, Kim led me to the deodorants. Was she hinting at something? I kept my armpits clamped. "What would you change about this section?" she asked.

"I'd stock it up," I replied. "There's a number of gaps on the shelves."

"Why is that important?"

Why'd you bloody think! "Because customers can't buy what's not there!"

"What else?"

"I'd tidy it up. Make sure all the products are facing the right way round." *Pathetic, desperate.*

"What else?"

What else was there? "Er, make sure the prices are clearly marked?" *Kill me now.*

"Anything else? What about cross-selling opportunities, perhaps?"

What could you cross-sell with deodorants? Nose pegs? Stain removal?

"Um, I'm not really sure-"

"What about razors?"

"What about them?"

"Do you think it would be a good idea to promote them here?"

Clearly it was. "Oh yes."

"Good, good," Kim nodded approvingly as she continued to scribble. "Last one! Can you select a product that you particularly like and tell me what it is you like about it?"

In a shop full of make-up? *Too easy.* I thought I'd better select something from the Blacks own-brand range 'Because you're worthless' so I settled on one of their foundation creams. I'd never used it, but what the hell, they're all pretty much the same. I focussed on the benefits: "It's so hydrating, lovely and light, thoroughly illuminating – like a face-lift in a tube! Oh yes, I use this one all the time."

"And how would you promote it to a Granny and how would this differ to a teenager?"

"Well, an older lady may be more interested in, er, looking more youthful, so I'd focus on that benefit and a teenager may be..." *may be what?* "they may want more spot coverage, perhaps, if they have greasy skin. I'm not saying all teenagers have bad skin, of course," I quickly added, not wishing to offend her. I realised, with horror that I hadn't picked up a foundation cream at all. It was fungal nail cream. At that moment, one of Kim's colleagues rushed over. "Kim! Sorry to interrupt, but there's a customer making a bit of a fuss at the pharmacy because her card's been declined. She's insisting on the manager."

"Oh, right. I'll be back in a minute, Kate."

I watched them head towards the pharmacy which was located at the back of the store and saw Kim trying to pacify an indignant middle-aged woman. I wandered over to listen in.

"How dare you insinuate that my account is overdrawn? It's your dreadful equipment that's faulty! I've plenty of money in my account! Heaps, in fact. Try it again."

I recognised that high-pitched whiny voice – it was Tory Melanie!

"I'm sorry Madam, but your card has been declined. Do you have any other forms of payment?"

"You can't possibly refuse my purchase; it's an outrage, *a disgrace*. I'll report you to, to the chemist ombudsman! My daughter needs her medication!"

On the counter were three Slim-Fast shakes, a packet of Senokot max strength tablets, and a yellow box with 'Kilo Trim' written on it.

"I'm very sorry, Madam. If you don't have any other means of payment, perhaps you could pop into the bank to see what's going on." Kim was impressively calm and assured.

"Oh, it's *outrageous!*" Tory Melanie was apoplectic. She snatched up her handbag and jabbed some numbers into her smartphone. As she stormed past me out of the shop, I heard her snap, "Guy, it's Mel again. Why haven't you returned my calls? It's about my investment; what's happened to my money-"

Oh dear. It didn't look as if Vera Wang could expect a visit anytime soon.

Kim and I returned to the make-up section but she told me she had everything she needed and the interview was complete. I didn't know if it had been more torturous for her or for me; she certainly shook my hand with huge relief. She said my interview had been "very positive", which I thought was pretty non-committal and that she'd call me at the end of next week after she had seen all the other candidates. There had, apparently, been a "massive amount of interest" in the role. I took that to mean "so it probably won't be you".

I left the store, passing Sultana Face who was tidying up the anti-wrinkle creams. Not really a great advert for them.

CHAPTER TWENTY-FIVE

"I've arranged to meet him on Friday, Kazza! I'm so nervous, but it's just for a drink. If it's too awful I'll just make an excuse and leave."

"Jesus Kate, you be careful; you've seen all those documentaries. I think I should come with you."

"No, don't be daft! We're meeting in the wine bar, it's all very public. I'll be fine."

"Well, keep your hand over your drink at all times in case he tries to put something in it and date-rapes you. And whatever you do, don't tell him where you live-"

"Bloody hell Karen! This was your idea, remember? If you thought it was so dangerous why on earth did you insist I joined a dating website?"

"I thought you'd enjoy a bit of cyber sex, of course! Swap a few dirty pics, indulge in some sexting and all that. Hardly anyone actually meets up, you know."

"Well, I want to meet a real person and have a real conversation; I don't want to hump my laptop or go down on my mobile. Anyway, it's all arranged now, so don't try and talk me out of it."

"Kate?"

"Yes?"

"For Christ's sake don't let him see that pre-historic Nokia of yours. At least scrape the moss off it first."

Friday night

I rushed home and leapt into the shower, belting out a Lady Gaga medley to keep my courage up. I was nervous, but really excited about seeing Mike - he could be The One! I dressed in my pencil skirt and black jumper again, the same getup as when I'd met Guy. It wasn't exactly my lucky outfit, but it was my newest. Would Mike actually turn up? Surely he would, he seemed so reliable; I was certain he wasn't the type to leave someone hanging. At the last minute, I swapped my M&S high-legged erection-killers for French knickers, just in case things went particularly well.

Cheltenham town centre was buzzing and I had to park in a street a good half-mile from the Montpelier Wine Bar, regretting wearing such high heels. I tried to walk elegantly but ended up hobbling like an old woman. I chanted my mantra to myself: "Men want a woman who is positive, upbeat and a blast to be around. They don't want a neurotic, chardy-swilling, lettuce leaf muncher who bleats on and on about her son-of-a-bitch ex-husband whilst viciously stabbing a toothpick into a gherkin."

There was a buzz of voices coming from the wine bar and I was met by a throng of people as I opened the door, most of whom gave me a quick glance then looked away. I shuffled my way apologetically towards the bar and caught sight of Mike seated on a bar stool with half a lager in front of him. Thank goodness - he'd turned up! He was wearing a pale blue shirt under a smart, light grey blazer and dark chinos; very nice.

"Hi, Mike!" I greeted him with a friendly smile.

"Kate!" he smiled warmly back and bent forward to kiss me on the cheek, which was all a bit awkward as he did this while remaining on his stool and ended up getting a mouthful of hairspray. "It's nice to meet you in person! What can I get you to drink?"

"Well, I'm driving," I said pointedly, "but I'm sure I'll be ok with a small glass of wine. I'll have a Chardonnay, please."

As he tried to catch the barman's attention, I pulled up a free stool and made a clumsy attempt to perch my bottom cheeks on the seat. It was just slightly too high, so I had to place one foot on a rung and wriggle myself up onto it. Bar stools are dreadful for posture; they crush you up and make your stomach look like a space hopper. I placed my handbag in front of my tummy, remembering to keep smiling.

"Here's your *small* one," said the barman, smirking at me. Cheeky sod. He'd never served me a small glass of wine before.

Conversation with Mike was a little stilted at first; "Well, here we are then!" "Yes, we meet at last!" but it soon improved into the relaxed friendly banter we'd enjoyed over the web cam. We both talked a lot about our work as we shared many similar issues and difficulties and he was very amusing when describing some of his colleagues. I noticed he was funny without being cruel, which was endearing so I tried to do the same; it took a good deal of effort. I kept the magic mantra in my head and when I slipped up and said something negative I immediately countered it with something positive: "I was saddled with this complete neurotic mess of a woman, she was absolutely useless ... oh, but at least she made super cakes, so actually, it was really great!"

I made my small glass of wine last as long as I could but I was dying for another one. It was all going so well; should I take a chance and let my hair down? I could always get a taxi home. But what if I went too far and started to slur and belch and tell crude jokes like I always did after a few too many glasses? No, best to try and appear demure at this early stage. Mike refused to let me buy him a drink which I thought was very gentlemanly and after my experience with Guy, somewhat of a relief.

"Look," he said, sipping his beer, "I know we said we'd just have a drink but I really am enjoying myself; would you like to get something to eat? The food here looks good."

"That would be really nice," I agreed, both surprised and delighted that he was enjoying my company. "As long as we go halves on the bill. That's the deal," I added firmly when I saw him about to protest.

"I think we should go downstairs to the bistro," he suggested. "The only free table up here is next to that strange looking couple and I think they're best avoided." I looked over to where he'd indicated and did a double take. There was a couple seated at a round table, both facing the bar. The woman was wearing a large, raspberry-coloured crushed velvet hat with, bizarrely, a peacock feather sticking up from one side. The hat was squashed right down over her eyes and a dark red scarf was pulled up almost to her nose but even so, I could tell it was Karen. The man with her had a ridiculous black bushy moustache and massive auburn side burns - James! Honestly, they looked utterly ludicrous. Realising they'd been spotted, James tried to bury his face in his pint glass and Karen seemed to find something fascinating to examine under the table. Recovering myself, I turned away from them and back to Mike, who was just dismounting from his bar stool. He all but disappeared. *Christ alive!* He was so short! I hadn't noticed whilst he'd been sat at the bar but now he was stood he only came up as far as my chest! His eyes were exactly level with my nipples.

I shot a desperate glance towards Karen and James. She had put her head down again but I could see her shoulders shaking uncontrollably and the peacock feather was bobbing about wildly. James still had his face in his glass but he appeared to be spluttering so much that his stupid moustache had slipped and was now dangling from his top lip. Feeling my face turning scarlet, I followed Mike through the bar and down the stairs to the bistro. Out of the corner of my eye I could sense that people were looking at us and nudging each other with amused grins. Poor Mike - he must have to put up with this all the time. Did he notice the unkind sniggers or had he become immune to it all?

We were shown to a table where I ordered a mineral water and then excused myself so I could escape to the sanctity of the Ladies. I didn't want to have a meal with him now; I just wanted to go home. I sat on the loo and covered my face with my hands. What was wrong with me? Why was I so shallow? He was a really nice guy, what did it matter if he was a bit on the short side? Looks didn't matter, personality did. Was I so insecure that I cared that much about what other people thought? Oh no! Oh God no! When I'd been talking about where I lived, I told him my house was so tiny it was only fit for a Hobbit-

"Kate? Are you in here?" It was Karen. "How's it going with Stuart Little?"

"His name is Mike, as you well know," I said irritably, flushing the loo. I emerged slowly from the cubicle, reluctant to face my smirking friend. "And you two look ridiculous."

"We thought we'd come incognito-"

"So what made you change your minds? You couldn't be more conspicuous if you tried! Where did that bloody feather come from? And James' moustache doesn't look the slightest bit real, his sideburns are a completely different colour!"

"Yes, he got those for a fancy dress party; he went as Bradley Wiggins."

"Jesus, the Scarlet Pimpernel's got nothing to be worried about, has he? Now, please leave me alone so I can at least enjoy my meal in peace."

"Oh yes, no problem," Karen leant cheerfully against the sink. "I'm not worried about you now. Even if he tries something you could easily overpower him. In fact, he's probably the one that needs protecting. Still, he's quite a handy height, isn't he? I mean, very convenient for-"

"Stop it!" I hissed.

"James reminded me of that joke, you know, the one where the woman goes to the doctor with chest pain and he says 'I'm sorry Madam, but I'm going to have to numb your breasts' and then he rubs his face in them - num num num-"

"*Bugger off* Karen! And take the cycling bandito with you."

I closed the door firmly behind me but I could still hear her laughing out loud. Mike looked up at me with huge relief when I rejoined him at the table. "Kate! There you are. I thought you'd, er, you'd, well, never mind. Here's your menu."

"Oh, isn't it small?" *Doh! Cringe.* "I mean, it's a limited selection ... I like that, actually, I don't like too much choice, or things that are, um, too big..." I trailed off. The easiness from earlier in the evening evaporated and our conversation became stilted and peppered with long silences. He ordered chicken and prawn skewers, which were delivered hanging vertically and embarrassingly, he had to stand up each time he wanted to reach the top of them. I picked miserably at my spicy sausage pasta then ordered the Tiramisu, saying jovially, "Oh, I never count calories! Life's too short, isn't it?" *Jesus Christ woman!* Then I ordered a coffee that I didn't want just so he didn't think I was in a tearing rush to get away from him.

When, at last, the meal was over, we stood awkwardly outside on the pavement. I refused his offer to walk me to my car saying it was parked "literally round the corner", thanked him for a lovely evening and lied that of course I'd love to do it again. That must have provided him with some kind of encouragement, as just as I lowered my head to search my handbag for my car keys, he seemingly thought I was leaning down for a kiss and made a sudden lunge at me, standing on his tiptoes to reach my mouth. I was taken completely by surprise. I was also trying to disguise a spicy sausage burp, so clamped my lips firmly together against his to avoid belching in his mouth. I felt his hot tongue prodding to get through the barrier but I clenched my jaw. When I could hold my breath no longer, I jerked my head away and to one side, exhaling my foul wind behind my hand.

"Gosh, sorry Mike, I thought I was about to sneeze."

"Ah, that was bad timing, wasn't it? Shall we try again?" He was standing very close and tried to put his arms around me, leaning forward again to kiss me. I had already started to back away and he ended up planting a cumbersome kiss on my collarbone.

"I really must go," I said, with excruciating embarrassment, edging out of his embrace. I actually patted him on the shoulder saying "Night night then!" as if he were a small child. I knew I should have been truthful but I was just too much of a coward. I hobbled and clattered my way back to the car, moving as quickly as I could, fearful he would drive past me and know I had lied about where I'd parked. When I finally reached the Focus, it was badly boxed in by a bully-boy BMW and it took me almost thirty manoeuvres to extract it. Biceps aching like hell, I set off for yet another depressing drive home at the end of yet another disastrous evening. How many more would I have to endure? How did single people stand it, or was it just me that had all the bad luck? I couldn't do this anymore; was anyone what they seemed? I could feel my last shred of courage packing its knapsack, ready to desert.

When I got home, I texted The Ex, saying I'd like to meet him for dinner at Chives.

Saturday

I turned on my mobile to find a voicemail message from Mike saying how much he'd enjoyed last night and when could we do it again? He'd also texted the same thing. Oh God. I was going to have to tell him I didn't want to see him again. What reason should I give? Sorry, but you're just not my size? I desperately didn't want to hurt his feelings, almost as much as I didn't want him to think I was the sort of shallow bimboid who cared about appearances and what other people thought. But I did care, so I was, as I'd long suspected, a shallow bimboid. Therefore, he was actually better off without me in his life. That thought made me feel a little better, so I took a deep breath and picked up the phone to call him. I put it down again; I couldn't do it. *Come on, man up. You've got to do the decent thing.* I picked it up again. Nope, I just couldn't do it. *You coward. You rotten, stinking, miserable coward.*

Should I text? No, that wouldn't do. What about email? Not much better, but at least I could write a longer message. I fired up the laptop and saw he'd already emailed me. Blimey, he really was keen. This was awful. I noticed Karen had emailed too. It read:

Morning Kate!
So, did you wake up feeling Happy? Or did Happy turn you down and now you're feeling Grumpy?
HI HO!
Give us a buzz
Kazza xxx

Very funny. I deleted it and started to type my message. It was incredibly difficult to write and I had to start again several times. Eventually, I went with:

Dear Stuart
I am so sorry not to have the courage to call you and I hope you will forgive my cowardice. Although it was really great to meet you and I very much enjoyed our evening together, I do not feel ready for a relationship at this time. I thought I would be when I joined the dating website but I'm afraid it is all a bit too soon.
I wish you all the very best for the future - I'm sure it won't be long until you find the perfect partner you very much deserve.
Kind regards
Kate

It was a bit of a lie but there was some truth in it too. I hit 'send' and got up to make a cup of coffee. As I stood at the kettle, pondering over the message, a horrid thought hit me. Oh no! Oh no no no! Had I written 'Dear Stuart'? Surely I hadn't? Heart in my mouth, I rushed back to the laptop and clicked on the sent items. I had! *Jesus!* I'd been thinking of Stuart Little when I wrote it! How awful. What the hell was he going to think? I desperately tried to remember how to recall a sent item and after much frenzied clicking, thought I'd managed it, but no; I got the message 'unable to recall item'. That meant he'd already read it.

I slumped on the sofa. Bloody Karen, this was all her fault. She'd called him Stuart Little. Poor Mike; how often did he have to put up with this? Would he think I was taking the piss out of him? I didn't know if I should email him again to say sorry or if that would make things worse. Why hadn't I just called him? It would have been awkward and embarrassing but it would have been the right thing to do. I stared at the screen feeling sick and after about ten minutes, a reply came back. Oh heck. I opened it, narrowing my eyes as if that was somehow going to protect me from the contents.

Kate

I was rather surprised to receive this email from you. Last night you told me that I was the only person you'd met up with. Presumably you told Stuart the same thing? Or perhaps you have been on so many dates you can't remember one from the other?

We both agreed that honesty was an essential part of any relationship so I find this particularly saddening, especially as we have both been lied to in the past. Or was that a lie too? As I do not feel able to trust you it is probably best that we do not see each other again. I feel

very concerned for you and your future - I will pray for you.
    Yours in great disappointment
    Mike

I will pray for you? I hadn't realised he was religious, but then, we hadn't discussed religion. He thought I was an untrustworthy, deceitful, lying, two-faced, satanic trollop, but at least he hadn't made the Stuart Little connection - *what a relief!*

Chapter Twenty-Six

I found an official-looking letter on my desk marked 'Private and Confidential'. I opened it up.

Dear Kate King   .

You are required to attend a formal meeting on Tuesday 17th at 10.00am in meeting room 4, Cheltenham following your failure to meet the required standards as detailed in your progress plan.

You are advised to seek representation to accompany you to this meeting. If you are unable to attend, please inform the hearing manager immediately.

Yours sincerely
Roger Fitzall
Hearing Manager

I stared at it in dismay. How could *Roger* be the hearing manager? They were supposed to be impartial! He hadn't even used the standard HR invite letter, he'd simply knocked up a memo. He may just as well have scrawled it on the back of a receipt from Tesco's. I had to assume the hearing was a week on Tuesday because he hadn't bothered to put the month in. Just over a week and I could be out of a job. I'd get one month's salary then that was it. Destitute, prostitute, *oh Christ*. Tears welled up but I forced them down. Can't cry in front of the troops. I picked up the phone and dialled the number for the union. I needed help. I needed a bloody miracle.

My phoned peeped. I had a text from my brother. *"Georgia in labour! Can u tell George? Cant contact him"*

What? Surely Georgia wasn't due for ages yet! Where the bloody hell was George? I rushed over to his desk and saw his iPhone lying on top of his FHM magazine. He'd missed twelve calls. Typical! He was always attached to the bloody thing and now, the one and only time he actually needed it, he'd chosen to bugger off somewhere without it!

"Where's George?" I snapped at Hissing Cyn. She didn't know. One of his team suggested he might have gone round to the Concerns teams to discuss a complaint with them. Hmmm. TCLS George proactively dealing with a piece of work? That didn't sound very convincing. I sent The Drain to search the fourth floor and The Snake to search the third while I headed to the canteen. No sign of him there. He wasn't outside in the fag hut or wondering aimlessly around the car park pretending it was his 'thinking time'. Where was he?

I took the back stairs and as I reached the landing between the second and third floors, there he was. Leant with one arm against the wall and the other up the jumper of a young blonde girl who seemed to have her hands on his-

"George!"

They sprang apart, both their faces flaming up. "Oh, Kate, I was just, er-"

"Yes, I can see what you were just doing, thanks George." *So this is where he disappears to.* "This is a bloody office you know, not a knocking shop. I thought you should know that Georgia has gone into labour."

The blonde girl stared at me. "What's that got to do wiv 'im?"

I looked at her sadly as George shook his head vigorously at me behind her back. "You'll have to ask George about that, won't you? But not now, you should be working. Who's your team manager?"

"I work in the kitchens."

"Right, well, off you go and for Christ's sake wash your hands before you touch any food." She shot TCLS George a furious look as she departed. "You'd better get to the hospital, George, you don't want to miss the birth. Of your child." Oh dear God. George was about to reproduce.

I met Big Andy on the stairwell and told him about my impending hearing. He boomed at me, the echoey stairs making him louder than ever. "It sounds like you're giving up, Kato! It's not like you to throw in the towel! Where have your balls gone? Aren't you the same Kate the Lion King that disarmed Psycho Simon when he went berserk in the canteen after he'd only found two pieces of mushroom in his omelette? That wasn't for the faint-hearted! No one else had the nerve to wrestle that frying pan off him. You've got to stand up to the bastards, Kate; bloody well fight for your rights!"

"I don't know if I've got any fight left in me, Andy; I'm so drained. I'm thinking that maybe I should just go quietly. After all, I can't do what he's asking me to, so it's not the job for me anymore, is it?"

"You can't do it because it's not humanly possible! And he bloody well knows it's not - he's been told to get you out before they announce our closure and have to pay you off. He's started on me too, you know. He's sent in a bunch of efficiency consultants; they're all over my Finance team like a dose of the clap. You know they've got me filling in a logging form which explains what I'm logging and why I'm logging it? So something that's been taking me fifteen minutes to do now takes the whole bloody day! How the hell is that efficient?"

I'd never heard Big Andy be so feisty before. He was rattled. I owed it to him to put up a fight. I wasn't going to topple into the illy tin on top of my long-lost colleagues like a spineless slug; I had to fight to stay out of the death trap. Even if I didn't win, it might at least make The GPS think twice before treating Big Andy and others the same way. It might. A little voice inside my head told me it might not.

As I waited for news of Georgia and the baby, Bridgend David called. "Hi Kate. I've got George's doctor report at long last. Guess what?"

"There's nothing wrong with him?"

"Correct. George first reported his OCD symptoms to his doctor two days before his hearing. There was no mention of it at any time before that so the doctor hasn't taken him very seriously by all accounts. I called HR for advice but do you know what they said?"

"Er, that it's not their decision, they're not there to give advice, they don't know why they exist and it's all up to you?"

"Spot on! So I'm as comfortable as I can be that I should dismiss George. I considered demoting him, but because of his sickness and lateness issues he's blown that possibility. I'll send George an invite for one week and I'll be down to do the dirty deed."

Could the timing be any worse? "You should know his partner's just gone into labour," I said sadly. "He's about to become a father."

"Oh. That's a shitter." I could hear David scratching his chin. He could do with a shave. "That doesn't change the outcome, though, but I could make the meeting for two weeks time, just to give him a bit longer?"

"Yes, that would be good." So George only had two weeks left. How long did I have?

I hadn't long been back at home when the doorbell rang. I gave a groan of frustration; I'd started to wrap Karen's birthday presents and had just managed to contain the hairy yellow cardigan within a sheet of wrapping paper. I opened the door to find Kieron standing in front of me, clutching a green tool bag. "Hi Kate!" he exclaimed cheerfully. "Stu said you had some problems with your plumbing?" *Not quite yet, but Tena Lady was lurking just around the corner.*

"Well, yes, I have, but I asked Stu if he could-"

"Ah, yes, but they're all at the hospital so he asked me to call round. There's no news yet."

I smiled and thanked him for coming, letting him in so I could show him the leaky shower. How much was this visit going to cost me? I would have paid my brother, of course, but he'd do me a friends and family rate.

I finished wrapping the cardigan and fired up the laptop, intending to catch up on some work emails while Kieron banged about in the bathroom. I saw I had one from The GPS entitled "Kate King Progress Plan." I opened it up to find a copy of my plan peppered with a detailed analysis of my performance and the words DID NOT MEET emblazoned at the end of every objective. It wasn't subtle. For the very first time in my life, I couldn't face a Marmite sandwich. Where was the nearest food bank? I'd better make enquiries.

Kieron appeared. "All done! The shower tray just needed sealing. Too easy! I noticed the bathroom door is sticking; shall I come back another time and have a bash at that?"

"Um," *Not unless you accept payment in kind.* "That would be great, but I'll have to let you know, if that's ok. How much do I owe you for this visit?"

"Oh, don't be daft! It was nothing. Don't worry about it."

"But I must give you something, for your petrol at least, or-"

"No, honestly, it's fine." We were stood by the front door but he was hovering. "Oh, I meant to tell you! Do you remember your stall at the fete? The balloon race? Well, my balloon ended up in Rosslare! That's in Ireland," he added when he saw me looking blank. "And as it went the furthest, I won the Pizza Palace meal-"

"Bad luck!"

"Aaand I was going to ask if you'd like to come with me."

I stared at him. He'd gone slightly pink. I could feel my face getting hot, too. Was he asking me out? On a date? Or was he just asking because he felt sorry for me? God, I was such a goon. Say something ... "Oh! Er, that's very kind of you, Kieron." *Kind? He hasn't just offered to drive you to the varicose vein clinic!* "Um-"

"As you bought the winning balloon for me, I thought it would be nice if you came too." *Ah, he was just being polite.* "It's

351

actually a meal for four, so I wondered about asking your brother and Kirsty to come, too." He saw my face and quickly added, "Or not. But I thought they could do with a night out, as they've been having a few, er, problems lately and I know you and Kirsty don't exactly see eye to eye, but it might be a chance to all have a fun night out together. Bury the hatchet, perhaps." He studied my face anxiously, fiddling nervously with his screwdriver.

"Kirsty would love to bury the hatchet alright," I said gloomily. "Straight into my skull. You know what a nightmare she is after a few drinks. Look, it's very sweet of you to think of it but are you sure you really want to waste your winnings on my dysfunctional family and other animals? I mean, wouldn't you rather ask some gorgeous girl to go with you?"

"I thought I just had." He fixed me with his lovely blue eyes. My knees went weak. Was he for real, or was he just messing around? I covered my uncertainty by laughing maniacally; I sounded like a car trying to start.

"Oh, you are funny!" I rubbed at my forehead in a hopeless attempt to cover my flaming face. "Well, if you're that hard up for a date I'd better say yes, then, hadn't I?"

"Great!" he sounded relieved. "Shall I book a table for Friday? I think Kirsty's shift at Aldi finishes at six, so if I book for seven she should at least turn up sober. What do you think?"

"Won't she want to be with Georgia and the baby?"

He laughed. "You have met Kirsty, haven't you? I think she and Stu will be keener to wet the baby's head. I'll pick you up, shall I? About six thirty?"

"Oh, er, yes, thanks, but don't you want to have a drink?"

"Tut tut! Trying to get me drunk on our first date, are you?" he laughed, picking up his tool bag. "My mother warned me about girls like you! I'll see you on Friday."

I saw him out and waved him off, lost in thought. So was it a date? Or just an act of kindness? Or of sympathy? Was he feeling sorry for a lonely, middle-aged woman whose house was slowly disintegrating around her (hair-sprouting) ears, along with the rest of her life? Or had he clocked the state of the house and realised it would keep him in business for years to come?

I asked Karen for an opinion when we met up for her birthday drinks. "Ooh, I know Kieron, he's lush! Did he actually say it was a date?"

"Well, he accused me of trying to get him drunk on our first date but he was laughing when he said it. He said his mother warned him about girls like me, but he was joking, of course."

"Ah! His mother? He's younger than you, isn't he?"

"Yes, a bit-"

"What's his relationship with his mother like?"

"What? How the hell should I know?"

"You've got to be careful, Kate, he may be suffering from Oedipus complex; it's extremely common, you know. Did he talk about his mother much? Does he seem fixated on her? What about when he adds milk to his tea, does he eye up your breasts and lick his lips-"

"*Jesus* Karen, he's only a couple of years younger than me! And I'm hardly the motherly type, am I?"

"Hmmm. Where's he taking you?"

"The Pizza Palace."

"I bet his mum used to take him there! If he asks you to

cut up his pepperoni and swoop it into his mouth like an aeroplane, run for your life."

"I really don't know why I asked you." I handed over her present. "Here you go. Happy birthday!"

I watched her unwrap the yellow monstrosity, getting my camera ready to capture one of those priceless "What the fuck?!" moments.

On my way into work, I received a text from my brother: "Girl Ellie Bo 7 lbs. Both ok. Am a grandad! Sort of!" Blimey, seven pounds? Wasn't that a normal weight for a baby? I thought Georgia's baby was born prematurely. I sent congratulatory texts to both my brother and to George when I got to my desk. I supposed I was technically an Auntie now. Step-aunt Kate. That sounded awful. I'd be wearing glasses on a string next.

My phone rang and I picked it up to hear Stalin Stan's stroppy voice in my ear. "There's a visitor for you. Alan Jenkins. I wasn't told about him, you know, it's not acceptable; Reception must be informed about all visitors, it's critical for the security of this building-"

"He's from the union, Stan, not Al-Qaeda. If you're worried about an attack, stick another cone out by the entrance. That should foil the bastards." I went down to Reception to meet the man who, I hoped, would be my saviour. I found a short, stout, crumpled-looking man attempting to flatten down wisps of sandy hair across his balding head.

"Alan? Hi, I'm Kate." I shook his clammy hand, ignoring Stan's red angry face glowering at me from behind his counter.

"Yes, yes, I'm sorry I'm late, both my trains were delayed. Signal failure this time, at Bristol. Usually it's the wrong type of leaves on the track at this time of year and then of course, it will be the jumpers over Christmas and into January. It's just one excuse after the other."

"I expect you could do with a coffee," I said, guiding him through the revolving doors. "The canteen is just through here."

"Well, I mustn't have coffee because of the effect it has on my restless leg syndrome, nor tea, of course. I'll just have a hot water with a slice of lemon and hope it doesn't aggravate my colon."

For God's sake. Why could I never meet anyone healthy? I got myself a strong cup of coffee and a lemon tea for Alan. I did ask Grinding Greta for a hot water and a slice of lemon but she snapped, "We don't serve cocktails." I sat down with Alan at a table in the corner and he produced a dog-eared copy of my action plan from a greasy cardboard folder.

"I've had a good review of your case on the train. Lucky there were so many delays really; it's quite a lengthy read, isn't it!" He snorted with laughter, changing it to a cough when he realised I wasn't going to join in. "No, seriously though, it's a very comprehensive plan with targets clearly set and thoroughly reviewed. We don't often see this level of detail and clarity, you know. It's like a breath of fresh air!"

Was he for real? He was supposed to be on my side! "But it was never a jointly-agreed plan, Alan. I haven't ever had a detailed discussion with my line manager about my performance, which surely you'd expect? I've never been set an informal plan so he's just skipped that bit and gone straight to formal. He hasn't followed policy at all."

"Hmmm, well, there is that, of course." He rubbed his temples. "But it's a bit difficult to see what our defence is actually going to be. He has clearly stated in the plan what the consequences of failure are so there's no getting away from that." There was a short, sharp squeak. What the hell was that? I glanced anxiously down beneath the table. Had it finally happened - were there rodents loose in the canteen?

"No," he continued with a sigh. "It's all pretty much sown up. We could try the old lack of support thing, I suppose. Have you had documented one to ones?" There was another prolonged squeak. He pulled out a grubby handkerchief and pressed it to his nose. "My sinusitis. Long train journeys wreak absolute havoc with it."

"I can't say I've had any support from Roger at all. He turns up, finds something to criticise, tells me it's not good enough then goes again. It's obviously a new style of management - hates, shoots and leaves. He returns a couple of days later to repeat the process. He doesn't provide any coaching or give me any clues as to how I can make the improvements."

"Have you asked him for support?"

"I do keep asking for more staff. My numbers are significantly down on last year whilst volumes are up and yet my targets are still increased. I'm told I can't recruit."

"Mmm, yes, the recruitment freeze is a nuisance, isn't it?"

A nuisance? Having a bit of an itchy bum was a nuisance. Not having enough people to support the business was disastrous; colleagues were knackered and fed up, customers were frustrated because everything took so long, systems didn't work, complaints were piling up. Oh no, sorry, *comments* were piling up...

"So what are we saying here, Alan?" I was beginning to lose patience. "That my best chance of being able to keep my job is to claim that I haven't been given the correct amount of support?"

"Well, I ... oh!" He looked at me, eyes wide with alarm. "Oh no! Oh no no no! Was there caffeine in this tea?" His left leg suddenly shot straight out and caught me in the shin.

"Ow! Bloody hell Alan!"

"Sorry, sorry-" his right leg kicked out this time, whacking the table's pedestal so hard that my coffee slopped all over his file. He leapt up and started striding around the canteen, lifting up each leg in giant, exaggerated goose steps. The canteen staff stopped dead in their tracks, staring at him in astonishment.

"Sorry about this, Kate," he called, as he kicked out. "Restless legs. Bit of a nightmare. Still, better now than when I'm in bed. The wife has to sleep wearing cricket pads, you know."

As I watched him perform his demented can-can, accompanied by his squeaking nostrils, I felt my last tiny bubble of hope floating away.

At home, I found a message on my voicemail from The Ex. "Hi Kate, hope all's well. I've booked a table at Chives for eight o'clock on Friday night, hope that's ok with you? I checked and they will have their spicy meatballs on the menu! Really looking forward to it. Bye."

Oh, *drat*. I was supposed to be going out with Kieron on Friday. Why had I agreed to it? I knew it wasn't a real date and the evening would only end in disaster again. The Bunny

Boiler would probably slice me up into six pieces like a bloody pizza. I didn't want to go to the crappy old Poxy Palace when I could get all dressed up and go to Chives. That pencil skirt wouldn't fit me forever. Chives had twinkly fairy lights and lovely waiters who pretended to flirt with you. Perhaps I should cancel on Kieron; he was a laid-back sort of chap after all so I'm sure he wouldn't mind. He'd probably be a bit relieved, even. But it had been so kind of him to ask us all and I'd already said I would go. *Buggeration.* The meatballs would have to wait. I dialled The Ex's number and left a message on his voicemail, asking if we could make it next Friday instead. I hoped he would pay. There was every chance I'd be signing on by then.

Friday

Hissing Cyn slithered over, eyes all glinty. "Have you seen George's tattoo, Kate? He had it done last night. I wondered what you thought of it?"

I looked at her suspiciously. "And what do you think of it, Cyn?"

"Well, it's not for me to say anything, of course, but I don't know what the company thinks of team managers with tattoos on their necks. I mean, it's not the sort of image Perypils wants, is it?"

George had a tattoo on his neck? I followed The Snake back towards George's desk where I could make out an angry looking red patch of skin on the side of his neck, just below his right ear. As I got closer, I could see it read 'Ellie Bo'. What on earth had possessed him? Why not on his arm or his chest? Or on the top of his head; that was all anyone ever saw of him as he constantly fiddled with his phone. And his other

scrolly bits. He looked like he should be in charge of the
waltzer at a fairground. He might be doing that sooner than
he realised.

"That looks sore, George," I said.

"Yeah, my mate did it," he said proudly. "He's thinking
about taking it up professionally. You know, when he gets
over the DT's and all that."

"How is Georgia? And Ellie?"

"They're at home. At her mum's, that is. They're gonna
stay one week there and the next week at her dad's. Alternate,
like. Until I can get a bigger flat."

I wouldn't hold your breath.

The Snake was hovering, hoping for a scene but I just
didn't have the energy. Besides, George would be gone soon.
And so might I. Meet Step-auntie Kate: jobless, manless,
homeless, gutless.

CHAPTER TWENTY-SEVEN

Friday night

I'd been in back-to-back meetings all day over the POQS issue and every single one of them had overrun. I drove home like an absolute maniac, getting in at ten past six. Damn it - there was no time to shower, Kieron was picking me up at half past. In a frenzy, I swished bronzing powder over my face and applied another clumpy layer of mascara. What was I going to wear? It was only the Pizza Palace so it had to be something casual. I whipped my skinny jeans out of the cupboard and managed to get them done up by lying flat on my back on the bed but when I sat up I just couldn't breathe. Sod it - they were no good. Nothing else for it; time for the fat suit. I grabbed a soft green tunic top and a pair of black leggings. The tunic used to be loose-fitting but now I could clearly see my stomach protruding. I looked like a snake that had swallowed a small dog. I struggled into a pair of M&S shapewear pants, which helped spread my stomach up to my rib cage so at least it looked a little flatter. Let's hope I won't be needing my kidneys this evening.

The doorbell rang. *Christ, he was here already.* I snatched up a bottle of perfume and gave myself a liberal squirting before dashing downstairs to open the door.

"Hi! Sorry Kieron, running a bit late! Day from hell."

"No worries." He came in and immediately started to cough. "Sorry," he spluttered, "something caught in my throat." Oh dear, I must have gone overboard with the perfume. It was in an unbranded bottle, a gift from Karen; swiped, I suspected, from the Shit-A-Brick stall. The way Kieron was gasping for breath I wondered if it actually contained Mace.

"Would you like a glass of water?" I asked anxiously. The date hadn't even begun and I'd already tried to gas him.

"No, no, I'm fine," he lied, mopping his eyes. "I'm afraid I've had to bring my van; my car's off the road." He was coughing again.

"Oh and I was expecting the five star treatment! Never mind, that's pretty typical of my luck!"

At least he was laughing now as he choked to death. I picked up my coat and we left the house; there was no sign of Mervyn, thank goodness, although a curtain twitched. I had to climb up into the van's passenger seat, relieved to note that there was a strong smell of wood glue. Surely that could overpower my toxic fumes? We set off towards town. Kieron's mobile kept ringing and he eventually turned it off.

"My ex," he said, apologetically. "She wanted me to have Max tonight but I said no. Now she's got the hump."

"Oh dear! Was it for something important?"

"Karaoke at the Rat and Parrot, most likely. She's always the same when X Factor starts, suddenly thinks she's Kylie. Anyway, we agreed I'd pick Max up tomorrow morning; he's staying at mine for the weekend but she wanted to go out tonight. She can't keep changing arrangements at the last minute, it's unsettling for Max. I put my foot down."

"It must be difficult."

"Well, it shouldn't be, not really." His face was impassive. "If you make plans you should stick to them. That way, everyone knows where they stand." I nodded in agreement, glad I hadn't cancelled on him. He shot me a sideways glance. "Do you still see your ex?"

I hesitated before answering. "I was supposed to be seeing him tonight." I looked at him. "But I decided not to." What would he make of that? I realised I was holding my breath.

"Oh, right," he said. "That's-" he spluttered, then started to cough again. That's *what*? Good? Alarming? Disturbing? This bloody perfume! I wound my window down a little, desperate for him to complete his sentence, but it was such a prolonged fit that by the time he'd recovered, the moment had passed.

The Pizza Palace was in full swing, even though it was only seven o'clock. A pretty young raven-haired waitress showed us to our table and we ordered some drinks while waiting for Stu and Kirsty. I hoped they wouldn't turn up and it seemed like my wish might be granted; by seven thirty there was still no sign of them. Kieron tried calling Stu, but it went straight to voicemail.

"Do you think something's happened?" I asked. "Perhaps Georgia's landed them with the baby to look after."

"I'm sure they would have called one of us," said Kieron, looking concerned. "Do you think we ought to go round there to check? Oh, no need, here's Stu now!"

I looked up to see my brother barging through the doors and peering blearily around the restaurant before spotting us. He staggered over and crashed down into one of the vacant chairs.

"You alright, Stu?" asked Kieron, tentatively.

"Am I alright?" he slurred. "Well, I will be soon." He beckoned to the waitress. "Large Jack Daniels, please, no ice.

Don't want to dilute it!" He leant forwards to kiss me on the cheek. "Jesus Sis! What happened? Doused yourself in petrol? Christ alive! You'd make an onion cry!"

"Er, yes, I might have been a bit heavy-handed," I muttered, not looking at Kieron. "What's going on, Stu? Where's Kirsty?"

"Well, that's the six billion dollar question, isn't it? Shall I tell you where she is?" he picked up my Chardonnay and took a large swig. "She's with another bloke! Oh yes! She's met someone else."

Kieron and I looked at each other. "Are you sure, mate?" he asked. "You're not confused, or, er-" *Just completely pissed?*

"She met him online. Been going on for weeks it has, behind my back. She knows I'm not very good on the computer but Georgia logged on and accidentally got into Kirsty's emails. And bam! There were about a hundred messages from this bloke. I knew something was up, I knew it." His drink arrived and he knocked it back, looking around to order another.

"But she's not actually seeing him?" I checked. "Is it just emails? And texts?"

"Cyber sex, Sis," he tried to focus on me. "It's just as bad. She's been *mentally* unfaithful. In she walked from work, like butter wouldn't melt, trying to get round me with an out-of-date trout that the fish counter was going to throw away and I fronted her with these messages. I'd stuck them all round the kitchen; Georgia printed them off for me."

"What happened?" I asked.

"Well, she could hardly deny it, could she? I'd got her bang to rights. She wasn't even sorry; told me this guy made her feel like a princess and I made her feel like a bag of spanners."

"I'm sure she didn't mean it, mate," Kieron tried.

"Oh, she meant it alright." He finished his second drink and sat swaying at the table. "It's all over. Do you want to see what the bastard looks like? Georgia found him on Facebook and sent his picture to my phone." He peered at his iPhone, jabbing at it with his finger. "There. Nothing special, is he? His name's David Zeller. What a wanky name. I bet it's not even his real one."

David Zeller? Why did that name ring a bell? I looked at my brother's phone and saw the familiar long unsmiling face, serial-killer eyes - it was my online eDates stalker. I couldn't say that, of course, I didn't want them to know I'd been using a dating website. How had he and The Bunny Boiler come into contact? Had she been using the website too? I could just imagine her profile: "Devil worshipper seeks like-minded gentleman for wining and dining, good conversation, romantic walks and slaughtering rabbits in cemeteries at midnight".

"I've sent the bastard a message, of course, several in fact. Well, it was Georgia that typed them. Do you want me to read them to you?"

"No!" we both cried.

"Best not mate, not in the restaurant." Kieron glanced anxiously around. "I think we'd better get you home."

"Home? I haven't got a home!"

"We'll go back to mine," I said, nodding at Kieron. "Come on Stu, up we get. Yes, yes, there's plenty of booze back at mine! Come on, let's go."

We helped Stu to his feet and Kieron supported him out through the doors while I settled up for the drinks. The fresh air didn't do him any favours and his legs buckled.

"I'll have to put him in the back of the van," panted Kieron. "There's not enough room in the front for all of us." He leant Stu against the van while he opened the back doors. I peered inside at all the tools and crates.

"We can't put him in there, Kieron, there's too many sharp things. He'll do himself a mischief the state he's in."

"But-"

"Put him in the front. I'll get in the back."

Kieron looked doubtful, but there really wasn't any choice. We got him into the passenger seat and put his seatbelt on. I crawled into the back and sat down on a bag of sand. It was pitch black when Kieron closed the doors. The van shuddered into life and I clung onto the edge of the bag for dear life. The tools clanged and rattled about alarmingly and when Kieron took a corner too sharply, something fell on my head causing me to cry out in pain. I fumbled around in the dark; the perpetrator had a long, wooden handle with a metal end - a hoe, perhaps? I rubbed my head, willing the journey to end. I felt very close to throwing up. Why the hell hadn't I cancelled? I could be in Chives right now, sipping Chablis from a glass the size of a goldfish bowl and nibbling on a stuffed olive.

At last, the van came to a halt and Kieron opened the doors. "Are you ok?" he asked anxiously. "Sorry about the scythe, let me help you out. There's an ambulance outside your neighbour's house- oh God, I've got to get Stu, he's wandering in the road." He disappeared, leaving me to shuffle on my bum towards the doors. Who was the ambulance for? It was outside Mervyn's. I could see Doris and Ernie stood anxiously by the open front door.

My tone-deaf brother was singing at the top of his lungs "I can't live ... if living is without you! I can't give! I can't live anymore!" as Kieron tried to shepherd him back towards the house. I rushed up Mervyn's drive. "What's happened?" I asked Doris. "Has Mervyn been taken ill? Or is it Sissy?"

"Um," Doris glanced awkwardly at Ernie and then had to step aside as two grinning ambulance men carried a stretcher out of the house. I saw a pair of Hush Puppies, a long flowery dress, hands with red painted nails folded over a sizable bust, long dark hair, a stubbly chin - and Mervyn's face. His orange lip-sticked lips were contorted in pain.

I looked at Doris, stunned. "His back's gone," explained Doris. "It's happened before; he has trouble with the suspenders, I think ... don't you worry, we'll go with him. He'll be fine." Ernie nodded swiftly and I realised I'd been dismissed. Neither of them seemed in the least bit shocked.

In a daze, I stumbled down Mervyn's drive and helped push Stu in through my front door. Kieron managed to get him upstairs by telling him there was a bottle of whisky in the spare bedroom. He crashed out on the bed like a starfish singing, "Don't you want me, baby? Don't you want me, oh oh oh."

"Shall I make him some coffee?" I asked from the safety of the doorway. Drunks always scared me; or actually, it was vomit that scared me. I couldn't even be in the same room as a bowl of carrot and coriander.

"No, I don't think that's going to help," Kieron replied, tugging Stu's shoes off. "I'll try and get some water down him; it might thin out the booze. I'd better stay with him for a while. He's not usually sick but just in case."

I was about to fetch a bucket when the doorbell rang.

My blood ran cold. *Please don't let that be The Bunny Boiler.* I'm too exhausted to deal with any more drama tonight. I'd like to squeeze into the cupboard under the stairs, shut the door on everyone and sleep for an entire year.

I opened the door to find The Ex stood there. He was very smartly dressed in a charcoal grey suit, white shirt and grey and silver striped tie. It was rather comforting to see such a familiar face on the weirdest evening ever.

"Oh, Kate, you are in!" he exclaimed. "I was just passing by, on my way back from an appointment and I saw an ambulance coming out of your road. I wondered if everything was ok? I thought you were out tonight?"

He looked full of concern. I was surprised; he never used to do evening appointments on a Friday. But then, this was a changed man. Perhaps he'd discovered a new work ethic. I sighed. "I have been out but things didn't exactly go to plan."

"Oh dear! Well, if you fancy it, I expect I could still get us that table at Chives. They don't stop serving until ten."

He looked so eager and hopeful. "You'd better come in," I said, standing back from the door. "I don't think I can really go to Chives in these filthy old leggings and to be honest, I haven't got the energy to change. The best I can do is a cheese toastie. How's that?"

He laughed, stepping into the hall. "Just like old times, then! We used to survive on a diet of toasties and fish finger sandwiches, didn't we?" *Yes, we did and you moaned like buggery every single time.*

"Blimey, what's that smell?"

"It's, um, cleaning fluids, I think," I said vaguely.

"I was working as a waitress in a cocktail bar when I met you!"

The Ex looked at me in alarm. "What the hell was that?"

"But now I think it's time I live my life on my own!"

"It's Stu. Bit drunk, I'm afraid. Another falling out with Kirsty."

"Ah. I thought that was his van outside."

"Oh no, that's not-"

"Now, you must have some wine open somewhere! You never serve cheese toasties without vats of vino to wash them down! Shall I get us a glass?" He was opening cupboards, searching for wine and glasses. It felt quite nice to have someone wait on me, even if it was only to pour a glass of wine. "So, you were out with Stu tonight, were you? I thought you were being a bit mysterious about your plans! Made me think you had a hot date! But it was only Stu..." He was humming as he busied himself, wiping up a couple of glasses from the draining board and opening a bottle of red. He wouldn't be humming when he tasted it; I'd got in on special at the Co-op.

"We were supposed to be meeting Stu and Kirsty at the Pizza Palace," I told him, cutting up some cheese. "But it was just Stu that turned up and he was in a right old state. He thinks Kirsty's having an affair. We didn't have much choice but to get him back here as soon as we could."

"We?"

"Yes, me and Kieron. He's upstairs, looking out for Stu."

The Ex looked up at the ceiling as if expecting to see through it. His face had fallen. "You and Kieron? Why was Kieron there?"

"Er, well, he'd won a meal for four so he asked me and Stu and Kirsty to go with him." I lined up six slices of wholemeal toast on the grill pan, taking care not to meet his eye. "Do you want Worcester sauce on yours?"

He wouldn't be thrown. "But why did Kieron ask *you*? He's got a girlfriend, hasn't he? Why didn't he ask her to go?"

"Because he won the meal at my stall. I was helping out at a school fete, you see and I paid for his balloon so I think he felt obliged to ask me." I knew that made no sense whatsoever. The Ex took a sip of his wine, unable to stop himself wincing at the acidic taste. I made a mental note to try it on the limescale around the bath.

"But you hate the Pizza Palace," he said, sounding sulky. "You always used to say you'd never go there because you didn't want to wake up attached to a life support machine. I can't believe you turned down Chives to go there. Why did you?"

Why had I? Had I felt obliged to go because of Kieron's generosity or was it because I thought there might be a chance that Kieron was interested in me? But why was I being forced to explain myself in my own home? I felt a stab of irritability.

"I thought it was very nice of Kieron to ask me," I said, folding my arms defensively. "And he's been absolutely brilliant since I moved in here; my saviour, actually. He's been round a couple of times to fix-"

"I bet he has! He fancies you!"

"Of course he doesn't! He's just a thoroughly decent guy."

"*Bollocks!* I never thought you could be so naïve, Kate! Come on, he's after you and the fact that you've got a house that requires constant running repairs is a dream come true for him. Provides the perfect excuse to keep popping round and playing the hero." He braced himself and took a glug of wine. "Look, it's not your fault, Kate. You've probably been friendly with him and he's read too much into it. Would you like me to have a quiet word with him? I don't mind."

I saw a sudden movement by the kitchen door. Kieron was standing there. Oh no, how long had he been there? How much of that had he heard? My face fired up. "Hi Kieron! I was just making toasties if you fancy one. How's Stu?"

He came into the kitchen and leant against the fridge, looking directly at The Ex. "He got through most of Don't You Want Me which was pretty impressive really, but then he tried to take on Stand By Your Man and fell asleep muttering 'sometimes it's hard to be a woman'." That made me think of Mervyn.

The Ex stood up straighter, pulling himself up to his full height. "Well, it's been very kind of you to look after him, Kieron, very kind indeed. I expect you'll want to get on your way now, won't you? Are you meeting your girlfriend later?"

"He's missed out on his pizza tonight!" I said quickly, not wanting to offend Kieron. "A toastie is the least I can do. Anyway, they're nearly ready now."

The Ex let out a burst of phoney laughter. "I'm sure Kieron doesn't want your burnt offerings, love! I bet he's got something much hotter waiting for him!" He turned back to Kieron. "Don't let us keep you."

The awkward silence was broken by the phone ringing. I couldn't answer it as I was trying to wrestle the cumbersome grill pan from the oven. Karen's voice burst into the room: "Hi Kate! I hope you can't get to the phone because the luscious Kieron is taking you roughly over the ironing board. Remember - a pity shag is better than no shag at all! I hope he doesn't shout 'Mummy' when he comes! You probably already know but I heard that Barringtons have laid off all their financial advisors, so your ex is out of a job. I thought I'd warn you in case the slimy bastard comes slithering around again. Do you fancy a spot of shopping tomorrow? If you can still walk, that is! Byeeee!"

In the deathly hush that followed, I laid the pan carefully down on the work surface. I couldn't look at either of them. The Ex spoke first. "Well, that was offensive," he said, sniffily. "I daresay she's pissed again, but really, there was no call for that. She was so rude. About Kieron, I mean. Obviously, *I'm* well-accustomed to her sense of humour." I turned to him. He took a sip from his glass and didn't meet my eye.

"Have you lost your job?" I asked him. He shifted uncomfortably.

"Barringtons has been going through a tough time, yes. Most companies have."

I looked at his fancy tie, his smart suit. "Why are you all dressed up? You never do evening appointments on a Friday." He didn't reply. "You've been for an interview somewhere, haven't you?"

"Oh, so you're Miss bleeding Marple now, are you!" He snapped sarcastically then quickly caught himself. "I mean, yes, I have been for an interview. With Charter Estate Agents; they're looking for an experienced mortgage advisor. It's a great opportunity."

"You never mentioned your job was in jeopardy. In fact, I recall you saying it was going really well."

There was a short silence. Kieron looked from one of us to the other, his face creased with embarrassment. The Ex pursed his lips. "I didn't tell you because I didn't want to worry you. And I didn't want it to cloud things. You know, us getting back together. It would just have made things, er, confusing."

"Yes, you're probably right. You telling the truth for once in your life would have confused me! God, how stupid am I, thinking you might have changed - you're still Billy Bullshit!"

He flushed. "You're over-reacting as usual. I simply wanted us to concentrate on how we felt, not about jobs and finances and stuff. That way, we'd be getting back together for the right reasons."

I studied his red shifty face. "What are the *right* reasons? To keep a roof over your head? You've lost your job and you're on your own so you thought you'd get back with me for a while so you had somewhere to live! Or were you planning on moving me into the flat as a lodger to cover the rent? One in one out!" A peel of hysterical laughter burst from me, making both men jump. "That's hilarious! And what would you have done when I lost *my* job? Lined up some other sucker? Worked your way back through all your exes until one caved in?" A thought struck me. "You didn't actually finish things with Debbie at all, did you? She left you when she found out your job was going. I bet once Paul had calmed down, she persuaded him to give things another go. I expect she was missing his six figure salary and triple platinum credit card."

He slammed his glass down. "You're being utterly ridiculous. I told her it was all over because I was still in love with you. If she's decided to go back to Paul, well, that's up to her."

The stupid half-smirk playing across his lips betrayed

him. It had been present the time he'd said his new golf clubs had only cost one hundred pounds and it was there each time he'd said "No, of course I'm not shagging Debbie! How could you even *think* such a thing?"

I shook my head. "I don't get it. You're not in love with me; you fell out of love with me some years ago. And don't try and tell me those sorts of feelings have come back; they never do. This has all been pretence! Calling round here, dressed in your finest, getting all nostalgic over the crappy cheese toasties that you detested; you just wanted someone to sponge off."

"That's rubbish-"

"Do you actually remember how to tell the truth?" I asked him. "It's all making sense now. All that drivel about missing me, booking tables at Chives, leaflets on dementia ... are you really on anti-depressants? I bet you're not, you don't seem in the least bit depressed. A boiled sweet would have more effect! You just wanted me to feel sorry for you."

"You're talking nonsense-"

"Am I? You know what, you're worse than those bloody slugs I've been fighting all year; sliming your way back into my life, leaving your horrid trail everywhere, doing your best to strip me of my juicy green shoots of recovery," I was talking crap now, I knew that, but if I stopped I thought I might cry. "Well, your little plan's failed, hasn't it? Why don't you go and find some other mug to, er, mug?"

I felt Kieron's hand on my arm and saw I was brandishing the cheese knife. He gently took it out of my hand and turned to The Ex. "I think you'd better leave."

"Don't worry, I'm going," he snarled. He took a step closer to Kieron. "I'd forgotten how hysterical she could become. She's still a bloody mad woman; totally irrational, just like before. I hope you know what you're taking on."

Kieron nodded. "The ironing board, hopefully."

The Ex hesitated, looking at me as if expecting a sudden change of heart but when it was obvious that wasn't going to happen he flounced out of the room and strode down the hall, slamming the front door so violently that the whole house shook.

"And tell the world you love him!" Stu made a brief contribution.

I felt utterly drained. "I'm so sorry you were involved in that, Kieron," I said, fighting back tears. "I can't believe how gullible I've been. *Again.* I'm such an idiot; a total loser."

He grinned. "You're no such thing, he's the loser. As well as a big fat slug."

I covered my face with my hands and groaned. "Did I really say juicy green shoots of recovery?"

"Yep! Disastrous line! Never mind, he got the message. Look, are you going to be ok or would you like me to stay for a bit?"

A bit of what? "Um, no, you get off Kieron, go and see your girlfriend. Thanks for all your help with Stu and for stopping me ruining a perfectly good cheese knife."

He gave me a funny look. "I haven't got a girlfriend. I wouldn't have asked you out if I did."

My heart skipped a beat. "Oh, er, I thought you were just being nice, you know..."

He laughed. "Then I'd have asked my mother! You should have said you didn't like the Pizza Palace; I can't stand it either! But the vouchers were a good excuse to ask you to go out with me; I've wanted to for ages. Look, I've got Max this weekend but why don't we do something next weekend? Go somewhere nice; somewhere there's no drunken brothers or leaking showers or slimy slugs? A proper date?"

I smiled at him. "And what about pity shags?"

He came close and put his arms around my waist. "Definitely none of those," he murmured looking straight into my eyes. He pulled me in close and I felt his warm lips on mine. Then he lurched suddenly away, overcome by another violent fit of coughing.

CHAPTER TWENTY-EIGHT

Sunday

I was eating my Crunchy Nuts very slowly, watching my brother pacing up and down the garden, talking to his demonic wife on his mobile. He'd stop every now and then to throw his arms in the air or put his hand to his head. The camellia kept a watchful eye on him. It had grown so much bigger and scared it would become pot-bound, I'd replanted it into the ground at the forefront of the jungle. To my amazement, it appeared to be flourishing. My mind was on Tuesday's hearing. What would I be advising a member of my team right now? I'd be hinting very strongly that they do themselves a favour and resign. At least I'd keep a clean reference if I did that. But go down without a fight? Let the bastards get away with it so they can do it to someone else? I couldn't do that - but did I have the stomach for a bloody battle?

Stu plonked himself down heavily at the kitchen table. "Jesus Christ, Sis," he muttered. "You'll never guess what's happened now."

"Go on."

"Georgia's baby isn't George's! Kirsty got suspicious about the dates and forced the truth out of Georgia. Turns out the real father is some spotty oik in her Modern Studies class. I think she wanted it to be George's cos he's got a good job and has his own place."

Not for long. "Oh, blimey. Does George know he's not

the father?"

"I should think so; it's all over Facebook."

"How's Kirsty?"

"She's finished with that Zeller wanker. Says she was going through a crisis; shock of becoming a granny, she reckons. She wants us to try again."

"Oh, that's good." I said, not even convincing myself.

An article in the Sunday paper jumped out at me:

When's a complaint not a complaint? Ask Perypils!

The FSA has been asked to investigate claims that Perypils Insurance has been falsely reporting the number of customer complaints it receives. A whistleblower at the company told this paper that a significant amount of complaints go unrecorded because of a management decision to redefine what constitutes a complaint.

The whistleblower told us: "I had a customer who was shouting and swearing and threatening to kill me because we'd given him an incorrect quote for his American Pit Bull, but my team manager told me not to record it as a complaint because, in her words, the customer was only 'informing' us about an error. Most of the staff here are so confused by what they should be classing as a complaint they often don't record anything at all. If you get the tiniest thing wrong your team manager jumps on you straight away and marks it down in your progress plan. Everyone's in constant fear of losing their job."

We asked the company to comment but we were told nobody from Perypils was available. We asked if they would send us the company's official definition of a complaint but they declined. The matter is now in the hands of the FSA. We hope they will also be investigating the company's ever-present intimidation tactics, which have long been threatening the well-being of its employees.

Well, well! I had a mole in the team. Who was it? Furtive Fiona? She was always whispering and glancing over her shoulder - and she had an extra thumb on one of her hands. Or was it Sweaty Sean? He would start to perspire whenever I got within twenty feet of him. Did he have something to hide? I put the paper down and watched my brother spreading a thick layer of Nutella onto his toast. What did it matter who the mole was? They'd only repeated what was actually happening. It was just another nail in my already tightly sealed coffin.

Monday

The departments were buzzing with thoughts on who the mole could be. Hissing Cyn informed me that I was currently the hot favourite!

"Why would I drop myself in it with the FSA, Cyn?"

The Snake's eyes gleamed at me. "I don't think it's you of course, but it's what people are saying. I thought you should know. Some of them think you did it to get Roger into trouble. No one would blame you - everyone hates him."

"I'm not the mole, Cyn, so you can tell Ben and Danny they can increase the odds on me. I daresay they've opened a book on it."

She looked disappointed. "Is George coming in today?"

"No, I'm afraid not." TLCS George had phoned in sick, saying he was 'grieving'.

"I heard about the baby, what a shock for him. He put a

photo on Facebook last night; he's had his tattoo amended. It says SmEllie Botty now."

I started to work through the monthly sales figures, trying to take my mind off tomorrow's hearing. We'd managed 106%, our best ever performance, but I knew it wasn't going to be good enough. Big Andy called me.

"Kate!" he said, sounding excited. "Can you come to the meeting room? I've got something to show you that you're not going to believe!"

"If it's that horrid thing you do with your eyelids, I've seen it a hundred times-" The dialling tone told me I was talking to myself. With a sigh, I made my way to the meeting room where Big Andy sat, grinning from ear to ear, his battered leather brief case in front of him on the table.

"You'd better sit down, old girl! You're not going to believe what you're about to see!"

I slid into a chair. "What's going on?"

Still grinning like a loon, Big Andy produced a tatty magazine from his brief case. My eyes widened as I realised what it was. "*Andy!* You can't bring a porno into work! And why the hell are you showing it to me? I don't want to look at stuff like that! Have you gone completely mad?"

"No, look at this, page forty-three, the lonely hearts ads. Recognise this person?"

I peered at one of the pictures under the heading 'Men Seeking Men'. It was of a man, eyes shielded by a peaked leather cap and exposing a very hairy chest under a studded leather jacket. The advert read:

"Calling all Hairy Bikers! Well-endowed, 35 year old man WLTM similarly hairy males to cook up a storm with! Likes being taken for long, hot rides and loves thick beards to hold on to. Will

379

consider discreet dress-up. Midlands based. Box 629130"

The man had a large, bushy moustache. His face looked very familiar. *Oh my God!* Was it-

"It's only bloody Roger!" Big Andy burst out, unable to contain himself any longer. "I knew I'd seen him somewhere before as soon as I met him! I just couldn't place it till now. I found the magazine under my son's bed ages ago. I had to flick through it to see what sort of stuff he was looking at, you see, and I remembered this advert as particularly creepy."

"Are you sure it's him? You can't really see his eyes-"

"You don't need to see his eyes, Kate, look at that bloody moustache! There's only one of those in this world, thank Christ!"

"But I can't believe it! Why on earth would he do something like this?" I looked at the date on the magazine. It was several years old. "You've kept the porno all this time?"

"Oh, er, well, let's not worry about that now. The point is, you've got him! Show this to head office and he'll be out on his arse! His very sore arse, I shouldn't wonder! And what about the press? If you took it to the tabloid that printed the story on Brett, well, they'd have a field day!"

I rubbed my chin. "But he's got a wife and kids, Andy."

"I know he has. But they'll stand by him, that type always does. I don't know why you're so worried about him; he's quite happy to throw you under a bus! I'm telling you, if the Board get wind of this there's no way the Chief Exec will survive another scandal. You could bring him down too, Kate; just think, you've got the power to wipe out both bastards!"

"I don't know-"

"You've got to think about yourself now, old girl, because no one else is going to. You've got responsibilities here, a mortgage, bills to pay, and what about all that make-up you need to cover your ugly face? That must cost a small fortune! And you're going to have to give in to plastic surgery soon or your tits will be round your ankles. You can save yourself with this; it's your lifeline."

"It's all a bit, well, sad, isn't it?"

"*Sad?* You've got to be kidding me! It's the funniest thing I've ever seen! He was supposed to be the great moralistic version of Bonking Brett, a devoted family man and pillar of the community and now we find out he likes them hot and hairy! All this time he's been trying to shaft you and all he really wants is someone to shaft him! Someone to roger Roger! It's bloody fantastic." He paused and looked thoughtful. "What do you think discreet dress-up involves?"

"*Ugh.*"

I lay awake all night, tossing and turning. Could I do it? Could I resort to blackmail to save my skin? I'd phoned Karen and her advice had been, somewhat predictably, "*Fuck yes!* Blow it up fucking billboard size!" But I didn't know if I could do it. I wasn't even convinced it was The GPS in the picture; why on earth would he risk public humiliation like that? Unless he was into that too, of course.

Big Andy had never asked me for anything before and I'd noted the desperation in his voice. It was not as if The GPS didn't deserve it. But that didn't make it right. What was I going to do? Could the union save me? A rep was going to be with me at the hearing and the good news was that Alan was on 'extended sick leave' so it wouldn't be him. Perhaps it would be someone more robust; someone who knew what they were doing and could give The GPS a run for his money. What state would I be in this time tomorrow night? Devastated or relieved? Either way, I was planning on being completely pissed.

I gave up on sleep around four in the morning and went downstairs, clicking the telly on. I sat down on the remote control and the shock caused it to suddenly start working. The Gay Rabbit Chat channel popped up. An omen, perhaps? Was it good or bad?

I arrived at work on Tuesday morning, realising incredulously, that it could be for the last time. The hearing was scheduled for ten o'clock. I simply couldn't concentrate on anything so I aimlessly scrolled up and down my inbox. I hadn't told anyone what was happening. Who was going to deal with all these emails if I left? Hundreds were pouring in from the risk and compliance teams, the aftermath of the newspaper article. What if I had to take the walk of shame? Escorted from the premises like a criminal - I didn't deserve that. How could this be happening to me! *Bloody bastards.* I choked back tears of self-pity. Surely the union rep would kick The GPS into touch?

The Drain was hovering. "Kate, would it be okay if I left early tonight? I've been summoned to a meeting with the school psychologist."

"Oh dear! Is everything ok?"

He sniffed. "It's a ridiculous over-reaction, if you must know. Just because my son tried to buy a shot-gun off the Internet; I think it's perfectly normal for boys to experiment with weapons and things, don't you?"

"How old is your son now, Martin?"

"Nearly seven."

As he headed off to the Gents, The Rock appeared. "Kate, I thought you should know that Joy and Pat are squabbling over the late shift tonight. It's Pat's turn, but she wants to swap because she's got her Wobwam group but Joy says she won't as her friend's coming round with a limited edition DVD of Schindler's List. She's been looking forwards to it for ages. Pat's now crying in the toilets."

"What's Wobwam?"

"I think it's 'We're Obese But We Aren't Morbid'. Something like that."

"Right. Well, thanks for letting me know. I'll sort it."

The Rock gave me a funny look. "Are you feeling alright? I thought you'd storm round there and bash their heads together."

I tried to smile. "I'm fine. And Jan; thank you for all your support. I really mean it. I probably don't say it as much as I should."

She looked alarmed. "Now you're scaring me! What's going on?"

"Oh, it's nothing to worry about. I'll tell you later."

At a quarter past nine, Stalin Stan called me to say Charles from the union was in reception. Charles! That was a good, strong-sounding name - the name of Kings, of fighters and saviours. Maybe everything was going to be alright! With a sudden surge of energy, I scooted down the stairs to collect him. A thin, stick-like man in a cagoule was sitting on one of the sofas, removing his cycling clips. I stopped and looked at him. His brief case had an elastic band round it. A high-pitched wailing sound caused him to fumble in his ear to adjust his hearing aid and his head jerked sideways with a violent twitch. I left him sitting there and walked slowly back up the stairs.

Ten o'clock loomed large. I had two white envelopes on my desk in front of me. With shaking hands, I picked them up and made my way to the meeting room, sick to the stomach with nerves. I knocked on the door, which was opened by The GPS. There was a small round lady seated at the table. "Come in, Kate," The GPS growled. "This is Sue Williams from HR."

Sue bared her teeth at me. "Hello Kate. We haven't met before, but we've spoken several times on the phone."

"Have we?"

"Oh yes. I don't know if you recall the last time; I certainly do. You didn't agree with one of my decisions and referred to me as a pen-pushing, menopausal woolly mammoth, still fossilised from the ice age."

"Right." I could almost hear my chickens clucking as they came home to roost. "Well, it's nice to meet you at last, Sue. And to discover I was at least half right."

Her smile snapped off. The GPS was looking up and down the corridor. "Are you on your own, Kate?"

"Yes."

"No union rep?"

"No." I'd told Stalin Stan to send Charles away. The GPS looked disappointed. I noticed he'd laid out pages and pages of copious notes on the table. He must have spent hours preparing for this meeting; probably couldn't sleep last night in his eager anticipation at ripping a weedy little union nerd to shreds. Now he only had me to bully. He sat down at the table on the same side as Sue and they both looked at me.

I wondered if they could hear my heart thumping.

"I'll kick off proceedings, shall I?" I said, trying to speak calmly. "I'd like you to have this." I chose one of the envelopes at random and slid it over to The GPS. He looked at it as if it were a turd, then slowly and deliberately picked it up and opened it. I watched him anxiously as he digested the contents. His face remained impassive. He cleared his throat and read it aloud.

"Dear Roger

Please accept this letter as formal notification of my resignation. I understand that I am obliged to give three months notice, however I would be grateful that in view of my thirteen years of unblemished service to the company, you would allow me to take this as paid leave, so that I have sufficient opportunity to find and secure a role elsewhere.

Yours sincerely
Kate King"

That wasn't what I'd wanted to write. There were a million different thoughts and emotions I wanted to express "Dear Bastard, I hope you die soon" etc but in the end, it just didn't seem worth the pain. The GPS looked across at me. "You're resigning?"

"Yes."

"And you're saying, in front of a witness," he nodded towards a smug-looking Sue, "that you haven't felt forced into resigning in any way? Or, by anyone?"

I let that one hang for a few seconds so they could be in

no doubt about my true feelings. "No."

"Good. Very well then. I think you've made a very sensible decision, Kate, in view of your *performance* issues. As to your request to take the notice period as paid leave," he shot Sue a sideways glance and I saw her give a quick shake of her head. "I'm afraid I can't agree to that. It's not within company policy and we need time to, er, to find your replacement. I can't allow our business to suffer."

Replacement my arse. They were closing us down. I pursed my lips. "I'd thought that in view of my *performance* issues, as you put it, you might wish to consider my early release?"

"I'm afraid it can't be done."

"I think Roger's been extremely gracious, Kate," chipped in Sue, haughtily. "He could still go ahead with disciplinary action, you know, even though you have resigned."

"I'm happy to halt disciplinary proceedings," said The GPS quickly. *Of course you are. You haven't followed policy and I'd have a strong case for unfair dismissal.* "It goes without saying that I expect your full co-operation and commitment whilst you work your notice period, otherwise your references could still be adversely impacted. Is there anything else?"

Was that it? After thirteen years of working countless unpaid hours with a broom shoved up every orifice, giving up weekend after weekend, deprived of sleep, bloated by stress, falling asleep at social gatherings because I was so knackered, changing holiday plans to suit those of colleagues, never taking time off sick, not even when I'd sprained my ankle and had to be wheeled round the office in my chair like Davros; was that really it? The end? And not even a thank you? They were already gathering their notes together, looking very pleased with themselves. I stood up to go, then turned round at the door.

"Oh, there was one last thing, Roger."

He looked up at me, irritation flickering in his eyes. "I thought you ought to have this." I handed him the second envelope. He snatched it impatiently, frowning at the inconvenience.

"What is it?" he snapped, tearing open the envelope. He looked at the contents and turned white. Sue looked at him expectantly but he didn't speak. She leant across to see what he was holding but he jerked it violently out of her line of vision.

The GPS slowly turned his horrified stare to meet my eyes. He swallowed. "Has, er, anyone else seen this?" His voice was almost a whisper.

"Andy's seen it," I told him, firmly. "But we haven't shown it to anyone else, of course; we wouldn't dream of it. But these things do have a nasty habit of getting out, don't they? You know what offices are like. And three months is a long time..."

Sue's mystified face swung from one of us to the other. The GPS swallowed again. "Yes, well, perhaps I was a little hasty with my decision. I mean, you have worked for Perypils for some time, haven't you? Perhaps I should take into account all your years of er, commitment to the company and make an exception; shall we say you can leave at the end of the week? How would that be?"

"Roger?" Sue queried. "What's going on?"

"Is the end of the week acceptable to you, Kate?" The GPS asked urgently, ignoring Sue.

I held his panicked eyes for a moment, watching beads of sweat gather on his forehead. "Yes," I said finally. "That would be acceptable."

I closed the door quietly behind me and leant against it for a moment. It was all over. Thirteen years of my life wiped out just like that - what had it all been for? What sort of mark had I made at Perypils when my services could be dispatched with so easily? I'd known skid marks that had left more of an impression. On the other side of the door I could hear Sue asking The GPS what was going on. I waited for him to tear her off a strip for daring to question him, but he remained silent.

"Kate! *Kate!* Thank God I've found you," The MC was running up the corridor, her face as white as a sheet. "I didn't know where you were! Stan on reception said a gang of inspectors have turned up from the FSA! They've come to do an unannounced audit; are they allowed to do that? He had to let them in because they had a, a *warrant* or something; they're on their way up here. What are we going to do?"

Behind her, the doors flew open and five stern-looking men in dark suits strode towards us. The MC shrunk back in terror and tried to hide behind me.

"We're looking for the manager of the complaints department," barked the leader of the pack. "I believe her name is Kate King."

I considered them for a moment. "I think you mean the *concerns* department," I replied, with a bright smile. "I'm afraid Kate's not available, but very fortunately, her line manager Roger Fitzall is on site today. He's in here." I pushed open the door to the meeting room and stood back to let the five inspectors inside. I just caught sight of Roger's shocked face as he was surrounded. I closed the door on them.

"Don't worry, Joy," I gave The MC's thin shoulders a

quick squeeze. "I'm sure Roger will be able to explain all his decisions to the FSA; you've done nothing wrong. Get yourself a cup of tea and go back to your team."

She departed gratefully and I returned to my desk, ready to start clearing out over a decade of blood, sweat and tears. What on earth was I going to tell the teams about my sudden departure? Would they be upset? Maybe they would be; perhaps they'd weep and wail and start up a petition begging me to stay. But that was cloud-cuckoo land. All they'd actually want to know is, "Will the new manager let us wear Ugg boots?" and "Can we still dress down at Christmas?" I felt bad about The Rock, though. I'd begged and begged her not to take early retirement and she'd eventually relented, staying on to support me. Now here I was, preparing to bugger off at the end of the week. A big fat rat deserting the sinking ship.

But at least I had the cushion of three months on full pay. Surely I would find another job in three months? I'd be willing to do anything, absolutely anything. Apart from estate agency, of course; I still had some dignity. Maybe I'd land the absolute best job in the world, but if James Martin didn't need another thigh masseuse perhaps I could get the second best and work as a taster for Cadburys. I'd love to make the chocolate fingers! That might get a bit repetitive, I suppose, but at least I would have fun pretending to be Willy Wonka. It didn't really matter about taking a drop in salary; I would be much richer just by getting away from the endless office sponsorship. And I had a date to look forward to on Saturday! Not an investment opportunity date or a head on a laptop date or a do you fancy a spot of dogging date but a proper date. With someone lovely. A nice, normal, *analogue* date.

I hadn't realised The Snake was behind me, silently gliding along as if on casters. "I shouldn't tell you this," she hissed, "but rumour has it that Andrea is the mole! You know her *friend*, the one she meets every lunch time, in the woods? Well, apparently his wife's brother's cousin knows someone who knows a journalist-"

The Blubber came rushing over, wringing her hands. "Oh Kate, I've got a customer on the phone, Mr Harris. He says he's been kept waiting for so long, the hold music has triggered his psychosis. He had to listen to 'Memory' twelve times. He's demanding two hundred pounds in compensation because he's just tried to hack through his kitchen wall with a tea spoon - whatever shall I do?"

I sighed. To think, in my next job, I may even get to work with the sane. "Pat, please tell Mr Harris that you've just consulted with your manager and after much careful consideration, she said to go screw yourself."

"Right, ok. Thanks Kate."

"Er, hang on Pat, I was joking! Pat! Pat, come back! PAT! *Oh God.*"

--The End—

ACKNOWLEDGEMENTS

With grateful thanks to my lovely family and friends for all their wonderful support and a particular mention to Libbie Payne and Lesley Lewis for being the most vocal! Thank you.

WORK WIFE BALANCE
Jo Edwards

Kate King is flailing to keep afloat. As her team bicker, finger-point and cheat their way through rumours of sackings and site closures, her ill-tempered husband is becoming increasingly embittered and secretive.

If things aren't bad enough, Kate also has to contend with the sudden appearance of back fat and an over-ambitious, attractive younger colleague.

Something has to give, but will it be her marriage or her job? And which does she care about more?

"Kate is a wonderful character, believable, likeable and with a nice line in funny put-downs. This is well-written, very funny and I raced through it, occasionally squealing in horror at the antics of Kate's colleagues." Daily Mail

FOGGY'S BLOG
Jo Edwards

Hello! I am Morten Astley Fogarty – call centre worker and all-round entertainer. Although I have an extremely rewarding career answering the phones at Perypils Insurance (customers are always telling me what a total brick I am), my ambition is to perform on the stage. I am, after all, named after two of the greatest singers of the 1980's.

My colleagues are a wonderful bunch and are always doing little things to brighten my day. Only yesterday, I returned from lunch to find they'd re-arranged the letters O, K, N, B on my keyboard. We always have such fun!

I am delighted to be able to share my unbelievable journey with you via my incredible blog.

ABOUT THE AUTHOR

Author Photograph ©Richard Edwards Photography

Jo Edwards lives and works in Hampshire, in the UK. She is always delighted to hear from readers – please visit her at:

www.jo-edwards.com

Pot-bound is the sequel to Jo's bestselling debut novel, Work Wife Balance.

For more information and links:

Other Weasel Green Press paperbacks:

Dulcie Feenan:
Christmas comes to Oddleton

J.A. Clement:
On Dark Shores series
1: The Lady & 2: The Other Nereia

Other Weasel Green Press e-books:

Dulcie Feenan:
Christmas comes to Oddleton

J.A. Clement:
On Dark Shores series
1: The Lady & 2: The Other Nereia

Parallels series:
The *Black-Eyed Susan*

Flight from Shantar

Song of the Ice Lord

A Sprig of Holly

All available from Amazon.

Printed in Great Britain
by Amazon